BAD LIAR

BAD LIAR

A NOVEL

TAMI HOAG

DUTTON

DUTTON

An imprint of Penguin Random House LLC

Copyright © 2024 by Indelible Ink Inc.
Penguin Random House supports copyright. Copyright fuels creativity, encourages
diverse voices, promotes free speech, and creates a vibrant culture. Thank you for
buying an authorized edition of this book and for complying with copyright laws by
not reproducing, scanning, or distributing any part of it in any form without
permission. You are supporting writers and allowing Penguin Random House to
continue to publish books for every reader.

DUTTON and the D colophon are registered trademarks of
Penguin Random House LLC.

ISBN 9781101985434

Printed in the United States of America

BOOK DESIGN BY PATRICE SHERIDAN

This is a work of fiction. Names, characters, places, and incidents either are
the product of the author's imagination or are used fictitiously, and any
resemblance to actual persons, living or dead, businesses, companies, events,
or locales is entirely coincidental.

For the loyal readers
who waited so patiently for this book
while my own story took a few unexpected plot twists.
Thank you.

AUTHOR'S NOTE

South Louisiana's French Triangle is a place like no other in this country—ecologically, culturally, and linguistically. I have done my best to bring some of that rich flavor of the region to my readers with the occasional use of common Cajun French words and phrases.

Cajun French is a patois as unique to Louisiana as gumbo, and as different from its mother tongue as it is similar. Evolving a world away from standard French as a language that was primarily spoken rather than written, it can differ in spelling and meaning, not only from Louisiana to France, but from one parish to the next. A glossary of the words and phrases used in this story can be found at the back of the book.

1

MOONLIGHT ON BLACK WATER, SHINING LIKE DARK GLASS IN the night. Tree branches reflected on the surface, silhouettes on shadow, silent sentinels of the swamp, draped in moss that swayed in the whispered breeze.

A shallow boat glided over the surface, the engine barely running, its low, throaty purr swallowed up by the wilderness with only nature there to hear as the boat slipped deeper into the night.

Fingers clutching the steering wheel, the mother sat in her car, staring at the house. A narrow, rickety little shotgun shack that had somehow stood there for more than a hundred years. A sagging roof to match the sagging, postage-stamp front porch. Narrow clapboard siding that hadn't seen a fresh coat of paint in a generation. The front windows were not quite square in the wall. No light shone through the dirty glass.

How had it come to this?

Her son's life had begun in comfort and security. A big house in a good neighborhood. A respected family. A bright future. Little by little that foundation had eroded, corrupted by things she knew now were beyond his control—mostly—though she had judged him and blamed him. Fought him instead of fighting for him, which would be a stain on her soul for the rest of her life, no matter if he forgave her or not—which he did, or so he said. Sometimes she thought he only said it because he was too weary of the battle to say anything else.

Her heartbeat quickening, she got out and looked all around, still clinging to the car door, just in case. This wasn't a good place to be. On the ragged outskirts of town, this was a neighborhood that quickly gave way to dirty blue-collar businesses—a welding shop, a scrapyard, a rusty corrugated metal warehouse that stored Mardi Gras parade floats. The old abandoned sugarcane processing plant was just down the road.

A row of small houses like this one squatted like toadstools, side by side on weed-choked lots, forgotten by everyone who didn't have to live this way. Those were the people who lived here—people not wanted anywhere else, people without the means to live anywhere else, the marginalized, the outliers, the forgotten. Her son.

There was no one around that she could see, although she was sure she felt the crawl of eyes on her. Just her imagination, she tried to tell herself. A train whistle wailed in the distance, a mournful sound echoed by an owl in a nearby tree. The sound of the owl unnerved her and stirred a long-dormant memory of a timeworn superstition that she would have said she didn't believe in. A folktale about owls being harbingers of death. Her stomach clenched, and a chill ran down her back just the same as she hurried to the front door.

She knocked and waited. And waited . . . And waited . . .

The mother's trembling fingers tightened on the doorknob.

The owl called a second time.

The wife reached out with trembling fingers and pinched off the blackened wick of a candle. *Happy birthday to me*—a thought steeped in sarcasm and sorrow. She was angry and sad and alone. Nothing new there.

This wasn't what her life was supposed to be. This hadn't been part of the deal. Not at all. She had fallen in love with the man of her dreams—handsome, smart, full of fun and promise. They had planned and plotted a life in a better place with a brighter future. They had had so much to look forward to, so many promises their dreams had held out for them, like shiny brass rings on the beautiful carousel of youthful romance.

But there she sat, alone in her kitchen, drinking warm chardonnay in the glow of the under-cabinet lighting, in a backwater town in south Louisiana. A place she didn't belong. A fact she was reminded of daily by people she didn't like and who didn't like her. People who had pulled her husband back here on the leash of obligation and loyalty, dragging her along, an unwanted accessory. She often wondered if he thought of her the same way and resented her for it. Was she the constant reminder of what he could have had, could have been, if he hadn't come back here and settled for so much less?

Of course he resented her.

No more than she resented him.

This was what her life had become, and she was sick of it, choking on it.

She didn't want to live like this anymore.

She wouldn't.

She wiped away the tears that clung to her eyelashes and reached across the kitchen island for her cell phone.

Happy birthday to me . . .

A predator attacked. Prey screamed. The swamp was alive at night, a tableau for the drama of life and death, survival and loss. The circle of life turned continuously, naturally, without sympathy or sentiment. One life fed another, which fed another, which fed another.

The choreography of nature was graceful, brutal, and honest, a dance carried out in moonlight and shadow.

The engine died. A spotlight swept low across the water.

Eyes glowed back.

The apex predator had arrived.

The lovers' hands pressed palm-to-palm, fingers intertwined as they slow-danced barefoot on the cool, damp grass. Black water and the gilded moon painted the backdrop, the bayou shining like polished obsidian in the moonlight.

The warm, smoky voice of a favorite singer set the mood with soulful lyrics—an intimate, heartfelt confession, a pledge of love and wonder. *"You're as smooth as Tennessee whiskey . . ."*

Their hips swayed together, touching, pressing into each other. His breath stirred loose tendrils of her hair. His lips brushed across her skin, traced the shell of her ear. She smiled. He sighed.

Whispered words. Breath caught and held. His mouth found hers. Her tongue touched his. Desire rose like a flame, burning, licking, igniting a deeper need, driving them indoors to the privacy of their bedroom.

The curtains billowed in the night breeze. Clothing fell, sheets whispered. His hand swept down the curve of her side. Her fingers dug into his shoulders. They moved together, slowly and gently, then with strength and passion. The pleasure built to a crescendo and took them both over the edge on a wave of bliss.

The lovers fell asleep one tucked into the other, wrapped up in each other in every way, his hand holding hers pressed against her heart.

The alligators came like Pavlov's dogs. They thrashed and snapped and devoured what was thrown to them, churning up the water, stirring up the smell of mud and blood and decay.

The pieces were small, bite-size, alligator fun-size, meant to be eaten in the moment rather than dragged away and tucked under a log to rot and tenderize. A heart, a liver, a foot, a hand.

And then it was done, the evidence gone. The spotlight went out.

The boat started back the way it had come, leaving nature to itself, as if nothing had happened. Leaving nothing but moonlight on black water.

2

"AIN'T NO REASON ON GOD'S GREEN EARTH ANYONE SHOULD ever find a murdered body in south Louisiana," Chaz Stokes proclaimed.

He lit a cigarette and took a deep pull on it as he leaned back against the side of a black Dodge Charger and surveyed the area through the dark lenses of his aviator sunglasses. A light-skinned Black man, he was tall and lean, built like an athlete and dressed like a jazz musician in loose-fitting gray slacks and a black-and-white straight-bottomed Cuban-style shirt.

"Umpteen gazillion acres of swampland, marshland, woodland, rivers, bayous, and backwaters, and this genius dumps a body at the end of a road," he said, exhaling twin streams of smoke through his slim nose. "This is just pure damn laziness."

He pointed toward a sign that had been posted by the state just off the end of the road: ILLEGAL TO FEED OR HARASS ALLIGATORS. "Could'a fed that body to the gators with none the wiser."

"If they were geniuses, we'd be hard-pressed for work, *mon ami*," Nick Fourcade said. He slid his backpack off his shoulder and set it on the trunk of Stokes's car.

"Still . . ." Stokes said, making a dismissive gesture with his cigarette. He frowned within the frame of his neatly trimmed mustache and goatee. "This ain't even sportin'."

"Unless you pull a suspect out your ass, that remains to be seen."

They stood near the dead end of a gravel-and-crushed-shell road a mile or so outside the drive-through town of Luck, where the wild began to swallow up what passed for civilization hereabouts on the western edge of the Atchafalaya Basin. The road petered out a dozen or so yards from a shallow slough choked with hackberry and willow trees. It was the sort of place where the occasional drug deal was made and where lovers came to escape scrutiny for a steamy tussle in a back seat or in the bed of a pickup truck. Kids came out here to drink, smoke dope, and bait gators, as was evidenced by the number of crushed beer cans and scattered, crumpled Sonic and Popeyes take-out bags.

Recent rains had left the ground soft, and a set of muddy ruts indicated someone had nearly gotten themselves stuck venturing too far off the gravel. Beyond the tracks, hidden by tall grass, a body lay waiting.

The morning was young and clear, with sheer scraps of clouds as thin as gauze contrasting the electric-blue fall sky. Too pretty a morning for a murder, Nick thought, watching a squadron of ducks flying toward the basin, though he knew all too well that nature made no concessions for human tragedy. The world turned; the seasons passed. Death was just part of the deal. The man lying dead at the edge of the slough mattered no more to the natural world than a rabbit snatched up by an owl in the moonlight. The sun would still come up the next day and the day after that.

The world of humankind was another matter altogether.

Dressed for a court appearance in a shirt and tie, he had been on his way to the sheriff's office to start the workday early when the call had come. He ran the detective division of the Partout Parish Sheriff's Office, a squad of six detectives, covering 816 mostly rural square miles, investigating everything from burglary to homicide.

He had hoped to get some paperwork done before heading to the courthouse.

He checked his watch and frowned.

"Nothing like starting a Monday off with a murder," Stokes remarked.

"So what's the story?"

"It's a dump job," Stokes said. "Looks like the victim ran into the wrong end of a shotgun—elsewhere. I'd say the killer backed in, thinking to dump the body in the water, sank down to his rims, said fuck it, and chucked the body into the weeds. Like I said: pure damn laziness."

"Any chance we might get a cast of a tire track?"

"Maybe. It's pretty squishy over there right now, but there's one or two might set up enough to be worth a try if we wait a bit for the sun to do its thing."

"You have a plaster kit?"

"I've got one in my trunk. You got any?"

"I think I might have two. Who called this in?"

"Swamper," Stokes said, nodding in the general direction of the blue-and-white sheriff's office cruiser parked a short distance ahead of his car. A bald, stocky deputy sat back against the hood of the cruiser, chatting animatedly with a small, wiry man in overalls and green waders, the pair of them smiling and laughing like old friends catching up at a Sunday picnic.

Nick hitched his backpack over one shoulder and headed toward them.

"*Bonjour*, Sergeant Rodrigue. *Ça viens?*"

He had grown up in a household where Cajun French was the default language of his parents, people proud to keep that language alive even when that idea had been unpopular in the mainstream. As was the case with many people in these parts, even his English was seasoned liberally with French.

"Our newly minted Lieutenant Fourcade!" Rodrigue boomed, his usual broad grin lighting his face beneath a bushy black mustache of epic proportions. "*Bonjour! Ça va*. I'm good, me. What a fine day we have in God's country, no?"

"*Mais oui*. That it is."

"Fourcade?" the swamper asked, squinting hard beneath the bill of a worn, dirty green Bass Pro cap. "You related to the Fourcades down Abbeville? Coy and them?"

"No, sir."

"Fourcade—that's not a Cajun name, but you a Cajun. I can tell," he declared.

"Through and through," Nick conceded. "And you are . . . ?"

"This here's my wife's third or fourth cousin or something like that," Rodrigue said with a chuckle. "Alphonse Arceneaux. My wife, Mavis, she's an Arceneaux on her mama's side. Alphonse, he found the body, him, and he called me."

"Why you didn't call nine-one-one?" Stokes asked, joining them.

Arceneaux looked at him like he was a fool, lines of disapproval creasing his narrow, weathered face. He might have been seventy or forty-five. It was difficult to say. His skin had been turned to tooled leather by years working outdoors in the harsh Louisiana weather.

"That's for emergencies!" he declared. "This ain't no emergency. That dude, he's *dead* dead, him. He as dead as dead gets. What's the hurry?"

"We'd like to catch the bad guy."

"Bah!" Arceneaux scoffed. "I told you, there wasn't no bad guy. There wasn't nobody but me, and I gotta stay here for y'all. I might as well call a friend, no?"

"You didn't see anyone?" Nick asked. "No car or truck?"

"*Mais non*, no nothing."

"How'd you come to find the body? You got a boat out there?"

"My bateau." Arceneaux pointed in the general direction of the water, though the boat was hidden from view by the tall grass.

"And what brings you out this way?"

"Running my traplines. Me, I lease this land. I come this way first thing in the morning and try to get my nutria before they get stole. This here land's too close to town. Lazy-ass town boys come out here and steal my nutria. Y'all need to do something 'bout that!" Arceneaux said, as if the raids on his traplines should take priority over a murder.

"We do dead people, not dead rodents," Stokes grumbled.

"Stealing is stealing," Arceneaux said. "Six bucks a tail this year. That's my livelihood they messing with!"

"I don't disagree," Nick said. "But you have to take that up with the Wildlife agents. That's their jurisdiction."

"Me, I'm gonna catch them rascals red-handed this year," Arceneaux promised, clearly relishing the idea. "Give them raggedy-ass thieves some Cajun justice!"

"Dude, don't promise violence on your fellow man in front of cops," Stokes cautioned.

Nick had already lost interest in the conversation. "Show me your boat."

Arceneaux led the way. "You don't wanna see that body first?"

"He's not going anywhere, is he?"

Even as he said it, a trio of stray dogs emerged from a thicket of trees, noses scenting the air.

"Goddamn it," Stokes muttered, moving off, pulling his sidearm. "I'll stay with the body. Git, you mangy mutts!" he shouted at the dogs. "Go on, git!"

He pointed his weapon off to the side and discharged a round, sending the dogs scurrying back toward the trees.

Nick followed Arceneaux and Rodrigue, glad for the boots he kept in his vehicle as they pushed through the weeds and the tall grass that had faded from green to blond with the approach of winter. There was no bank to speak of, just softer and softer ground that gave way to water.

They broke through the vegetation where Alphonse Arceneaux's snub-nosed bateau floated, a shallow, flat-bottomed aluminum boat as weathered as its owner's face. A pile of dead nutria lay in the nose of the boat—ugly, orange-toothed swamp rats bigger than cats. They were the scourge of the wetlands, non-native invaders devoted to tearing up the root systems of the marsh grasses, creating erosion in the delicate ecosystem that seemed threatened at every turn these days.

A rifle lay propped near the morning's harvest.

"You hunting with a .22?" Nick asked.

"When I need it. Me, I'd rather use ol' Black Betty and save the ammunition," Arceneaux said, reenacting clubbing something. "I run a hundred fifty traps, me. Not going 'round filling the swamp with shot when there's no need."

"You got a shotgun on board?"

Arceneaux laughed and tipped his cap back on his head. "What kind of damn *couillon* hunts nutria with a shotgun?! That's a good one! Talk about!"

Rodrigue laughed along as Arceneaux pantomimed shooting and exploding a nutria to kingdom come.

"How'd you come to find the body?" Nick asked.

As expected, the corpse wasn't visible from this spot, nor was the road. Nothing but a waving sea of grass and the occasional glimpse of Stokes's dark head a dozen yards away.

"I had me a bad oyster last night," Arceneaux confessed, "and I got me a touch of the *fwa* this morning. Got out the boat to relieve myself and that's how I come to find a dead dude. How 'bout that?"

Rodrigue shook his head. "We got us a case of the diarrhea to thank for the discovery of a murder victim! I been doing this a long time, and that's a first for me!"

"Did you recognize this dead man?" Nick asked.

"*Mais non*," Arceneaux said, shaking his head. "That dude, his own *maman* ain't gonna recognize him. You'll see. It's bad. *Pauvre bête*," he murmured. "May God rest his soul."

He crossed himself, picked up the small crucifix he wore on a chain around his neck, and pressed a kiss to it with chapped lips.

"Closed-casket bad," Rodrigue said. "Somebody was mad mad at that guy. Maybe a drug thing or some kind of feud. Something personal."

"You don't know him, either?" Nick asked the deputy as they made their way back through the grass toward the body. "He ain't your fourth cousin twice removed?"

"I wouldn't know him if he was my own brother," Rodrigue said. "We gotta hope he's still got his wallet in his pants. Only God gonna know him now."

Ran into the wrong end of a shotgun, Stokes had said. There was no pretty version of that.

"Did you touch the body?"

"No, sir."

"Did Stokes?"

Rodrigue laughed. "He's just here for show, ain't he?"

"I heard that!" Stokes shouted. "You know I leave the bodies for you, Nicky. You get so testy otherwise."

Dressed in jeans, socks, and nothing else, the decedent had landed on his back with his arms outflung in a pose reminiscent of da Vinci's *Vitruvian Man*. He was a tall Caucasian male, over six feet, Nick reckoned. Fit, broad-shouldered, narrow-hipped. His left hand and wrist were blown to shreds. His right hand was damaged as well, but less so. Defensive wounds. The hands had probably been held up in a vain attempt to shield his face from the shotgun blast.

His face and head were almost completely destroyed, a bloody, unrecognizable mess of shattered bone and pulverized tissue. The small remaining portion of the right side of his face was speckled with the tiny red stippling caused by the impact of the fine plastic filler used in buckshot loads. Judging by the damage, the shooter had been standing maybe six to eight feet away from the victim. Personal, Rodrigue had said. Indeed.

It didn't look real, what was left of this person. Absent the life force, and so badly damaged, a body ceased to seem human. The reality was so shocking, so hideous, the observer's mind automatically wanted to discount what it saw.

The man's right eye stared up at him, brown and cloudy, hopeless, lifeless. Flies had begun to swarm on the wounds to feed and lay eggs, but the maggots had yet to hatch. He couldn't have been lying there more than a few hours, Nick reckoned.

He pulled on a pair of purple latex gloves from his backpack and squatted down beside the corpse in the damp grass. The body was cold to the touch but not stiff. The greenish discoloration of the skin on the abdomen and the beginning of bloat told him the man had been dead for a while. A day or two, perhaps. Decomposition was under way. Rigor mortis had come and gone.

Buzzards had begun to circle overhead. Thank goodness for Mr. Arceneaux's bad stomach. If he hadn't come along when he did, the corpse would have become a feast. Mother Nature recycling her own.

Nick glanced up at Arceneaux, who was staring off into the distance, pointedly not looking at the body. The reality was beginning to set in.

"*Merci*, Mr. Arceneaux. We'll need to have you come into the sheriff's office and make a formal statement. Later today, if possible. Finish running your traplines, then come in and see Detective Stokes here."

Stokes stepped forward and handed the man his business card, instructing him to call first.

Rodrigue walked Arceneaux back to his boat. When they were out of sight, Stokes said to Nick, "I'm gonna tell you what right now: I know exactly what happened to our dead friend here."

"I'm glad to hear it," Nick said, walking carefully around the body, snapping photos with the digital camera from his backpack. "Do you have evidence to back up this theory?"

"This guy here got caught doing some other dude's lady. I'll bet you a hundred bucks."

Nick looked at the body and its state of semidress, jeans half undone. That was probably a sucker bet, but preconceived ideas were dangerous things in a homicide investigation.

"You know what they say about an assumption," Nick said. "It'll make me kick your ass."

"That ain't what they say."

"It's what I'm telling you."

"Whatever. You mark my words," Stokes promised. "This here is all about a chick. If I'm lying, I'm dying."

"Let this be a cautionary tale, then," Nick remarked.

"I don't know what you mean by that."

"Really, Romeo? You standing here in the same clothes I saw you in yesterday. And how is it you came to arrive at this scene before me when you live a good twenty minutes in the other direction?"

Stokes frowned. "I was visiting a friend in the area," he said stiffly.

"Mm-hmm. At the crack of dawn. Mrs. Who-was-it-this-time?"

"That is not your business, my friend."

"It'd be good if I had a starting place for the investigation when you go missing thanks to a jealous husband," Nick said, squatting down beside the body again to search through the man's pockets for any indication of identity.

"And might I say for the nine hundreth time, this judgy side of you is not appealing, Nicky," Stokes complained. "Oh, wait. There *is* no other side of you."

"Good thing you don't want to date me, then, yeah?" Nick said dryly. "And I'm married and everything. Just your type."

Stokes, ever the ladies' man, had, in the last year or so, shifted his love-life strategy to affairs with married women, on the theory that they were only starved for great sex and weren't out to snag him for a husband, as most of the single women in his dating pool were—or so he claimed. Though any woman who thought Chaz Stokes was husband material needed her head examined as far as Nick was concerned. The apple of his own eye, Stokes was as faithless as a feral tomcat.

"Ha ha," Stokes said, irritated. "All this sassy-ass humor. You're a regular comedian today. You must have gotten laid last night."

Ignoring the remark, Nick carefully pulled out the contents of the dead man's right front pocket. Nine cents, a gum wrapper wadded around a hard knot of chewed gum, and a felted piece of lint that had been jammed down in the pocket corner for a very long time. He slipped the items into a plastic bag and handed it to Stokes, then slid his hand under the man's hip and felt for the shape and bulk of a wallet.

No such luck. Not that he was surprised. A man dressing that hastily, not even managing shoes, his wallet was likely sitting on a dresser or nightstand somewhere. But he slipped his fingertips into the hip pocket anyway and was rewarded with a business card he worked gingerly out of the pocket and into the light of day.

Mercier & Sons Salvage
673 Canal Road
Luck, Louisiana

Handwritten in the upper-left-hand corner was an amount: $2,875.

"Got a name?" Stokes asked, peering down over Nick's shoulder.

"No, but $2,875 could be a motive, if there was cash that went with this card."

Nick had certainly known people to be murdered for a lot less. A man walking around with a big wad of cash, flashing it in the wrong bar . . .

Mouton's roadhouse wasn't far down the bayou from here. The kind of place where brass knuckles were a common fashion accessory and every man—and most of the women—carried a gun or a knife. People looking for trouble looked at Mouton's. Poachers, thieves, drug dealers—all made themselves at home there.

"Could be he picked up a hooker, got wasted by her pimp," Stokes speculated.

"Could be."

"I'm telling you, my friend, this'll end with a woman."

Nick arched a dark brow. "You know the only difference between you and this guy?" he asked, nodding to the faceless corpse.

"Fashion sense?" Stokes quipped.

"Timing."

3

TIMING. LIFE WAS ALL ABOUT TIMING, ANNIE BROUSSARD RE-flected as she waited for the traffic light to turn green. Time: a complex and delicate dance of nanoseconds orchestrated by an unseen force beyond the ordinary person's control or understanding.

A schedule, a plan, a timeline—all were just illusions people were allowed to believe in to let them feel like they were in control of their lives. A million tiny things happened every day to direct the dance. Move a split second faster here, hesitate briefly there, and the outcome could change dramatically. That annoying delay could save you from being in the wrong place at the wrong time, avoiding catastrophe. Life was all about timing.

The driver behind her beeped his horn. The light had turned green.

She drove down the main drag of Bayou Breaux, with its eclectic mix of brick and clapboard buildings. Several dated as far back as the mid-eighteenth century, before the first Acadian refugees—the people who would eventually come to be known as Cajuns—had arrived as exiles from Canada. Some businesses boasted second-story galleries reminiscent of New Orleans' French Quarter, with ornate wrought iron railings and window boxes trailing ivy and the last geraniums of the season. Some had been restored over the years; others looked like they hadn't seen a coat of paint since God was a child. All of it passed by Annie unnoticed. Her mind was elsewhere.

This would be her first day on the job in weeks. It seemed like forever since the night she'd been attacked. It seemed so long ago that memory might have been a dream—no, a nightmare, as surreal as any horror movie.

Don't go there without me. She could still see the text in her mind's eye. But it had been getting late, the tail end of a terrible day. Tired, wanting to make that one last stop and be done, she had run out of patience.

R U coming or what?

She had sent the message, then sent it again, trying to annoy Nick into answering, but no answer had come. Impatient, she had typed:

Going on . . . Need this day to be over . . .
Come when you can . . .

What if she had waited just a little while longer?

If just one person involved in that series of events had made a different choice that night, someone who had died might have lived, but someone who had lived might have died. She might have died. It could have been her family grieving, her son without a mother. The possibilities tumbled in an endless cycle in her battered brain these days—what if this, what if that?—driving her crazy to the point that she questioned every decision she had to make no matter how trivial, trapped in a state of anxiety over potentially making the wrong choice.

Her doctor assured her this was not abnormal. She had suffered a serious concussion. Her brain was sorting itself out, healing, rewiring itself, rebalancing its chemistry. Add to that the post-traumatic stress that came in the aftermath of what had happened, the shock of the things she had seen. She needed to be patient with herself, and patience was all about time. Too much time.

She had already tried once to go back to work too soon and had ended up on an additional two weeks of doctor-ordered rest—no activity, no working out, no driving a car, no heavy lifting. Not able to read a book or to follow the plot of a TV show for the pounding in her head, she had nothing to do but lie around and think. What if this? What if that?

The pain and the anxiety chased each other around and around in her head like two squirrels racing up a tree. She tried to distract herself with positive thoughts—the fact that what had happened had given her and Nick a reboot at a time when their marriage had been struggling a bit. Nothing like a near-death experience to refocus on the things that were truly important in life. She smiled a little now, thinking about the night before, the two of them slow-dancing on the lawn, making love and falling asleep together. So comforting, so peaceful . . . until her brain had awakened her shortly after to spin and fret and keep her up . . .

Sick to death of herself, she felt an almost giddy sense of excitement as the law enforcement center came into view. She needed to get out of her own head and get back to work. She needed the distraction of other people's problems. She needed to make herself useful to humankind. Even if she spent the day doing nothing but counting paper clips, it would be better than being alone with her endless thoughts.

Later she would wonder, what if she had waited just one more day?

"I need to speak with the sheriff," B'Lynn Fontenot announced.

She sounded authoritative, in complete control of herself. What a joke. She was trembling inside like a terrified Chihuahua. Her mouth was parched. Her heart was pounding. She'd been accused more than once in recent years of having a loose screw. She felt as if that screw was about to fall free and let her come apart like a cheap watch, springs and gears flying to every corner of the Partout Parish sheriff's outer office.

"Do you have an appointment?"

The woman on the other side of the counter—Ms. Valerie Comb, according to the nameplate on the countertop—was a very deliberately put-together package wrapped in too-tight clothes with a shellac of too much makeup and Aqua Net. Her hair was streaked white-blond with harsh dark lowlights and cut in a severe, angled style B'Lynn's daughter, Lisette, referred to as the "Internet Karen," Woman Most Likely to Demand to Speak to a Manager. A sure red flag for trouble.

Ms. Comb's gaze ran down B'Lynn from head to toe like a cold shower of disapproval, taking in the dull brown hair that had barely seen a brush in days, taking in the dark circles under bloodshot eyes and the lines of strain etched permanently into her face. She looked like hell because she'd been through hell. She had given up trying to hide it long ago.

"No, I don't have an appointment, as I'm sure you know," B'Lynn started, unable to keep the irritation out of her voice. "But it's imperative I speak with him—"

"Sheriff Noblier is a very busy man," the secretary declared condescendingly. "If you'd like to make an appointment—"

"I don't want to make an appointment," B'Lynn snapped as the tension wound tighter inside her. "This is urgent. I—"

"If you have an emergency, I can direct you down the hall to the sergeant's desk," Ms. Comb said with maddening calm.

"I have been down the hall," B'Lynn said, her small hands balling into fists at her sides. "Days ago. They didn't help me. I want to speak to the sheriff."

"Well, I'm afraid I can't help you unless—"

"No," B'Lynn interrupted curtly. "You *won't* help me."

Valerie Comb arched a penciled brow. "I beg your pardon?"

"You have made no effort to help me," B'Lynn said. "You haven't even *pretended* to help me. The least you could do would be to pick up the damn phone and *pretend* to speak to the sheriff before you blow me off."

Ms. Comb gave a little huff of offense. "Ma'am, I have no idea why you're speaking to me this way."

Because I'm terrified. Because I'm angry. Because I haven't slept in days.

B'Lynn didn't know if she was being unreasonable. Maybe she was. Maybe she was being rude and unfair. She knew she was beyond caring. Her frustration and her fear hadn't just sprung up at the start of this conversation with the sheriff's secretary. It had begun days ago, weeks ago, years ago. The pressure had been building all that time. Just in the last week alone she had been discounted, dismissed, patronized, and ignored by people she had gone to for help. Fair or not, Ms. Valerie Comb, with her overabundance of attitude and blue eyeshadow, was on the last shred of B'Lynn's final remaining nerve.

"At any rate," Ms. Comb went on, tipping her head back to look down her slender nose, "Sheriff Noblier is out of the office this morning."

"I don't believe you." The words blurted out of B'Lynn's mouth before she could even realize she was thinking them.

"Excuse me?"

"I don't believe you."

She couldn't believe the sheriff wasn't in his office because she needed him to be in his office. She had nowhere left to turn.

Her heart was racing, her pulse pounding in her ears. Panic swelled in her chest like a balloon, making it hard to breathe. She went to the closed door of Sheriff Noblier's office and banged on it with her fist. She tried the knob without success, twisting it, yanking at it, tears welling in her eyes.

"Ma'am! I'm going to have to call a deputy!"

Valerie Comb sounded faraway, in another dimension. The last of B'Lynn's control crumbled. Tears spilled over, and she gasped for breath even as she pulled at the doorknob with one hand and pounded on the door with the other.

Oh, my God. Oh, my God. He's not here. He can't help me. No one can help me.

"No, no, NO!" she cried.

"Ma'am! Ma'am!" the secretary shouted, rushing out from behind her counter.

B'Lynn spun around and bolted for the hallway, pushing past Valerie Comb, knocking her sideways. She was beyond thinking rationally now, running in blind panic like an animal. Her surroundings took on a macabre, distorted funhouse quality. The faces of the people she passed twisted in shock. Her legs felt like rubber, her arms as heavy as lead. Her lungs were on fire.

She pulled up in front of the desk sergeant's counter. Two uniformed deputies in the area behind him turned to stare at her.

"Help me!" B'Lynn sobbed, pounding her fists on the counter. "Why won't anyone help me?! Oh, my God! Oh, my God!"

The cry stopped Annie in her tracks. She was only cutting through the squad room to go to the HR office because she had an insurance question. A question she could have gotten answered over the phone, but it was a beautiful morning, and she was happy to walk over to the main building from the Pizza Hut, as they called the small separate building that housed the detective division. Maybe Katy in HR would be ready for a coffee and they could catch up.

The sound of anguish seemed too big to have come from the small, dark-haired woman. Hooker, the desk sergeant, three times her size in all directions, stood flat-footed, his little pig eyes as wide as they would go.

"I'll help you, ma'am," Annie said, rushing forward as the woman doubled over, sobbing. Annie caught hold of her shoulder and sank to the floor with her. "Are you ill? Do you need medical attention?"

"She's out of her mind!" Valerie Comb exclaimed. "She was demanding to see the sheriff. She nearly knocked me flat!"

Annie ignored the secretary. "Do you need an ambulance, ma'am?"

"No. No," the woman said, shaking her head, struggling visibly to pull herself together. She wiped the tears from her cheeks with trembling hands and drew in a shaky breath. "I'm fine."

"'Fine' seems like a stretch," Annie said. "Do you have an emergency? Should I be sending deputies somewhere?"

"I wish I knew."

"I'm Detective Broussard," Annie said. "Let's go sit down and you can tell me what's going on. Can you stand up, ma'am?"

The woman nodded and pushed to her feet on shaky legs. Annie rose with her, steadying her.

She must have been around fifty or so, Annie thought, petite, birdlike, with delicate features. Deep worry lines bracketed her mouth and creased her brow.

"What's your name, ma'am?"

"B'Lynn," she said softly. "B'Lynn Fontenot."

Annie glanced back at Valerie Comb's sour face. "Valerie, could you please bring us some coffee? Thank you so much."

Without waiting for a response, she led the way to the interview room across the hall. B'Lynn Fontenot took the seat on the far side of the small table and wrapped her black quilted jacket around herself as if she were freezing. She swept a hand back over her shoulder-length hair self-consciously, as if to smooth away the tangles and wipe away the gray streaks.

She looked rough, like she hadn't slept, or maybe she drank or had a drug habit. Maybe she was panicking because she needed a fix. Maybe she was shivering because she was going into withdrawal. But if B'Lynn Fontenot was a drug-seeking addict, then she would have gone to the ER, not to the sheriff's office.

"Can you spell your name for me, ma'am?" Annie asked as she took her seat and settled in with the yellow legal pad and pen that had been left there.

"Fontenot. F-O-N-T-E-N-O-T. Beverly Lynn. B-E-V-E-R-L-Y L-Y-N-N. I go by B'Lynn."

"I don't mean any offense, Ms. Fontenot, but I have to ask: Are you under the influence of any alcohol or narcotics right now?"

The woman's laughter was sudden and slightly hysterical. "Oh, my God! I wish! I wish I was on drugs and this was all some kind of bad trip! Wouldn't that be nice? Or maybe this is all just a bad dream, and I'll wake up, and everything will be . . . different," she said, her voice trailing off. "I wish . . ."

"I'm sure I seem like a lunatic," she said. "I'm sorry. I just . . . I'm just at the end of my rope," she said, her voice tightening and trembling, tears rising again in her eyes, "and I don't know what else to do."

"It's all right," Annie assured her. "What is it you need our help with?"

"My son is missing. My son is missing, and no one seems to care but me."

Oh, God, not another case with a kid, Annie thought, anxiety tightening like a fist in her chest. She wasn't sure she could take another. The last one had nearly done her in, literally and emotionally.

"How old is your son?"

"He's twenty-seven."

The fist released, and she could breathe again.

"And what's his name?"

"Robbie. Robert James Fontenot III."

"Where does he live?"

She gave an address. A run-down area of blue-collar businesses over by where the Mardi Gras floats were stored, not far from the old sugarcane processing plant. Who the hell lived over there? People who had no choice.

The lining of B'Lynn Fontenot's jacket was signature Burberry plaid. Expensive. The diamond engagement and wedding set she wore carried larger-than-average stones. Why did her son live in a shithole?

"That's within the Bayou Breaux city limits," Annie began.

B'Lynn's back stiffened. "Don't tell me I need to go to the Bayou Breaux police," she said sharply. "I have been to the Bayou Breaux police. Several times. They told me a twenty-seven-year-old man doesn't need his mother's permission to go somewhere."

And they were correct. Robbie Fontenot was an adult, free to come and go as he chose, with or without the knowledge and consent of his mother. But that didn't mean he couldn't be missing.

"When were you last in contact with your son?"

"Halloween. I spoke with him on the phone around three. He was supposed to meet me for dinner the next day, but he didn't show up and I didn't hear from him. I haven't heard from him since."

Nine days.

"And he hadn't said anything about taking a trip anywhere?"

"No."

"Have you spoken to any of his friends?"

"I don't know Robbie's friends anymore," she confessed. "I don't know if he has any."

"Does he have a girlfriend? A boyfriend?"

She shook her head.

"Where does he work?"

She glanced away. "He's . . . between jobs."

Annie wrote *unemployed* on her legal pad.

"So he could have just decided to—"

"He didn't."

"He normally stays in touch with you?"

"He calls me every day, twice a day."

"You're close."

"We have a deal," B'Lynn said plainly. "He calls me every day, twice a day, and we have dinner on Sunday. Every Sunday."

Deal?? Annie noted.

The door swung open, and Valerie Comb came in with a single mug of coffee and two thimble-size containers of fake creamer. She gave Annie the side-eye as she set the cup on the table in front of B'Lynn.

"So sorry, Annie, I couldn't carry everything," she said with saccharine sweetness.

"That's all right, Valerie," Annie replied with a phony smile. "I wouldn't have drunk it anyway."

Valerie narrowed her eyes and pressed her lips together in a pissy line as she turned on her high heel and left the room.

"She doesn't like me," Annie confessed casually when the secretary had gone. "I know too much about her sordid past."

"She doesn't like me, either," B'Lynn said as she peeled back the tops on both creamers and dumped them into the coffee. Her hands were still trembling. She wrapped them around the mug and raised it to her lips. "But I did call her a liar and almost knock her flat."

"She's been called worse," Annie said. "She said you wanted to see Sheriff Noblier. Do you know him?"

"I've met him. My husband knows him, has supported him in the past. I was hoping if I could appeal to him directly, maybe something would happen."

"Your husband, he didn't try to reach out to the sheriff himself?"

"No."

A short answer with a long story behind it, Annie suspected.

"Robbie's father isn't involved in his life anymore."

"So your son wouldn't have reached out to him?"

"No."

Annie wrote *Divorced?* but didn't ask the question yet, glancing again at the rock on the woman's left hand. Remarried, perhaps, not that it mattered.

"This deal you have with your son," Annie started, trying to pick her way through a minefield of wrong words. Why was a grown man that much under his mother's thumb? She needed the story without putting the woman on the defensive. "Tell me more about that. It seems very formal. Is there a reason behind it?"

B'Lynn frowned and looked away again, considering her answer. Would she tell the truth? Would she tool the truth to suit her needs? It was a straightforward question, Annie thought. There should have been a straightforward answer.

"My son has had his issues."

"What kind of issues?"

She set the mug down a little too hard and smiled a brittle smile. "Here we go! This is where I tell the truth and you stop listening, and nothing more happens because you've made up your mind. That's exactly what happened with the town police. That's exactly what happened when I came here the first time."

"I can't help you if I don't know the whole story," Annie said.

"And when you know the whole story, you won't want to help me."

"You don't know that," Annie said, leaning forward, resting her forearms on the table. "I'm a mother, too. And I literally came into work this morning because I wanted to be able to help someone. That's why I do what I do. But I need to have all the facts—good and bad."

B'Lynn Fontenot stared at her for a long moment, pretending to weigh her options when she actually had none.

"My son has a drug problem," she began. "He's had a drug problem off and on for a long time. He's been in and out of trouble, in and out of jail, in and out of rehab. He's been clean recently," she hastened to add. "He's been checking in with me every day, twice a day. That's our deal since he got out of rehab this time. I'll help him out with money, and in any other way I can, but he has to stay clean, and he has to stay in touch."

"How long has he been out of rehab?"

"Five months, and he's been doing well. He had a job at the lamp factory, but they had layoffs recently . . ."

Annie kept her expression carefully neutral. An addict just out of rehab needed stability and little successes to keep them encouraged and moving forward one small step at a time. Losing a job might easily have been enough of a stressor to send Robbie into a depression, looking for an escape, looking for something to numb the pain of his disappointment.

"He was looking for another job," B'Lynn said. "He was optimistic. He told me he had a line on something."

"Do you know what?"

"He didn't say."

"You heard from him on Halloween at what time?"

"Around three in the afternoon."

"Did he have plans for the evening?"

"Not that he said."

"There's a lot of parties on Halloween," Annie pointed out. "Monster Bash going on downtown," she said, referring to the huge annual street festival that took over downtown Bayou Breaux for the holiday every year, where costumed revelers wandered from bar to bar, street vendor to street vendor, enjoying food and drink and live music. "Old patterns are easy to fall back into."

B'Lynn shook her head, her jaw set at a stubborn angle. "He knew better. He's been on the straight and narrow. He was optimistic, upbeat. He's been talking about going back to school part-time, working toward getting his degree."

Or so he told his mama, who was helping him out financially. It was painful to watch the range of emotions pass across her face— anger, determination, hope, fear—an endless cycle for the mother of an addict.

"Does he have a car?" Annie asked.

"Yes. It's a blue Toyota Corolla, eight or nine years old." She rattled off the tag number by heart.

"Is it registered to him or to you?"

"It's in my name. For the insurance."

"And you gave this information to the police?"

"Yes, of course."

Meaning there should already have been an order for local law enforcement to be on the lookout for the car.

"When did you first report him missing?"

"Last Tuesday. I never heard from him that Sunday. I waited through Monday, hoping, thinking . . ." She shook her head. "I went to the police first thing Tuesday morning. They weren't interested in helping me. They said Robbie would turn up. He didn't. I went back on Thursday, and they said it wasn't a crime for him to go wherever he wanted. Then I came here, and I was told it was a city police matter and that he'd likely turn up on his own when he was ready."

"Who did you speak to here?"

B'Lynn scowled, gesturing toward the door. "That man at the desk."

"Sergeant Hooker," Annie said, doodling an angry face on her legal pad. "Did you report the car stolen?"

"No," B'Lynn said, confused. "Why would I? It's Robbie's to use."

Annie hesitated to answer, trying to formulate the right words.

B'Lynn's eyes widened. "Do you mean to tell me the police will look harder for a stolen car than for a missing person?"

"That's not exactly how I'd say it," Annie said. "But you already know the police think your son is free to go wherever he wants. However, he is not free to go in a stolen car."

"Then the car is stolen!" B'Lynn said urgently. "It's definitely stolen!"

"Okay. We'll file that report right away."

"But not the missing persons report?"

How to say that a drug addict gone off on his own wouldn't be considered as much a priority as a suspect in a felony theft? Annie chose not to try.

"So you spoke to Robbie late in the day on Halloween, and he said he didn't have any plans. Did you believe him?"

It wasn't hard to imagine an addict, down on his luck, feeling blue, catching up with some old buddies at a party. Life seemed so much better high. Maybe just this one night . . . He'd get sober again the next day . . . Then one pill became two or someone offered to share a needle . . .

B'Lynn didn't answer, which was answer enough. She wasn't sure. She couldn't be sure.

"What's his drug of choice?"

"Oxycontin, or anything like it."

"Heroin if he can't get it?" Annie asked.

Painkillers eventually became a difficult habit for a lot of people to sustain. What might have started as a legitimate prescription for a necessary drug quickly became an addiction. But prescriptions ran out, and addicts turned to other sources. Demand kept the street price high—$30 to $50 a pill, depending on strength and brand name. Those who couldn't afford the cost of pills from dealers often turned to heroin for a more affordable high. But heroin was now often cut with fentanyl, a synthetic opioid fifty to a hundred times more potent than morphine. Overdoses were depressingly common.

The mother shook her head. "He doesn't do needles. It's practically a phobia. He would never inject anything. He might try something else, but he wouldn't shoot up."

Annie said nothing, mentally ticking off the long, depressing list of the many other things an addict might try.

"I know what you're thinking," B'Lynn Fontenot said softly. "I've thought it, too. I'm not unrealistic, Detective. I know what addicts do. I know the promises they make and break. I am well aware he could be lying dead somewhere.

"Ten years we've been struggling with this—Robbie's addiction. There's nothing I don't know about dealing with an addict. My son has disappointed me and disappointed himself again and again. And I know exactly how pathetic I'm gonna sound when I say this, but he was *truly* doing better this time. He was trying *so* hard. We were trying hard together, and I'm not gonna give up on him now, no matter where he is or why he's there. But I need help. *Please* help me."

Ten years. Robbie Fontenot had been seventeen, just a boy, when addiction had taken hold of his life. And here was his mother, a decade later, still fighting for him, begging for help.

Annie had started the day wanting the distraction of someone else's problems. B'Lynn Fontenot had a boatload of them. *Careful what you wish for, Annie*, she thought. This situation wasn't liable to have a happy ending.

"I'll help you, Mrs. Fontenot," she said simply, though she had a feeling there wouldn't be anything simple about it.

B'Lynn Fontenot blinked back tears. "Thank you."

"Do you have a key to his place?" Annie asked.

"Yes."

"Okay." She nodded, pushing to her feet. "Let's go."

4

"HOW DID IT START?" THE DETECTIVE ASKED, GLANCING OVER at her from the driver's seat as they waited for an opening in traffic to pull out of the law enforcement center. "Your son's addiction. How'd it start?"

B'Lynn took a deep breath and sighed, wondering how many times she'd told this story over the years. Too many.

Once was too many.

"Robbie played football in high school. He blew out his left knee during a practice at the beginning of his senior year. He had to have reconstructive surgery."

She left out the details of an injury so devastating, they had feared for a time he might lose his lower leg. She left out the part of the story about how talented her son had been, how he had been courted by college scouts. He'd had a bright, exciting future, such big dreams, so much to look forward to, and in a single moment all that opportunity was gone. The college scouts disappeared. Fans and fair-weather friends faded from his life. His classmates kept moving forward at the breakneck pace of senior year and all the activities that entailed, while Robbie's life stopped hard, then crept forward, defined by grueling hours of physical therapy and time spent with tutors as he struggled to catch up academically. He lost who he had been. Depression had descended on him like a dark cloud and swallowed him whole.

"He got hooked on the painkillers," the detective prompted as they drove toward downtown. It was a statement, not a question. She clearly knew the gist of the story. The way things were in the world, she had doubtless heard many different versions of the same basic tale.

"His doctor prescribed Oxycontin post-op. I didn't like the idea, but my husband said not to worry. It wouldn't be for long. Just to get him past the worst of it. But that's not how it worked out."

"What does your husband do?"

B'Lynn felt her lips turn in that too-familiar ironic smile. "He's a doctor. Was. Was my husband," she hastened to clarify. "He's still a doctor."

The detective cut another glance in her direction, looking at her wedding ring, B'Lynn thought, wondering why she still wore it, no doubt. That was a long story of her own bitterness and stubbornness, and her vindictive and pointless desire to aggravate and embarrass Robert. Detective Broussard didn't need to hear about that.

"You remarried?" she asked.

"No."

"Have you spoken to your ex about your son being missing?"

"I texted him. He hasn't heard from Robbie. They don't speak. They haven't had a relationship for a long time. Robert can't accept having a failure for a son. It reflects badly on him."

That was unfair, to a certain extent, but B'Lynn didn't care. Her anger toward her ex was one of the few indulgences she allowed herself these days. Blaming Robert made her feel less bad about herself, briefly distracting her from her own failures as a parent.

They had gone through the nightmare of Robbie's addiction together at first, a united front. She, the dutiful doctor's wife, had let her husband take the lead, going along with his ideas on treatment facilities and parenting style. Mr. Tough Love, taking the hard line, eventually cut their son off after one too many relapses, one too many transgressions. She had gone along with it, exhausted and at her wit's end, ground down by the experience and by Robert's domineering personality. If she lived to be a thousand, she would never forgive herself for it. And she would certainly never forgive him.

"I'll need his contact information anyway," Detective Broussard said, hitting the blinker and taking a left. "Does he live here in town?"

"No. He lives in Lafayette."

He had established his career at Lafayette General Orthopedic Hospital when Robbie was small, but they had chosen to settle in Bayou Breaux, where B'Lynn had grown up, wanting to raise their kids in the sanity and security of a small town, where life was simpler and bad things didn't happen—or so they had naively believed. But bad things didn't require a minimum population or draw a line at a maximum income level.

"What kind of doctor is he?"

"Orthopedics." Which had made the situation with Robbie's injury and rehab ironically worse than if his dad had been an internist or a gastroenterologist or any other kind of doctor. Robert had been a specialist first and a father second at a time when his son had needed love and support and understanding more than expertise and judgment.

B'Lynn looked over at the detective. She was young—in her early thirties, maybe—with dark hair and dark eyes. Pretty in a girl-next-door kind of way. *I looked like that once*, she thought, not quite believing herself. It seemed so long ago in so many ways.

"You said you're a mother, too," she said.

Broussard nodded. "He's five. Just started kindergarten this fall."

B'Lynn immediately flashed back to Robbie's first day of school, how cute he'd been in his new clothes, carrying a little dinosaur backpack that seemed almost as big as he was. So sweet, so innocent. She pressed her lips together, afraid to open her mouth for fear of something grim and cynical tumbling out, like *Enjoy him while you can.*

"Such a cute age," she said at last.

Looking ahead, she could see the big, rusting corrugated metal warehouse looming off to the left in the distance. Her landmark for Robbie's downtrodden neighborhood.

"It's just up here on the left," she said, pointing.

The street was narrow and badly in need of repaving, forgotten by the city long ago. The shabby, narrow shotgun houses squatted beneath the oak trees like toadstools in the weed-choked yards. Four in a row, side by side, with shedding paint and sagging porches and roofs that looked like they wouldn't make it through the next big hurricane. Yet Annie knew the buildings had somehow managed to stand there since the days of hoopskirts and slave labor, when this land had been part of a long-gone plantation. Funny, the things that lasted to serve as reminders of the past.

"It's the first one," B'Lynn said.

Annie pulled into the two sparsely graveled tracks that denoted a driveway and cut the engine.

"I budgeted a certain amount of money toward his rent," B'Lynn explained. "This is the place he picked. He said he liked the privacy— meaning he didn't want to live anywhere I could easily spy on him."

"Would you?" Annie asked as they got out of the car. "Spy on him?"

"That's tempting after all we've been through," B'Lynn admitted. "I mean, here we are. I looked away for a minute, and he's gone."

"Is the lease in your name or his?" she asked, thinking ahead to any procedural no-no's of a search of the premises.

"Mine. Needless to say, Robbie's credit score isn't exactly stellar."

Annie mounted the steps to the sad little porch. She stood a bit to one side and knocked, trying not to recall the deputy who had gotten shotgunned through the door of a drug house some years before.

"Hello?" she called, knocking a second time, then listening for any sound of movement. She thought she heard a faint scraping sound, then instantly wondered if she had imagined it. "Hello? Sheriff's office. Anybody home?"

A wave of anxiety rolled through her as she waited for an answer. Silly, she told herself. This was just a welfare check. No big deal.

Don't go there without me. Nick's text from the night of her attack flashed through her mind's eye. She remembered feeling tired and impatient. She had just needed to make a quick stop to deliver some news, then head home. No big deal. What could go wrong?

Everything.

"Are you all right?"

B'Lynn Fontenot's voice startled her back into the moment.

"I'm fine," Annie said, but her hand was trembling a little as she put the key in the lock. The last time she had walked into a strange house, she had left it by ambulance.

Holding her breath, she pushed the door open, still standing slightly to the side, her right hand resting on the butt of her sidearm, her heart rate picking up as she braced herself for something that didn't happen.

The anxiety ebbed. She breathed again as she looked down the dark side hall. True to the name of the architecture, you could have shot a shotgun in the front door and not hit a thing on the way out the back door . . . which stood wide open.

A person emerged from the last room down the hall. A short body on skinny, wide-set legs, arms wrapped awkwardly around a good-size flat-screen TV as they hurried for the back door.

B'Lynn gasped and shouted, "Thief!"

"Stay here!" Annie ordered. She drew her weapon and hustled after the burglar. "Sheriff's office! Stop right there! Stop!"

The thief continued out the door, off the back porch, and hung a staggering right, heading toward the house next door, struggling with the grip on the television, shouting, "I didn't do nothing!"

"You're stealing a TV!" Annie said, incredulous. "I'm looking right at you!"

The thief glanced back over a hunched shoulder to hurl an angry "Fuck you!"—a crucial mistake that threw momentum and balance out of alignment and sent him/her—Annie still wasn't sure—into a drunken spiral that ended with a strangled cry and a thud. Like a character in a cartoon, the perpetrator fell backside-down, feet up in the air, dirty flip-flops flying off into the weeds, and lay moaning, trapped beneath the television like an upended turtle.

"Oh, for God's sake!" Annie grumbled, pulling her phone out of her pocket to call for backup.

"You're under arrest," she announced, looking down at the thief as she waited for the call to connect.

A woman, she decided, though it could have gone either way. Limp, shaggy dishwater-blond hair. A wide, flat face with the sunken features and bad skin of an addict. She struggled to get out from under the television, skinny arms and legs flailing. Shoving the TV off her chest, she revealed a bleached-out red Fuck Your Feelings T-shirt. Charming.

"Don't you even think about getting up!" Annie snapped, pointing a finger in warning. Her call went through, and she identified herself and requested a deputy to come to the address.

"Where's my son?" B'Lynn Fontenot demanded as she came off the porch and made a beeline for the thief. "Where's Robbie?"

"How would I know?" Fuck Your Feelings grumbled, struggling to sit up, grimacing as she felt the back of her head.

"Please stand back, Mrs. Fontenot," Annie said, stepping in her path. "I'll ask the questions. Why don't you take a seat on the porch?"

"I don't want to take a seat," B'Lynn snapped. "I want to know where my son is!"

"That's my job to find out," Annie said. "Please let me do it."

She turned back toward the thief, who had begun to crab-walk backward toward the next house, as if she thought she might sneak away in broad daylight with a sheriff's detective standing three feet away.

"What do you think you're doing?"

"You told me not to get up!"

"Are you high?" Annie leaned down, looking for dilated pupils. "Are you high right now?"

"No, but I wish I was," the thief said belligerently. "You can't arrest me for wishing!"

"I'm arresting you for stealing that TV."

"It's mine! I loaned it to that guy."

"That's a bald-faced lie!" B'Lynn shouted, pacing back and forth maybe ten feet away, arms crossed tight over her chest. "I gave that TV to Robbie. It came out of my guest room. I have the serial number at home."

The thief made a face. "Who keeps the serial number for a TV?"

"You're friends with the guy that lives here?" Annie asked. "What's his name?"

"Uh . . . Donnie?"

"Wrong."

"I call him Donnie."

"Why would you loan a TV to a guy you don't even know his name?"

"I'm nice that way."

"Uh-huh." Annie rolled her eyes. "You're a regular ray of freaking sunshine, you are. What's your name?"

"I don't have to tell you nothing! I know my rights!"

"No doubt by heart. But I'll refresh your memory, just the same."

Annie recited the Miranda warning as she pulled her handcuffs off her belt. "Stand up, please."

"Fuck yourself."

"You're not doing yourself any favors here being an ass to me,

Sunshine," Annie said, going around behind her and bending down to cuff one wrist and then the other.

"Not doing you any favors, either."

"And here I'm probably the nicest person you're gonna meet to-day," Annie said as a car door slammed in the distance.

She glanced down the narrow space between the two houses, expecting to see a sheriff's office cruiser; instead, a town cop in uniform came walking up, hand resting on the butt of his sidearm.

"Everything all right back here, ma'am?" he asked with a pleasant smile. He was maybe thirty and built like a small bull. His gray uniform shirt was tailored tight over his bulletproof vest. His jaw was square, his face all sharp angles capped with a head of blond-tipped dark hair. Annie recognized him from around town. Danny Perry. People called him Hollywood. It wasn't a compliment.

She held up the badge she wore on a ball chain around her neck. "Detective Broussard. Sheriff's office."

"What you got going on here, Detective? You need help? Oh, hey, Rayanne," he said to the thief. "What you got yourself into now?"

"You know Little Miss Sunshine here?" Annie asked.

"Oh, yeah. Rayanne Tillis. Me and Rayanne go way back, don't we, Rayanne? How many times have I arrested you?"

The thief made a face at him. "I'd tell you to stick it up your ass, Danny, but you'd probably like it."

"She's a charmer," Perry said. "What's she done this time?"

"Caught red-handed stealing a TV from this house."

The officer raised his eyebrows, pretending to be impressed. "B and E. You're moving up in the criminal world, Rayanne."

"What's her usual?" Annie asked.

"Oh, you know, possession, shoplifting, the odd twenty-dollar blow job."

"You never complain," Rayanne remarked.

The officer narrowed his eyes at her and then turned back to Annie. "For the record, I have not partaken."

Annie just looked at him, unamused and unconvinced.

"What brings you to town, Detective?" he asked. "Something going on I should know about?"

"Yes, you should know about it," B'Lynn Fontenot snapped, coming in from the side. "You *would* know if you had any interest in doing your job."

Perry looked ambushed. "Ma'am?"

"This is Mrs. Fontenot," Annie said. "Her son lives in this house right here."

"Except that he's been missing more than a week, and y'all have not done one damn thing about it!" B'Lynn stepped right up to the officer. She looked ready to punch him. Annie wasn't entirely sure she wouldn't.

"You don't know about Robbie Fontenot being missing?" Annie asked. "Is this your regular patrol area, Officer Perry?"

"Well, yes, but—"

"But what?" B'Lynn demanded. "But you don't give a rat's behind?"

"No, well, no, that's not it at all," Perry stammered. "I came over here with Detective Rivette on a welfare check a few days ago. We didn't find any reason to be concerned."

"He's *MISSING*!" B'Lynn shouted directly into his face.

Perry frowned and puffed himself up, trying too late to project an air of authority. "Ma'am, please calm down."

Annie cringed.

"Calm down? *Calm down?!*" B'Lynn raged. "My son could be dead by now because of you people, because of your gross incompetence and abject lack of humanity. And you tell me to *calm down*? I am all out of Calm Down!"

She was red in the face, eyes wet with tears she refused to let fall. Annie gently rested a hand on her shoulder. Her small body was vibrating with fury and fear and helplessness.

"Come on, B'Lynn," she murmured. "Let's just get on with it. I want you to go in the house and have a look around. Don't touch anything. Just look and see if anything is missing or out of place. Can you do that for me?"

B'Lynn drew in a sharp breath and stepped back, fighting to compose herself for the umpteenth time that morning. Annie watched her walk back to the house, then turned to the officer. "Let me give you a few words of wisdom, Danny. Never in the history of the world has an upset woman ever calmed down because a man told her to calm down. Don't ever do that."

"Well, but I just—"

She held up a hand to cut him off just as a sheriff's office cruiser came down the alley. "No mansplaining necessary, thank you. She's a mother who can't find her son."

"He's an addict with a record—"

"She's well aware of that. He's still her son."

Perry huffed a frustrated sigh as he watched the radio car approach. "So, you're just taking this over?" he said, making a vague gesture toward the house.

"Looks that way, yeah," Annie said casually, though she had the distinct feeling she was about to kick over a small hornet's nest.

Cops were territorial animals, and the Bayou Breaux PD, a much smaller agency, was ever in the shadow of the sheriff's office. Only the governor of Louisiana had more power than a parish sheriff, and Gus Noblier had been sheriff a very long time. He had finally retired, only to be pressed back into service after the death of his successor, no doubt much to the consternation of Chief of Police Johnny Earl. The two men had disliked each other for a decade or more, constantly butting heads. While the agencies coexisted and cooperated with each other by necessity, that rivalry was always just under the surface.

"Rivette's gonna be pissed," Perry announced.

"Why?" Annie asked. "I'm just taking something off his plate he didn't want in the first place. He should send me flowers."

"You're making him look bad."

"How's that? I didn't make Mrs. Fontenot show up at the

sheriff's office this morning, begging for help. What was I supposed to do? Throw her out in the street? Y'all don't even think this is worth investigating, do you?" she asked. "Robbie Fontenot is just another addict who up and left or OD'd somewhere. I'll probably come to the same conclusion. I'll just be kinder about it, that's all."

The deputy got out of the cruiser and came across the weedy lawn toward them. "Hey, Annie, whatcha got?"

"Young Prejean," Annie greeted him. If the poor kid had a first name, nobody cared. He was called Young Prejean because he was the younger of the two Prejeans in uniform for the SO. He was twenty-two, wide-eyed and fresh-faced with a pathetic tuft of billy goat whiskers masquerading as a goatee on his chin.

"I need you to take this lady in for me," Annie said. "Put her in a holding cell. Don't book her yet."

Young Prejean looked around the yard, tilting his head like a confused puppy. "What lady?"

"You can suck my ass, Deputy Dog!" Rayanne Tillis shouted as Annie gestured toward her. "And I didn't steal nothing! I was just borrowing it."

Annie arched a brow at her. "I thought you were loaning it to him."

"I did, Miss Stick Up Your Ass. And now I'm loaning it back to me."

"Oh, Lord help me," Annie grumbled. To the deputy she said, "This is Miss Rayanne. Don't let her work her feminine wiles on you."

"Watch out," Danny Perry warned. "She'll bite, too."

"Oh, hey, Danny," Young Prejean said. "She a friend of yours?"

"Frequent flier."

"How come we're taking her, then?"

"'Cause I said so," Annie said, wrinkling her nose as she picked Rayanne's filthy flip-flops out of the grass. "Don't strain yourself thinking about it. I'll be along directly. Miss Rayanne and I need to have a chat."

"Hell to the no!" Rayanne declared, then made an ugly bulldog face at her. "I got the right to remain silent."

Annie rolled her eyes. "That hasn't stopped you so far. Come on now, get up and put your shoes on."

She helped the woman to her feet and patted her down, blinking hard at the unpleasant smell of sour sweat and stale sex.

"You got anything sharp in your pockets gonna stick me?"

"I hope so."

"You need to think on being friendlier to me, Rayanne," Annie advised. "I can make your life easier or harder. Your choice."

She handed off her thief to Young Prejean and started back toward the house. Dismissing Danny Perry, she said, "I'll call Rivette when I get back to my desk," dreading the idea.

Welcome back to work, Annie, she thought as she climbed the back steps. She'd caught a case, caught a burglar, and started an interagency war, and it wasn't even noon.

Her phone pinged the arrival of a text message.

Have you counted all the paper clips?

Nick.

Not yet, she typed, adding a smiley-face emoji, and left it at that.

What he didn't know could wait. He wasn't liable to be happy about this situation. As her boss, he would take the brunt of any blowup over the potential turf war. As her overprotective husband, he would have preferred to wrap her in cotton wool and tuck her away someplace quiet than have her digging into a missing person's case with potential drug involvement.

Oh, well.

5

B'LYNN WAS STANDING IN HER SON'S TINY BEDROOM AT THE back of the house, looking small and lost and drained in an unguarded moment. As soon as she saw Annie, she pulled herself up taller and put on her game face like a warrior putting on armor. She had to be exhausted, bone-weary after a week of worry and anger, fighting to get anyone to listen, much less care, about her missing son.

"They haven't done a goddamn thing!" she said, pointing toward the backyard. "He's been gone more than a week and they haven't done a goddamn thing!"

"I'm sorry, B'Lynn."

"It's not your fault. You're the first person to even listen to me."

"Have you looked around?" Annie asked. "Is anything missing?"

"I don't know. It's hard to tell," B'Lynn said, turning around in a circle.

The room was messy but not dirty. The bed was unmade, a tangle of blue sheets, a single pillow. A side chair held a pile of cast-off clothes.

The closet door stood open. An assortment of shirts hung on the rod. A gray roll-aboard carry-on-size suitcase sat on the floor, tucked back in the corner behind a pile of sneakers. If Robbie Fontenot had taken a trip, he was traveling light.

Annie pulled on a pair of gloves and opened the drawer of the single nightstand, bracing herself for a stash of pill bottles, but there were none. There was nothing but a half-dozen foil packs of condoms, which made her wonder again about the possibility of a girlfriend or boyfriend. Or maybe he preferred to pay for his pleasure with his friendly neighborhood prostitute, Rayanne. Could be that was how she knew about the TV.

On top of the nightstand, a cheap glass ashtray held a few spent butts.

"Is Robbie one to keep cash around?" she asked, bending over for a quick look beneath the bed, checking for a stash or a body, finding nothing but dust.

"He's unemployed. Where would he get any cash to speak of?"

Selling drugs. Selling himself. Fencing stolen goods. The list of unlawful cash sources rolled through Annie's head, but she said none of it.

"What about any valuables? Watches, rings, neck chains—anything like that?"

"We gave him a nice watch when he graduated from high school," B'Lynn said. "He sold it to buy drugs."

On the dresser, a plastic dish held loose change and a matchbook from the Quik Pik convenience store on the south side of town.

"Is he a drinker?"

"He's not supposed to be. I know he'll have a beer now and again, but other than that, he doesn't drink in front of me."

"No DUIs on his record?"

"When he was eighteen he totaled his father's Porsche. He was drunk and high. That prompted his first trip to rehab," B'Lynn said as they moved from the bedroom to a bathroom the size of a phone booth. She stood in the doorway while Annie checked the medicine cabinet. "He lost his license for two years the next time it happened, but it hasn't happened since . . . that I know of."

As young bachelor bathrooms went, this one was better than average in terms of cleanliness. It smelled of mildew, but so did the rest of the old house. A used bath towel hung over the shower curtain rod instead of being left in a crumpled heap on the floor. The toilet seat was up, but the bowl was flushed. The medicine cabinet held a razor, shaving foam, a bottle of Advil, a bottle of mouthwash. No hard drugs. Of course, Rayanne Tillis could have helped herself to any prescription bottles on a prior visit.

The tiny kitchen was suspiciously tidy. Someone had taken the trash out. There were no dirty dishes in the sink, no food left out on the counters. Nothing had boiled over on the 1970s vintage stove and been left to crust over. Junkies generally lived in squalor, their only concern being their next high.

Annie glanced at B'Lynn. "Is this the way he left it?"

"No," she admitted. "I washed a few dishes and took out the trash last week."

Took out the trash and any evidence that might have been in it.

"I wasn't going to leave it and get roaches. This place is bad enough as it is."

"You didn't take any pills out of here, did you?" Annie asked bluntly. "Or drug paraphernalia?"

"No. Absolutely not. What good would it do me to lie about it?"

"None," Annie said. "But that doesn't stop people doing it."

In her experience, people often preferred to hold on to a fairy tale about a loved one than admit a brutal truth, to protect the loved one's reputation or simply to protect their own feelings. B'Lynn Fontenot didn't strike her as one of those people, but at the same time, she was a mother wanting to believe her son was staying on the straight and narrow when he had run his life into a ditch again and again.

"I quit lying to myself about Robbie a long time ago, Detective," she said wearily. "I'm sure as hell not going to lie about him to you. I want him back, whatever state he's in. I'm not going to sabotage the effort by painting a pretty picture."

"Good."

They moved on to the front room of the house, a small living room with stained wallpaper, old linoleum, and furniture that stank of decades of cigarettes. There was a conspicuous blank spot on a console table where the television had been and a disconnected gaming station on the shelf beneath. There was nothing personal in the room, no photos, no mementos.

"I don't see his laptop anywhere," B'Lynn said. "It's a silver MacBook."

An item to list on the search warrant for whatever shithole Rayanne Tillis lived in, Annie thought. That was something, anyway. Or he might have made a habit of taking the laptop with him when he left the house, considering the neighborhood he lived in.

The house wasn't giving her much else to go on. It hadn't been tossed. There was no evidence of a violent struggle. There was no wall calendar with a big red circle around the date Robbie Fontenot had disappeared, no cryptic scribbled note with a phone number or a name on it. Those were things people Robbie Fontenot's age kept in their smartphone instead of conveniently leaving them lying around the house for the cops to find.

It looked like he had simply gone out and not come back. Danny Perry had been telling nothing but the truth when he said the welfare check executed by himself and Detective Rivette had given them no cause for concern. The only interesting part of that story was that Rivette had shown up at all. A simple welfare check was not usually of any interest to a detective. Maybe Rivette was making more of an effort than B'Lynn realized.

"All right," Annie said on a sigh. "Let's go."

"That's it?" B'Lynn asked. "Aren't you going to dust for fingerprints or something?"

"Aside from the TV thief, this doesn't appear to be a crime scene."

A hint of panic crossed B'Lynn's face. "Oh, here we go again! There's no crime!"

"I can't process the house as a crime scene when it doesn't appear a crime has been committed here," Annie explained calmly. "My time will be better spent pursuing other leads. Does your son have a bank card or credit cards? Where would those statements be kept?"

"As far as I know, he only has a debit card. He does his banking online," she said.

"What about his cell phone? Is it part of your family plan?"

"Yes."

"Good," Annie said, knowing it was only good if Robbie Fontenot was using the phone his mother provided for him and didn't have another she knew nothing about, or wasn't using a burner phone for drug business. There were a lot of very unhelpful possibilities, and the possibility that a twenty-seven-year-old man with a history of drug abuse was walking the straight and narrow was the least likely of them all.

They locked up the house, and as they started across the weed-patch lawn for Annie's vehicle, an unmarked city police sedan pulled up on the street.

"Did Detective Rivette ask you for any of this information?" Annie asked. "About Robbie's phone, his credit cards, any of that?"

"No," B'Lynn said, staring at the car as Dewey Rivette got out on the driver's side. "He didn't ask me a damn thing."

"Let me talk to him," Annie said.

"I don't have anything more to say to that man."

That was certainly a lie, but Annie could only hope B'Lynn would contain herself for the time being. She pulled in a deep breath and started toward the detective.

Dewey Rivette was in his mid-thirties, an unremarkable sort of guy—medium height, medium build, medium-brown $20 haircut. In his khakis and a button-down shirt, he had the slightly rumpled look of a single man who had never mastered the steam iron. Spoiled by his mama, no doubt. He had a round face and the petulant expression of a cranky toddler.

"What the hell do you think you're doing here, Broussard?" he demanded as he walked up to stand toe to toe with her.

"Good morning to you, too, Detective Rivette," Annie said calmly. "I'm here doing my job. How about you? Did you just drop by to say hello?"

"Am I supposed to be amused?" he snapped. "You come waltzing in here to take my case, and I'm supposed to be amused by you?"

"Well, I've never known you to have a sense of humor," Annie remarked. "So, no, I shouldn't think you'd be growing one now. And just what case are you referring to? Because when I looked, Robbie Fontenot had not been reported missing, his car had not been reported stolen, and according to his mother, you have done jack shit to find him, which is why Mrs. Fontenot came to the sheriff's office first thing this morning, begging for someone to help her."

"We took her complaint."

"And did what with it? Line a birdcage?"

"We put a BOLO out on his car."

"Oh, goodness!" Annie feigned amazement. "I hope you didn't strain yourself getting that done!"

Rivette scowled. "I can do without your sarcasm."

"Well, then you should probably leave, because I've got a bucket of that stuff for you, Dewey Done-Nothing."

His face had begun to redden in blotches. "I took her complaint. I did a welfare check." He ticked these points off on his short, stubby fingers. "If you've been inside the house, you saw for yourself there's no reason to think anything other than that he just left."

"So, case closed!" Annie said, dusting off her palms. "Pat yourself on the back, Dewey! What do you care what I'm doing, then?"

"You can't just come into town and do whatever the hell you want!"

"Actually, yes, I can. Last I checked, Bayou Breaux is in Partout Parish, which is my jurisdiction, not just yours, town boy."

"My investigation is ongoing," he insisted. "Mrs. Fontenot can't just go shopping for another law enforcement agency because I didn't return her every fucking phone call."

"Seriously? Are you new to the real world?" Annie asked. "Because you didn't return her every fucking phone call, Mrs. Fontenot came to the SO this morning to speak directly to Sheriff Noblier, as is her right."

Rivette suddenly looked sick. "She spoke with Sheriff Noblier?"

Annie said nothing and let his imagination run off.

"Fucking hell," he muttered.

"Yeah, I hope you wore your chain mail drawers today," Annie said. "I imagine Johnny Earl is gonna be looking for someone to sink his teeth into after Gus calls him."

"Jesus Christ." Rivette turned around in a little circle with his hands on his head as if trying to stop his brain from exploding. "You're making me look bad!"

"Don't be such a child," Annie snapped back. "I'm not doing anything to you. B'Lynn Fontenot came to the SO looking for help. I'm helping her. The fact that you didn't is a *you* problem, not a *me* problem."

"What was I supposed to do?" he asked. "The guy is an adult. He can go where he wants. There's nothing to say anything happened to him at all!"

"Nothing except for his criminal record and his history of drug abuse."

"I asked around. I looked," he insisted.

"Asked who? Looked where?"

"Around!"

"*Around* is not a person or a place," Annie pointed out. "You drove around to the local shithole bars looking for his car? Checked a couple of drug houses? What?"

"I don't need to tell you!"

Annie rolled her eyes, exasperated. "What are you? Five years old? A person is missing, and this is how you behave?"

"I can't pull a lead out of my ass!"

"I'm sure not," Annie said. "There's no room for one, what with your head shoved up there."

"Robbie Fontenot done picked up and left!" he argued. "That's what's happened, and who can blame him? He's a grown-ass man with his mama watching him like a hawk every minute of the day. I'd run off, too, with her breathing down my neck."

"Then why don't you, and we can all be happy?" Annie suggested. "You think this is a nothing case, then leave it alone. I may well come to the same conclusion, but I don't mind holding Mrs. Fontenot's hand along the way."

"And what am I supposed to tell Chief Earl?"

"I can't solve all your problems for you, Dewey," Annie said. "Tell him you had no case. Tell him you're still on it. I don't care what you tell him. I'm gonna do what I'm gonna do, and B'Lynn Fontenot is no longer your problem."

She stepped back and gave him a little salute. "You have yourself a beautiful day!"

Rivette stood there, red-faced with his hands on his hips. She could feel his eyes boring into her back as she went to her vehicle. She tried to feel sorry for him for a second without much success. He had blown off a mother worried for her son, as if Robbie Fontenot didn't deserve that concern, or as if B'Lynn should have been past caring. Whatever little effort Dewey Rivette had put into this was no more than half a tick past outright laziness. He deserved whatever ass chewing Johnny Earl might give him.

She was halfway back to her vehicle when the passenger door opened and B'Lynn popped up like a jack-in-the-box. Her laser stare blasted right past Annie.

"You're a tool, Dewey Rivette!" she shouted.

"I guess you had something more to say after all," Annie said as she rounded the hood of the car. "I appreciate that you didn't rush over and punch him in the throat. Though I admit I would have enjoyed watching that."

"His day may yet come," B'Lynn muttered, settling back down in the passenger seat.

One way or another, Annie thought as she started the car and shifted into reverse. She watched Dewey Rivette in the rearview mirror as she drove away, standing in the sorry little yard like a lost soul, growing smaller and less significant by the second. She hoped he would stay that way.

6

THE HUGE SIGN MUST HAVE BEEN THIRTY YEARS OLD, WEATH-
ered and worn, painted and repainted over the decades. It was
mounted on cut-down power poles fifty yards before the driveway.
MERCIER & SONS SALVAGE AND SWAMP TOURS with an airboat-load
of bug-eyed cartoon tourists gaping at an alligator down in the
right-hand corner, the gator's jaws open wide, ready to snap on the
first person to fall out of the careening boat.

The business was crammed onto ten acres of land on both sides
of the old canal road on the butt end of the town of Luck. The marine salvage and tour business were located on the canal side, auto
salvage on the other side. The property was a wasteland of decrepit
boats and wrecked cars, rusted metal, and rotting wood contained
inside the confines of high chain-link fencing crowned with a con-
certina wire overhang, like a prison yard for junk.

Nick pulled in at the gate with the red arrow pointing to the office and parked in front of the first of three large World War II–era
Quonset hut buildings—half-round cylinders of time-worn,
weather-beaten galvanized steel.

"Man, I hate these places," Stokes griped, unwrapping a stick of gum as he got out of his car. He looked around and made a face.

"Look at that mess," he said, nodding toward the corral of trashed cars gutted of their engines, stripped of their tires, hoods up or missing, doors hanging open. "There could be anything out there. Rats and snakes. For sure there's snakes. And trunks full of drugs and dead bodies for all we know."

Nick cut him a sideways look. "You're up to date on your tetanus shot, yeah?"

"I don't know why I put up with you."

"Because you have no choice."

"Well, it sure ain't your sunny disposition."

The door and two long horizontal windows of the building marked OFFICE were fitted with iron bars for security and plastered with redneck bumper stickers and product logos for Pennzoil and Snap-on tools, support for the NRA, Browning rifles, and Ducks Unlimited. A hand-lettered sign proclaimed: WE REServE THE RIGHT TO REFusE ServicE TO ANyBoDy!!

"Like it's a freaking five-star restaurant," Stokes quipped. "I didn't know junk dealers could be so choosy."

A bell rang as they opened the door and went inside, though whether it could be heard over the blaring country music was debatable. The smells of oil, grease, and sweeping compound made a thick perfume that assaulted the senses. Long rows of tall industrial metal shelving were crammed with all manner of engine and car parts, household plumbing fixtures, pipes of all descriptions, light fixtures, and electrical wiring.

At the front of the space, a long cypress-wood counter that looked like it might have come out of an old-time drugstore marked off the office section of the building. Several chrome-legged stools with ripped vinyl seats invited customers to sit and shoot the breeze. Behind the counter, more shelving was piled with precarious mountains of paperwork and thick catalogs. A doorway led into what looked to Nick like a small private office—more shelves stuffed with who knew what.

A woman's harsh voice called out from inside the little room: "Turn down that goddamn music! *Merde!* I can't hear me think! Do you hear me, Luc Mercier?!

"*Mais ça c'est fou!* 'Course he don't hear me 'cause of that goddamn radio," she muttered, coming out of the office. "Damn *couillon.*"

She was a tall, rawboned woman, thin and sinewy with wide hips and a lean, unadorned face. Her hair was steel gray and scalp short. She stopped in her tracks and stared with narrowed eyes at Nick and Stokes. Men with badges hanging around their necks were not her regular customers.

"Lieutenant Fourcade, Sheriff's Office," Nick said. "This is Detective Stokes."

The woman said nothing as the color drained from her face. She stood frozen, as if she were afraid to move, afraid to breathe.

"You say something, Mama?" a man's voice called. Luc Mercier emerged from the murky darkness of the shelf rows, thirtyish, six feet of stocky muscle, with a day's growth of dark beard, and a shiner on his right eye.

"Can I help you fellas?" he asked, wiping his meaty hands on a greasy rag.

"Turn off that goddamn radio!" his mother shouted, snapping out of her state of suspended animation.

He turned on his heel and headed back down the first aisle to kill the music.

The woman turned back to Nick. "Is it Marc?" she asked. "Was it a car wreck?"

"Ma'am?"

"My son Marc. Marc Mercier. Is he dead?" she asked, and crossed herself over the front of her bib overalls.

The picture of the faceless body flashed through Nick's mind, the body he'd sent to the morgue at Our Lady of Mercy with a John

Doe toe tag. The mystery could be solved right there and then, which was way more than he had hoped for—and not at all what this woman wanted to hear. That was how quickly lives could be turned on their heads, upended and tumbled all over the place, like dice from a cup. Just like that.

"We ain't heard from him since Saturday," the woman went on. She turned toward her present son as he came back. "I told you! I told you something terrible happened! And would you listen to me? Hell no!"

He threw his hands up. "Well, what the hell was I supposed to do about it? Drive up and down every goddamned road in the parish looking for him?"

"You don't ever listen to me!"

"Oh, I hear you! Jesus Christ! My ears are ringing all damn day with it!"

Nick held a hand up like a referee and barked, "*Arrête! C'est assez!* We need to begin here again, yeah? There's been no car crash I know of. Let's start there."

"Jesus," Luc Mercier muttered half under his breath. "Going off half cocked for no damn reason, as usual."

"Shut your mouth!" his mother snapped.

"What happened, then?" she asked, turning back to Nick. "What are you doing here?"

"What's your name, ma'am?" Nick asked, opening his notebook and clicking his pen.

"Kiki Mercier."

"And how old is your son Marc?"

"Twenty-eight."

"What's he look like?"

She hooked a thumb in the direction of her other son. "Like this one, but taller."

"How tall?"

"Six foot two," Luc said, his straight, thick brows drawing together in suspicion. "Why would you ask that?"

Tall enough, Nick thought. He would have brown eyes, like his mother and his brother and the corpse.

"What kind of vehicle does he drive?" Stokes asked.

"He's got a brand-new flat black Ford Raptor truck," Luc answered.

"Sweet ride! You know the tag number?"

"No."

"What kind of tires on it?"

"BFGoodrich all-terrains," he said, looking from one of them to the other with growing suspicion. "What the hell kind of questions are these?"

"If he's missing, we need to be looking for him, right?" Stokes said. "Have you reported him missing?"

"No. We figured he'd turn up. He ain't been gone that long," Luc said irritably.

"Marc don't ever miss work," Kiki said. "We didn't hear from him yesterday—and they were supposed to go duck hunting."

Luc rolled his eyes, impatient with the whole conversation. "I was late getting there. He left without me just to be an asshole. I guarantee it."

"*Mais* yeah, Marc being gone is all about you," Kiki said sarcastically.

"Duck season ain't started yet," Nick said.

"We was just going out to get the blind cleaned up and ready, and work the dogs some, that's all," Luc said. "Shoot some geese, maybe, or snipe. I was supposed to meet him at the Corners at five thirty in the goddamn a.m."

"And?"

He made a face. "I was late, because fuck that shit. I had a hangover."

"You ain't never been on time in your whole goddamn life," his mother remarked, "including when you was born."

"Yeah, well, that wasn't no surprise, then, was it?" Luc shot back. To Nick he said, "He'd done gone by the time I got there."

"Did you call him?"

"So he could chew my ass? No, thank you. I turned around and went home."

"And he didn't call you, ask where you're at, when you're getting there?"

"No. Because he was pissed, and better to sit out there in the boat by his own damn self and pout so he could bitch about it later."

"What kind of boat?"

"Seventeen-foot War Eagle Blackhawk with a modified V-hull."

"Where do y'all hunt?"

"We got some property on the marshes, on the western edge of the parish. I drove out there later—"

"I made him go," Kiki said. "Marc could'a been out there drowned, for all he knew."

"Well, he wasn't, was he?" Luc shot back. "He wasn't there at all."

"I tried to call him to come over for supper last night," Kiki said. "My calls, they went straight to voicemail. I tried to call that useless wife of his, but she wouldn't answer the damn phone!"

"Could they have gone somewhere together?" Nick asked.

Luc made a scoffing sound, as if the suggestion was absurd.

"Me, I called her work this morning," Kiki said. "They told me she was in a meeting."

"What's the wife's name, and where do they live?" Nick asked.

"Prissy Missy," Kiki muttered.

"Melissa," Luc answered. "Twenty-eight Quail Trace, Bayou Breaux."

"Her Royal Highness," Kiki grumbled, building up another head of steam. "Luck ain't good enough for her."

"Bayou Breaux ain't good enough for her, neither," Luc said. "Maybe Marc had enough of her bullshit and left. Who could blame him?"

"He wouldn't just up and go and leave his baby!" Kiki insisted. "Maybe she killed him!"

Luc rolled his eyes. "Don't be ridiculous!"

"Well, where's he at, then?" she demanded. "I told you something was wrong! A mother knows. I feel it in my bones! And here's the sheriffs, right here now! So who's ridiculous?"

Luc Mercier looked past her to Stokes and Nick. "Wait a minute. If you ain't here about Marc, and you don't know nothing about Marc or where he's at, then what are y'all doing here in the first place?"

Nick opened his phone and pulled up a photo of the business card he had pulled from the dead man's pocket. "We came across this card in the course of an investigation and were hoping you might be able to shed some light as to who might have had it or to what that written amount might refer."

"What kind of an investigation?" Kiki asked.

"Routine," Stokes said. "We're just clearing up the little details."

Luc Mercier stepped closer and squinted at the photo. "Probably an estimate."

Kiki peered at the photo, frowning. "That's Marc's handwriting. He makes his eights like that, like two little circles."

"Like a kindergartener," Luc grumbled.

"Does that amount mean anything to you?" Nick asked.

"Why didn't the person who had it tell you?"

"There was no one there to ask," Nick said calmly. "It's just a thing we found. Could mean nothing at all, but if you know anything about it, that could be helpful pointing us in a direction."

Luc shrugged. "Could be anything. We deal with all different kinds of people—contractors, commercial fishermen, car dealers . . . Could be for anything."

"If y'all did a deal for that amount in the last few days, you'd have a receipt for that, yeah?"

"Should have," Kiki said. "Me, I'm behind on my paperwork, though. We've been busy, and shorthanded. I was gone down Jeanerette Friday and Saturday to a visitation and a funeral. My cousin Gerry Gaudet, she died of cancer."

"Sorry for your loss," Nick said automatically. "So, who was working in here Friday and Saturday?"

"Just Marc in here," Luc said. "I was running swamp tours all day, both days."

"Evie Orgeron," Kiki said. "She minds the tickets and whatnot for the swamp tours over on the dock. She don't come in here, though. And Noelle was here."

"Helping Evie," Luc clarified.

"Who's Noelle?"

"My daughter," Kiki said.

"She's got Down's syndrome," Luc explained. "She likes to help on the dock, cleaning the boat up and whatnot. Marc was the only one working the desk Saturday."

"If there's a receipt in this amount, you'll have the name of the customer, right?" Stokes asked.

Luc Mercier shrugged. "If they bought something from us and paid with a credit card or a check, yeah. If we bought something from them, there should be a record."

Should be. Nick suspected there were probably few records of any cash transactions, people being people, not wanting to give the government a cut of their hard-earned business. And then there was always the possibility the customer had been a thief. Stolen catalytic converters brought a pretty penny, and copper was always a hot commodity. Thieves targeted construction sites and ransacked vacant houses and fish camps, stripping out all the copper they could get their hands on. It was hard to trace and easy to sell—particularly to a dealer not fussy about sources or paperwork.

"If you could check and let us know, we'd appreciate it," he said.

"What kind of an investigation did you say this is?" Kiki asked.

"I'm not free to say at the moment."

"Oh, my God," she murmured, pressing a hand to her flat chest. "He's dead, isn't he? Marc's dead."

"We don't know anything of the kind, ma'am," Nick assured her, not wanting to reveal too much too soon and cause what could very well turn out to be unnecessary anguish. There was also the matter of needing to speak with Marc Mercier's wife, who was his legal next of kin. She would be the one asked to identify his body if it came to that, or to provide something for a DNA sample.

The wife, the woman whose mother-in-law thought her capable of murder.

"Do you have any reason to think he could become a victim of foul play?" Stokes asked. "Does he have shady friends or dangerous habits? Drugs? Gambling? Anything like that?"

"Everybody loves Marc," Luc said with just enough of an edge to make Nick wonder where he'd gotten that shiner. The remark was also curiously not an answer to the question.

"Is he a party kind of guy?" Stokes asked. "Did he maybe go out Saturday night? He could be sleeping off a good time at a friend's house."

"He likes to pass a good time, like everybody," the brother said. "But his wife was still pissed off about Halloween."

"Why was that?"

"He wanted to go to Monster Bash with some friends. She had an opinion about it. He went anyway. Been in the doghouse since."

"Marriage problems often come with girlfriends and boyfriends attached," Stokes said. The voice of experience. "Is he seeing anybody outside the marriage?"

Luc Mercier made a little shrug and glanced ever so slightly away. "Not that I know of. Not that I'd blame him."

"You don't like his wife," Nick stated.

Again with the shrug. "She don't like us."

"We're not good enough for her," Kiki said. "She thought she could take Marc away from us. She thought wrong. His daddy got sick and we needed him, he come back to us, sure enough. If it wasn't for the baby, I'd tell her to pack up and go back to her people."

"Where's she from?" Stokes asked.

"Philadelphia," she said, as if the name left a bitter taste in her mouth.

A woman not only taking her son away from her, but a Yankee to boot.

"How'd they meet?"

"In college. Marc, he went to Tulane on a scholarship," Kiki said proudly.

Luc turned his head just enough that she couldn't see him roll his eyes.

"Have you had problems with any customers lately?" Nick asked. "Not to suggest anything improper, but times are hard. People try to make a buck any way they can, sometimes with things that don't necessarily belong to them, yeah?"

"We don't trade in stolen goods," Luc said flatly.

"Have you refused anybody that's brought stuff in recently? Somebody who might nurse a grudge?"

"No."

His answer was too quick and too definitive. South Louisiana was a place overflowing with hot heads and quick tempers. Grudges could be held for decades, for generations, even. Tempers could flare up with the slightest provocation, the barest hint of an insult. And the Merciers had seen fit to post a sign in their front window telling the world that they could refuse to do business with anybody. With two exclamation points, no less.

Nick looked up and glanced around, spying one camera over the desk, pointed toward the door. "Is that hooked up?"

"No."

"Marc wants us to put in a new system," Kiki said. "He says it's not even hard these days—"

"We got dogs on the property at night," Luc interrupted. "Don't nobody mess with them. That was good enough for Daddy."

"What you talking about?" Kiki snapped. "He put that camera up back in the nineties—"

"Damn thing was busted more often than not," Luc said. "That ain't worked in years. We keep it for show, and that's enough."

"You just don't want new 'cause it's Marc's idea," Kiki grumbled, pulling her iPhone out of a pocket on her overalls. She tapped the screen and began scrolling. "You don't never grow up.

"Here! Here," she said, turning the phone around so Nick could see the photo she had stopped on. "This is Marc and his truck. You can see the tag."

The photo showed Marc Mercier, tall, athletic, good-looking, posing next to his new big-boy toy with a wide grin splitting his face. *Everybody loves Marc . . .* He had that look about him, like life was easy and doors opened before him like magic. All he had to do was smile that smile.

"Can you text me that picture, *s'il vous plaît*?" Nick asked. He handed a business card to the mother. She immediately typed his cell number into her phone and sent the photo.

"He's a good boy, him, my Marc," she said. "You gonna find him for me, yeah?"

"We'll do our best, ma'am," Nick assured her, then turned to Luc. "Step outside with us for a moment, Mr. Mercier."

"I got a tour group coming in ten minutes," Luc Mercier said, squinting hard as they went out into the bright light.

He walked a few yards away from the front door of the building, stopping at the nose of a black Dodge Ram 2500 pickup. Spotless, Nick noted, freshly washed and hand-dried.

"Nice truck," Stokes remarked, looking down the length of the pickup, his gaze dropping to the tires. "That black is a commitment."

"Less trouble than a woman," Mercier returned. He shook a cigarette out of a pack from the pocket of his denim shirt and hung it on his lip as he leaned back against the front quarter panel of the truck.

Out of eavesdropping range, Nick thought, glancing back to see Kiki Mercier peering out the window at them, eyes narrowed as if that might sharpen her hearing.

"Getting late in the season for swamp tours, no?" Nick asked.

Luc shrugged as he lit up. "We run as long as the weather holds and the tourists want to go out and see an alligator."

"When I was a boy, it'd be cold by now," Nick remarked, settling his sunglasses down on the bridge of his nose. "The gators would be digging in for the winter about this time."

"Yeah," Mercier said. "Gotta love that global warming."

Global warming and gator baiting. Tour guides routinely fed the gators from their boats, so much so that some of the animals became programmed to swim toward the boats instead of away from them as they would have naturally done. The ready food source ensured that the tourists got their money's worth. The animal rights activists tried every few years to get the practice banned, but to no avail. Practicality won the day in Cajun country. People needing to feed their families trumped the needs of alligators every time.

"Me, I'm thinking a brother knows some things about a brother that a mother might not know about a son, yeah?" Nick said. "I wanted to give you a chance to speak freely."

"About Marc?" Mercier exhaled a stream of smoke. "What's to say?"

"You get along with your brother?"

"We get along like brothers do. Sometimes yes, sometimes no."

"He give you that shiner?"

He laughed but glanced away. "That'd be the day. Fighting is the one thing I'm better at than him."

"You don't seem all that upset about him being missing," Stokes said.

"Well, I just don't think it's anything, that's all. He probably had a fight with his wife, and he's gone to cool off somewhere. It wouldn't be the first time."

"He's up and gone before?"

"He's spent more than one night on my couch."

"What do they fight about?" Nick asked.

He heaved a sigh. "She don't wanna be here. She didn't marry no junk man, and she don't wanna live in Asscrack, Louisiana."

"But he does?"

"For now." He picked a fleck of tobacco off his tongue with his thumb and flicked it away. "Daddy got brain cancer. Marc came home to help with the business."

"How long ago was that?" Stokes asked.

"About a year ago. She's had enough."

"And your dad?" Nick asked.

"He passed back in March."

"But your brother's still here."

"He's still saving us," he said, his mouth twisting in an ironic smile. "That's Marc, always the hero."

Brotherly resentment, the loss of a parent, a strained marriage— a combination of stressors that could be a recipe for depression, Nick thought. But it wasn't depression that had shot the face off his morning victim and dumped him like a sack of trash on the side of the road. Still, he had to ask.

"Has he seemed depressed? Is there a chance he might have hurt himself?"

The brother laughed. "Marc? Hell no! Everybody loves Marc, but don't nobody love Marc more than Marc does. You think he'd blow his pretty brains out? I don't think so."

Stokes shot Nick a look at the mention of a potential cause of death. Neither of them cared for a coincidence.

"You have any idea where else he might have gone?" Nick asked. "If he decided to drown his sorrows, where would he go?"

"Voodoo Lounge, Blue Bayou . . . Wherever two or more are gathered in his name."

"Mouton's?"

"No. That's not his crowd."

"Is he a hard drinker?"

Mercier shrugged. "Compared to what? He likes to toss back a few, like anybody."

"And you're sure he doesn't have a girlfriend?"

"None that I know of," Mercier answered, putting his attention to neatly rolling up the sleeves of his shirt, revealing an elaborate and colorful sleeve of tattoo ink.

"Your brother got ink like that?" Stokes asked.

"No. Marc, he wouldn't mess with perfection."

"What about the wife?" Nick asked. "She got a boyfriend?"

"I don't know. Mama thinks she's got something going on with her boss."

"What do you think?"

"I don't give two shits, but I don't think Will Faulkner bats from that side of the plate, to be honest."

"Where does she work?" Stokes asked.

"She manages vacation rental properties for Bayou Realty."

"Y'all have a fishing camp Marc might have gone to?" Nick asked.

"Yeah, down the bayou on Lake Aucoin. He could be there if Missy didn't Airbnb it up full of out-of-town sports this weekend," Luc said, his attention going now to the road as a van pulled into the property on the bayou side. His tour group. "There's never enough money to suit the princess."

"You didn't go down there and check?" Nick asked.

He heaved a sigh. "Me, I only got so much patience for Marc's bullshit temper tantrums. I got a business to run, and I can't just drop everything and go looking to see where my little brother's sulking this time.

"I gotta go," he said, pushing away from the truck.

Nick handed him a business card. "If you hear from him, give me a call. We'll put out an alert on his vehicle."

"You do that," he said as he dropped the last of his smoke on the crushed shell and ground it out with the toe of his boot. Done with the conversation, he got in the truck and fired up the diesel engine to drive thirty yards across the road.

"How about that?" Stokes said as they watched him go. "Start the day with a Who Is It, now we got us a What the Hell, and it's only lunchtime. What do you think the odds are our dead guy and our missing guy are one and the same? Could we get that lucky?"

"You know I don't believe in luck, me," Nick said, glancing back to see Kiki Mercier duck inside from the window. "Human nature, though . . . that's something else again."

He let the thought trail off. In his experience, crime almost always turned out to be depressingly, stupidly simple. Criminal masterminds were the stuff of movies and TV. People did what they did for simple reasons—money, lust, jealousy, fear. Pick a thread and follow it to the end. Luck was seldom necessary.

7

BAYOU REALTY, ONCE HOUSED ON THE FIRST FLOOR OF A small historic building in downtown Bayou Breaux, had grown and prospered its way to one of the newer business complexes on the north side of town. A cluster of single-story Caribbean-style brick buildings, Bayou Professional Park boasted an architecture firm, a mortgage and title business, a trio of accountants, and an interior design firm, with the realty office the centerpiece of the complex.

Nick parked in the lot and sat for a moment, sorting through his thoughts. What to say, what not to say to Melissa Mercier. He had a corpse with no ID, no vehicle nearby, no cell phone, and no face. The business card with a dollar amount written in Marc Mercier's hand found in the pocket of the dead man could have been an estimate given to a customer, but it could just as easily have been a price given *to* the junk dealer by someone wanting to sell something.

He had nothing concrete to indicate the body was that of Marc Mercier, and if it turned out to be Marc Mercier, the wife would be on the list of potential suspects, if what his family members had said was anything to go by. To try to glean as much information as possible while giving away as little as possible was the best tack, but that would be a tricky dance to accomplish.

Word that a mutilated body had been found south of town would be burning up the gossip grapevines by now. Stokes had already texted him to say KJUN radio had the news on the air.

Alphonse Arceneaux had unknowingly bought them some time ahead of the media by calling his friend Sergeant Rodrigue directly, but the subsequent callouts to deputies and the crime scene unit had been picked up by police scanners, and two TV news vans had shown up as they had processed the scene. Though they had been kept at a distance and had been given no official comment to run with, the lack of details wouldn't stop them from going on air with what little information they had. There was a chance Melissa Mercier had already heard the news.

A young woman with a bright pageant-girl smile lighting her face greeted Nick from behind the reception desk as he walked into the office.

"How can we help you to have a great day today, sir?" she asked as if the prospect thrilled her.

"I'm here to see Mrs. Mercier."

She looked puzzled for an instant. "Mrs.?"

"Melissa Mercier."

"Oh! Melissa!" She waved a hand at him, laughing. "We just aren't so formal here!"

"I'll just go back to her office, then," Nick said, as if he had been there many times before. The receptionist let him go, turning her attention to a ringing telephone.

"Bayou Realty, Shavon speaking. How can we help you to have a great day today?"

He passed through an open area of comfortable couches and chairs and coffee tables strewn with glossy real estate ads, then went down a hallway past a pair of small conference rooms with open doors. Laughter floated out into the hall several doors down— a man and a woman sharing a joke.

"What would I do without you to cheer me up, Will?" the woman asked in an accent not from Louisiana.

Nick stopped outside the open office door. The man stood near the window, tall, lean, and handsome, in his mid-thirties with a full head of deep auburn hair and a wide white smile. The woman sat behind the desk, just a few feet away, beaming up at him. They looked like a toothpaste ad. Her honey-blond hair was swept back from her delicate face in a ponytail that bounced when she laughed. She caught sight of Nick in the corner of her eye and turned and looked at him expectantly.

"Can I help you?" she asked pleasantly. She was pretty with a heart-shaped face and big green eyes. Her mouth tipped up slightly higher on one side than the other, a charming quirk.

"Melissa Mercier?"

"Yes?"

"Lieutenant Fourcade with the sheriff's office," he said, holding up his badge. "I need to ask you a few questions."

What was left of her smile fell away and the color left her face. She sat up straight.

"Oh, my God, has something happened? Is it Marc? He's crashed that stupid truck, hasn't he?"

"No, ma'am."

"Is he in jail?!" she asked, incredulous.

"Maybe let the man speak, Miss," her friend said gently, resting a hand on her shoulder. "This could be nothing.

"I'm Will Faulkner," he said to Nick. "I'm the boss around here most days."

"Mr. Faulkner." Nick acknowledged him with a nod, noting that his hand lingered with comfortable familiarity on Melissa Mercier's shoulder.

"Mrs. Mercier, have you been in contact with your husband today?"

"No, I haven't. Why?"

"When was the last time you spoke with him?"

"I really wish you'd answer my question," she said anxiously. "Has something happened to Marc?"

"Not that I'm aware of," Nick said. "His family is concerned, though. They say they haven't been able to reach him."

"Oh, my God," Melissa muttered, suddenly exasperated as she sat back in her chair. "They called the sheriff's office? Seriously?"

"They say they haven't heard from him since Saturday. Have you?"

"No, I haven't, but—"

"And is that normal?"

"I wouldn't call it normal, no."

"But you're not concerned?"

"I didn't say that!"

"Whoa!" Will Faulkner said, holding up a hand and taking a half step forward, putting himself ever so slightly in front of Melissa Mercier. "Let's slow this down and start from the beginning here. This is sounding like an interrogation."

"Not at all," Nick said calmly. "I'm just trying to get a sense of things. Have you been in contact with Mr. Mercier?"

"Me? No."

"Are you friends?"

"I've known Marc for years."

An answer that wasn't an answer.

Nick stared at Faulkner for a moment, letting the silence hang to see if he would say something more, wanting to see how uncomfortable he might become with the scrutiny. Faulkner glanced at Melissa and took a step back.

"When did you last speak with your husband?" Nick asked.

"Saturday night."

"About what time?"

"Six thirty, quarter to seven."

"And then what?"

"He left. We had an argument," she admitted quietly, "and he left."

"Have you tried to contact him since?"

"No," she said, pressing her fingertips to her temples as if to rub at a sudden headache. "Because I was angry. I'm still angry. And now I'm scared, too."

Tears filled her eyes, and she looked down at the desktop.

"Mrs. Mercier, would you be more comfortable having this conversation in private?" Nick asked.

She shook her head, composing herself. "No, it's fine. There's nothing about Marc and me Will doesn't already know. He's probably sick to death of hearing about it, though."

"Not at all," Faulkner said, touching her shoulder again to reassure her. "That's what friends are for."

"What was the fight about?" Nick asked.

She sniffed and swiped at an errant tear. "He came home pulling that stupid boat and announced he was going to go hunting yesterday with his brother, but yesterday was my birthday, and I thought I should outrank shooting things." She forced a sad, crooked smile. "Turns out, I don't. Marc stormed out. I assumed he went to Luc's house."

"Luc says he hasn't seen or heard from him," Nick said. "And when he didn't come home last night, what did you do?"

"I made myself a nice dinner and had a glass of wine," she said with a touch of defiance.

"His mother says she called you last night and got no answer."

"I wasn't interested in making my evening worse by having a conversation with Kiki."

"At that point you were still not concerned about your husband's whereabouts?"

"No. I didn't expect him to come home, just to spite me."

"And you didn't wonder where he might be at? Or did you have an idea?"

"Like I said, I thought he was with Luc. Anyway, Marc has a lot of friends," she said, "and plenty of places to stay."

"Did you call any of those friends looking for him?"

"No." She shook her head again. "The first time Marc did this, I called everyone I could think of, looking for him. I called the area hospitals, thinking he might have had an accident. I was beside myself. I was six months pregnant at the time . . . And when he came home, he was angry with me for calling his friends and making a big deal out of nothing."

A fresh sheen of tears glazed her eyes as she looked up at him. "I don't make a big deal out of nothing anymore."

There was a lot of pain in that statement. Hurt feelings, hurt pride. She was a young bride with a new baby. She wanted to be the most important person in her husband's life, but that didn't seem to be the case. Luc Mercier had said Melissa didn't want to be there in south Louisiana, but her husband had been lured back to help his family, and the family and the place were hanging on to him. She had to feel very alone there . . . except for her good friend, Will Faulkner.

"I'm sorry to ask," Nick said, "but do you think he's seeing someone?"

"Yeah," she said with a bitter laugh. "All his old friends from high school. I had an adult husband who was smart and ambitious, and then we moved here, and he magically turned into an eighteen-year-old boy with mommy issues and a bunch of overgrown adolescent drinking buddies. Of course, he calls them *business connections* now, and hanging out with them is *networking*."

"That's Marc reliving his glory days," Will Faulkner remarked. "It's sad when a guy thinks he topped out in high school."

"He didn't, though," Melissa argued. "That's what makes this so frustrating."

"I understand the family has a fish camp down on Lake Aucoin," Nick said. "Could he have gone there?"

"No. We had renters there for the weekend. They checked out late in the day yesterday."

"So he could have gone there last night."

"I suppose he could have, but my cleaning crew should have been there this morning. No one mentioned anything to me."

"Is he into any kind of risky behavior?" Nick asked. "Gambling, drugs?"

She looked confused. "Drugs? Marc? No, nothing like that."

"Is there anybody he hasn't been getting along with?"

"You mean besides his brother? Or me?"

"The brothers don't get along?" Nick asked, opening that door a crack.

"Luc resents him for coming back here," she said. "Marc's the golden boy of the family, if you didn't already catch that from his mother."

"But Marc and Luc, they were still going hunting together?"

"Oh, sure. Hunting and fishing transcends all. If there's a living creature they can kill, the Mercier boys are right there for it. Don't ask them to agree about anything else, though."

"How has it been for him, coming back into the family business?"

"It was a mess when we got here," she said. "His dad, Troy, had let things go for who knows how long. He'd been ill for a couple of years already. Luc doesn't have any interest in dealing with paperwork, and Kiki had her hands full trying to take care of Troy and Noelle."

"A lot of pressure on Marc, then, to straighten it all out, yeah?"

"Yes. I offered to help him sort out the business accounts and the tax situation, but that wasn't well received."

"Not well received by whom?"

"Any of them," she said. "Mercier Salvage is Mercier business, and I'm a Mercier in name only, so . . ." She shrugged. "Never mind my business degree."

"So it all fell on Marc," Nick said. "That's a lot of stress, yeah? His dad was dying. He's saddled with the business problems. Family tensions. A new baby. An unhappy wife. That's a lot. Is there any reason to think he maybe just didn't want to deal with it anymore?"

Melissa stared at him for a moment before the realization of what he was saying fully hit her, and she gave a little start, as if she'd had an electrical shock. Her green eyes widened.

"Marc wouldn't hurt himself!" she said, but a hint of uncertainty in her voice made it sound slightly more like a question than an answer. She glanced up at Will Faulkner as if for reassurance, then turned back to Nick. "He wouldn't. That's ridiculous! Why would you even suggest that?"

"I'm not suggesting anything," Nick said. "I have to be open to all possibilities."

"Well, *that* is *not* possible!" she said, trying to sound emphatic instead of on the verge of panic.

"Really, Detective," Faulkner said. "That's some pretty wild speculation. Marc's off on a temper tantrum. He's probably sitting out in the basin somewhere, shooting ducks and perfectly happy to think he's got people worried sick. He's made himself the center of attention even when he's not here."

"So there's no reason to think Marc might have come to harm by his own hand or anyone else's?" Nick asked.

"Who would want to hurt Marc?" Faulkner asked.

"No one," Melissa snapped. "It's ridiculous. This is all ridiculous!"

She snatched up her iPhone from the desktop and made a call, setting it to speaker, looking at Nick while she waited for the connection to pick up. The call went straight to voicemail.

"This is Marc. Leave a message."

"It's me," Melissa said. "You need to call me back, Marc. People are worried sick about you. Your mother called the sheriff's office, for God's sake! I'm sitting here with a detective who's asking me if someone might have killed you! Call me. Call *someone*, damn it! Let us know you're all right, you selfish prick!"

She ended the call and covered her face with her hands for a

second before looking up at Will Faulkner. "Oh, my God, I shouldn't
have said that! What if something *has* happened to him? He could
be dead in a ditch or drowned in the swamp, and I'm sitting here
pissed off at him for being a jerk!"

Faulkner squatted down beside her and squeezed her hand.
"Let's not panic."

"Why did we have to come back here?" Frustration and anger
and fear boiled up and spilled over. "God, I hate this place!"

"I'm sorry this is upsetting for you, Mrs. Mercier," Nick said.

"Are you?" she asked, getting to her feet. Needing to burn off
some of her anxious energy, she shifted her weight from one foot to
the other even as she wrapped her arms around herself to hold herself together. "Why are you asking these questions? Would somebody want to hurt Marc? Would Marc hurt himself? What aren't you
telling us? Marc's dead, isn't he?"

"I don't know that," Nick said. His free question time was up. He
would have to tell her, and she would react, and everything would
shift, but there was no avoiding it. "This morning a body was found
along a dead-end road outside of Luck."

Melissa went still. Her face blanched chalk white. She pressed a
hand across her mouth, as if to keep the emotion welling inside her
from spilling out.

"Is it Marc?" Will Faulkner asked.

"We don't have a positive ID at this time."

"Didn't Kiki give you a picture of him?" Melissa asked. "I-I can
give you a picture of him."

She scooped up her cell phone with trembling hands and fumbled
to bring a photo up on the screen. "This is him," she said, shoving the
phone at Nick. "Is it him? Oh, my God!"

Will Faulkner stepped close and put an arm around her shoulders to steady her.

"I'm sorry there isn't a better way of saying this," Nick began.
"But due to the nature of the injuries, we are unable to make an
identification from a photograph."

Melissa's eyes widened, and a strange, primal sound of anguish wrenched itself out of her as her knees gave way. Her boss held on tight as he helped her slide back down onto her chair.

"Does your husband have any identifying marks on his body?" Nick asked. "A tattoo, a scar, a birthmark, anything like that?"

"Oh, my God. I can't believe this is happening," she said to herself. She was hyperventilating now, and a sheen of perspiration glazed her face. "Um, he . . . has a . . . scar . . . on the back of his left hand. He fell out of a tree. Deer hunting."

She indicated the left hand. The hand Nick's victim had held up in a vain attempt to block a shotgun blast.

"He broke his wrist," Melissa added. "Our freshman year. I didn't really know him that well at the time. He had a cast on his arm. He played it up to get sympathy from girls," she said with a sad little smile of remembrance. "I fell for it."

She curled over on herself as if she were in pain and started to cry. Will Faulkner bent down and murmured something to her as he pressed a clean handkerchief into her hand.

"What about his truck?" he asked Nick.

"There was no vehicle at the scene."

"So what was this? Some kind of carjacking?"

"We don't know at this point," Nick said. "And I want to be clear, Mrs. Mercier: We don't know that this is or isn't Marc. Your husband may be alive and well. I encourage you to keep trying to call him and contact whatever friends you think might be in touch with him if he's just gone off on his own for a time."

He placed a business card on her desk. "And call me if you hear from him."

Melissa nodded and dabbed at her eyes with the handkerchief. She rose slowly to her feet, still shaky. "If you'll excuse me, I'm going to the ladies' room to try to pull myself together . . . or just fall to pieces. One or the other."

"Do you want me to walk you?" Faulkner asked.

She shook her head. "No."

"Do you want me to get Shavon to go with you?"

"God, no. I don't need her trying to help me have a great day to-day," she said sarcastically. "I just need a moment alone."

Nick stepped aside to let her pass. Her emotions seemed genu-ine. Uncommonly honest, he thought. In his experience, people more often than not tried to paint an image of perfect normalcy when speaking to law enforcement, no matter what a train wreck their lives might actually be. They lied, even about things that didn't matter, because they were afraid of being judged or because they wrongly assumed the cops were out to get them, even when they'd done absolutely nothing wrong. But Melissa Mercier was either hon-est or one of the better actresses he'd come across.

"Well, this day has certainly taken an unexpected turn," Will Faulkner said as they followed Melissa into the hallway. She turned left. Faulkner turned right. "Can I buy you a free cup of coffee, Lieutenant?"

"Thank you," Nick said, following him to another office. If Faulkner had something more to say, he would listen.

"Have a seat," Faulkner offered as he went behind his desk and busied himself with an expensive-looking espresso machine tucked into the built-in cabinetry. "I don't want you getting the wrong idea about Melissa."

"What idea would that be?"

"That she doesn't care about Marc or that remark about hating it here . . . I mean, she does hate it here, but not without reason. I don't want you to hold that against her. This place doesn't always make strangers feel welcomed, and Marc's family hasn't helped with that. They'd just as soon she leave Marc and the baby here and go back to Philadelphia, never to be seen or heard from again. Marc's mother would swallow him whole to keep him here if she had to. Melissa is the enemy."

"And what is Marc's feeling on being here, staying here?"

"I don't know," he said, dropping a pod in the coffee maker and punching a button. "He's stuck in the middle. This has been a rough year for both of them."

"You're good friends, yeah?" Nick asked.

"We all went to Tulane—Marc, Miss, and I," he said, raising his voice a bit to be heard above the hissing and spitting of the espresso machine. "Of course, I was years ahead of them, but I worked with a group of the business students in a mentorship program when they were there, and we got to know one another. Little did any of us know at the time they would end up moving back here. That wasn't the plan. They graduated and moved up north, went to work for Missy's dad. He has an investment firm. I would never have expected them to come back. Then Marc's dad got sick, and everything changed.

"Cream? Sugar?" he asked.

"Black is fine, *merci*."

"I get it, you know?" he said as he handed Nick the steaming mug. "The mixed emotions of coming back to the hometown when you thought you were getting away. You thought the world was your oyster; then suddenly here you are, right back where you started. That's not easy."

"That's what happened for you?" Nick asked, glancing around the room. One entire wall was covered in framed photos and award plaques and civic commendations for good works in Bayou Breaux and around the parish. Will Faulkner had a full life here.

"Yep. You know my older sister, Lindsay, she started this business. She and her partner, Pam Bichon. That's one sad story after the next."

"I remember."

Pam Bichon had been brutally murdered, a case that had taken Nick down a rabbit hole of obsession—the killer's and his own. Less than two years later, Lindsay Faulkner had fallen victim to a serial rapist and died from her injuries.

"I came back when Lindsay died," Will said. "I had a good job in

New Orleans, had a life there, but someone had to deal with this business, and our parents were just broken by it all . . ."

"And you ended up staying."

"I did. I was back and forth for a while," he said, dropping another pod in the coffeemaker. "I still have business interests in New Orleans. But I'm from here. My family is here, old friends are here. Bayou Breaux was growing, and I saw opportunities . . . So I see it from both sides—getting pulled back but wanting to outgrow the place at the same time. Torn between duty and desire," he said, dropping a pair of sugar cubes into his mug.

"Is that Marc?"

He sighed as if he were long since tired of the subject of Marc Mercier.

"Marc's a good guy," he said. "He is. I just get frustrated with him on Missy's behalf. Marc needs to be the hero. He always has. Leading the high school football team to victory in the state championships, winning a scholarship to Tulane, being the first in his family to get a college degree. Of course it's all commendable, but sometimes it's at the expense of others, you know?

"I can't fault him that he came back when his family needed him, but it's been awful hard on Melissa. She doesn't know anyone here but me. She doesn't fit in here. Small-town life is not as easy as people want to believe. In fact, it can be damned complicated. She might as well have moved to France. It's just as foreign to her.

"She never thought they'd be here this long. She believed they would be moving back up north at the end of the summer. She was ready to start packing. Then she read in the local paper Marc had volunteered to coach youth football this fall. It was big news, you know. The hometown hero saving the day for a team whose coach— Marc's old coach—had a heart attack. Marc couldn't say no to him, but then he didn't have the nerve to tell Missy. That went over like the proverbial lead balloon, let me tell you."

"I can imagine."

"My mother always says wives don't like surprises unless they come in a box from a jewelry store."

"You gave Melissa a job when they moved here," Nick said. "What does she do for you?"

"She needed something to do or she'd lose her mind," Faulkner said. He took a sip of his coffee and sighed. "I'm lucky to have her. She manages my vacation rentals, takes care of the marketing, booking, all of it. It's something she can handle even with having the baby and all. I'd be happy to have her stay for my own selfish reasons," he admitted. "But I understand why she'd rather go."

"And if Marc didn't want to go with her?"

He shrugged. "Marriage is hard—or so they tell me."

"You're single?"

"Much to my mother's chagrin," he joked, then sobered. "This dead body. Do you think it's Marc?"

"I don't know," Nick said, setting his cup aside as he stood to go. "But I'll find out who it is, and I'll find out why he's dead, and I'll find out who made him that way. Thank you for the coffee, Mr. Faulkner. And thank you for your time."

8

THE PIZZA HUT, A LOW SNOT-GREEN CINDER BLOCK BUILDING with bars on the windows and doors, had originally been the offices of a road construction business back in the seventies and eighties. The property had been swallowed up by the expansion of the law enforcement center in the early nineties and the building given over to the sheriff's office's small squad of detectives. It had been christened the Pizza Hut due to the amount of pies delivered there on a regular basis.

The large front office housed a bullpen of half a dozen beat-up Steelcase desks loaded down with computers and paperwork and the assorted oddities cops collected as souvenirs over their careers. Annie sat at her desk in the middle row, picking the fried shrimp out of a po'boy, hoping the calories would bring a fresh surge of energy. The morning had drained her.

Only two other desks were occupied. Wynn Dixon sat in the back of the room, deep in concentration as she hammered away at her keyboard. A tall, athletic woman with a shock of short hair recently dyed purple for LSU homecoming, she was their designated tech person. The desk to Annie's right was occupied by Deebo

Jeffcoat, their guy on the Acadiana multiagency drug task force. In his early thirties, he was small and wiry, with a greasy mullet and an atrocious, scruffy neck beard he had grown as part of his under-cover meth-head look. Eyes closed, grooving to the music on his AirPods, he bounced in his seat, playing imaginary drums with a pair of pencils.

Annie thanked God for keeping Nick out of the office for the time being. She wanted a clearer picture of what she was dealing with regarding the disappearance of Robbie Fontenot before she had to make her argument to pursue the case on her own.

She started with the story of Robbie Fontenot as told by his ar-rest record, an unsentimental version of a drug addict's history, from possession to petty theft. She inserted B'Lynn's version of the story between the lines, the weight of a mother's sadness pressing down on her heart even as her trained detective's eye marked the cold hard facts.

He had been in and out of jail at least as much as he had been in and out of rehab. Never for very long. Never for very much. His pos-session charges never crossed the threshold for serious prison time. He had never been charged with the intent to sell a controlled sub-stance. His stealing had never risen to the level of a felony.

Curious, Annie thought, though what she really meant was "sus-picious." All those not-quite-enough charges sent up little red flags in her mind. Robbie Fontenot was the son of a doctor, a white man with money and connections, a man who had known and supported Sheriff Noblier for long enough that his ex-wife felt she could appeal to him personally on her son's behalf.

She grabbed her phone and punched in the number B'Lynn had given her for Robbie's father. The call went straight to voicemail. She left a message asking for him to call her back at his earliest con-venience, and wondered if he would. According to B'Lynn, he had been divorced from his son longer than he had been divorced from his wife.

It might have been easy to judge him harshly for that, but Annie had seen many versions of the addiction story, all of them sad, all of them difficult. She tried to reserve judgment on Dr. Robert Fontenot, even if her instincts as a mother conditioned her to side with the child. She had never been the parent of an addict, but she had dealt with enough of them to know that it was no easy path, not even for families with every advantage at their disposal.

Still, she couldn't help but think that if Robbie Fontenot had been of a different complexion and from a different part of town, he would have been doing hard time. A chronic abuser who sometimes augmented his income by theft—the state penitentiary at Angola was chock-full of them. He was either too smart or too valuable to someone to be shoved out of society to toil in the fields at the notorious prison unaffectionately known as the Farm.

Ten years an addict. That was a lot of hard life experience with people constantly at odds with the law—and with people enforcing the law. She looked at the names of the arresting officers over the years, both from the SO and from Bayou Breaux PD, some cops she knew and some she didn't. The name of Officer Derwin Rivette jumped out at her from an arrest five years past. And another arrest two years before that, long before Dewey had made detective.

So Dewey and Robbie Fontenot were not unknown to each other, she thought, nibbling on a shrimp. Was there enough familiarity there for Dewey Rivette to know where Robbie Fontenot might go, who he might hang out with, do business with, buy drugs from? Or were the arrests just two in a pile of hundreds Rivette must have made over the years?

She thought about how many arrests she had made as a patrol deputy and how many of them had been memorable. Some had been, for sure. Cops on the job long enough all had, as Danny Perry had said of Rayanne Tillis, their frequent fliers, the repeat offenders who stood out for one reason or another. Were two arrests two years apart reason for Robbie Fontenot to qualify for that status with Dewey Rivette?

She picked up her cell phone and brought up the photo B'Lynn had texted her. It was a recent picture taken in a kitchen, Robbie smiling reluctantly as he stood with his arm around an elderly woman. Probably the day he got out of rehab, Annie imagined, coming home and hugging his grandma. The kind of obligatory picture every mother would take. He was a good-looking young man with an angular face, high cheekbones, and straight brows over weary, wary dark eyes. Eyes that belonged in a much older face, Annie thought. Ages-old, seen-too-much, heart-wrung-out kind of eyes. The windows to a soul that had weathered a hard road despite its privileged start.

She wondered if sometimes that wasn't as painful in its own way as a dirt-poor start to a hardscrabble life. Robbie Fontenot had grown up a much-loved child of comfort and opportunity. Smart, talented, he had the world rolled out in front of him like a red carpet. On his way to big things until that red carpet had been yanked away. He had lost it all. Thrown it away, some would say, though addiction wasn't as simple as choice. Resentment of privilege more often than not erased the sympathy of casual observers to a train wreck life. That was just how people were—jealous and petty. But life was only black and white to those lucky enough to never have been faced with real adversity. Strife was a layered and complex thing, no matter how much money you had.

As a mother, Annie could look at Robbie through B'Lynn's eyes and see the face of a five-year-old, as innocent as a puppy, as sweet as pure love. She could imagine him as that teenage boy, his mental maturity scrambling to grow into his tall, lanky developing man's frame. She could imagine his hurt and disappointment as his dream was dragged away, leaving him bereft and wondering who he might be without that success. He'd been thrown down a hard road with no preparation, with no one to feel sorry for him but the woman who had brought him into the world. And Annie surmised that even his mother's love had been conditional during the worst of it. That was what addiction did—it shredded the fabric of even the strongest relationships.

Guilt was at the core of B'Lynn Fontenot's worry now. She held it tight inside her, thinking it couldn't be seen behind her shield of determination, but it was there, part of the aggregate of the foundation of motherhood. That was why she was still there now in her son's life when everyone else—including his father—had long since given up on him.

Annie sighed and rubbed a hand across her forehead, trying to massage the tension away in the hopes of cutting a headache off at the pass. She didn't have time for it now.

With a few keystrokes, she brought up Rayanne Tillis's record on her computer screen. As Danny Perry had said, possession, shoplifting, and the odd twenty-dollar blow job. A petty criminal, the same as Robbie Fontenot was a petty criminal, though Annie doubted Rayanne's mama was beating anybody's door down trying to get her help or steer her onto a better life path.

Rayanne claimed not to know Robbie, but she had known he wasn't at home. She had found her way into his house—which B'Lynn swore had been locked up when last she'd been there. Somehow she couldn't picture Rayanne picking a lock.

She looked over at Deebo Jeffcoat, still grooving to his tunes. He had abandoned his pencil drumsticks to play a mean air guitar solo.

"Deebo!" Annie called. "Deebo!"

She grabbed a fried shrimp and tossed it at him, bouncing it off the side of his face. He jumped a foot off his seat and looked at her wide-eyed, shocked to be brought back to the mundane reality of the office. Annie pantomimed pulling AirPods out of her ears.

"Hey, Annie. What's up?" he shouted, following her instructions by plucking the earphones out and killing the noise.

"Do you remember a pillhead named Robbie Fontenot? You collared him for possession three or four years ago."

"Him and a few hundred others."

She held up her phone and showed him the snapshot. "He got out of rehab a couple of months ago. Have you seen him around?"

He squinted at the photograph and shook his head. "I don't think so. Why?"

"He's missing."

"Missing from where?"

"Here in town. Hasn't been seen or heard from since Halloween."

"A missing drug addict?" He shrugged. "Go figure."

"He just got out of rehab a couple of months ago. His mother says he's been clean."

"That's what mothers always say. It's their job," Deebo said. "He's probably told her he's clean, but he's an addict and addicts are liars by default, and they make liars of everyone close to them, too. If his mother has been through this enough times, she'll tell you he's clean in the hopes you won't just write him off."

"That's sad but true," Annie admitted on a sigh. "And she'll think it's a good lie because it serves a good purpose."

"And the addict is a bad liar because his lies only serve himself, or so he thinks as he spirals down that hole. What's this one into?"

"Oxy."

Deebo made a pained face. "I hope he's got a trusted source. We're up to our asses in fentanyl overdoses these days. Every goddamn thing is laced with fentanyl. I don't get it myself," he confessed. "These dealers are killing off their customers, but there's no shortage of them, I guess. The high is too seductive, and nobody thinks they'll be the one to die. I'd buy stock in Narcan if I had money. That shit should be in vending machines on every street corner. Have you checked the morgue at Our Lady?"

"Not yet."

"They found a dead body down by Luck this morning," he said. "Maybe that's your guy."

"What?" The word came out on a hard breath, like she'd been punched in the stomach.

"White male. Twenty-five to thirty-five. You didn't hear?"

"I've been busy all morning."

She felt sick at the idea that B'Lynn Fontenot might have finally found someone willing to help her on the same morning her son's corpse was discovered.

"Was there a vehicle?" she asked.

"Nope. The body was dumped. No crime scene. No witnesses—so far, at least."

"Any obvious cause of death?"

"Shotgun blast to the face."

"Oh, Lord."

"Makes me think there ain't one," Deebo said. "It's a cruel world. I spent last night with the parents of a kid who OD'd on heroin and choked to death on her own vomit. Wasn't no higher power looking out for her.

"You gonna eat that sandwich or peck it to death?" he asked, his attention on her po'boy.

"Help yourself," Annie said, shoving her lunch toward the edge of her desk as she stood up. "I'm going over to the jail . . . and then to the morgue."

She thought of B'Lynn as she walked across the yard toward the jail. What would her reaction be if the news was that her son had run afoul of someone with a shotgun? Shock? Sadness? Disappointment? Anger? Relief? All of the above? In the last ten years she had probably braced herself for the worst outcome many times, only to have hope restored, only to have to start the cycle all over again. No wonder she looked wrung out.

Three trustees were washing sheriff's office vehicles outside the garage. Annie glanced at them as she passed. They all had mothers somewhere, just like Robbie Fontenot. Just like Deebo's dead junkie from the night before. Too bad Hallmark didn't make a Mother's Day card for *Sorry, Your Kid Screwed Up*.

She had called ahead to the jail and asked that Rayanne Tillis be taken from the holding cell to an interview room to wait for her. Annie watched her now on a video monitor down the hall, reading her body language. Rayanne paced around the small white room, restless, anxious, looking like she wanted to crawl out of her own skin and melt under the door to escape. She sat down at the little table that was bolted to the wall, stood up, turned around, did another circuit around the room, then stopped to pick at the acoustic foam on the back wall.

She would be thinking about how much she wanted to get high, and thinking about how that wasn't going to happen anytime soon, and starting to panic a little bit. She hadn't asked for an attorney yet. Annie suspected she had held off in order to make sure she got fed lunch. That timing could work to Annie's advantage if she was lucky.

Don't say the L word. Don't say the L word . . .

Rayanne went back to the chair, sat down, pulled her feet up on the seat, looked up at the camera, and gave it the finger.

Annie went down the hall, paused outside the interview room, took a deep breath, and opened the door.

"Don't say anything!" she said as she walked in. She held up a hand as if that might forestall any statement from her prisoner.

"I ain't gotta talk to you!" Rayanne shouted, popping up from the chair.

"That's exactly right. Don't say anything. Listen for a change."

"I don't gotta do that, neither!" she said, jutting her chin out defiantly. "I know my rights!"

"Before you repeat them back to me, do you want to get out of here?" Annie asked.

Don't say the L word, don't say the L word. One mention of a lawyer and their conversation would be over.

"I can get you out of here," she said, "but you have to shut up and listen for a minute."

Rayanne squinted at her. "You done arrested me! You ain't gonna let me go! You're full of shit! You're just messing with me, bitch."

"I'm not," Annie said. "You can shut up and listen to me for a minute, or I can turn around and walk out of here and you can stay a guest of the parish. Your choice, Rayanne."

She took a step backward toward the door. Rayanne shifted her weight from one dirty foot to the other, her expression wavering between suspicion and belligerence.

"Why would I trust you?" she asked.

"You got nothing to lose by listening, so why wouldn't you?"

Rayanne wrapped her hands in the stretched-out hem of her Fuck Your Feelings T-shirt and rocked side to side, thinking. "This is some kind of trap."

Annie shook her head. "No trap. This is just us talking. Maybe something good comes of it, maybe not. Up to you."

Rayanne glanced up at the camera on the wall above the door. "Who's watching us?"

"Nobody's listening in," Annie said. "Why would they? We're talking about a petty burglary. You haven't even been charged with anything yet. Maybe you won't be. Mrs. Fontenot got her TV back. And there wasn't any sign you broke into that house—"

"I didn't break in!" Rayanne insisted. "I just went in the back door. It was open."

"So what am I supposed to charge you with?" Annie asked. "Trespassing? This ain't worth the paperwork to me. If I can convince Mrs. Fontenot to let it go, you'll be a free woman."

Rayanne turned around in a little circle, contemplating her options. She chewed on a dirty thumbnail and stared at Annie. "What do you want?" she asked. "You ain't gonna just let me go for no reason."

"All I want is an honest conversation."

"You'll use it against me."

"How? If you haven't done anything worse than I know about, how will I use it against you?" Annie asked. "I'm trying to get you out of here with no charges."

"Why?"

Annie gave a small shrug. "Maybe I think you deserve a break, Rayanne."

"Yeah, right."

"All I see every day on this job is people getting knocked down in life. Maybe I can give you a hand up, and maybe you do something good with it. And you'd save me doing a lot of paperwork, so . . ."

"You think that bitch would drop the charges?"

"I think if I can put it to her right. If I can tell her you were help-ful to me . . . She's pretty pissed right now, though."

"Rich bitch," Rayanne muttered.

"What makes you think she's rich?" Annie set her notebook and phone down on the table and took a seat.

If Rayanne Tillis didn't know Robbie Fontenot, how did she know anything about his mother?

Rayanne glanced away and shrugged. "She got that look, that skinny rich bitch look."

"If she's rich, how come her son is living on your street?"

"How would I know? Maybe she don't like him."

"She's worried sick," Annie said. "She hasn't seen or heard from him since Halloween. Have you?"

"I told you, I don't know him!"

"But you've seen him around, yeah? Coming and going."

"I guess."

"You live right next door. You must look out the window every once in a while. When do you remember seeing him last?"

"I don't."

"You knew he wasn't home this morning, though."

"His car was gone. It's been gone. I thought he maybe just up and left. People do," she said defensively. "All the time. They can't pay their rent and they just leave, and they leave all their stuff, and somebody might as well have it."

"Have you seen anyone else going in and out of that house?"

"Like who?"

"Like anybody. Friends of his. Girlfriends. Family."

Rayanne squirmed a bit on her chair, scowling down at the floor. "Am I supposed to be the neighborhood watch or what? I don't know nothing about that house."

"Have you seen the cops going in and out of there?" Annie asked. "Your good friend Danny Perry?"

"Oh, yeah," she said on a harsh laugh, "'cause I should rat out cops! That's a good one!"

"Rat them out for what?" Annie asked calmly, though her heart beat a little bit harder at Rayanne's choice of words. "Robbie Fontenot was reported to the Bayou Breaux police as a missing person. I would expect them to go to his house. I just don't get the impression that they're taking this seriously. That's why I wonder have they been around."

"Oh, well . . . I guess I seen them there once or twice."

"Danny Perry?"

"Yeah . . . He's around."

"Do you know their detective? Dewey Rivette?"

"Why would I know a detective?" she asked, laughing again as she looked up at the camera on the wall. "Like I'm some kind of criminal mastermind or something. Can I get a cigarette?"

"There's no smoking in here," Annie said. "Sorry. I'll make sure you get a pack on your way home."

"When's that gonna be?"

She was getting restless, shifting around in her seat. Annie wondered if it was her need for a smoke or her discomfort with the line of questioning. Either way, the clock was running down on her chance to get any useful information from Rayanne Tillis.

"You said that back door was open this morning. Mrs. Fontenot says that door was locked last night. You didn't see anybody over there this morning messing with it?"

"No. I was having my beauty sleep," Rayanne said, and she struck a pose like a model and smiled, showing off a dental wasteland of yellowed, snaggled, and missing teeth.

She might have been pretty once, Annie thought. The physical transformation brought on by addiction was like a time-lapsed horror show of sinking features, skin lesions, sores and scars, rotting teeth and gum disease. Rayanne Tillis was only twenty-three years old. She could have passed for forty-three.

"Rayanne, did you take anything else out of that house this morning besides that TV?"

"No!"

Annie held her hands up in surrender. "It doesn't matter. I'm not gonna hold it against you if you did. Just tell me now. If you did, we'll take it back. No harm, no foul. Nobody needs to know."

"I didn't take nothing!"

"Then I won't find anything in your house when I take you home—like a laptop computer, for instance?"

"Fuck you!" Rayanne bolted up out of her chair and started pacing, agitation winding her tighter and tighter. "No, I don't have no fucking laptop computer. And now I don't have no TV, neither. This has been a fucking day, and I ain't got nothing to show for it!"

She bent over, snatched a filthy flip-flop off one foot, and hurled it at the camera on the wall with amazing accuracy.

"Fucking cops! I want out of here!" she shouted at Annie. "You said you'd get me out of here! You fucking liar!"

She grabbed her other flip-flop and threw it at Annie, who batted it aside before it could hit her in the face. She jumped up out of her seat as Rayanne started toward her, her face twisted with rage.

That fast, the door swung open and a deputy the size of a minivan burst into the room, shouting at Rayanne, "Hey! Back off! Right now!"

Rayanne pedaled backward, leaning around him, red-faced. "You lying bitch! You said no one was watching us!"

"I said no one was *listening* to us," Annie said. "That doesn't mean you get to assault me!"

"I didn't touch you, you lying cow!"

The deputy stepped in front of her again. "You need to sit down and shut up, miss."

"Kiss my ass, you fat fucking whale!" Rayanne barked back. "I don't take orders from you!"

The deputy glared at her. "You're gonna take an order right now and shut your filthy mouth."

"Deputy, it's all right," Annie said calmly. "We've just had a little misunderstanding, Miss Tillis and I. Give us another couple of minutes here."

He looked at her like she was out of her mind.

"She's not armed—other than the flip-flops," Annie pointed out. "We'll be fine."

The deputy looked from Annie to Rayanne and back. "Something happens to you, ma'am, Lieutenant Fourcade will cut my liver out and eat it with onions."

"Nothing's gonna happen," Annie assured him, her gaze steady on the woman. "Isn't that right, Rayanne?"

Rayanne had retreated to the farthest corner of the small room to sulk, her stringy hair falling around her face like a shabby curtain.

"Miss Tillis will be going home shortly," Annie said.

The deputy shook his head in amazement. "Whatever you say, Detective."

"Thank you."

"I'll be right outside the door."

Annie nodded. "Thank you."

He threw one last disapproving look at Rayanne. "You mind your manners," he said as he backed out of the room.

Rayanne gave him the finger—but only after the door had shut.

Annie drew a slow, deep breath and sighed as he closed the door. "You realize I could have him take you back to a cell."

Rayanne rolled her eyes. "Yeah, you're a regular Saint Annie of the Bayou."

"A simple thank-you will do."

"Oh, please. It's not like you don't want something for it. You're just like everybody else—give something to get something. Else you wouldn't give me the time of day."

"Well, I haven't gotten anything besides a headache so far," Annie pointed out, rubbing at the tension in the back of her neck.

Rayanne pursed her lips and batted her eyelashes. "Boo-fucking-hoo. Can we go now?"

Trust was something Rayanne had little of, and she wasn't going to give it away.

Annie picked up her things and moved toward the door. "I'm gonna step out and make a phone call to Mrs. Fontenot. And if she agrees to drop the charges on the TV, I'll drive you home. I told you I'd get you out of here, and I will. I keep my word, Rayanne. I hope you'll remember that in the future."

"You live here alone?" Annie asked as Rayanne preceded her into the shabby little shotgun house—a twin to the one next door. Squalid as it was, she still had a hard time imagining Rayanne Tillis being able to afford the rent on her own. Twenty-dollar blow jobs didn't add up fast, and drug habits were expensive.

"I had a roommate." Rayanne shook a cigarette out of the pack Annie had bought her at the Quik Pik, along with a bag of junk food and a thirty-two-ounce vat of Diet Coke. She lit up with a Bic lighter off a chipped, cluttered end table.

"What happened to her?"

She took a deep drag, blew out a long stream of smoke, and shrugged. "She just didn't come back one day. I don't know where she went. I don't care. She was a lying hoebag anyway. I heard she maybe OD'd."

"What's her name?" Annie asked.

"What do you care?"

"Someone should."

"Why?" She looked at Annie, puzzled for a second, then took

another drag on her cigarette. On the exhale she said, "Beth. Beth Unger."

People in Rayanne's life were transient and disposable. She didn't value herself, no one valued her, she didn't bother to value anyone else. It surprised her when someone else did.

"How long has she been gone?"

"I don't know. A month or so," she said, pacing back and forth behind the worn-out rust plaid sofa that looked like a relic from the eighties. "She used to talk about moving to New Orleans. Maybe she did."

"Did she take her stuff with her?"

Rayanne didn't answer.

Annie glanced around the front room, with its furniture that belonged in a landfill. The place smelled of cigarettes, mold, and mice. It was a mess. Dirty drinking glasses and take-out food wrappers sitting around on every surface. An overflowing ashtray on the coffee table. Looking through to the kitchen, she could see dirty dishes and food left out on the counter. The sour smell of neglected garbage drifted in. The place was a cockroach paradise.

On the upside, she didn't see anything sitting around that might have come from Robbie Fontenot's house.

"Do you have a job, Rayanne?"

"I got laid off."

"From where? The lamp factory?"

"Don't you have someplace else to go?" Rayanne asked irritably, tapping the ash off her smoke into an open beer can.

"Why?" Annie pushed back. "Are you expecting guests or something? I sprung you out of jail. I brought you home. I bought you cigarettes. I think you can answer a question or two. Did you get laid off from the lamp factory?"

"Yeah. So? Who cares?" she complained, pacing. "Shit job. Shit pay. Now I get unemployment. Works for me!"

"Robbie Fontenot worked at the lamp factory. Did you know him from there?"

Rayanne rolled her eyes dramatically and heaved a sigh worthy of a teenager. "I done told you a hundred and ten times already: I don't know him! Jesus Christ!"

"All right," Annie conceded. "I'll let you get on with your busy social calendar. But I want you to call me if you see anything going on next door," she said, handing her a business card. "Can you do that one thing for me, Rayanne?"

Rayanne took another pull on her cigarette as she looked at the card, frowning.

"And you call me if you need me. For anything," Annie said. "I mean that."

"Sure. Whatever."

Annie let herself out, breathing the fresh air deeply to flush the smoke out of her sinuses. Farther down the street to her left, some kids were riding their bikes around in circles, popping wheelies. Nothing much else was going on. There were no houses directly across the street, so no doors to knock on for possible witnesses to anything going on at Robbie Fontenot's place. She wondered if that might have been a deliberate choice on Robbie's part. B'Lynn had said he didn't want her spying on him, but he might not have wanted anyone else watching him, either.

She walked next door to his house and went around the back. Standing on the sagging porch, she looked across the alley, where another shitty house with peeling paint squatted in a yard full of weeds.

Just looking at it, she couldn't know if the place was inhabited. The building looked like someone should have pushed it with a bull-dozer into a hole. But that was certainly no guarantee that someone didn't call it home. Not in this part of town.

The curtains were drawn on the back window. The back door was covered with a rusted white security screen door.

Trying to ignore the low-level hum of anxiety in her head, Annie crossed the alley. The windows along the side of the house were covered with weatherworn warped plywood sprayed with random vulgar graffiti. The front yard was as weed-choked as the back, and strewn with litter. Someone had chucked a blown-out tire into the tall grass to collect rainwater and grow mosquitoes. There were no cars parked out front.

Same as in the back, the curtains were drawn on the front window, and the front door was decked out with a rusty white security door, a twin to the one around back. There were no obvious signs of life. Still, Annie's heart beat a little faster as she climbed the steps.

She wondered how long before her situational anxiety would wear off. It was only her first day back on the job. She should have been more patient with herself, but the irrational fear that it might not ever go away had taken root in the back of her mind. She criticized herself for that, too.

She raised her hand to knock on the door, pausing as something caught her eye, just to the right of the doorframe—the button for a video doorbell.

That seemed a very odd thing on a house that appeared abandoned. No one could be bothered to mow the lawn, but someone had gone to the trouble of installing a security gadget. Why?

Drug house, she thought. Conveniently located on a block of addicts.

She went ahead and rang the bell, her pulse whooshing in her ears as she stepped to the side of the door and waited. No one came. She made herself ring it a second time, watching for a twitch of the front window curtains, but there was none. Somewhere, someone might have been watching her on an app on their phone, but nothing happened.

A kid of about ten or so cruised past on a bike as she stepped down off the front stoop, staring at her openly as he went by. Annie watched him make a wide U-turn and come back, still staring at her.

"Do you know if anybody lives here?" Annie asked as she walked toward him.

The kid turned the bike in a slow circle. He wore a dirty white

New Orleans Saints T-shirt, and his dark hair stood up every which way, like he'd stuck his finger in a light socket.

"I don't talk to no po-po," he said, and he gave her the finger and took off, standing on the pedals, the bike swaying side to side as he raced away.

Good little lookout, Annie thought. It made her sad to be so cynical about a little kid, but it was a real possibility. If he was, he would report to some higher-up that there was a cop poking around, asking questions. She could ask Rayanne about the place, but she doubted she'd get an answer. At any rate, she'd used up her time with Rayanne Tillis for one day. If she pushed too hard, she would never get anything out of her.

She walked back down the side of the house and around the back, taking a closer look at the back porch, looking for and spying a white security camera the size of a deck of cards, mounted up high on the wall. It was angled to spot anyone coming up on the back porch. Whether Robbie Fontenot's back door might have been in its line of sight was anybody's guess, but it was worth finding out.

Her phone pinged to signal the arrival of a text message as she walked back to her vehicle. Nick.

At the PH. Where are you??

Somewhere you won't like, she thought with a little knot of dread forming in the pit of her stomach.

On my way back, she typed, adding a smile emoji, as if that might soften him up. *Fat chance*, she thought, heading back to her vehicle.

9

"YOU'VE BEEN AWFULLY BUSY FOR SOMEONE WHO WAS SUP-posed to be counting paper clips today, no?" Nick said, closing the door behind her as Annie walked into his office. The space was spare and impersonal, organized immaculately down to the last detail, a perfect reflection of its occupant: private and carefully compart-mentalized.

Annie cringed a little inwardly at the undertone of irritation in his voice.

"Yeah, I got sidetracked into serving the public," she said, turning to face him.

He had left the house that morning looking crisp and pressed and ready for court. Now his shirtsleeves were rolled up, the knot in his tie had been pulled loose, and he had undone the collar button of his shirt.

"I gather your day hasn't exactly gone to plan, either."

"*Mais non*," he confessed. "Got called to a dead body on my way in."

"What happened to court?"

"They cut a deal. They didn't need me after all."

He looked her over from head to toe, his dark gaze intense, missing nothing—not in a sexual way, but assessing, judging, looking for any sign she wasn't physically fit to be there. Annie pulled her shoulders back and stood up as tall as she could, the way people were said to do when facing off with a panther. That was her husband—the human embodiment of a big cat: powerful, athletic, intense.

"How you feeling, 'Toinette?" he asked softly, stepping closer.

Annie held her ground, looking him dead in the eyes. "I'm fine."

He frowned, his brows drawing together above his aquiline nose. "Me, I don't quite believe you. You look tired."

"*You* look tired," Annie countered. "Maybe you should go home and have a lie-down."

"How's your head?"

"It's fine."

"Fine. You know I don't like that answer," he complained. "That word doesn't tell me anything, yet you toss it out like a shiny object, as if it might distract me when you know better. Should I have to interrogate you like a suspect?"

"I don't know," Annie said softly, widening her eyes and batting her lashes. "Will that involve some kind of restraints? Lieutenant Fourcade, you shock me!"

He wagged a finger at her. "Don't you try plying me with your womanly wiles, Antoinette."

"You didn't seem to mind that last night," she murmured, taking another step toward him.

He gave her a warning look. They had always been scrupulously careful to draw a line between their professional and personal relationships, for the sake of both their reputations and the emotional balance of the squad.

"We're at work," he reminded her. "And I'm your boss."

"Then you should act like it," Annie said, stepping back, pleased with herself for getting him to make her point for her. "I'm no different than any other employee coming back from time off. You wouldn't have Deebo or Chaz in here, asking them if they were tired from five hours of nothing much."

Nick arched a brow. "'Nothing much'? I hear you suddenly have a missing persons investigation going on, and you somehow managed to arrest someone this morning. Me, I wouldn't call that *nothing much*."

"I'm a highly productive member of your team, then. You should be so pleased."

"*Tête dure*," he grumbled, going behind his desk.

"My hardheadedness is what you love about me," Annie said, taking a seat.

"Not at the moment," he muttered, settling into his chair.

"I'm concerned for your well-being as your boss, and, yes, as your husband," he confessed. "And I admit I'm having a hard time drawing the line between those two roles just now, which is a bigger problem than you want to realize."

"I do realize," Annie said quietly.

The issue sat between them all the time, like a small elephant only they could see. The night she had been injured on the job, he had made several decisions as a husband rather than as her superior. Decisions he would not have made if the fallen officer hadn't been his wife. Nothing that had changed the outcome of the case, but those choices bothered him, nevertheless. The walls between his carefully constructed compartments had been breached, and he didn't like it. Not one bit.

"We've made this work for a long time," Annie reminded him. "And work well."

He had recommended her for the detective squad when she had still been in a uniform. He had mentored her. They had worked hundreds of cases since, all without a problem until that one night.

Don't go there without me . . .

But she had.

He said nothing for a moment, and she couldn't read him. She doubted he was thinking anything positive, but in the end, he just moved on.

"Tell me how you came to be involved with this missing person situation," he said, "after you promised me you would behave yourself if I let you come back to work."

"I didn't go looking for trouble, if that's what you're thinking."

"*Mais non*, you never go looking for trouble, 'Toinette," he said, "but when trouble comes calling, you are seldom out of earshot."

"I swear I was minding my own business," Annie said. "I was on my way to HR. This woman was literally on the floor in front of Hooker's desk, sobbing, begging for help to find her son. Was I supposed step over her body and keep going?"

"This is a missing child?"

"No. He's an adult. Hooker needs his ass kicked, by the way," she added. "Today was the second time that woman had come here looking for help. He turned her away last week."

"Why would he do that?"

"He told her it was a BBPD matter because she had gone to them first."

"So this is their case?"

"They don't want it," Annie insisted. "There's no missing persons report anywhere. They didn't do anything more than a welfare check and put out a BOLO on his car. Dewey Rivette couldn't be bothered to return the mother's phone calls, for God's sake. He never asked her for the most basic information."

"So you just snatched their case away from them."

"What case?" Annie challenged. "They weren't doing anything! Dewey as much as told me he thinks this is an addict who just took off, and God knows he's probably holed up somewhere doing drugs or he's already OD'd, and he's dead someplace. And that may well be true, but that doesn't mean we shouldn't try to find him."

"You spoke to Rivette directly?"

"Yes."

"And he's happy to have us take this over?"

"No," Annie admitted. "Like any man with the maturity of a three-year-old child, he only wants the toy he was ignoring after someone else picks it up. He's done fuck all in a week, but he was Johnny-on-the-spot to yell at me while I was at the missing man's home."

"So he *does* want the case."

"He does want me to butt out so he can continue to tell B'Lynn Fontenot there's nothing to be done," Annie said, her frustration rising. "He's lazy and a misogynist, and time's a-wasting, so yes, I took his case away, if that's how you want to look at it."

Nick heaved a sigh. "It's not about how I want to look at it. Tell me about this missing guy."

"Robbie Fontenot. He's twenty-seven, recently out of rehab, longtime opioid abuser. He has a close relationship with his mother, speaks to her daily. She says he's been on the straight and narrow, and she watches him like a hawk. She hasn't heard from him since Halloween."

"Halloween," Nick repeated. "So he might have gone to a party, fell off the wagon. Addicts do what addicts do . . ."

"Maybe so," Annie conceded. "What does it matter? We shouldn't try to find him because he's an addict?"

"Did I say that?"

"No."

"But he's an adult," he pointed out, "and free to do as he will."

"That doesn't mean he can't be missing!" Annie argued.

"*C'est vrai,*" he said. "But you can't just hijack a case."

"Oh, please," Annie said, rolling her eyes. "You would have done the exact same thing if you'd seen this woman, and you would now be scraping Dewey Rivette off the bottom of your shoe. So spare me the bullshit lecture on professional courtesy.

"Anyway," she added, "it's not like we don't have jurisdiction. If Rivette was doing his job, we should have been in on it anyway. So I don't see the problem here."

Nick shook his head. "You kicked over a hornet's nest and you claim not to hear the buzzing. Johnny Earl will be on the phone to Gus, and there'll be hell to pay."

"Don't be so sure about that," Annie said. "The mother came here this morning to speak to Gus in person. Her ex-husband is some old crony of his, a campaign supporter from back when. Do you think Gus would have turned her away? I don't. I think he would have especially jumped at the chance to make Johnny Earl's head spin. He just happened to be gone to Baton Rouge this morning is all."

"Why the husband didn't come to Gus in the first place?" Nick asked.

"*Ex*-husband," Annie corrected him. "He's not in the son's life anymore. It's been a long road with this kid. The addiction started in high school, and I gather they've been to hell and back too many times. The marriage broke up. The husband lives in Lafayette now. Anyway, the mother went to the police thinking they would help her, *because that's what they're there for.* When they didn't, she came here, and Hooker bounced her back to them. The poor woman is at her wit's end, Nick. I just want to help her. Is that so wrong?"

Nick swiveled back and forth in his chair, his expression inscrutable.

"I'll get him in the NCIC database," Annie said. "I'll request his phone records, financial records. Talk to his employer. Talk to people he worked with, see if I can find out who his friends are . . . Somebody must know something."

She took a big breath and sighed. "Of course, this might all be moot anyway if my missing guy turns out to be your dead guy in the morgue."

"That would be simple for us," Nick agreed. "Two birds with one stone."

"If that's him, his murder is already our case, and we'll need to do the background investigation anyway," Annie pointed out.

She hated the thought of Robbie Fontenot being dead—murdered, no less. "I can't tell you how much I don't want that to be the case. His mother has been through so much, and she's fighting so hard for her son."

"There aren't a lot of happy endings to be had for stories like hers," Nick said. They had both seen too many of those stories to delude themselves.

"I at least want her to have someone on her side to help cushion the blow if it comes to that," Annie said. "I get the impression she doesn't have much in the way of a support network. Ten years dealing with addiction. The husband bailed. People don't like to ride that roller coaster if they don't have to."

"This body in the morgue," Nick said. "It has no face to speak of. One brown eye. Dark hair."

"That fits."

"That fits ninety percent of the local population. How tall is your guy?"

"Six-two, athletic build."

Annie wanted him to stop her there, to tell her his victim was a short guy with a potbelly, but he didn't. Her heart sank a little lower as she began to imagine breaking the news to B'Lynn.

"He has a surgical scar on his left knee," she added. "And his prints are on file. He's been in and out of jail."

"We'll know quick enough if he has that scar or doesn't," Nick said, rising. "Let's go find out.

"I've got a potential missing person myself," he said as they walked down the hall.

"Connected to this dead guy?"

"Don't know. We were following a lead—a business card from a junkyard found in the dead man's pocket—and come to find out someone from that business is missing since Saturday night."

"So he could be your dead guy?"

"I don't know," he said, opening the front door and holding it for Annie to pass. "Marc Mercier. Right age, right size, right coloring. No prints on file, no tattoos, distinguishing marks—not sure. But I don't want to bring the family in to look without good reason. If he can be eliminated from consideration some other way and spare them the trauma, better for all concerned."

"Marc Mercier. That name sounds familiar."

"He was in the local paper a few weeks ago. Maybe you saw him there," he said as they headed to his SUV. "The savior of youth football in Bayou Breaux, much to the surprise of his wife."

"What's that mean?"

"Marital strife. It's a long story, but the short version is the marriage is in trouble. They had a fight Saturday night. He stormed off. He was supposed to meet his brother out at the Corners early Sunday morning. They were headed out west to some hunting land. The brother was late. There was no sign of Marc when he got there. Hasn't been seen or heard from since," he said, pulling open the passenger door for her.

"If he was at the Corners," Annie said, climbing into the vehicle, "he should show up on Uncle Sos's security video."

The Corners was a local institution. A combination convenience store, café, bait shop, landing for swamp tours, and boat launch for sport fishermen, it had been run for decades by Sos and Fanchon Doucet, the people who had raised Annie after her mother's death when Annie was just nine years old—and before that, truth be told. Sos and Fanchon had taken in Marie Broussard when she had been lost and pregnant and prone to long bouts of depression. Annie had been raised calling them uncle and *tante*, her family by love rather than by blood.

"We could run out there tonight for supper," Annie suggested as Nick got behind the wheel. "They'd love to see Justin, and Uncle Sos will be in his glory to help with an investigation."

A small smile tugged at the corner of Nick's mouth. "*C'est vrai.* I can hear him now, telling his cronies how he helped solve the case."

With his own parents long deceased, Nick had grown to love Sos and Fanchon almost as much as Annie did, spending time on the water fishing with Sos when he could, helping him with his boats and with repairs around the place. Sos considered him as much a son as he considered Annie a daughter.

Sos and Fanchon had never been blessed with children of their own, but that hadn't stopped them from making a family of nieces and nephews and strays. The love they had for that family was fierce and unconditional. There was nothing they wouldn't do to protect or save one of their own, and their love never wavered, even in the hardest of times.

A wave of emotion rolled over Annie as she thought of them. Tears welled in her eyes. She cursed herself for forgetting her sunglasses. Sudden strong emotions had been a side effect of her head injury. Her doctor told her that would eventually subside, but while it lasted, she hated it. Nick watched her like a hawk for any sign of an issue, any reason he could add to his arsenal of why she shouldn't be going back to work, and there she was on her first day back, ready to burst into tears in front of him.

He glanced over at her then as they sat at a red light.

"You all right, *bébé*?" he asked, reaching a hand over to touch her shoulder.

"Just thinking I'm awfully lucky," she said, blinking back the tears as she checked her phone for any sign of a callback from Robert Fontenot II. "Not everyone has family that loves them."

"*Mais non*," he agreed, stroking a hand over the back of her head. "We're lucky, that's for true."

"That's why I want to help B'Lynn Fontenot. She's fighting tooth and nail for her boy when no one else will. His father can't even be bothered to return my phone calls."

"That's a hard road, dealing with an addict," Nick said. "People do what they have to do to survive it."

"I know, but can you imagine any circumstances where you'd just give up on Justin? Just cut him out of your life like he never existed?"

"No, but you should know not to pick sides before you even meet the man, no? That's your mama bear claws coming out."

"I suppose you're right about that."

"I imagine you left a few marks on Dewey Rivette," he teased.

"Maybe one or two," Annie admitted, finding a weary smile.

"Me, I would have paid money to see that."

"So you're not mad at me after all?" Annie ventured.

He made a noncommittal sound as he cut her a glance, his eyes hidden by the mirrored lenses of his sunglasses. The jury was still out.

In the center of the driveway leading up to Our Lady of Mercy hospital, a pristine white statue of the Virgin Mary greeted all comers with open arms. A groundskeeper knelt at her feet, using a hand clipper to trim the low ring of boxwood that circled her base. Built in the seventies during the oil boom, the L-shaped two-story hospital was still the pride of Partout Parish, with its manicured gardens and broad, oak-studded lawn sweeping down to the bayou, the one institution that had withstood the economic roller-coaster rides of every decade since.

Nick pulled the SUV into a parking spot reserved for sheriff's office vehicles near the entrance to the ER and cut the engine.

"Come here, *chère*," he said, leaning toward her. She met him halfway, and he kissed her softly, sweetly.

"I love you," he murmured.

She sensed a *but* coming at the end of that sentence, but he didn't voice it, and she decided to take that as a positive for the moment.

"Let's go get this over with," he said.

The small flock of reporters loitering outside the ER entrance jumped to attention as Annie and Nick approached. They all cackled at once, parroting the same question: "Detective Fourcade! Do you have an ID on the body?"

"Not yet," Nick said, not slowing down. "You'll know as soon as I do."

"Are there any leads?"

"What about missing persons?"

"Is this drug related?"

A uniformed deputy stepped forward to clear the way for them to pass through the glass doors. The noise died by half as the doors swished closed behind them.

They passed through the emergency room waiting area, where half a dozen people of varying ages and maladies sat looking miserable as they waited their turn—an elderly man holding a bloody rag to his forehead, a teenage girl with a tearstained face clutching an injured arm against her body.

One woman caught Annie's eye as familiar—someone she'd dealt with on a domestic call. The woman quickly turned her face away, embarrassed, ashamed, not wanting the attention of a cop. That was part of the job—not being a welcome sight, people avoiding eye contact in public. Also part of the job: automatically assuming the worst, wondering if a black eye or a broken arm was the result of violence.

"Someone you know?" Nick asked as they turned down the hall that led to the morgue.

"Yeah. Just another reluctant customer."

"At least they're out front and not back here," Nick said as he pulled the morgue door open.

The room was all white tile and stainless steel, sterile and silent. A twentysomething man in purple scrubs with a shock of red hair sat using a gurney as a desk, his nose buried in a book as he scribbled notes. He glanced up as Nick spoke his name.

"Caleb, we need to have a look at that body, s'il vous plaît."

"Sure thing." He stuck his pen in his textbook and hopped off his stool. He was built like a fireplug, with the muscular arms of a man who spent too much free time in the gym. An easy smile split his square face. "Hey, Annie, how you?"

"Hey, T-Rouge, I'm good," Annie said. "How's your mom and them?"

His family were cousins to the Doucets by marriage. Annie had known Caleb McVay all his life.

"Mostly good. Nonc Claude, he's got the shingles on his face," he said, going to a wall of small stainless steel doors. "I told him before to get the vaccine, but he wouldn't listen. Why listen to the medical professional in the family when you can get your medical advice from conspiracy nuts on the Internet? He thinks vaccines are a government plot to install tracking devices in everyone. Meanwhile, he's walking around with a cell phone twenty-four/seven."

"What can you do?" Annie asked with a shrug.

"Well, you can't pick your relatives," Caleb said with a laugh, opening a door and rolling out their murder victim. "Here you go. We got everything done you needed done ASAP—fingerprints, photos, X-rays, pulled blood, fluids. The only personal effects was his jeans and his socks. Detective Stokes bagged that stuff and took it."

"Autopsy when?" Nick asked.

"First thing in the morning."

Annie took a deep breath and braced herself. The victim wasn't the worst she had ever seen—not even close. She'd seen bloated bodies pulled out of the swamp, half eaten by wildlife. She'd seen the bodies of people who died alone in the dead of summer in an attic with no air-conditioning. Her first murder victim was a woman who had been nailed to a wood floor, tortured, and eviscerated. Still, there was always a jolt of shock seeing what was left after one human being had snuffed out the life of another.

"That's nasty," she muttered, staring at what was left of this man's head. It was a sight from a horror movie, one brown eye staring out of a shell of shattered bone and pulverized flesh.

"No mystery what killed him," Caleb remarked, leaning back against the wall and setting his hands at his waist.

"*Mais non*," Nick said. "The secret is who he is and who did this to him."

"Well, he's not Robbie Fontenot," Annie said with no small amount of relief as she looked at the dead man's bare knees. "No surgical scars."

"Robbie Fontenot?" Caleb asked. "Why'd you think it was him?"

"Is he a friend of yours?" Annie asked.

"Not mine. He went to school with Eli. They both played football for Sacred Heart.

"Man, that kid Robbie was a baller," he said. "He would have been a Division I quarterback if he hadn't blown out his knee."

"Is Eli still friends with him?"

"Nooo," Caleb said, shaking his head. "Robbie ran off the rails way back when. Drugs. In and out of jail. Eli bumped into him in town not long ago. He only mentioned it because he hadn't seen him in so many years. He was shocked the guy was still alive. I guess I shouldn't be surprised if this was him, all things considered."

"Where's Eli at now?" Annie asked. "Is he still in Houston?"

"He moved to Lafayette this summer. He's a civil engineer for the city."

"You bunch of brainiacs," Annie teased, pulling out her phone and entering Eli McVay as a new contact. "Your folks must be pleased he's closer to home. What's his phone number?"

Caleb recited the number. "Why you looking for Robbie Fontenot? Is he wanted for something?"

"He's missing," Annie said. "Have you heard anything about him recently?"

"No. We don't run in the same circles."

"Do you know for a fact he's still into drugs?"

He shrugged his meaty shoulders. "Those tigers don't change their stripes as a rule, do they?"

So everyone but Robbie Fontenot's mother wanted to think.

"If you happen to hear anything about him, you call me, all right?" Annie said, handing him a business card.

Caleb tucked the card in the breast pocket of his scrubs. "Sure, but all I do these days is study. Unless he shows up here, I'm not liable to be much help."

"I'm gonna hope for his mama's sake, then, I don't hear from you," Annie said. She turned to Nick, but his attention was still on Caleb.

"Caleb, do you happen to know Marc Mercier?" he asked.

"Sure, I know Marc." His blue eyes widened suddenly, and he turned to look at the body on the gurney. "You don't think this is Marc, do you?"

"I don't know. Could it be?"

"No!" he said, incredulous at the idea. "It can't be!"

"It can't be because the body doesn't look like him," Nick asked, "or it can't be because you don't want to believe it could be him?"

"Well, I ain't never seen Marc naked, for starters," Caleb said. "And I don't know what to say about that head. That doesn't even look real, let alone resemble an actual person. If you put Marc's face on that mess, could it be him? Maybe. But who would shoot Marc? Why?"

"He's not a man with enemies?"

"Hell no. Nice guy, fun guy, give-you-the-shirt-off-his-back kind of a guy. Everybody knows he moved back here to help out his family."

"You know him well?"

"I know him to say hey. He was Eli's friend. I was just the little brother. They were the big men on campus at Sacred Heart, that football team. Marc led them to the state championship. They were my idols."

"They all knew each other?" Annie said. "Eli and Robbie Fontenot and Marc Mercier? They were all friends?"

"Eli and Marc were always tight. And Robbie to a lesser degree before his life went south. I remember Robbie was more of an introvert—quiet, serious."

"Was Marc Mercier into drugs?" Nick asked.

"No," Caleb said. "Him and Eli were student leaders of the DARE program, and they took it to heart. Not that they didn't drink their share of beer back then, but drugs? No. If I remember right, Marc had lost a cousin to an overdose or something like that. He was dead set against drugs."

"So when Robbie went down that path, his friends weren't going with him," Annie said.

"Not Eli's crowd, that's for sure."

That had been the start of the Robbie Fontenot life avalanche, Annie thought: the injury that had taken away his sport, the drugs he had become dependent on to numb the pain, the social isolation of losing his peers and disappointing his family. Down the slippery slope he went.

"Have you seen Marc recently?" Nick asked.

"I saw him on Halloween at Monster Bash," Caleb said. "He was dressed up as Hawkeye, you know, from the Avengers, with the bow and arrows and everything."

"Was he with anyone?"

"The Incredible Hulk. Dozer Cormier." He rolled his eyes. "That was some typecasting there."

"Dozer. That's a nickname?"

"Yeah. The Bulldozer. Then it got shortened and everyone just called him Dozer. They still do. I don't even remember what his real name is."

"Does he live around here? Do you know what he does for a living?"

"I don't really know him other than by sight. You can't miss him. Bald head like a cinder block and he's the size of a farm implement."

"You didn't see Robbie Fontenot by chance that night, did you?" Annie asked as Nick stepped away to look at his phone.

"I don't think I'd know him," Caleb said. "It's been years."

Annie pulled up the photo on her phone and showed it to him. He frowned and shook his head. "Sorry."

"*Merci*, Caleb," Nick said, turning toward Annie. "We've got to go. Gus is back."

10

"IS HE IN A BAD MOOD?" ANNIE ASKED AS THEY HEADED BACK down the hall toward the ER.

"He's got the caps lock on," Nick said, showing her his phone screen.

GET YOUR ASS TO MY OFFICE ASAP.

"Shit," Annie said. "He's heard from Johnny Earl."

"That's a good bet, though he's just generally in a bad mood these days."

"Sorry I'm adding to that."

"No, you're not," he said, cutting her a look, a hint of a smile turning one corner of his mouth.

His wife had a long and consistent history of doing the right thing (in her mind) first and apologizing later. She was as stubborn as the day was long when it came to her beliefs about anything. She would stand in the face of a roaring lion if she had to. She had stood up to him more than once when no grown man would have. That attitude got her in trouble as often as not, but he loved her for it fiercely.

"No," she admitted. "I'm not sorry. I'm not sorry at all. I just wish it wouldn't be a problem."

"It won't be, not after the initial explosion."

"The shrapnel is so unpleasant, though."

"Me, I'm more concerned about what we've got going on here. Your missing person and my missing person just happened to know each other?"

"Could be a coincidence."

"You know how much I like that word," he said. "Not at all. And Marc Mercier's wife told me he spends his free time with the guys he went to high school with."

"I asked B'Lynn about Robbie's friends. She said she didn't know if he had any left. With his drug history and your guy's anti-drug history, it wouldn't seem like they'd be hanging out in the same circles."

"But your Mr. Fontenot is allegedly clean now, yeah? It's a decade on since high school. If he's making a fresh start, runs into old buddies . . . who knows?"

"Well, we know that body on the slab in there isn't Robbie, and Robbie's been gone more than a week. Your guy disappeared when? Saturday?"

"*Mais* yeah, but *gone* doesn't necessarily mean dead or missing. I've requested Marc Mercier's dental records. If there's enough jaw left on the one side of the mouth of our corpse, we might be able to compare. Otherwise we're waiting on DNA results to eliminate him. Christ knows how long that'll take."

"You need to text me a picture of him," Annie said. "I'll show Robbie's neighbor and his mom."

"Same here. Text me that picture of your guy."

They turned the corner into the ER waiting area. Beyond the big glass doors, the gaggle of reporters had grown while they'd been inside. There were TV cameras now as the afternoon countdown to the five-o'clock news began. As the doors slid open, the reporters shouted a chorus of all the same questions they had asked before.

He hated dealing with the media, but he stopped to address them nevertheless. They had their uses, and he had his responsibilities.

"I have no new information for you regarding the identity of the victim found outside of Luck this morning. As I stated earlier today, the victim is a white male, age twenty-five to thirty-five, with dark hair and dark eyes. If anyone in the public has any information, please call the sheriff's office tip line. That number is three-three-seven—"

"You lying son of a bitch!"

Kiki Mercier had pushed her way to the front of the small crowd. Now all eyes turned toward her in her bib overalls and work boots, her short hair standing up in ragged tufts, as if she'd been pulling at it.

"I asked you was he dead and you said no," she said, stepping forward. "He's dead in there right now, isn't he? That's my Marc in there, and you wouldn't tell me!"

"Mrs. Mercier," Nick said quietly, well aware the TV cameras were rolling, "I don't know any such thing."

"You're lying!" she cried, tears welling in her eyes as she took another step forward. "You told that bitch wife of his! You told her, but you wouldn't tell me. I'm his mother! I want to see him!"

She was close enough now Nick could smell the whiskey on her breath.

Luc Mercier rushed up behind her, red-faced. "Jesus, Ma, stop it! You're making a fool of yourself!"

"Don't you talk to me like that!" Kiki snapped. "You'd be only too happy if your brother was dead!"

"For fuck's sake, shut up!" Luc said, his voice low and tight. "You're drunk!"

"Don't you tell me what to do, Luc Mercier," she barked back. "You're only here to drive the damn truck."

She turned back toward Nick, losing her balance and falling against him. "I want to see my son. Right now!"

Nick turned, pulling Kiki with him. He looked to Annie and said, "Find us an empty room. Quick." To the uniformed deputy standing sentry at the doors, he said, "Keep these people out here."

Behind them, the shouted questions of the reporters rose to a crescendo.

Annie dashed ahead of them, through the ER waiting area and down the hall, knocking on the door of an examination room then swinging the door open and motioning for them to come.

"I had to hear it on the radio," Kiki said angrily as Nick ushered her into the room. "That there was a body found practically down the road from us. You stood right there in our place and didn't say a goddamn thing!"

"I didn't say anything because we don't know anything, Mrs. Mercier," Nick said. "I've got an unidentified body. I don't know if it's Marc. I don't know who it is."

"Let me see him!" she shouted. "I know my own son!"

"No," Nick said. "That's not how this is happening."

"You went to Melissa," Luc said. "Has she been here? Where the hell is she? Or can't she be bothered?"

"I'll be blunt with you," Nick said. "This victim took a shotgun blast to the face."

Kiki gasped as if she'd been struck. "No!"

"No one is identifying him by sight," Nick said. "This body was dumped. I don't have a vehicle; I don't have an ID of any kind. Yes, I went to Marc's wife. She is his legal next of kin. I had to get the information from her for Marc's dentist in Philadelphia to send his dental records for comparison."

"Oh, my God, she's killed him!" Kiki wailed, falling against the exam table. "I told you she killed him. Her and Will Faulkner. And now they gonna take my grandbaby away from me!"

"Mrs. Mercier," Annie said, reaching out to lay a hand gently on her shoulder. "Why don't you take a seat and we'll talk about your concerns."

Kiki jerked backward. "Who the hell are you?"

"Detective Broussard."

"I don't want to *talk about my concerns*, Detective Broussard," she said, sneering at the idea. "I want to see my son!"

She shoved Annie hard into the cabinets and bolted for the door.

Nick blocked her, grabbing her by the shoulders and trapping her back against the exam table. Fueled by rage and panic, she was shockingly strong.

"Let me go!" she screamed, twisting in his grasp. "Let me go, damn you!"

"Stop it!" Nick ordered. "Be still, or I'm putting you in handcuffs!"

He glanced over at Annie. "Are you all right?"

"I'm fine," she said, even as she pressed her fingertips against her eyebrow to stem the flow of blood from a cut.

"Jesus Christ, Ma!" Luc Mercier exclaimed. "What are you doing? What the hell is wrong with you?"

"I'm here to fight for your brother," she said. "What are you doing? Nothing!"

"Fight for him how? Fight for him for what?"

"You don't love your brother!"

"Oh, for fuck's sake! You're out of your damn mind!"

"*C'est assez!*" Nick barked, pulling Kiki's attention back to him. "Enough!"

She went still, and he loosened his hold on her shoulders, not trusting her enough to let go altogether.

"I understand that you're upset, Mrs. Mercier," he said. "But you just assaulted a sheriff's detective. You're intoxicated and violent, and I would be well within my rights to arrest you. Is that what you want? You want to go sit in jail? I will happily accommodate you."

Kiki huffed a sigh, still agitated. "You'll arrest me, but you won't arrest Prissy Missy, and I'm telling you she killed my boy!"

"I'm done explaining myself to you," Nick said.

He looked to Luc Mercier, the errand boy and chauffeur and apparent constant source of disappointment to his mother, and couldn't help but feel sympathy for him, having to deal with a daily dose of this woman.

"You're gonna take your *maman* out of this building by another door," Nick said. "Speak to no one, and go home now or she's going to jail until she's sober, and you can deal with the aftermath of that. Those are your choices, Mr. Mercier."

"Might as well ask me would I rather be gouged with a stick or hit with a hammer," Luc grumbled. He looked at his mother. "I should let them lock you up, if for no other reason than I wouldn't have to listen to you bitching on the drive home."

"Don't you dare!"

"Don't worry," he said. "You'd only be worse after jail. I'll take you home and you can drink yourself into oblivion tonight, fretting about your one worthy child. If there's a God, you'll choke to death on your own vomit later."

"Oh, you'd like that," Kiki snapped.

"I would, yes."

"You're an ungrateful, spiteful man."

"Well, look who I learned from."

"*Arrête!*" Nick snapped. "I've had it with the both of you!" He stepped back, hands raised. "Go! Go home. Now, before I change my mind. I'll be in touch as soon as I know whether or not the body in the morgue is Marc's."

"These family meetings are so heartwarming," Annie said, pressing a tissue to her bleeding eyebrow as they watched the Merciers walk away down the hall toward the main entrance of the hospital.

"To hell with them," Nick grumbled, turning his attention to her. "Are you all right, *chère*? You're bleeding. Let me see."

"It's nothing," she said, but she let him look and fuss as he muttered a stream of curse words in French. "It's just a little cut. I'm fine."

"You hit your head!"

"No. I just caught the edge of the cabinet with my eyebrow. Really, I'm fine."

He scowled at the cut. "I want you to get it looked at. That might need a stitch."

Annie drew breath to object, but he cut her off with a stern look.

"No arguments, 'Toinette. We're at the damn hospital. Have a nurse look at it while I go outside and deal with the press."

She sighed in resignation. "All right."

They walked together back to the ER, Annie turning to the triage desk as Nick went through the double doors to face the reporters waiting outside. She gave the nurse at the desk a peek at her bleeding eyebrow and then followed her back into the treatment area, where the physician's assistant came to look at the wound.

"Please tell me I don't need stitches."

"You don't need stitches," the PA said. "We'll just clean it up and put a butterfly on that, and you'll be all set. It won't take a minute. Just have a seat here."

Annie hopped up on the end of a gurney to wait. The treatment bays were divided by curtains but open to the work lane, which was cluttered with various carts and machines pushed up against the wall. Privacy was minimal. She could hear conversations on either side of her—a mother consoling a daughter over a broken arm, a man complaining about his insurance, a nurse giving someone instructions about resting an injury.

". . . Are you sure you don't want to speak to a deputy, Mrs. Parcelle?"

Annie sat up straighter. Tulsie Parcelle, the young woman who had tried to duck her notice in the waiting area when she and Nick had first come in.

"No! There's no reason for that," the woman scoffed, laughing. "I just had an accident, that's all. Quit making such a fuss!"

Annie hopped down off the gurney and walked down the work lane. Two beds down, she found Tulsie Parcelle, her right arm in a sling, cradled gingerly against her body. In her early twenties, petite and curvy, she was a pretty girl when she didn't have a black eye or a busted lip. She had a heart-shaped face with tiny blue eyes that disappeared when she smiled. Her honey-blond hair hung in a thick braid over one shoulder.

"Hey, Tulsie," Annie greeted her, keeping her tone light and conversational. "I thought that was you in the waiting room. How are you?"

"I'm good!" the girl answered stupidly, as if she wasn't sitting in an ER with her arm in a sling, looking like she'd been on the losing end of a brawl.

"What'd you do to yourself?" Annie asked, as if she had never been called to the Parcelles' farm on suspicion of Cody Parcelle knocking his wife around.

Tulsie had refused to press charges that day, insisting her husband hadn't touched her, that she'd had an accident handling a young stallion. The story had smelled like so much horse manure to the deputy who had responded to the 911 call. Annie had agreed with him, but without a complainant or a witness, they'd had to accept the girl's story.

"Just a stupid accident!" Tulsie said now with another nervous laugh. "I was pulling down some hay. Cody, he bought a whole load of those big hundred-pound bales. I don't know what he was thinking. They're way too big for me to deal with! It's like me trying to wrestle an alligator. I wrenched my shoulder pretty hard, but I'll be fine!"

She spoke in exclamation points, as if the extra emphasis and forced smile would sell her story.

It could have been true, Annie conceded, but if she'd gotten hit in the face with a bale of hay, there would have been scratches, not just a black eye and a split lip. More likely was Cody Parcelle backhanding her across the face and yanking her around by one arm, but if Tulsie wasn't ready to tell that story, there wasn't anything Annie could do about it.

"Better ask Cody to get those bales down for you from now on,"

Annie said. "A hundred pounds apiece? That's almost as big as you are!"

"Oh, well, you know us farm girls," Tulsie said, trying to smile again with her fat lip. "We just figure things out!"

She was trying so hard to sound lighthearted and carefree that she came across as frantic, verging on hysterical.

"Yeah, well, still," Annie said. "Us short girls need to know our limitations, right?

"I didn't see Cody out front," she said. "He didn't come with you?"

She glanced around as if Cody Parcelle might be lurking nearby, half hidden by a curtain. "You didn't drive yourself here with that bad shoulder, did you?"

"No, I—"

"Because it's really not okay for you to drive like that," Annie said. "I'd be happy to give you a lift home—"

"No, no, not necessary!" the girl protested, smiling, laughing, sliding down off the gurney. "Our hired hand brought me. They're waiting out in the parking lot."

"Oh, well, good," Annie said. "But, you know, if you ever need help, you just call me."

She handed the girl a business card, and they both knew her offer had nothing to do with the attack of a hundred-pound hay bale.

Tulsie shoved the card into the pocket of her jeans, her eyes already on the exit. "Sure. Thanks, Annie. I need to get going. There's chores to do before supper!"

"You take care," Annie said.

"I will!"

The girl all but bolted down the work lane, nearly colliding with the PA coming back to tend to Annie's eyebrow.

The nurse who had been helping Tulsie leaned toward Annie and murmured, "Funny how that girl can look everywhere but right in your eyes."

"Yeah," Annie agreed. But it wasn't funny to either of them. It wasn't funny at all.

11

AUGUST F. "GUS" NOBLIER HAD RULED AS KING OF PARTOUT Parish for two decades before his retirement. A reign of consecutive terms blemished by one election loss to the skullduggery of a political rival who had subsequently left the office in a cloud of scandal, only to be replaced by Gus for another dozen years after. It was a tenure unlikely to be repeated.

He was a figure as big as his reputation—rawboned and rough-edged, full of bluster and bombast and too much fried food. He stood behind his desk with his hands on his hips and a scowl on his face. He had dressed for his day of meetings in Baton Rouge in full uniform, though he had jerked loose his necktie now at the tail end of the afternoon. He looked tired and irritated.

Between the shocking circumstances of the death of his successor, Kelvin Dutrow, and the fact that Dutrow had never promoted a chief deputy to the official position of second-in-command, the governor himself had asked Gus to come back and take control until the situation could be sorted and settled. Gus had done so grudgingly, out of a sense of duty, and he had made no bones about his intention to leave as soon as his replacement was in place.

As impossible as it had been for anyone to imagine him relinquishing his hold on power in the first place, retirement had suited Gus just fine. He had filled his days with his horses and his hobbies and helping his wife in the garden. He had claimed not to miss the spotlight or the endless headache of holding office, though Annie secretly wanted to believe otherwise.

Gus Noblier had been a constant in her professional life since she had come out of the police academy. He had hired her as a patrol deputy and promoted her to detective, serving as a mentor of sorts along the way. He had filled a similar role for Nick, hiring him after Nick's career in New Orleans had crashed and burned like a derailed train. He had known Nick's father and had taken on Armand Fourcade's son at a time when no one else would have touched him.

He stood looking at Annie and Nick now like they were a pair of ill-behaved students who had been sent to the principal's office.

"Imagine my surprise," he said, "when I'm sitting with the governor at Sullivan's, about to cut into my beautiful Delmonico steak, and my phone starts blowing up with Johnny Earl having a tantrum because one of my detectives has chased one of his off a case. Imagine my indigestion."

"That's what you get eating red meat," Nick said.

Gus's scowl deepened as red began to creep up his neck. "Are you trying to be amusing?"

"No."

"Because I am not in the mood to be amused by anyone, least of all you, Lieutenant." He turned his eagle-eyed glare on Annie. "And you must be eating your Wheaties these days, young lady. First day back on the job and you're sinking your teeth into the town boys like a terrier with a rat, running their detective off his case in their jurisdiction."

"I didn't run Dewey Rivette off his case, sir," Annie corrected him. "He didn't have a case. He wasn't investigating anything. He's just a big baby who showed up mad because he thought I was about to make him look bad."

"Weren't you?"

"I don't have to lift a finger to make Dewey Rivette look bad. He does all that heavy lifting on his own. Anyway, Bayou Breaux is as much our jurisdiction as it is theirs, as you yourself have pointed out many times."

His attention went back to Nick. "And I suppose you're gonna make excuses for your wife's behavior?"

"*Mais non,*" Nick said calmly. "No excuses are necessary. Detective Broussard, she did nothing wrong."

"You gave her the okay for this?"

"Me, I was otherwise engaged at the time with a murder victim. At any rate, my detectives don't need permission to investigate crimes. It is their job after all, is it not?"

"Don't get cute with me," Gus grumbled. "I'm trying to orchestrate a smooth change of power in this office. I don't have time to be starting World War III with Johnny Earl."

"*C'est triste,*" Nick said. "That's sad, for sure, considering butting heads with Chief Earl has always been your favorite way to pass a good time, yeah?"

"Now, listen here—"

"Don't bother to deny it. I don't know how you stood it this long out of office not being able to wind up Johnny Earl 'til his head spins. It seems to me the only real problem here is that you were caught unaware. You never did like to play defense."

"Well, the best defense is a good offense," Gus conceded as he took his seat. He heaved a sigh and gestured them toward chairs.

"Have you actually spoken with Chief Earl?" Nick asked.

"Without knowing the particulars of the situation? Hell no!"

"Then there is no problem, is there? You're just cranky because the governor didn't tell you what you wanted to hear today, and you're gonna be stuck with this job longer than you want to be, yeah?"

Gus made a rumbling sound low in his throat like distant

thunder. "That I'm sitting here this minute dealing with you is already longer than I want to be here."

Annie glanced around the office. When Gus had reigned, this room had been a veritable time capsule of the history of Partout Parish. The walls had been covered in photographs of Gus with every important or self-important politician and minor celebrity in south Louisiana, as well as dozens of commendations and awards and framed newspaper and magazine articles featuring Gus. Every available surface had been piled with old files and weird relics he had collected over the years: lacquered alligator heads, giant ceremonial ribbon-cutting shears, a jar full of tiny plastic baby dolls found in decades' worth of king cakes.

When he had come into office, Kelvin Dutrow had stripped the room bare and then built his own wall of fame, all of it gone now, thrown away and forgotten. The wall had remained empty, save for the dozens of empty picture hooks. Gus had made no effort to bring anything personal back into the room. The sense of impermanence was subtly unsettling.

"I wanna dig Kelvin Dutrow up and kill him myself for leaving this office in the lurch," he grumbled. "No chief deputy, and the next obvious choice don't want the job, not that I blame him."

Nick, who had hated Kelvin Dutrow on first sight and had never changed his mind, wisely chose to say nothing in the moment. Gus had handpicked Kelvin Dutrow to succeed him. That his choice had turned out to be a bad one was not sitting well with him. He now found himself in a hell that was, at least in part, of his own making, but he was more than willing to take some of that frustration out on anyone handy if they displeased him.

"This is a missing persons case," Annie said, turning them back to the topic at hand. "We should have been brought in immediately, not left to wait until a family member came to us out of desperation."

Gus sighed and rubbed a big hand over his face and back over his silver crew cut. "Is this family member the same woman Valerie tells me attacked her this morning?"

Annie rolled her eyes. "She did not attack Valerie. If Valerie didn't wear her skirts too tight and her heels too high, she could have easily gotten out of the way."

"Out of the way of what?"

"B'Lynn Fontenot," Annie said. "She came here this morning hoping to appeal to you directly. She said her ex-husband is an acquaintance of yours—Dr. Robert Fontenot."

"Bob Fontenot?" Gus said. "There's a name I haven't heard in donkey's years."

"He moved to Lafayette."

"I know."

Something in the way he said it gave Annie pause, like those two simple words might be only the very tip of a substantial iceberg.

"You haven't heard from him lately?" she asked.

"No."

"His son is missing."

"Is he?"

Another two icy chips off the same block. There was a story there, and Gus wasn't wanting to share it.

"He's been missing since Halloween," she pressed on. "So far, the only person who has any sense of urgency about it is his mother—and I include the BBPD and our own desk sergeant in that statement. Dewey Rivette has done nothing, as far as I can see."

"The Fontenot boy isn't this body you've got laying in the morgue at Our Lady?" Gus asked.

"No, sir. Definitely not."

"And we may have another possible missing person," Nick said. "Marc Mercier, who hasn't been seen since Saturday. He and Mr. Fontenot knew each other, as it turns out."

"Then who is this corpse? Marc Mercier?"

"We don't know yet. I've got to get his dental records and hope there's enough mouth left on that corpse for comparison. He took a shotgun blast to the face. It'll probably come to DNA to identify him, and where do we even start with that if it isn't Marc Mercier?"

Gus slapped a hand down hard on his desktop. "What the actual hell is going on in this parish? I leave for one day and come back to all this mess? Missing persons. Unidentified murder victims . . ."

"*Mais* yeah," Nick said dryly. "As I recall, there was no crime at all when you were sheriff before."

"Smart-ass. The world's going to hell on a sled," Gus declared. "You think this is somehow all connected, do you?"

Nick gave half a shrug. "I have no idea at this point."

"I spoke with Mrs. Fontenot after we left the morgue," Annie said. "She remembers Marc Mercier from when the boys were in school. They ran together before Robbie had his accident, but not after. He lost most of his old friends. They graduated, moved on with their lives. She doesn't know who his friends are now. He doesn't share with her. But she's never heard him mention Marc Mercier in recent memory, for whatever that's worth."

Gus frowned. "Try to find people in this town who *didn't* go to school together. Doesn't mean much."

"I still don't like the coincidence," Nick said. "For now these are three separate investigations that may or may not intersect. But if it turns out there's a connection, I would sooner not be tripping over the BBPD as we investigate.

"Annie filed the missing persons report, she'll enter Mr. Fontenot into the NCIC database, and she's already working on a possible witness. As far as I'm concerned, this is our case going forward, and Dewey Rivette can devote himself to solving the crime wave of shoplifting in downtown Bayou Breaux."

Gus sat back in his chair and heaved a sigh as the wheels of his mind turned.

"If you had been here this morning," Annie began, "what would you have told Mrs. Fontenot? Would you have turned her away? Would you have told her that her son isn't our problem because of his address, because you didn't want to offend Johnny Earl?"

"No," he said wearily. "I don't reckon I would have. But that doesn't make this any less of a can of worms."

He swiveled his chair slowly back and forth as he stared out the window, as if it was a portal into the past.

"That boy caused his parents a world of grief," he said. "And here he is, still doing it."

"We don't know that he's done anything," Annie said. "All we know at this point is he's gone. Where and why, I don't know. Could be no fault of his own at all."

"The result is the same," Gus said. "Here's his mama, hysterical with worry, begging for help, running herself ragged, I expect. She's dragged him out of hellholes before. She's gotta be thinking he's dead or worse."

"*Mais* yeah, and she could be right," Nick said. "That doesn't mean we shouldn't look for him. And, given the shit show this office has been in recent months, stepping up in a public way to take over a case the BBPD fumbled could be a good PR move, no?"

Gus laughed, a big, loud belly laugh. "How unlike you to consider the public image of this office! Since when do you give a rat's patoot about appearances?"

"I don't," Nick admitted. "You know that all too well. I only care about the work. That's why I have my job and why you have yours."

Gus pursed his lips and nodded. "I can't deny this office could use some good publicity. I don't like having to get there via a minor crime wave, but showing people we have control of the situation surely can't hurt us."

And if that show of strength came at the expense of his rival, all the better, Annie thought, but she kept that thought to herself.

The sheriff turned his eagle eye on her. "I'm gonna hope for everyone's sake this case has a positive outcome, but I'm gonna tell you what, Annie, you've cut a big hog in the ass here. Robbie Fontenot was nothing but trouble and disappointment back when, and there's no reason to expect something better now."

"I know," she said. "But it's not always nuns and schoolteachers who need us."

"No. That's true," he said on a sigh. He raised a big hand as if to give a benediction. "Give my regards to Mrs. Fontenot," he said by way of dismissal. "I'll deal with Johnny Earl."

"Thanks for having my back, boss," Annie said as she and Nick walked across from the main building toward the Pizza Hut.

The sun was puddling against the western horizon like molten gold, casting the world in a burnished glow as the last of the afternoon slipped away. The pleasant warmth of the day had gone with the light. She wished for the jacket she'd left in her vehicle.

Nick glanced down at her. "I didn't do you any favors, *chère*. This is the best way to proceed."

"I'm glad you're a control freak, then. It sometimes works to my advantage."

"Why do you think Dewey Rivette is so bent out of shape about this that he would go to his chief?" he asked. "He could have just stepped back and saved himself the headache. Or he could have welcomed our help and kept his hand in. Why make such a fuss?

"If he's made no progress and had no real interest in the case, then he had to expose himself to Johnny Earl as being incompetent," he said. "Why do that? Why wouldn't he be just as happy to let it go?"

"I don't know," Annie admitted. "I looked at Robbie Fontenot's arrest record. Dewey collared him a couple of times back when he was still in a uniform. Not for anything much, mind you, and it was years ago."

"Could Rivette be running him as a CI?"

"I wonder that, too. But if Robbie Fontenot is his informant, wouldn't that be all the more reason for him to take a genuine interest in finding him?"

"Maybe he doesn't need to find him because he already knows where he's at."

"Then why make himself look like an incompetent fool?" Annie asked. "It'd be one thing if nobody cared this kid is missing, but Dewey's had B'Lynn Fontenot calling him on a daily basis. Why wouldn't he try to at least make it look like he's doing everything he can?"

"Well, I doubt Dewey's ever won any prizes for his intellect," Nick said, pulling open the outer door and holding it for her. "But this is curious nonetheless."

"Yeah. Stay tuned," Annie said as she walked through into the bullpen. "I have a feeling the shit has only begun to hit the fan where Dewey and the BBPD are concerned."

"There he is!" Chaz Stokes announced. He stood leaning a hip against the counter next to the coffeepot, his porkpie hat tipped back on his head. "Our own star of the afternoon news himself!"

Nick scowled. "What are you doing watching afternoon television? You have a murder to investigate."

"I happened to be investigating in a place with a television," Stokes said, "and there you were, nose to nose with that Mercier woman. She needs her own show: *Crazy Housewives of Asscrack, Louisiana*. That's some must-see TV right there!"

"How like you, Chaz," Annie said, irritated, "making fun of a woman in an emotional crisis. She thought her son was dead in the morgue. Put a laugh track to that, why don't you? Hilarity ensues as a man gets his face shot off and his mother loses her mind with grief. Belly laughs all around!"

"You're in the wrong building, Broussard," Stokes said. "The Fun Police meet two doors down. Or you could get a sense of humor."

"I have a great sense of humor," Annie countered. "You're just not funny."

He made a face at her like he was ten years old. Annie rolled her eyes like an annoyed little sister.

Their mutual dislike went way back. He was the kind of man

who believed his looks entitled him to the adoration of all women everywhere. If a woman didn't agree, she went immediately from potential date to enemy in his eyes. He had dogged Annie pretty hard when he had been new to Bayou Breaux and Annie had been a green deputy and the only woman driving a patrol car in the parish, before she and Nick had become an item. When she had turned down his advances, Stokes had become her bully, spurring on co-workers in their campaign of sexual harassment against her. It had been a miserable time in her life.

Her relationship with Nick and her promotion to detective had put a stop to the worst of it, no one in their right mind wanting to run afoul of Nick's temper. And times and attitudes toward women in policing had changed in the years since. Old grudges had softened, and she and Stokes had learned to coexist. That was as good as it would ever get. He still managed to irritate the shit out of her by merely breathing the air.

"Listen up!" Nick barked, getting the attention of everyone in the room. "As of right now, we've got three cases that will take precedence over everything else we've got going on. The unidentified murder victim found outside of Luck this morning; the disappearance of Marc Mercier, last seen Saturday night; and the disappearance of Robbie Fontenot, last seen on Halloween, both white males in their late twenties.

"These three cases may or may not be related. We know that Mercier and Fontenot knew each other in high school. Whether or not they've had anything to do with one another recently, we don't yet know. We do know that the body in the morgue is not Robbie Fontenot. I've requested dental records on Marc Mercier for comparison, or we may have to rule him in or out by DNA.

"Annie is the lead on Fontenot. Chaz is the lead on the DB. I'll take Mercier. Wynn, we'll need cell phone records for both Fontenot and Mercier."

"Do we have case numbers?" Dixon asked.

"On Fontenot, yes," Annie said.

"I'll have a case number for you on Mercier before I leave to-night," Nick said. "For now, we've got a BOLO out on Mr. Mercier's vehicle, a new black Ford Raptor pulling a seventeen-foot modified V-hull boat. Mr. Fontenot's vehicle—a blue Toyota Corolla—has been reported stolen. I've given all the basic information to the press, but we need to get photos of both men released to all media outlets. Wynn, I'll put that on your plate, too.

"Deebo," he said, turning his attention. "Annie's case may have a drug connection."

Jeffcoat nodded. "We've already spoken. Whatever you need, Annie."

"I need to know about a possible drug house on Lafourche over by the Mardi Gras warehouse," Annie said. "Do you know that neighborhood?"

"Sure. Used to be Two Deuce Krewe territory, if we're talking about hard drugs," Deebo said. "But not for a while now. They move around. Did you see something?"

"The house is across the alley from where Robbie Fontenot lives," Annie said. "It looks like it could be abandoned, but it's also got bars on the doors and it's tricked out with security cameras."

"And you want to knock on the door and ask can you see their security footage?" he asked. "There's a good way to get your head shot off."

"I want to know what I can know about it," Annie said. "Robbie Fontenot is a recovering addict. He's supposedly been clean since he got out of rehab recently, but if his next-door neighbor is a dealer, that's the most obvious rabbit hole to go down. As for the cameras, the one on the back porch could possibly catch anything going on at the back of Robbie's place. That's what I'm most interested in."

"You've been in his house," Nick said. "Were there any signs of a struggle?"

"No. I can't say he was taken from there, but I'd sure like to see any comings and goings," Annie said. That she was most curious about any comings and goings of Dewey Rivette, she kept to herself.

"I'll find out what I can," Deebo offered.

"Thanks."

"Find out who owns this supposed drug house," Nick said. "It's likely a rental property."

Annie nodded.

He turned to Stokes. "Has Alphonse Arceneaux come in to make his statement?"

"Yeah. He didn't have anything useful to add. He's still more hot under the collar about kids stealing his goddamn nutria. He gave me a list of suspects for that," he said with a dismissive eye roll.

"Check them out."

"What?" Stokes scoffed. "Are you fucking kidding me? Are we the swamp rat police now?"

"Use your head for something other than a hat rack," Nick snapped. "If someone is raiding his traplines, they're getting out there earlier than he is. Maybe they saw something. Check them out. Bring them in. They're potential witnesses. What else did you manage to do today besides catching me on TV?"

"As you know, there's no houses on that road out to where the body was dumped," Stokes said, "so no doors to knock on, no witnesses. We can't know if the vehicle that brought him out there came north out of Luck or south out of Bayou Breaux, or came from any one of a dozen side roads in between.

"The tire tracks at the scene are probably from a pickup," he went on. "Hopefully, the casts are clean enough to get a make on the tires. That'll take days or weeks to hear back. In the meantime, we can check security cameras on the south end of Bayou Breaux and the north end of Luck on the off chance this mystery truck stuck to a main drag hauling a murder victim around, and then we track down every pickup we see on the video."

"The autopsy will be first thing tomorrow," Nick said. "We'll have a more accurate time of death, but he was out of rigor and decomp had already started, meaning he was probably killed on the weekend. But he wasn't laying where we found him all that time, that's for sure. You only need to look at video from last night. We can borrow a couple deputies to help with that. There can't be but four or five businesses on either end of that route with cameras. And check any houses along the way for cameras on garages or video doorbells."

Stokes nodded. "We won't have a full tox screen back anytime soon, but I asked for a quick blood alcohol. If he'd been drinking, I think bars are a good place to start asking questions. Any altercations over the weekend, any guys seen stepping out with other dudes' ladies, that kind of thing. I still say that's what this will come down to. Why else is he only half dressed?"

"Don't rule out the chance that he could be gay," Annie cautioned. "Remember Ronald Dominique? Twenty-three victims, all men and boys."

"Thanks, Broussard," Stokes grumbled. "That's all we need. A serial killer."

"Don't shoot the messenger," Annie said. "We've got two men missing and a dead body, all white males from the same age-group. I'm just saying."

"Let's not get ahead of ourselves," Nick said. "For the moment, these are three separate cases. Let's keep it simple but keep our minds open.

"We'll set up the conference room. I want to lay these cases out side by side on the whiteboards. Then, if there is a connection, we're more apt to see it right away. And if there's not, we'll see that, too."

He glanced at Annie and nodded for her to follow him down the hall to his office.

"Serial killer," he muttered as they went.

"That wasn't my point," Annie snapped, her patience worn thin by the day and by Chaz Stokes. The adrenaline that had carried her through the afternoon had run out. She wanted to lie down and take a nap, right there on the spot, but didn't even dare to express her exhaustion to Nick lest he seize the opportunity to tell her she shouldn't have come back to work. She had to thank her lucky stars he was too preoccupied at the moment to notice.

"I know that wasn't your point," he said, holding the door for her. "But think about it. We've got an unidentified body and two missing persons, all white males in the same age-group. How long before some true crime podcast junkie jumps on that and sets fire to social media? It's probably happening as we speak."

"It's not like you to care about such things."

"I don't care for myself, but I don't like it for Gus," he said, shaking his head. "Bad enough that he had to come back to this job at all, but now this mess . . . He doesn't need the pressure. He should be home driving Arnell crazy, not dealing with multiple high-profile cases while eating steak with the governor. He's gonna end up having a heart attack."

"I guess we'd better solve these cases, then."

"I want an ID on that body by the end of the day tomorrow."

"If it's your Mr. Mercier, hopefully the dental records solve that mystery," Annie said. "And with all the local news coverage, if some other poor soul from the area has gone missing, we should be hearing about it. If this guy isn't from the area and he just got dumped there, that's a problem."

"That seems unlikely, given the location," Nick said, taking his seat behind his desk. "That's a spot locals go to. It's not near a major highway."

"Fingers crossed he's a local, then, as odd as that is to say. I'm just relieved he's not my guy." She checked her watch and sighed. "If we're done, I'm gonna go pick up Justin."

She started to turn toward the door.

"You leave that drug house to Deebo."

His words spun her around and pulled her back. She felt her temper stir and rise. "That's why you asked me back here. To tell me that."

He had already turned his attention to his computer screen, dismissing her.

"This is my case," she said. "I've got a missing person possibly involved in drugs, but I'm supposed to avoid the neighborhood drug house? How is that supposed to work?"

"Like this," he said, not looking up. "You don't mess around with that house until Deebo does the intel. That's an order."

"Is that an order you would be giving to anyone else in this office or just me?"

"Just you," he admitted.

"That's not right."

"Too bad. Deal with it."

"Nick—"

"Don't argue with me, Antoinette."

Now he looked up at her, dead serious. Any sane person would have shut their mouth and backed away.

"Me, I don't want to have this conversation twice today," he said. "Deebo is our drug task force guy. He's got the best contacts in that world. He can deal with the drug house. That's a sound management decision, and that's that."

Annie weighed her options, not that she really had any. She wasn't going to win this fight, and pushing back would only make him dig in.

"Yes, sir," she said with a little salute. "I'm going to go now and pick up our son. Is that all right with you? Because, statistically speaking, driving a car will be the most dangerous thing I do today."

"Not if you stand there and push your luck with me, it won't be," he said in a completely empty threat.

"Oh, what're you gonna do?" Annie asked. "Lock me in a tower?"

"Maybe. Do you know of one?"

"No, but if you find one, I want a room with a view," she teased.

Nick fought a smile. "Because God forbid you should have to mind your own business for a time."

"What kind of detective would I be if I minded my own business?" she asked, coming back around his desk.

"Well, you'd be safe," he said, looking up at her. "That's all I want, 'Toinette. To keep you safe. You can't fault me for that."

"I don't," she whispered, leaning down to kiss his cheek. As much as she wished her safety didn't have to be an issue, she appreciated his concern and his desire to protect her.

That thought brought the memory of Tulsie Parcelle, with her split lip and black eye, cradling her injured arm against her body as she hustled out of the ER, ashamed and afraid.

"I count myself very lucky," she said. "I'm off now. I'll see you at the Corners. Try not to be late. This day has been long enough as it is."

12

HE STOOD IN THE UPSTAIRS HALL JUST OUTSIDE THE DOOR OF his old room, a silhouette in the moonlight. Faceless, but she was sure it was him. She recognized his outline, tall and lean, the set of his shoulders, the tilt of his head.

Exhausted, she had fallen asleep in her clothes on his bed. She lay still now, afraid if she moved, he would go. She wanted to hold on to the feeling of relief, to the rare sense that maybe everything would be all right after all. She had thought he was lost, but there he was. The nightmare was over.

"I'm here, Mama," he said.

"You sound so far away," B'Lynn murmured.

"I'm right here. With you."

"I didn't hear you come in."

"I didn't want to wake you."

"Come sit down."

He made no move to come closer. The wind moved through the branches of the live oak in the backyard, and the moonlight coming in through the hall window rippled over him, and for a split second she thought she could see his face and his sad, sweet smile.

"Where have you been?" she asked. "I've been worried about you."

"I've been right here," he said.

"No," she said, not to correct him, but to stave off the fear that was rising in her chest. "No, no, no."

"I'm sorry, I can't stay."

"Don't go," she said, her heart pounding. "Please don't leave me. I want to help you. Whatever it is, we can deal with it, Robbie. You can make it this time."

"You can't help me now," he murmured. "I'm so sorry, Mama."

He took a step back deeper into the shadows.

"No, Robbie, no. Don't leave me. Not again. Please!"

"I'm sorry, Mama." He sounded so far away. Miles away. "So, so sorry . . ."

She could physically feel him pulling back, pulling away from her, and then he was gone.

B'Lynn sat up with a gasp, her heart racing. She leapt off the bed and ran into the empty hall. The wind blew again, and the dancing branches of the oak tree created a strobe effect with the moonlight in the hallway. She was alone. He was gone . . . if he had ever been there at all.

It had to be. He had to have been there. She was so sure.

The wind rose again. Something banged downstairs.

"Robbie!" she called, racing down the stairs, stumbling, barely catching hold of the banister to prevent falling headlong to her death. "Robbie, wait!"

In her hurry to catch him, she missed the last step, turned her ankle, and went down in a heap, crying out. She scrambled clumsily to her feet and ran down the hall to the kitchen.

She had left the under-cabinet lights on, bathing the lower part of the room in a warm yellow glow. The room was empty. The only sound was the hum of the refrigerator. She rushed through into the laundry room and out the back door onto the porch. There was no one.

"Dammit, Robbie!"

Pulling in a big, deep breath, she launched herself down the steps and ran barefoot, wincing, limping hard, across the cool, damp grass to the gate in the tall privacy fence at the back of the garden. The latch was undone. She pulled the gate open and looked down the alley.

There was no car, though she thought she caught a glimpse of red taillights at the end of the street. Her lungs burning, her legs feeling heavy, she hobbled to the end of the alley to try to see, but if there had been a car at all, it was gone by the time she got clear of the trees.

"Dammit!"

She rubbed at the throbbing pain in the elbow she had banged against the hardwood floor in her fall. A maelstrom of emotions swirled through her—panic, frustration, hope, desperation, doubt.

Had he really been there? she wondered as she walked back to her yard and closed and latched the garden gate. Had he come and gone through this gate, or had the gardener neglected to fasten the old latch? How many times had she scolded Robbie as a child, as a teenager, about making sure that latch caught? Back when they had a family dog that had delighted in escaping the yard to run amok through the neighbors' gardens.

"Robbie Fontenot, you latch that gate! If Bubba gets out one more time . . ."

Had she dreamed it? she wondered, pulling back from the old memory. Had she just dreamed the whole thing? It had seemed so real. The sense of his presence, the sound of his voice . . . the sadness in it, the sadness in his eyes. *You can't help me now . . .*

She pressed a hand to her chest as if her heart physically hurt as she climbed the back porch steps. All the aches and pains from her fall began to make themselves known. She felt exhausted. She felt a thousand years old.

How many times in the past twenty-seven years had she flippantly tossed out the phrase *That boy will be the death of me*? When had she started to believe that might be true? The first time he

OD'd? The third time he'd gone into rehab? The fifth time he'd called her from a police station? The last decade of her life had been consumed by her son's addiction. How much more could she stand?

The wind rose again, shaking the oak tree and stirring the wind chimes in her memory garden. A chill went through her as the sweat evaporated from her skin. People liked to say the chimes in a memory garden were rung by the spirits of the lost loved ones being remembered there. B'Lynn wanted to scoff, but she had been born and raised on generations of south Louisiana superstition that even her hard-earned cynicism couldn't completely erase. Maybe she wanted to believe it. But that thought gave rise to another: Had she been visited by Robbie or by his spirit? *You can't help me now . . .*

Tears rose and crested in her eyes on a wave of dread.

"Stop it. Stop it!" she ordered herself, combating her fear with anger directed at herself. She had to keep her wits about her. Panic didn't help anything.

"Go inside, B'Lynn," she muttered. Nothing good would come from wandering thoughts of ghosts and spirits.

Should she call Detective Broussard? And tell her what? That she might have hallucinated Robbie being in her house? That she couldn't tell reality from wishful thinking? That she might have seen taillights going down the side street? She hadn't seen the car, if there had even been a car. She couldn't say it was Robbie's car if she wasn't sure there had been a car at all.

As she opened the back door to go inside, she realized it had been unlocked when she came out. She had just pulled it open and dashed out without thinking. It should have been locked. She always locked the doors before she went upstairs at night, always. She was a creature of habit and routine by nature. She had her nightly rituals of checking the doors and turning out the lights. Sure, she'd had a couple of glasses of wine after supper, but had she really missed locking this door?

Robbie had a key . . .

She made a point of locking it now, staring at the dead bolt as she turned it, trying to imprint the act on her memory. Maybe she was getting Alzheimer's. Hard to say if that would be a curse or a blessing at this point in her life. There were days when she was just so tired and done with it all. Drifting away into oblivion had a certain appeal.

That thought came with a terrible nip of guilt. Whatever went on with Robbie, she still had a daughter to live for. Lisette was in college. She had her whole bright young life ahead of her. She had yet to go out in the big world and make a career, and fall in love, and have a family of her own. B'Lynn's life would, presumably, at some point, take on that extra layer of being a grandmother and a mother-in-law. She had another life to look forward to.

She tried to envision herself as one of those "active seniors," joining clubs and traveling the world with a gaggle of friends her own age. Hard to do, seeing as she didn't really have friends anymore. She wasn't good company. The things most women her age talked about seemed frivolous and unimportant to her. And God knew, no one wanted to hear about Robbie's latest misadventure due to drugs. Most people she knew preferred to keep her at arm's length, as if her son's addiction and the trouble that came with it might somehow be contagious.

She couldn't really blame them. She wouldn't have wished any part of her struggle now on anyone—except her ex-husband, of course. She was not at all above wishing he could know this misery. But Robert had cut ties long ago and severed himself from all responsibility. How nice for him. The asshole. (Not a word she would have used aloud, having been raised by proper Southern ladies, but she didn't hesitate to think it.)

She wondered if he had bothered to return any of Detective Broussard's calls, but she doubted it. Robert had a narcissist's ability to deny anything that might inconvenience him. He disguised it as being decisive and in charge. Admirable alpha male qualities. It never failed to amaze her how much of his toxic behavior she had taken as a gift wrapped in a big red bow instead of seeing it for what it was: a big red flag. And all of it to the detriment of her children, Robbie in particular. She would never forgive him for that. Or forgive herself for allowing it.

All too late to cry about it now, though she couldn't—or wouldn't—let it go.

"Are you gonna take that mad with you to the grave, *chère*?" her grandmother would have said. "It won't keep you warm in the ground."

Needing to sit down, to gather her thoughts and steady her nerves, B'Lynn poured herself half a glass of red wine from the open bottle on the counter near the stove. She sat down at the kitchen table, on a chair that had already been pulled out.

Had she left it that way when she'd gone upstairs? That wasn't any more like her than leaving the back door unlocked, but it was something she had corrected Robbie for a million times.

Always in a hurry, he was the kid who left doors open, gates open, chairs pulled out. He was always gone, on to the next moment, the next adventure. What got left behind left his mind. His focus was always forward as he dashed off to football practice, basketball practice, baseball practice, running out the door with half a sandwich in one hand, in too big a hurry to sit down and finish a meal.

As sad as she was, she smiled at the memory. So many good memories from those years in this house.

She sipped her wine and looked around the kitchen and thought of all the family meals she'd made there, the holiday gatherings, the laughter, the love.

She thanked her lucky stars and her maternal grandmother for willing the house to her and insisting it be in B'Lynn's name and her name only, years before any hint of trouble in her marriage, Mamere Louisa having always possessed a healthy, hard-earned distrust of men in general. When the end of B'Lynn's marriage had come, she had at least had her home. By Louisiana law, an inheritance was considered separate property, not community property to be divided among the combatants in a divorce. In the end, Robert had packed up his Porsche and gone, leaving her to the comfort of this house and its generations of memories.

It was a gracious old Queen Anne Victorian, built in 1886 with the requisite gables and wraparound porch, located in a neighborhood of similar homes, in the part of town historically populated by doctors and lawyers and successful businessmen. It had been in her mother's family all that time. B'Lynn would pass it on to her daughter when she died. Eventually, some descendant wasn't going to want the house and its expensive upkeep, but she would be long gone before that happened. The idea of all those memories dying was too sad to contemplate.

There was enough history in this house to fill a book, and in fact, one of her great-aunts had written one that sold a few copies every year down at the historical society. There was an entire chapter on the supposed ghosts that haunted the place. B'Lynn couldn't confirm any of the tales herself, though now she wondered if she hadn't encountered one tonight.

You can't help me now . . .

No. She couldn't think that he might be dead. She'd been on that roller coaster all day, first hearing about the murder victim found outside of Luck, then holding her breath waiting for a call from Detective Broussard to confirm or deny the awful possibility. She desperately needed to hang on to the renewed hope that had come after that call. He wasn't on a slab in the morgue at Our Lady; therefore, she wouldn't believe he was dead.

Better to think he'd actually been there and gone tonight than that he was gone and never coming back. But whether he'd been there or not, she wasn't sure what to do next. If she told Detective Broussard what had happened, what then? Would law enforcement stop looking for Robbie if they believed he'd been to the house? Would B'Lynn admit to the detective she'd taken half a sleeping pill earlier and be accused of hallucinating the whole thing? Would a detective see the bottle of wine on the counter with two-thirds gone and decide she was a drunk? God knew, they probably thought she was unstable anyway after her performance at the sheriff's office this morning.

No. She wasn't going to say anything to Annie Broussard about any of it. What difference would it make if Robbie had been there or not? She still didn't know where her son was. She still needed help finding him. That was the bottom line. It wouldn't be a lie, exactly, not telling, just a sin of omission, a religious technicality. If that kept the investigation going, that was a good thing.

B'Lynn checked the clock. It was nearly one in the morning. She was exhausted, but the wheels of her mind were spinning now. Even on half a sleeping pill and a glass of wine, she wasn't going to sleep anytime soon. She would lie awake and wonder, if he'd been there, where had he gone? Back to his place?

She rinsed out her wineglass and went in search of her shoes and car keys.

Melissa woke with a start from a fitful sleep, her heart racing, her pulse pounding in her ears. She held her breath and tried to listen beyond the *whoosh, whoosh, whoosh*.

The wind had come up outside, shaking the trees, creating a creepy black-and-white show of moonlight and shadows on her bedroom walls like something from an old Hitchcock movie. She had forgotten to pull the drapes closed over the sheers on the sliding patio door, and now she suddenly felt exposed and vulnerable.

The overwhelming feeling of being watched crawled over her, sending a shiver down her back. She wanted to leap up and run to close the curtains, but at the same time she felt too afraid to do so. What if she went to the window and someone was looking in? What if the sense of a presence was what had awakened her in the first place? And if she turned the bedside light on, she would only be more exposed to anyone standing outside.

Now she began to wonder if the door was locked. She had gone out that door earlier to sit by the small firepit and have a glass of wine with Will. What if she hadn't locked it when she had come in?

She wished now she had asked him to stay. To hell with how that looked to her nosy neighbors. What did it matter if they saw a strange car in her driveway overnight? She didn't give a shit what these people thought of her. What did she care if a bunch of Louisiana hicks thought she was a whore, or believed she'd killed her husband, or anything else? She was moving back to Philadelphia as soon as she could manage to make it happen.

If someone didn't break into her house and kill her first.

She tried to tell herself that was a ridiculous thought, even as she glanced around for something to arm herself with. The story of Will's sister being raped and murdered in her own home just blocks away from there sat in the back of her mind, stirring her anxiety. Lindsay Faulkner had no doubt thought that would never happen to her, either.

The only thing within reach was her TV remote. Melissa snatched it up and held it in her hand like a club.

The baby monitor on her nightstand came alive, and she startled at the sudden sound of her daughter stirring and whimpering.

Madeline. What if someone had come into the house and was now across the hall looming over her baby in her crib?

The baby began to cry.

Melissa glanced at the patio door, then at the door to the hall-way. Her imagination raced to picture herself on the way to Madeline's room and some black-clad, faceless assailant rushing in through the patio door, running up behind her, knocking her to the floor, her stupid TV remote flying out of her hand, useless.

From somewhere out in the house came a loud *Bang!* Melissa jumped out of the bed, her heart pounding like a hammer in her chest.

Should she call 911? Where was her phone? She usually charged it on the nightstand overnight, but it wasn't there. Where had she left it? On the vanity in the bathroom? In the kitchen? Or had she left it out on the patio table? She'd had a little too much wine. She'd been slightly tipsy when Will stood up to go. She might have just left the phone out there when she'd gone to see him out.

Shit.

Tears rose in her eyes as the baby's cries became louder and more insistent. Was someone right this minute across the hall, lifting her daughter from her crib with the intention of taking her? She wouldn't put that past Kiki, who had spent half the day and all evening blowing up Melissa's phone. *Where is Marc? What have you done to Marc? Why aren't you on TV pleading for Marc to come home?*

Drunk. Hysterical. Vicious. Lunatic. Bitch. Stealing Madeline from her crib would be just something she would do.

Her instincts overriding her fears, Melissa threw the TV remote on the bed and ran for the door. No one was taking her daughter without going through her.

She bolted across the hall into the nursery, where a night-light cast a warm glow. There was no Kiki, no masked assailant, just Madeline sitting up in her crib, wailing as she tried to gnaw on her tiny fist.

Melissa scooped her daughter up and held her close and tight. Madeline was warm and wet, uncomfortable and inconsolable. She wailed and wriggled in Melissa's arms, wrenching herself one way and then the other. She'd been fussy for days now as a new tooth worked its way through her sore, swollen gum.

For a moment, Melissa forgot about anything else but her baby's comfort. Madeline needed changing and some ointment on her gums. She would get her comfortable, calm her down, sit and rock her back to sleep.

Bang!

That fast, she went back to panic mode.

She needed to find her phone. Oh for the days when every house had landline phones in practically every room. She had one device to connect her to the outside world, and no idea where she'd left it.

"I'll be back, sweetheart," she whispered to the baby, kissing her cheek and setting her back in her crib.

She went to the door of the nursery and stood there for a moment, trying to listen as the baby wailed behind her. She stuck her head out into the hall and looked both ways, seeing nothing but darkness.

"Fuck this shit," she muttered.

She went back into the nursery and snatched up the child-size baseball bat Marc had bought in anticipation of having a son. He had insisted on keeping it for Madeline, willing to settle for a tomboy until they could have another baby.

"As if," Melissa muttered, creeping back out into the hall.

She found the light switch and flipped it on. If she was going to be murdered in her own home, she at least wanted to see her killer.

There was no one in the hall.

Had she left her phone in the kitchen after Will had gone? She had brought their wineglasses in and rinsed them out. Maybe she'd left the phone on the counter. Bat in hand, she walked toward the heart of the house.

"If you're in here to kill me, I already called the cops!" she bluffed loudly.

She paused at the entrance to the dining room and listened for anyone scrambling to get out a door or climb out a window. She thought she heard a muffled sound, like something shuffling or thumping. Maybe out on the porch that wrapped around the entire house.

She flipped the dining room light on. Nothing. No one.

Bang!

She jumped at the sound, much closer now than it had been before.

Outside, the wind came up again.

Thump, thump. Bang!

"Oh, for fuck's sake!" she muttered as sudden relief washed through her.

She knew what that sound was. This had happened once before, back when they had first moved in.

The house, built in the nineties, was done in the Caribbean plantation style, with French doors and windows all around, each of them fitted with a set of shutters. Not the decorative fixed kind, but fully functioning shutters, able to be closed and locked in the event of a hurricane. It seemed a ridiculous expense to her, considering they were miles inland from the Gulf of Mexico. Will argued that people there liked the authentic historical details. Touches like working shutters and the wrought iron holdbacks that kept them open set this development apart from the cookie-cutter tract homes of the same era in other parts of town.

When she and Marc had first moved in, one of the holdbacks (called shutter dogs for reasons she couldn't fathom, like many things in the South) had worked itself loose in the brick wall, allowing the shutter to move with the wind, rattling and banging against the side of the house during a storm. Obviously, the same thing had happened again.

She went to the French doors and turned on the porch lights. There was no one lurking outside the door. The wind came up slightly again, and again she heard the *thump, thump, thump.* She unlocked the door and stuck her head out.

As the wind came up again, she could see one of the shutters by the living room door moving, the shutter dog clearly pulled quite far out of its mooring in the brick. She would have Will send his handyman tomorrow to fix it. She would ask, at least. If he could find the guy, if the guy wasn't gone fishing or out killing animals, maybe he would show up in a day or three, or next week, or next month. People there had their own sense of time and their own sense of what was important or necessary or an emergency. In the meantime, she would shove a big plant pot in front of the shutter to hold it back against the wall.

Her anxiety pushed to the back of her mind by her annoyance, Melissa set the baby baseball bat on the dining room table and went out onto the porch. Barefoot, dressed in a T-shirt and boxer shorts, she was instantly cold. Another thing she hated about this place: the weather. It was always too hot or too cold or too humid or pouring rain. She conveniently ignored the fact that Philadelphia had more than its share of shit weather, too, including snow, which she also hated.

As she pushed a heavy planter with a giant fern toward the offending shutter, she wondered where she would be right then if she had chosen to go to college in California instead of at Tulane. Probably sitting in San Francisco, enjoying actual culture, or living in the wine country, married to a successful restaurateur or the scion of a fabulous winery. She sure as hell wouldn't be in Louisiana, cursing the day she'd married the son of a junk dealer.

This wasn't at all how her life was supposed to have turned out—nor Marc's, for that matter. Or so she thought. She thought he had wanted away from this place and these people. She thought he wanted more from life than small-town friends and reliving his high school glory days. She thought he had wanted the life they had been building in Philadelphia. But maybe he'd been miserable all along in a place where no one knew him, where no one cared that he'd led his high school football team to the state championship, where no one in their circle of acquaintances wanted to go hunting or fishing all weekend, and he would never be a headline in the local newspaper for helping out his old coach. Maybe that life had been as much his mistake as this life was hers.

As she stood back and looked at her solution to the shutter problem, one of her father's gems of sage wisdom played in her mind: *Don't hang on to a mistake just because you spent a long time making it.*

The wind came up again, and the big oak tree beyond the patio moaned as it rattled its branches, an eerie, otherworldly sound that scratched at Melissa's nerves. She stared out into the darkness of the yard that was intermittently illuminated by silver light as clouds scudded across the moon.

The sense of being watched came back to her, and goose bumps raced down her arms. She hugged herself against the chill and stood very still for a moment, her imagination racing. She told herself she was being ridiculous, that she was just on edge and letting her imagination run away with her.

She spotted her phone then, lying face down on the little patio table on the pavers just off the porch. Her heart beat a little faster at the idea of going off the porch to get it. She didn't want to move away from the house, but she couldn't leave her phone there, either.

It sat there on the patio table like a piece of bait, waiting for her to step off the relative safety of the porch.

"Just get it, Melissa," she muttered.

She dashed off the porch, grabbed the phone, and rushed back inside, her heart racing a hundred miles an hour. Her hands were trembling as she closed the door and turned the dead bolt.

"You're so ridiculous," she told herself. "Pull it together, girl."

Even as she tried to tamp down her nerves, the phone rang, and she shrieked and dropped it like a hot rock on the floor.

Kiki, she thought. Goddamn it. Calling at this hour to continue her drunken tirade. Melissa bent down and picked the phone up, turning it over expecting to see Kiki's info on the screen. But she didn't recognize the number.

She never answered calls from strange numbers. But a call in the middle of the night . . . Maybe it was that detective—Fourcade. Or bad news. What other kind of call came in the middle of the night? Someone had found Marc . . .

She slid the bar on the screen and answered. "Hello?"

There was nothing but silence on the other end of the line.

"Hello?"

No one spoke. She heard what sounded like the wind rattling the branches of a tree.

Tears filled her eyes as unease crawled over her skin like a hundred snakes.

She ended the call and immediately brought up her contact list and tapped one. The phone on the other end rang three times before a sleepy voice answered.

"Hello? Miss? Are you okay?"

"No. I'm scared. Will, can you come over?"

"I'll be right there."

13

MARC MERCIER NEVER MADE IT TO THE CORNERS SUNDAY morning.

That truth kept replaying in Nick's head as he scrolled on his laptop looking for any information on Mercier, trying to get a broader sense of who Marc Mercier was.

It was nearly midnight, but the wheels of his mind were still turning too fast for sleep, overstimulated by everything that had gone on during the day, too wound up even to successfully meditate, his usual go-to to decompress.

The lamp on Annie's nightstand burned low, helping temper the more intense light of his computer screen. The house was quiet, but the wind was up outside, rattling the branches of the live oaks out in the yard. It was the kind of night he liked, snug in his home with his family, knowing they were all safe and healthy and secure, no matter what was going on outside. He couldn't say the same thing for Marc Mercier, who had never shown up for his scheduled rendezvous with his brother Sunday morning and hadn't been seen or heard from since.

Where the hell was he?

Favorite son, local hero, man who put his life on hold to help his family and his community . . . How did that guy go missing? That wasn't a man who just up and left. Quite the opposite. Even if he wasn't getting along with his wife at the moment, he had a new baby at home. He had friends. He had people who relied on him. He had made plans to meet his brother. He was driving a vehicle pulling a boat. How did that guy just disappear?

But Marc Mercier had never arrived at the Corners Sunday morning. That was a fact.

Nick and Sos had sat in Sos's office after supper and gone through the security video from the parking lot. No sign of Marc Mercier or his truck.

The office was cramped but tidy, the desk pushed up against a wall with a large window looking out into the café, speaking to Sos's need to be in on everything. He couldn't bear the idea of isolating himself, even just to do his paperwork. He wanted an eye on his business, his customers, and his wife, who was still recovering from a stroke she had suffered in the summer.

"What are we looking for?" Sos asked as he took his seat behind his desk, eager to be part of the investigation, as Annie had predicted.

Even in his early seventies, Sos was fit and naturally athletic. He was built like a shortstop, with strong shoulders and a flat belly. People liked to tell him he resembled the actor Tommy Lee Jones, to his unending delight. He swiveled his desk chair back and forth like a dog wagging its tail.

"A black Ford Raptor towing a boat," Nick said, pulling a chair around. "Marc Mercier's rig."

"I'm telling you, he wasn't here," Sos said. "Sunday morning? *Mais non.*"

"How well do you know him?"

"I know the Mercier boys. I knew their papa, Troy. He was a good man, him, God rest his soul. Give you the shirt off his back."

"This would have been early," Nick said. "Between five and six in the morning."

Sos shook his head. "What you think? I'm laying in bed? Me, I'm up early on the weekends, you know. All the out-of-town sports coming to hunt and fish. They need bait. They need ammunition. They need fuel. They need directions. They need the bathroom. Me, I do every damn thing but wipe their asses for them," he said with an easy laugh. "That's the one thing nobody's ever asked for! *Dieu merci!*"

The Corners had been a mainstay on the bayou for decades. Miles from town on the edge of the basin, it had begun as an old-time general store, serving the rural population: farmers, swampers, commercial fishermen. Over the years it had evolved and expanded to its present incarnation as convenience store, café, swamp tour boat landing, with Sos and Fanchon Doucet at the helm for nearly half a century.

"You were busy Sunday?" Nick asked.

"Oh, yeah. You know how it is this time of year. T-Crapaud, he was working Sunday, too. And Sharelle Dupuis, she come in to make the breakfast biscuits. Those are big sellers for us on the weekends, those breakfast biscuits!"

"So, if it was busy and if he just pulled his rig in at the far edge of the parking lot, but didn't come in to the store, you could have missed seeing him, no?"

"I suppose," Sos conceded. "But why would he do that? Marc, he would come say hello. He would come get a coffee. Why he would stay in his truck like he don't know me? Bah! No!"

"He was supposed to be waiting for his brother."

"I never seen him, neither."

"Really?" Nick asked. "Luc said he was here. He says Marc was gone by the time he got here."

Sos shook his head. "Me, I never seen him. And Luc, for sure, he would have come said hello, him. They're good boys, them boys. They was raised right. Look at Marc, coming home to help with the business when his papa was dying. And he was just in the paper for helping out Coach Latrelle with the youth football."

"He'd been fighting with his wife, fighting with his brother, might have been hungover. He might not have been feeling social. Especially at that hour," Nick said, commandeering the mouse and clicking on the icon for the security system. "Let's have a look and see what we can see."

"All right," Sos agreed as Nick clicked on the camera view of the parking lot. "I'm gonna be big disappointed, me, if he's on here and he didn't come say *bonjour* to me that day."

Nick didn't bother to say that, in his experience, people were endlessly disappointing. Sos was an eternal optimist. The glass was always half full as far as he was concerned. Even if it was all but empty, just a drop or two was enough to give him hope.

There were times Nick envied Sos his optimism and the cushion it provided from some of life's sharper edges. It had absorbed the blows of Fanchon's stroke and buoyed Sos through her rehab. Nick had wished for a fraction of that faith when Annie had been injured, instead of the bone-on-bone kind of pain he had experienced fearing he might lose her in part or entirely. Wasted worry, as it had turned out, but he hadn't found a way to let go of it, nevertheless.

"Do you do business with the Merciers?" he asked.

"Over the years, sure."

"What kind of business do they run? Honest? Aboveboard?"

"*Mais* yeah," Sos said in that slightly overly bright tone that told Nick the Merciers were probably just as honest and aboveboard as they needed to be.

Not an uncommon attitude in these parts, where people bristled at government interference or regulation of any kind. If a Cajun didn't think a rule was practical, then it didn't apply. That went for the laws of man and the church. The Cajuns had spent 250 years finding a way to make a life in some of the most inhospitable country imaginable. They didn't need any outsiders' opinions or approval.

"They baiting gators for their swamp tours?"

Sos shrugged, the picture of innocence. "I dunno."

He wasn't going to rat the Merciers out for doing something he was probably doing himself.

"You ever hear of them dealing in stolen copper, cat converters, anything like that?" Nick asked.

"No. Troy, he was an easygoing guy. He didn't like trouble, didn't like people who made trouble. And Kiki, she'd run a man off with a shotgun if she didn't like the look of him. Nobody mess with Kiki!" He laughed. "She's a pistol. Talk about!"

Still annoyed with Kiki Mercier for pushing Annie, Nick refrained from comment. He kept his attention on the computer screen, fast-forwarding the video from the arrival of one vehicle to another. Truck after truck, SUV after SUV, no black Ford Raptor pulling the Mercier brothers' boat. People came and went, none of them Marc Mercier or Luc Mercier. Hunting dogs ran in and out of the frame, their owners giving them the chance to stretch their legs before continuing on to their destination for the day.

"I told you," Sos said. "He wasn't here."

"That's interesting in itself," Nick said. "Why wasn't he here? He set it up. He named the time and the place. He's normally a reliable guy. Where's he at?"

He went to close the app at the 7:13 a.m. mark when a figure crossing the parking lot caught his eye and made him pause. A bald head the shape of a cinder block. A man the size of a farm implement.

He paused the video. "Do you know who this is?"

Sos squinted at the screen. "Mmmm . . . Big dude. He might be a Cormier. Them boys all got that side-by-side icebox look about them."

"He didn't come in and ask after Marc?"

"Not to me. You might ask T-Crapaud or Sharelle. If that dude came looking for breakfast biscuits, she gonna remember him for sure. He looks like the Incredible Hulk."

Dozer Cormier, as described by Caleb McVay. Not in a Halloween costume, but dressed in a camouflage jacket, just another hunter stopping by the Corners before heading out for a day of shooting. It might have meant nothing. Luc Mercier hadn't said anything about anyone else meant to join him and Marc that day. And, for sure, eight out of ten men in the parish were hunters, at least.

Sos had lost interest and was looking out the window into the café. Fanchon and Annie sat at the table where they'd had their supper, Annie hugging the woman who had raised her, resting her head lovingly on Fanchon's shoulder, both of them smiling as they watched Justin acting out some five-year-old silliness, hopping and dancing, beaming at his chance to be the center of all attention.

"Our girl, she's doing good, no?" Sos said.

"Fanchon or 'Toinette?"

"Both, I reckon. We're lucky men," Sos said with a smile, patting Nick on the shoulder. "I could'a lost my Fanchon this summer, but here she is, gonna be right as rain. And Annie's back at work. You good with that?"

"Her doctor gave her the okay," Nick said.

"That's not an answer," Sos pointed out astutely.

Nick shrugged. "It wasn't my choice to make. As you well know, she has a mind of her own. She wanted to go back to work. She was going stir-crazy at home."

"Time for another grandbaby, I think," Sos said, chuckling. "That'll keep her busy. You can do something about that!"

Sos had been lobbying for them to have more children since Justin was still in diapers. Not that Nick was against the idea.

He looked over at Annie now, in bed beside him, curled up with her back to him. They had always planned on having two children, but as logical as the timing might have seemed, he also realized it was the worst possible time to broach the subject. She wanted to be back at work in part because she was good at it, but in part to reassure herself of that fact.

She had made a bad choice for a good reason that night in September. It had been late in the evening, and she had gone to deliver good news to a worried mother. No one could have foreseen the madness that unfolded that night. And yet, he knew she blamed herself for not waiting for him to go with her to that house and for turning her back for the briefest second on a woman she knew to be unstable. She had paid physically for those choices and continued to pay in the form of lost confidence and PTSD.

Nick couldn't undermine her struggle to conquer those feelings by suggesting she didn't need to go back to the job or that she wasn't needed on the job, even if his strongest instinct as her husband was to keep her home and safe. He knew from his own experiences exactly what it was like to struggle with anxiety and self-doubt on the job. He had spent months struggling to climb out of the mental and emotional black hole his experiences in New Orleans had dumped him into. The shadow of anxiety and depression had never completely gone away, visiting him still in his darker moments. He had learned to control it, to head it off at the pass, to work through it, but that shadow never left for good. It hung out on the periphery, like a wolf, stalking, waiting for an opportunity.

He didn't want that for Annie. He would do whatever he could to help her get to the other side of this experience, conflicted or not. She was his partner, his anchor. They would get through this together and come out stronger for it.

Their marriage had been on a roller coaster this year, with both of them struggling independently over the summer—him dealing with a particularly troubling and difficult sexual assault case and Annie dealing with Fanchon's stroke and the possibility of losing the woman who had raised her. Both of them had been stressed and exhausted, which resulted in his being exceptionally blunt and short-tempered and Annie being hypersensitive, taking everything he said the wrong way. For the first time in their marriage, it had felt like they had one wheel off the tracks, dragging them toward the ditch. The silver lining of her injury had been to snap them both out of that nonsense. There was nothing quite like a near-death experience to reset one's priorities in a hurry.

Annie rolled over now with a sigh and looked up at him. "Why are you still up?"

Nick closed his laptop and set it aside on the nightstand. "Just doing some research on Marc Mercier."

"Learn anything?"

"No. Nothing new. And that's enough of it for tonight."

"Was this light bothering you?"

"No, *bébé*, you know that light doesn't bother me."

"I know you say it doesn't."

"Because it doesn't," he insisted. "I kind of like it now, truth to tell. I can look over and watch you sleeping."

"In the rare event I do," she said.

He could hear the strain of frustration in her voice. She had struggled with sleep since her head injury, a primitive part of her brain fighting to keep her from fully letting go of consciousness. The resulting exhaustion only added fuel to the anxiety that never seemed to entirely go away. Keeping a soft light on seemed to help somewhat with getting her to sleep, so that was what they did, but Annie took it as a sign of some kind of weakness and rode herself for it unnecessarily.

"Come here, you," he whispered, reaching for her. She snuggled in against him, her head finding the hollow of his shoulder. He kissed her hair. "My little puzzle piece," he murmured, tightening his arms around her. "You were out pretty good there for a while."

"Yeah. God forbid my brain should let me get away with that for too long."

"Don't be so hard on your brain, *chère*. It thinks it's doing the right thing, keeping you safe."

"I keep telling it I'm good now, that I'm not gonna die if I go to sleep. It's not listening."

"It's only as stubborn as you are," Nick said. "Don't fight with it so hard."

"I'm just so tired of it."

"I know, *bébé*. But it will pass. You have to be a little more patient with yourself, that's all."

"I'm not good at that," she admitted. "I feel like such a burden, and it's all my own fault."

"You have to let that go, 'Toinette," he said quietly, pulling back and tipping her chin up to look in her eyes. "You can't blame yourself for something someone else did. That woman made her own choices that night. You don't need to keep paying for them. She's the one going to prison. You don't need to go with her. Let that go."

"That's easier said than done," she whispered. "I made my choices, too, that night."

"What good does it do to punish yourself?" he asked. "None. No one else is keeping score. What happened happened. It can't be changed now, and you can't move forward if you're only looking back."

"How'd you get to be so wise?" she asked with a crooked little smile.

"The hard way. The universe had to knock it into my head with a ten-pound hammer," he confessed. "I'm trying to save you the experience."

"Thank you," Annie murmured. "You turned out okay."

"I married well," he said, smiling back at her. "It made me a better man."

She leaned up and pressed her lips to his. "I love you."

"*Je t'aime, mon coeur. Tu es mon coeur*," he whispered. "Go to sleep, now, *chère*. I'll keep you safe."

She sighed, and the tension left her body as she slowly drifted off, and Nick fell asleep counting her heartbeats.

14

THE MORNING SKY WAS THE COLOR OF A DOVE'S WING, BACK-lit by the diluted yellow of a hidden sun. From a distance, the water looked like mercury, rippling quicksilver, moved by the unseen hand of God . . . or a school of fish, or the sudden departure of a wood duck. Same thing, really, Nick thought.

He spotted Luc Mercier's truck parked on the water side of the property, near the small cabin-like building from which the Merciers ran their tour operation. He breathed a sigh of relief, wanting to avoid Kiki for the moment. She would be angry and impatient at his lack of information, a mood probably exacerbated by a hangover, but investigations seldom ran at a pace that satisfied the family and friends of victims—if indeed Marc Mercier was a victim of anything.

He turned in the driveway and pulled alongside the black truck, noting that it was no longer spotless and spit shined as it had been the day before. Now it was coated with a fine white dust. Someone had drawn a smiley face on the rear quarter panel.

Music was drifting out the open door of the little cabin, some old-school BeauSoleil—"Parlez-Nous à Boire"—a rollicking two-step that seemed overly energetic for a quiet, gray morning. Out in front of the cabin on the broad wooden deck, a plump girl in bib overalls danced by herself, singing along off-key in a garbled mix of nonsensical English and faux French.

Nick stuck his head in the cabin. *"Bonjour. Ça va?"*

A small older woman with cat-eye glasses and a head of curly black hair looked up from reading a magazine at the counter. *"Bonjour! Ça va!"* she greeted him, a sweet smile lighting her round face. *"Ça viens!"*

"Bon. Ça va. I'm Lieutenant Fourcade from the sheriff's office. You're Mrs. Orgeron?"

"That's me!"

"I'm looking for Luc Mercier. Is he around?"

"Mais non. He's out on the boat, him."

"He got a tour this early?"

"No. He's just out doing whatever men do on boats," she said. "He's outta my hair, but he said he'd be back soon. He gotta be somewhere at ten."

Nick checked his watch. "I'll wait, then."

"You ain't found Marc yet?" she asked.

"No, ma'am."

"This ain't like Marc to worry people," she said, shaking her head. "Kiki, she's sick over it. He come back now, she gonna kill him for making her worry so!"

"When did you last see him?"

"Saturday morning, early, but just from over here. I saw him and Luc in the yard on the other side. We were busy that day. I didn't speak to him."

"How's he been lately?" Nick asked. "He's got a lot on his plate, no?"

"That's Marc. He can't tell nobody no. He's all the time taking too much on. He always been that way."

"What's his mood been like lately? Happy? Down? Upset about anything?"

She frowned a bit. "He got too much responsibility on him. And that wife . . ." She rolled her eyes. "She's not from here."

"I hear she wants to move back to Philadelphia."

"*C'est bon!* She should go then, her! Won't nobody here miss her, that's for true!"

"What about the brothers? They been getting along?"

She pursed her lips and shrugged. "They're brothers. They fight like a couple of damn *couillons*. What's new?"

"What they been fighting about lately?"

"What don't they fight about? If Marc says white, Luc says black. They always been that way. That's nothing new. That's just how they are. Don't mean nothing."

Her cell phone lit up and rang. She glanced over at it, unsure if she should pick it up or not.

"Go ahead," Nick said. "I'll wait outside. Thank you for your time. *Merci.*"

He went out the open door and around to the deck where the girl was still dancing—until she caught sight of him. She stopped abruptly and stared at him, her hands clutched together against her chest, her small almond-shaped eyes as wide as they would go in her round face.

"*Bonjour,*" Nick said. "You must be Noelle."

It was difficult to pinpoint her age. She might have been a teenager or she might have been twenty-five. She had beautiful smooth skin and thin, dark shoulder-length hair pulled back from her face with a couple of ladybug barrettes like a small child might wear. She watched him with a child's wariness of strangers.

"That's good music, no?" Nick said, smiling. "You like to dance to that?"

"I can two-step!" she said proudly.

"I saw. You're a good dancer."

"Can you dance?" she asked.

"I do all right. Who taught you to dance? Your brothers?"

"Sometimes. And my papa. He danced with me all the time."

"Did he?"

"He's dead, though," she said. "He died. He's gone to be with Jesus and Mary and Joseph."

"I'm sorry to hear that."

"I was sad," she admitted. "Did you know my papa?"

"No, I did not. I've heard he was a very nice man."

She said nothing for a moment, as if she were trying to make her final decision on his trustworthiness. Nick waited, looking out at the water. A cormorant bobbing on the surface suddenly dove under, coming back up with a small fish, which was quickly swallowed whole. The bird shook its head as if to hasten the fish's trip down its gullet, then made its way up onto the end of the dock and spread its wings wide to dry off.

From the corner of his eye, Nick watched Noelle Mercier take a cautious step closer.

"I heard you're a hard worker here," he said.

She nodded. "I help clean up the boats, me," she said. "And I sweep. I'm a good sweeper, me."

"I bet you are. If you're a good dancer, you'll be a good sweeper, too."

"I sweep at home, and I sweep here, and I sweep the office every day."

"Really?" Nick asked. "You sweep the office across the road, too?"

Noelle nodded. "Every day. It's a very important job."

"I agree."

She came a step closer. "What's your name?"

"I'm Nick. I'm here to see your brother Luc."

"You're the po-po," she said, giggling, pointing at the badge he wore on a chain around his neck.

"I am."

"Luc, he don't like the po-po!" she said with a big smile.

"Doesn't he?" Nick asked. "Why is that?"

"I don't know, but he says bad words when he sees one."

"Well, he's not in any trouble or anything," Nick said. "I just need to ask him some questions."

"Can I see?" she asked, pointing to his badge.

"Sure."

He lifted the chain over his head and put it around her neck to her absolute delight—and to his. Sweet child. So innocent. Unspoiled by what passed for world wisdom among so-called normal people.

In the distance, Nick picked up the whine of an airboat motor.

Noelle lifted the badge with both small hands and looked at it with wonder, then danced away in a clumsy waltz around the deck to "Valse de Grand Meche," singing her own made-up lyrics. Oh, to be so happy for such small pleasures, Nick thought.

The airboat was in sight now, swaying gracefully over the surface of the water. The engine noise was as loud as a small airplane as it approached. Luc Mercier sat high up on the driver's chair, guiding the boat in. He cut the engine back fifty yards out and brought it in expertly alongside the dock.

Like many of the swamp tour boats Nick had seen, this one was a homemade affair with two rows of salvaged automobile bench seats for the tourists and a big ice chest bolted to the deck for refreshments or bait. He imagined people not from there might look at the vessel askance and wonder at its safety, but there wasn't a Cajun on the bayou who didn't take better care of his boat than of himself. Fancy seats and bells and whistles were unimportant here.

Mercier pulled his safety earmuffs off as he looked from Nick to Noelle and back, stone-faced, his eyes hidden by a pair of aviator sunglasses and a beat-up red ball cap pulled down low. He climbed down from his perch, tied the boat off, and came up on the dock, bolting the cormorant, which took flight with an offended squawk.

"What the hell do you think you're doing here, Fourcade?"

Nick could feel the fury in him, coiled tight like a heavy spring. He could see it in Mercier's fists as they closed and opened, the hands of a man who couldn't wait to hit something.

"I don't know what you mean," Nick said calmly. "I have a few questions for you."

"I mean *this*," he said, pointing at his sister, who had stopped dancing and stood with Nick's badge still in her hands even as she watched her brother with a wary expression.

Luc turned to her. "What you got there, Noelle?"

He didn't wait for her to answer, but snatched the badge out of her fingers and glared at it, then at Nick, then back at Noelle. "Give me that right now," he snapped.

Tears welled up in the girl's eyes. "Nick let me wear it! He's my friend!"

"Your friend?!" Luc barked. "He is *not* your friend."

He lifted the chain from around her neck and flung the badge in Nick's direction, his ferocious glare still on his sister. "Go in the building."

"I didn't do anything wrong, me!" Noelle wailed.

"Go inside!"

The girl ran bawling around the corner, met with a hug at the door by Evie Orgeron, whose expression should have burned a hole clean through Luc Mercier.

Nick bent and picked his badge up off the rough wooden planks of the deck. "What the fuck is wrong with you?" he asked quietly, taking a step toward Mercier, his anger held tight as a fist in the center of his chest. "Why you treat your sister like that? She's done nothing wrong."

"Don't you talk to me about my sister! Here you are, trying to take advantage of a retard!"

"Don't use that word."

"I'll use whatever word I want, and you can get the hell off my property!"

Nick took another aggressive step forward, prompting Mercier to do the same, his fists balled and raised to waist level.

Nick chuckled low in his throat, a sound that had nothing to do with humor.

"You gonna take a swing at me?" he asked, his voice barely more than a whisper. "Please do. I will put your sorry ass face down on this deck, and I hope to God there's some loose nails sticking up where you land. And then I'll drag your bleeding ass to jail for assaulting an officer and hope you haven't had a tetanus shot."

Mercier glared at him, but any words he had seemed caught in his throat. Still, he didn't back down.

"You wanna try me?" Nick asked. "'Cause now, me, I got a bad mood on, and I will be only too happy to turn you inside out for making that little girl cry."

"You're the one trying to take advantage," Luc accused.

"I did no such thing. I came here to ask you questions, not her. But while we're on it, maybe you wanna explain to me why she would tell me so proudly that she sweeps the office across the road every day when you told me nobody but Marc was in the office Saturday. You wanna tell me about that? Because now I'm thinking you're a liar, and I'm wondering what else you lied to me about."

"I don't want you bothering her!" Luc barked. "She don't need to be talking to cops, getting questioned like a suspect! She's just a child!"

"Oh!" Nick said, feigning amazement. "Now you're telling me you're trying to protect her, then you turn around and yell in her face and scare the hell out of her and make her cry? That don't fly, Mr. Mercier. Better oil up those wheels in your brain and come up with a better story than that."

Head down, hands on his hips, Luc Mercier took a step back, and then another. He turned toward the water, the muscles working in the back of his jaw like he was chewing on a tough piece of meat.

"Is that your pride you're chewing on?" Nick asked. "Choke it down, *baw*, because you're gonna apologize to that girl in front of me. Now, you and I are gonna have us a conversation, and you had better hope I find your answers satisfactory. Do you understand me?"

Mercier scowled and looked away. "This is how you treat people, Fourcade? My brother's missing. My family are the victims here, and this is what you do?"

Nick laughed out loud. "Now you're gonna play the Poor Me card? Spare me. You're starting to bore me, Mr. Mercier. You should at least make an effort to be more original in your phony outrage.

You were wrong, and you know you were wrong. I guess we should at least take that as a positive sign that you're not a sociopath."

Mercier sucked in a deep breath and sighed, still too stubborn to surrender, but not clever enough for a snappy comeback.

"Why you don't want your sister talking to me?" Nick asked. "What's she gonna say you don't want me to hear? Has she seen something? Heard something?"

"She got the mind of an eight-year-old child," Luc said. "She don't always understand what she sees or hears."

"Like what? Like you and Marc having a fight Saturday? Like Marc punching you in the face?" Nick suggested. "I don't care that he did, if he did. I hope he enjoyed it, 'cause I sure as hell would. I'm only interested in the why and what you did about it after."

"Nothing," Luc said. "I did nothing."

"So are you telling me now the two of you came to blows?" Nick asked. "That's how you got that shiner. But it don't mean nothing. And I'm supposed to swallow that? Seriously?"

"We're brothers. We don't always get along," Mercier said. "I don't know what planet you're from, Fourcade, but around here, that's normal."

Nick didn't argue. Bayou country was a place of strong opinions and hot tempers, to be sure. Though violence among family members was hardly the norm, that didn't mean it wasn't the norm for the Mercier boys.

"What did you fight about?"

Luc made an exasperated gesture with his hands and sighed again. "We disagree about things."

"What things?"

"Everything. Every fucking thing. How's that?"

"Not good enough, that's how that is," Nick said. "You disagree over Tony Chachere's or Slap Ya Mama seasoning, you don't punch your brother in the face for it. What did you fight about?"

Luc thought about it for a minute, still looking out over the water. Finally, he said, "I been running this business more or less since Daddy got sick. Long before Mr. Local Hero deigned to come back here. I didn't need his help then, and I don't need his help now. He can take his snotty wife and go back north. Don't nobody need him here."

He pulled his cap off and scratched his head. "That don't mean I want him dead or anything. Just gone."

"Well, he is gone, isn't he?" Nick said.

Mercier said nothing to that.

"Marc never made it to the Corners Sunday morning," Nick announced, then waited for a reaction.

"What do you mean?" Luc asked, doing a good job of looking confused. "That's where we were meeting."

"I mean, he was never there. And neither were you."

"The hell. How do you know?"

"I know because Sos Doucet is my de facto father-in-law, and I made sure there are surveillance cameras all over that property. Your brother was never there Sunday morning, and you never came looking for him. Why would you lie to me about that?"

Luc muttered a curse, looked away, and sighed. "Because I wasn't gonna stand there in front of my mother yesterday and say that I never went, that I blew Marc off. I don't need her chewing my ass any more than she already does. Saying I was late was bad enough."

As lies went, that one was for a good reason at least, Nick thought, but a good lie was still a lie.

"Marc's wife says he left home Saturday night around six thirty, quarter to seven," Nick said. "Where'd he go?"

"I don't know. I told you," Luc said. "I haven't seen or heard from him since Saturday afternoon."

"Where were you Saturday night?" Nick asked.

"I had some supper and watched the LSU game. Hit a couple bars after."

"Which bars?"

"Club Cayenne. Things got a little fuzzy after that."

"Were you there with anybody?"

"No. I don't need company to watch naked girls dance."

"Any girl in particular?" Nick asked.

"Their names aren't exactly important to me."

"Think hard. You might want one of them to remember you were there."

Mercier shook his head. "I don't know. I don't remember. I didn't know I'd need an alibi."

"And Marc wasn't there?"

"Hell no. He's too afraid of Melissa to go to a titty bar. You ought to be grilling her," he said. "She probably killed him and ate him. She's the last one seen him, ain't she?"

"That we know of," Nick said. "Do you know a guy named Robbie Fontenot?"

"Robbie Fontenot?" Luc said, pulling a face. "What about him?"

"You know him?"

"Not to speak of. Him and Marc played football together. Didn't nobody pay money for me to go to Sacred Heart. All my friends are from low places."

"Did Marc ever mention him recently?"

"Not to me. Why?"

"Robbie Fontenot happens to be missing, too."

"What?" Luc laughed. "You think they run off together?"

"I don't know," Nick said flatly. "Might they have?"

"Don't be ridiculous!" Luc blustered. "I don't know nothing about Robbie Fontenot and which side of the plate he bats from, but Marc ain't no fag. I'd'a beat that out of him a long time ago."

"That's not how that works," Nick said.

"Whatever. Marc is not a homosexual. He's got a new baby at home, for Christ's sake!"

"What about Dozer Cormier?"

"What about him? He's not a homosexual, either."

"Do you know where I can find him?"

"He works construction for Donnie Bichon."

"Dozer and Marc are tight?"

He shrugged. "I guess. I don't run with either of them."

"You haven't spoken with him to ask him has he seen Marc?"

"No."

"Have you done anything at all to try to find your brother?" Nick asked.

"Ain't that your job?" Luc asked.

"You really don't give a shit where he's at, do you?" Nick said.

"I know Marc," Luc said. "He's gone off somewhere to pout and sulk, and when he decides we've all missed him enough, he'll come home so we can fall all over ourselves with joy."

"Or he never comes home at all," Nick said. "And what then?"

He looked away, frowning. "Life goes on one way or the other, doesn't it?"

That was how deep the resentment went, Nick thought. Down to the roots. Luc Mercier resented his brother for everything he was—the favored son, the popular athlete, the kid whose parents sent him to Sacred Heart, the college graduate who had his pick of lives. He could go away. He could come back. People loved him either way. While Luc was the guy who never went anywhere but to a titty bar ten miles from home, alone on Saturday night.

Luc was the one who stayed and worked the family business, and looked after his parents, and had no aspirations to leave this place or these people. And for his loyalty and his trouble, he was taken for granted and treated like hired help.

That was a big chip to carry on his shoulder all day every day while Marc walked around in his own beam of sunshine. That had to be exhausting.

The tension and anger and defensiveness had gone out of him now. He just looked tired and sad.

"How's your *maman* today?" Nick asked quietly.

"Hungover and hell to be around," Luc admitted. "She thinks y'all ought to call out the National Guard and the Cajun navy to

search for Marc with helicopters and infrared cameras and subma-
rines and bloodhounds and all."

"Search for him where?" Nick asked. "I can't line people up across
the state and look at every square inch of Louisiana south of I-10.
We need a starting place, a sighting of him or his vehicle or the boat
or a likely place he might have gone.

"I can tell you we've alerted all law enforcement agencies, including the Wildlife agents, to be looking for him. All media outlets have
been notified, including television and social media," Nick said. "It
may seem to you that we don't have the sense of urgency you would
like to see, but we're doing what we can with what we've got. And I
will share as much information with your family as I can."

The main thing families wanted in a situation like this was information, to feel included in the loop of the investigation. Shutting
them out only fostered their frustration and anger. The trick was
giving them enough to placate them without giving them anything
that might compromise the investigation. At this point, Luc Mercier
was as much a person of interest in his brother's disappearance as
he was a family member.

Luc nodded and sighed, calmer. "Did you get them dental records?"

"Yes. We hope to have a comparison by this afternoon. No guarantees, though. There's a lot of damage to the face."

Could he have done that? Nick wondered. Shot his own brother
right in the face? The notion seemed both impossible and yet all too
logical—the need to obliterate everything about that person.

"What about DNA?" Luc asked, pulling a cigarette out of his
shirt pocket and hanging it on his lip. "Ain't that the be-all-end-all?"

"It is, but it takes time to get results back. This ain't television,
where you get all your answers by the end of the hour. Labs are
backed up, short-staffed, underfunded. There's a whole line of cases
ahead of this one with people waiting on those answers, too."

Luc lit the cigarette, took a deep drag, and exhaled. "Mama, she'll lose her mind if that's Marc. She had it in her head she could make him stay here. She can't stand the idea of losing that grandbaby."

"And which way is Marc leaning? Stay or go?"

"Whichever direction the wind is blowing in the moment. Marc wants to please everybody. I got it all over him there," he said with a bitter smile. "Me, I don't give a shit who I piss off. The more the merrier."

Ironic, Nick thought, that Luc was the Mercier who held grudges and made enemies, but it was the golden boy gone missing.

"I'll be in touch when I know something," he said. "Let's go see about that apology to your sister."

15

THE PARCELLES' CIRCLE P RANCH WAS LOCATED ON A GRAVEL side road down the bayou and two miles west of Bayou Breaux. Twenty acres carved out of the scrub, a horse barn that hadn't seen a coat of paint in a decade, a collection of pipe corrals, a riding arena with a rusty steel roof for shade, and a newer double-wide mobile home. A professionally done sign stood at the entrance depicting the Circle P logo and three silhouettes of horses performing different tasks. Beneath the horses in neat lettering:

TRAINING SALES LESSONS
CODY & TULSIE PARCELLE

Annie pulled in and parked at the end of the barn next to a white Chevy pickup with rust eating at the wheel wells. A motley pack of dogs of all sizes came running, announcing her arrival at the top of their lungs with barking and yipping and the mournful bay of a coonhound.

She sat for a moment, gathering her thoughts, fighting off the threat of nerves. She was only there to check on Tulsie and to make Cody Parcelle aware that he wasn't living in a bubble. The plan was to drop in early in the day, to make her presence known, then quickly move on. She wasn't there to push or prod, accuse or threaten. This was just an appearance, a courtesy call or a reconnaissance mission, depending on point of view.

There shouldn't have been any danger involved, but domestic situations could be unpredictable and volatile. She knew that first-hand. She knew of more than one law enforcement officer who had been shot answering a domestic call. She herself had witnessed a prim-and-proper churchgoing woman shoving a chef's knife into the belly of her abusive ass of a fiancé, as smooth as you like, as if she was just passing him something.

She could have skipped coming there. Tulsie Parcelle had not asked for her help. In fact, she was not liable to be happy to see Annie. But Annie wanted her to know that help was available just a phone call away, that she wasn't being abandoned to her fate in a bad marriage to a bad guy.

Her choice to come there had not been popular with Nick for the obvious reasons. He would have rather sent someone else, or no one at all, arguing that Annie had made her point with Tulsie at the ER and that her focus needed to be on Robbie Fontenot.

She had debated not telling him she was going, playing her con-versation with Deebo Jeffcoat over and over in her mind. Would it have been a good lie or a bad lie, this lie by omission? Did it matter? A lie was a lie, and she didn't want that between them, no matter how valid her motivation might have been.

She texted Nick then—*At Parcelles'*—and got out of her vehicle. The dogs came wiggling and jumping, yipping and sniffing. They would likely be the only ones there happy to see her.

Country music was blasting in the barn. "Hell on Heels," a fierce anthem of mercenary female independence by Miranda Lambert and the Pistol Annies. A pitchfork full of pine shavings and horse shit sailed out of an open stall door into a waiting wheelbarrow in the barn aisle. Annie went in that direction, careful to stay out of the line of fire.

The person cleaning the stall was small with short dark hair and an angular jaw. Since they were in jeans and boots and a T-shirt that revealed taut, muscular arms tattooed in kaleidoscopic colors, it took Annie a second to realize it was a woman in her early twenties. She paused mid-lift of the pitchfork and stared at Annie with large dark eyes.

"I'm Detective Broussard with the sheriff's office," Annie said. "Is Tulsie around?"

"Why?"

"Because I want to see her."

"Did something happen?"

"Like what?"

"I don't know," the young woman said with a shrug, sticking the pitchfork business-end down and leaning on the handle. "Cops don't usually stop by with good news, do they?"

"I suppose you've got a point there," Annie conceded easily. "I saw Tulsie at the ER yesterday. I just wanted to check and see if she's doing all right. And what's your name?"

"Izzy Guidry."

"Guidry? Where you from?"

"Eunice."

"You related to any of the Guidrys around here?"

"I don't have no family," she said bluntly. "Tulsie's down in the arena."

"On a horse?" Annie asked, incredulous. "She shouldn't be doing that with that shoulder."

The girl looked at her like she was stupid. "Horses don't ride themselves."

Annie didn't know what to say to that. True that the Parcelles were running a business here. This ranch was no hobby, and horses were not toys that could just be put away to wait for a convenient time to ride them. But still.

"Is Cody around?" she asked, now wanting to give him a piece of her mind about letting his wife ride with a shoulder injury when he was a big strapping young man, perfectly capable of doing his share of the work and his wife's as well if necessary.

"He's gone to Houston," Izzy said, pointing across the aisle to a poster tacked up on the wall advertising the tenth annual East Texas Performance and Stock Horse Auction. "His uncle runs that sale. It's a big deal. He'll be down there all week."

"When did he leave?"

"Sunday. He'll be back next Tuesday or Wednesday."

"Ah," Annie said. "That's why Tulsie was wrestling with the hay bales."

Izzy Guidry gave her an odd look. "We do that every day. You think girls can't lift a bale of hay?"

"Seems those bales are almost as big as you are," Annie said, looking at one sitting on the floor just down from the stall.

"So?" Izzy said, clearly getting frustrated with Annie's lack of understanding of what it took to run a place like this.

"You were here when Tulsie got hurt, then?"

"I drove her up to Our Lady."

"And what day did she get hurt again?" Annie asked, working out the timeline in her head and trying to reconcile it with the stage of color of Tulsie Parcelle's bruises.

"Yesterday," Izzy said, narrowing her eyes. "I thought you said you saw her."

"Yeah," Annie said. "I lose track of time. I'll go down to the arena and say hey. Nice to meet you, Izzy."

"Sure," the girl said, and went back to picking shit.

Cody being gone was both a disappointment and a relief, she had to admit. She had wanted to send him a message, but if he wasn't there, then he wasn't an immediate threat, either. She pulled her phone out of her pocket and texted Nick:

Cody P out of town.

She glanced around the yard as she walked, taking in everything involved with running a horse farm, wondering at the expense of it all. A tractor with a front-end bucket loader, a manure spreader, a four-wheel ATV. Two horse trailers were parked alongside the barn, a long gooseneck trailer that looked like it must be able to hold half a dozen horses, and a smaller trailer that could hold two next to it. Parked beside the trailers was an older blue Ford Escape SUV with a decal on the back window that read: *Cowgirl Up!*

Annie wondered if that was part of the reason Tulsie stayed with a man who abused her—because she thought she had to be cowgirl tough and take what her man dished out? Just like she thought she had to ride with a wrecked shoulder or wrestle with hay bales as big as she was. This was her lot in life and what she'd signed up for, and she would stick it out come hell or high water because that was what a cowgirl did. Stand by your man, no matter what. Such a bill of goods, Annie thought, sad for her.

Tulsie was making the rounds of the shaded arena on a little palomino with a flowing white mane and tail, trotting for a stretch, then cantering for a stretch, then back to the trot and back to the canter. She held her reins in her left hand, her right arm still in the sling from the ER. She spotted Annie along the rail and slowed to a walk, leaning down and hastily swiping away tears on the sleeve of her western-style shirt.

Annie wished Cody had been standing nearby so she could have turned and kneed him in the balls, just for the satisfaction of hearing the breath leave his lungs.

"Hey, Tulsie!" she said brightly.

"Hey, Annie."

"I didn't think I'd see you on a horse today," she said as the girl rode up on long reins and came to a halt.

"They don't work themselves."

"Would he forget how to be a horse if you took a day or two off?"

"She's coming back from an injury," Tulsie said. "We have to do her rehab every day. It's a strict schedule from the vet. There's no such thing as taking days off from that. Anyway, I only need one hand to ride her."

"Still," Annie said. "Couldn't your hired girl do it?"

"Better me ride and Izzy clean the stalls. I can't use a pitchfork with one arm."

Annie shook her head. "You horse girls are something else. Cody is looking obsolete here," she teased. "Does he realize y'all don't actually need him?"

"I'm sure he doesn't think that."

"Have you told him you got hurt?" Annie asked.

"He's gone to Houston," Tulsie said, "helping his uncle with the auction."

"Have you spoken to him since this happened?"

"I tried to call him last night, but he didn't answer," she said. "He's busy. They've got horses shipping in all day and half the night. He doesn't have time to hear bad news from me."

Why bother telling him something he already knew, anyway? Annie thought as she looked at the girl's facial bruises, which seemed a couple of days ahead of schedule on the color progression from black to green. This beating had most likely been Cody Parcelle's parting gift to his wife Saturday night or Sunday morning, not something that had happened the day before.

"What could he do about it anyway?" Tulsie asked.

"He could call somebody to come help you while he's out of town."

"We can't afford another hired hand," she said. "Me and Izzy manage fine. It's not that big of a deal."

The horse stamped at a fly and tossed her head, then stretched her neck to sniff at Annie, her big liquid brown eyes full of curiosity.

"I need to keep going," Tulsie said. "Did you come here for a reason?"

Annie touched the horse's velvet nose gently as she weighed her options, deciding to go with the truth.

"Tulsie, I'm sure you realize I don't believe your story about how you got that black eye and busted lip," she said calmly. "Those bruises are days old, not from yesterday."

"That's not true!" Tulsie said, shocked at the accusation. "It happened just like I said! Ask Izzy!"

"Then why aren't you all scratched up from the hay?" Annie asked. "Me and my cousins, we used to help our *nonc* Claude with his horses in the summer. And the thing I remember most from handling hay was getting scratched up from it. If that big bale hit you in the face hard enough to give you a black eye, you'd have scratches to go with it."

The girl looked on the verge of full-out panic now, scrambling mentally for an alternate story.

"Don't bother trying to bullshit me," Annie said, keeping her voice even and calm. "I came by to see how you're doing and to let you know that you're not living in a vacuum here. I know this isn't the first time Cody's hurt you, but maybe now is the time—while he's away—that you need to think about your options. Do you want to stay in a relationship with someone who treats you bad? You don't deserve that."

Tears welled up in the girl's eyes, and she looked all around but at Annie. Looking for escape routes, Annie thought. When she spoke, out came the same tired laundry list of excuses Annie had heard a thousand times over the years from a hundred different Tulsie Parcelles.

"It's not how you think. I love Cody. He's not a bad guy. I mean, sometimes he has a temper, but so do I, and—"

Annie held up a hand. "Just stop. You can tell that story to yourself, to your friends and family, but don't bother telling it to me. I've heard it all a million times, but I know what I'm looking at. The bottom line here, Tulsie, is that it's not ever okay for him to physically hurt you. Period. That's a serious crime, and I can and will arrest him for it."

"I don't want that!" She was hyperventilating now, terrified at the prospect of her husband's arrest and probably already projecting

ahead to what would follow in the aftermath of that, how badly
Cody would react and what actions he might take in retribution
against her.

"My marriage is none of your business!" she said. "Why can't you
just leave us alone?"

"Because I know that the next time I get called out here, you
might be dead," Annie said bluntly. "And I'm sure you don't want to
hear that or think it could happen, but if you don't believe it could,
you need to go have a long look in a mirror."

"You don't understand anything!" Tulsie snapped. "Cody is a
good husband. We've built this business together. I don't need you
messing things up. Just go!"

"Hey, Tulsie?"

Annie turned her head as Izzy Guidry approached.

"I just came to see if you want Poco up next," she asked, her expression perfectly neutral.

"Yes," Tulsie said, wrangling her emotions. "Thank you, Izzy. I'll
be ready for him in about fifteen minutes."

"Okay. Perfect."

The hired hand turned and started back for the barn. Annie
watched her go, remembering the first time she had been called to
the Parcelles'. The original 911 call that day had been anonymous.

She turned back to Tulsie. "You think on what I said, Tulsie. I
don't want to see you hurt or worse. And there are more people than
you know who will help you. All you have to do is call."

"Yeah, well, I won't, so just go on."

The old saw about leading a horse to water came to mind as
Annie walked back toward the barn. Or maybe more accurate was
the story her *nonc* Claude had told the kids every summer about
trying to rescue horses from a burning barn and how the terrified
animals had fought to stay in their stalls rather than flee to safety.

She stepped into the barn aisle as Izzy Guidry led a bay out of a
stall and brought him to the grooming area.

"Izzy, can you give me Cody's phone number?"

"I don't have my phone on me," she said, snapping the crossties on the horse's halter.

"You don't know your boss's number?"

"Who memorizes phone numbers?" Izzy asked with half a laugh. "This ain't 1995. Anyway," she said, picking a stiff brush off the cluttered shelves and setting to work on the horse, "I deal with Tulsie more than Cody."

"How long have you worked for them?"

"'Bout nine months."

"Are they good people to work for?"

"I'm still here."

"I was out here on a call a while back," Annie said. "I didn't see you."

Izzy shrugged. "Must have been my day off."

"Did you actually see Tulsie get hurt yesterday?"

"Nope. Happened before I got here."

"So it happened early in the morning, but you didn't bring her to the ER until afternoon?"

"She didn't want to go. I had to talk her into it."

"Do you think it happened the way she said?"

"Why wouldn't I believe her?"

"Those bruises look older to me," Annie said.

"Maybe she did it Sunday night at night check," Izzy suggested. "I wasn't here then."

"Maybe *she* didn't do it at all," Annie suggested.

The girl bobbed her eyebrows up but kept to her task, brushing the horse. "I don't know. It's not my place to ask."

Annie said nothing, weighing the question of how far to go. Izzy Guidry didn't seem the gossipy type, and she was clearly loyal to Tulsie. Would that mean glossing over Cody's faults because that was Tulsie's preference? And if they weren't that close, was it Annie's place to feed her suspicions about her boss? It was one thing for her to confront Tulsie, but to drag her employee into the conversation . . .

"You get along with Cody?" she asked, deciding to feel her out.

Izzy shrugged but didn't look up. She ducked under the horse's neck and disappeared around the other side. "Well enough. I don't see that much of him. He works most days."

"Works elsewhere? What does he do?"

"His dad's a contractor. They do remodels and whatnot. He gets home about the time I'm getting done feeding in the afternoon. He rides after supper, after I'm gone. When he's around, he don't have that much to say to me. I just do my job, stay in my lane."

"I get the impression you don't care for him," Annie said. "Why is that?"

"It don't matter," Izzy said after a moment's consideration, carefully choosing her words. "His checks cash fine whether I like him or not."

Annie stepped around to the other side of the horse and back into Izzy's line of sight. "I've only met him the one time. He strikes me like the kind of man who needs to be right even when he's wrong."

A bitter little smile twisted the girl's mouth. "Aren't they all?"

"True that," Annie said, pulling a business card from her pocket. "Hang on to this. In case you ever need it . . . for any reason."

Izzy took the card, looked at it, and stuck it in the pocket of her jeans.

"I'm an ally here, Izzy," Annie said. "Keep an eye on her for me, will you?"

"Sure."

Annie walked out of the barn, escorted by three of the farm dogs to her vehicle. She started the engine and sat there for a moment, looking around at the place Tulsie and her jerk of a husband had built. It wasn't fancy by any measure, but it was clear they had worked hard on it and took pride in it. The fences were mended; the weeds were cut. Two half whiskey barrels flanked the entrance to the barn, planted with well-tended red and white geraniums.

We've built this business together.

Even if her marriage wasn't worth saving, all Tulsie's hard work had gone into this place. She didn't want to risk losing it, even if it meant risking her life. She no doubt believed she could work around her husband's ego and his temper, stay under his rage radar, and keep riding her horses and living her dream, even if the other half of her life was a nightmare.

She might get half of what they owned in a divorce, Annie thought, but what did that amount to? The place was probably mortgaged to the hilt. Nonc Claude had always been fond of saying if you wanted to make a small fortune in the horse business, you had best start out with a large one. If Cody went to jail for assault, there went his income from his construction job, and where would Tulsie be? Selling up.

Those were her choices: a knuckle sandwich or a shit sandwich. She was left starving either way.

16

"OH, MY GOD IN HEAVEN, WHAT HAVE I DONE TO DESERVE this?"

Nick chuckled low in his throat. "Donnie Bichon, as I live and breathe. How the hell are you?"

It was Bichon's turn to laugh. "Like you give a bright shiny fuck!"

They went back. Their history had begun with the brutal murder of Donnie's estranged wife, the case that had eventually brought Annie into Nick's life, making it a twisted thing to be somehow grateful for. He admitted to making Donnie's life a particular sort of hell during it all, not that Donnie hadn't deserved most of it. He'd been a legitimate suspect right up until he wasn't. The ne'er-do-well cheating husband on the brink of losing everything if his wife had divorced him. The perpetual screwup who had never missed the chance to make a wrong choice.

"Don't tell me you still have hard feelings," Nick said, prowling the office like a restless cat.

Donnie's personal space in the Bichon Bayou Development offices looked the same as he remembered—like the office of a genteel hunt club with antique oak furnishings and expensive wildlife prints in frames on the burgundy walls.

Donnie hadn't changed much either, though hard lessons had etched some lines into his perpetually boyish good looks. He was tall and lean with sun-bleached brown hair and a tan that spoke of excessive time on the golf course. He had played basketball in college and still had that slight hunch to his shoulders that made him look like he was ready to drive to the basket at any moment.

"Why would I have hard feelings?" he asked affably, spreading his arms wide. "I remember so fondly that time you stuck my head in a toilet and flushed. Those were the days!"

"You came out all right in the end," Nick said.

"I did indeed. Truth to tell, I turned my life around after that, though you'll forgive me if I don't thank you effusively. I'm not so evolved that I can't still hold a little grudge."

"Fair enough," Nick conceded. "How's Josie?"

"She rules my life, that little girl," Donnie declared with a broad smile as he leaned forward and tapped a finger on the framed photo of his now-teenaged daughter. "Look at that. Pretty as her mama, and she's on the A honor roll every quarter. Fixing to take her SATs, if you can believe that. Obviously got her smarts from Pam."

"Obviously."

"She straightened her daddy out, that's for sure. She'll rule the world one day. I have no doubt."

He settled into the oxblood leather chair behind his desk and swiveled back and forth.

"Please have a seat, Detective. You're giving me motion sickness, prowling around like you do. Do you need to be on Ritalin or something?"

"I'm looking for Dozer Cormier," Nick said, running his fingertips over the head of a carved wooden mallard on the credenza. "I'm told he works for you."

"Dozer? Sure. He works on Tommy Crawford's crew, framing

and whatnot. I try to hire those Sacred Heart boys when I can. You know, support the alma matter. Why? What's he done?"

"Why would you think he's done something?"

"In my experience, you specialize in accusing people of crimes they didn't commit," Donnie said without any rancor at all. "Whose murder do you want to pin on him? That body y'all found yesterday? Or are y'all trying to clear cold cases?"

"He's not a suspect in anything," Nick said evenly. "I'm told he's a friend of Marc Mercier."

"So am I," Donnie confessed, making his eyes go wide. "Is that a crime now?"

"Not yet. How do you know Marc?"

"He was a Sacred Heart boy, an athlete, and I put a word in for him with the right people at Tulane when the time came."

"How benevolent of you, Donnie," Nick said. "At the risk of ruining your reputation as a feckless narcissist."

"Never let it be said that tigers can't change their stripes," Donnie said pleasantly.

"Have you seen Mr. Mercier recently?"

"On the news last night. They say he's missing. Is that gonna be my fault? Or Dozer's? Lots of people know Marc. You're spoiled for choice here, Fourcade."

"How many of them would want him gone?" Nick asked.

"None that I know of. Marc's a good guy. There's no reason for him to disappear that I can think of."

"That's the mystery," Nick said. "I'm hoping Mr. Cormier might be able to shed some light on that."

"Yvonne, my office manager, can get you his phone number and address. That crew is working down in Luck today," Donnie said. "Imagine that. Luck is getting a subdivision! When I was a kid, Luck wasn't nothing but a wide spot in the road and a fish canning plant. Next thing you know, they'll have indoor plumbing and everything down there! It's gonna end up being a suburb. Progress."

"So they call it," Nick remarked. "When was the last time you actually saw Marc in the flesh?"

"I saw him Halloween night at Monster Bash. Him and Dozer. I was working the Rotary Club shrimp boil booth."

"What can you tell me about Dozer?"

"Well, he's a big dumb lummox with a bad disposition when he drinks, but he'd give a friend the quadruple-XL shirt off his back," Donnie said. "He's a hard worker if he's supervised and lazy as the day is long if he's not."

"And him and Marc are tight?"

"They always have been. Dozer was Marc's left tackle in high school senior year. Mr. Blind Side. He ate defensive linemen for lunch and picked his teeth with their bones. I thought he had a shot at the NFL, but college and Dozer didn't mix. He couldn't spell 'SAT,' let alone pass it—not that that ever stopped a good football player from getting into a Southern university. He just couldn't keep himself out of trouble."

"What kind of trouble?"

"Drinking, fighting, flunking. The usual."

"You hired him, though."

"He took the twelve steps a few years back—as did I a few years before him."

"Congratulations," Nick said honestly. "Good for you, Donnie. I mean that."

"Thank you. I was as big an idiot as they come when I was drinking—as you well know. All that business with Pam's murder and everything that happened after . . . I needed to pull my head out of the whiskey bottle and get my shit together if I was gonna be a proper father to my daughter, save my business, and grow the fuck up."

"That's hard work. Takes a lot of courage to step up like that."

"Yep. I've been sober nearly six years now, and I'm damn proud of it," he said. "The program didn't stick entirely for Dozer, but he's good enough for day labor. I keep an eye on him. He'll go off the rails on the weekend, but he doesn't miss a day's work, and that's something."

"Tell me," Nick said, "do you do any business with the Mercier brothers?"

Donnie shook his head. "No. We're strictly new construction. Don't have any real need for the scrap business."

"You're not knocking down old houses or anything like that?"

"No. That's more trouble than it's worth to me. There's a couple small contractors around do that, and I leave it to them—K and B, Parcelles', Melancon brothers."

"What about copper theft? Has that been a problem on your end?"

"Oh, my God, yes!" Donnie said, rolling his eyes. "We have to guard that stuff like it's Fort Knox. And it's not just copper, it's every damn thing. Can't hardly leave anything on a jobsite, and the Bayou Breaux PD . . . Don't get me started on them! They're a goddamn clown show. My warehouse is in the city limits, you know. Next to over where they store the Mardi Gras floats.

"We hired private security," he said. "It was the only thing to do. Drives costs up, but so do thieves. And still we lose materials. All the time. That's the world we live in, sad to say."

"Sounds to me like you've got somebody inside stealing from you."

Donnie sighed. "I hate to think it. I'm good to my people. Most of them have worked for me for a good long while. That's saying something in this business."

"Those materials are insured, yeah?" Nick asked. "You get reimbursed, or you get to write off the loss at least, right?"

Donnie gave him a perturbed look. "Are you gonna accuse me of insurance fraud?"

"No," Nick said. "Some people don't think of it as stealing if the owner gets compensated for the loss. That's how to rationalize stealing from people who trust you."

"That doesn't really comfort me," Donnie said. "I want to think better of my fellow man. This just pisses on my optimism."

"You know what they say, Donnie," Nick said, pulling a business card from his pocket. "You want loyalty, get yourself a dog."

He held up the card and placed it on the desk. "You call me directly the next time it happens."

Donnie arched a brow. "What about the town cops?"

"Fuck 'em."

Donnie laughed. "You're the dog in this story! I'll hold you to it. Who would'a guessed we'd be having this conversation all these years down the road? Life is a kick in the head, man!"

"*C'est vrai*," Nick conceded. "That's for true.

"Talking about Sacred Heart boys," he said. "Have you seen Robbie Fontenot lately?"

"Robbie?" Donnie sighed. "Now, there's a sad story. I had heard he was back in town, and then I saw him Halloween night as well."

"With Marc and Dozer?"

"No. They don't run together that I know of," Donnie said. "I imagine on account of what happened."

"Because of Robbie's drug use?"

"I reckon it goes back to when Robbie blew out his knee. I was actually there when it happened. A lot of people used to show up to watch their practices then because, I'll tell you what, Robbie Fontenot was the real deal. That was gonna be his year. He was being courted by every college in the Southeastern Conference, and plenty others. They wanted him at Alabama, but I think he was leaning toward LSU. His daddy was an LSU alumnus. But shit happens. You know, it's a rough sport with big, strong young men. Even then, Dozer weighed 350 pounds if he weighed an ounce. He fell into Robbie on a play and down they went. Robbie didn't get back up. That'd be like having a small elephant fall on you.

"It was just an unfortunate accident, but I don't think anything was the same with any of them after that. Marc took over as

quarterback and the team still went on to win the state championship, but Robbie was gone, in more ways than one. Dozer—I think
that's still at the heart of his problems, truth to tell. He never has
forgiven himself. You gotta do that if you're gonna move on," he
said. "I've told him. That's part of the twelve steps: admit your mistakes and make amends. He can't bring himself to do it. I think
there's a lot of shame and guilt at the heart of that, and that's a
shame in itself."

"Life is a journey," Nick said, thinking of the conversation he'd
had with Annie the night before. "We can't make it for someone else."

"Nope," Donnie said, shaking his head. "It's hard to watch people
struggle, though. I think of what a shit show I was back in the day.
My poor family, having to watch me drive my life off a cliff."

It was hard to reconcile the Donnie Nick had known back then
with the man before him now. Despite his many faults, Donnie had
always had a certain likable quality about him, with his good looks
and self-deprecating humor, but Nick would never have imagined
the man he knew then possessing the inner strength to turn himself around.

Every once in a great while, people were surprising in a good way.

"So, you saw Robbie Fontenot on Halloween night," he said,
turning back to the matter at hand. "About what time was that?"

"Must have been around ten. I couldn't swear to it, though. We
were busy."

"Was he with anybody?"

"He was talking to some town cop."

"Really?" Nick asked. "What'd that look like? Like he was in
trouble?"

He shrugged. "I don't know. I just figured par for the course for
Robbie. He's got a long drug history. The cops know it. He knows
they know it. Around and around they go."

"He's not one of your AA reclamation projects?"

"People have to want help before they'll accept help," Donnie
said. "Robbie . . . I don't know. He was always kind of a loner, that

kid. A world of talent, but a puzzle. His folks did everything they could—rehab and whatnot. That Oxy, man, that is some bad shit. I've known too many people got hooked on that, and mostly not through any real fault of their own. They say it's as bad as heroin for addiction.

"I saw on the news Robbie's missing, too," he said, frowning. "I hate to say it, but my first thought was that he's probably dead somewhere. Playing with that shit, your luck runs out eventually."

"This cop he was talking to that night," Nick said. "Did you recognize them?"

"No. I just saw a uniform. I didn't really look. I was busy slinging shrimp and sweet tea. That was a hell of a party. Were you there?"

"No," Nick said. "Me, I don't like crowds. Get that many drunks together, that's just work waiting to happen for me."

"True enough," Donnie said, rising as Nick started to move toward the door. "I heard you married that Broussard girl, the deputy."

"I did."

Donnie shook his head, chuckling as he opened the office door. "I liked her. Man, she deserves way better than you!"

"She does," Nick agreed, smiling, "but she's my wife nevertheless."

"Good for you. Kids?"

"We have a little boy. He's five already."

Donnie gave him a look as they walked down the hall. "I'm not the only tiger changed his stripes."

"*Mais non,*" Nick confessed. "You're not."

He held his hand out, a peace offering long overdue. Donnie took it.

"I'm glad to see you're doing well, Donnie," Nick said. "Not everybody comes out the other side."

"Same to you."

"You call if you need me," Nick said. "Thanks for the info."

17

FYI: BETH UNGER IN LAFAYETTE JAIL 6 MONTHS FOR DUI.

Annie typed the text and hit send. She had told Rayanne Tillis she would look for her missing roommate, despite Rayanne's claiming she didn't care. The answer to Beth Unger's disappearance had been easily had with a few mouse clicks. Hopefully, following through on her promise would gain her a few trust points.

She had weighed the relative merits of getting a search warrant for Rayanne's place on the chance of finding Robbie Fontenot's laptop but had decided against it. If she searched the house and found nothing, she would also lose whatever slim chance she had at getting Rayanne to tell her anything she might have known about the comings and goings at Robbie's place. If she found the computer, she could use potential charges as leverage to get answers, but she felt that Rayanne was much more likely to get mulish and uncooperative, and there would be no going back from that breech of what little trust she'd built.

Rayanne was an addict. Rayanne was a thief. Rayanne was a liar. But Rayanne Tillis was also her one possible source of information. She needed to cultivate this relationship.

She had stopped at the lamp factory on her way back from the Parcelles' to find out what she could about Robbie's employment there, and Rayanne's as well. It had come as no surprise to her that Rayanne hadn't worked there long enough to collect unemployment as she had claimed. Nor was it a surprise that she had been fired rather than laid off, having repeatedly shown up late or not at all or in no condition to work. So if Rayanne hadn't been earning a paycheck or collecting unemployment, how was she paying her rent?

She probably qualified for food stamps but not welfare. As a low-income individual, she possibly could have gotten rent assistance from the parish, but applying for that required a certain amount of organization and initiative Rayanne didn't seem to possess. Where was her money coming from?

She was an addict. No dealer would have trusted her with any serious amount of product to sell. She might have sold some of her own supply to help with the cost of her habit, but that wouldn't amount to much. She was a sometimes prostitute for men who wanted it quick and cheap, not a high-priced call girl or a plaything for a sugar daddy. Danny Perry or Dewey Rivette might have been tossing her a few bucks here or there for information, but she wasn't selling state secrets for thousands.

The house she lived in—and Robbie Fontenot's house as well—was one of four on that block owned by local slumlords, the Carville brothers, Roy and T-Rex (so-called not because he resembled a dinosaur, but in the Cajun tradition. Because he was named after his father, who was also called Rex, the prefix _T_ was added, _T_ being a shorthand for _petite_. They were Rex and T-Rex, and T-Rex would be called that regardless of size or age until the day he died).

The Carville brothers ran a number of dubious businesses that skirted the bounds of legality, including Club Cayenne, the topless bar over on the industrial edge of town—not far from Rayanne's neighborhood, as it happened. But Rayanne was not a candidate for pole dancing.

Roy Carville was currently on bail awaiting trial for having installed spy cams in a number of his rental properties and selling the bedroom/bathroom videos of his unsuspecting tenants on amateur porn sites on the Internet. Annie wondered if Rayanne's home had been checked for cameras. Or Robbie's, for that matter. She doubted the Carville brothers discriminated on gender or sexual orientation or anything else. That investigation had gone on while she'd been out nursing her concussion. She would ask Nick about it later.

Even as she made that mental note, her phone pinged with a text from him.

FYI: RF seen at Monster Bash talking to a
BBPD uni.

Annie texted back:

Any idea who?

No. Check any CCTV cameras near Rotary Club
booth.

The Rotary Club booth was always set up for festivals in the parking lot of Evangeline Bank and Trust. The bank's cameras would be good, if the subjects had been standing in the right spot. If not, there was a camera across the street on the post office and one on the side entrance of the hardware store. She would start with the bank, but not until after she'd seen B'Lynn Fontenot.

The Fontenot family home was located on Belle Terre Drive, Annie's favorite street in town, lined on both sides with live oak trees that created a thick green canopy over the broad street. The homes were old and gracious with dense, fragrant gardens all around. There was an air of quiet gentility about the place, as if no one who lived there could possibly have any cares at all. But of course they did. A big house did nothing to ward off the same kind of problems any family might have. Old money was the same as any when it came to buying trouble like drug addiction. Money didn't prevent lives or families from being torn apart. It just made the trouble look better from a distance.

She had passed by the Fontenot house many times in her life, always enchanted by the wraparound porch, the steep roofs and gables that gave it a fairy-tale quality. The color scheme of pumpkin and cream with cranberry trim only added to the charm. Many times she had imagined sitting on that front porch swing, rocking the day away, sipping on a sweet tea, listening to the songbirds in the thicket of laurel trees that ran down the side yard. She had never imagined the lives of the people inside that house being anything other than perfect.

B'Lynn answered the door looking like she hadn't slept, her dark hair swept back into a messy ponytail. The delicate skin beneath her eyes was purple, matching a bruise rising on her cheek.

"Are you all right?" Annie asked. "You look like you've been in a fight."

"I'm fine," B'Lynn said, stepping back and holding the door. "I turned my ankle and took a fall last night. Just clumsiness on my part. I was half awake. Come in, Detective. I've made coffee. I certainly need it. I imagine you could use a cup yourself."

"I won't say no."

"Do you have any news?" she asked, leading the way down the hall. She walked gingerly, like she was trying valiantly not to limp, her left arm cradled carefully against her side.

"Not to speak of, no. Are you sure you're all right? I can run you to the ER if you need."

"I don't think they have a cure for clumsiness. I'll be fine in a day or two."

"How'd that happen again?" Annie asked.

"I missed the bottom step coming down the stairs. There's no one here to beat me up, Detective, if that's what you're thinking. I do a good enough job of that all by myself."

Annie made no comment. Her encounter with Tulsie Parcelle was making her paranoid.

"Have you found out who that body is?" B'Lynn asked. "That's all they're talking about on the news today. That body and is it Marc Mercier. Is it?"

"We don't know," Annie said. "We're hoping to match or rule out Mr. Mercier with dental records today."

"His people can't identify him?"

"Like I told you yesterday, the injuries are pretty devasting."

"God help me, I'm just relieved it's not Robbie," B'Lynn said, going into the large, bright, butter-yellow kitchen. "I saw Marc's mother all but attack that detective outside the hospital. I know that feeling—just wanting to shake an answer out of somebody. I'm sorry for her. Have a seat, Detective."

"Please, call me Annie. Can I help with something?"

"No, I've got it," she said, lifting the old-fashioned percolator coffeepot from the stove and bringing it to the table. The aroma of rich, dark Community Coffee scented the air like perfume as she poured it into the waiting mugs.

"Just like home," Annie said. "My *tante* Fanchon, she won't ever give up her percolator. Best coffee there is."

"I find some comfort in clinging to old ways," B'Lynn said, settling into a chair. She looked small and fragile, swallowed up in an old blue plaid flannel shirt with the sleeves rolled to her elbows. "Feels like family even though they're long gone. This was my grandmother's coffeepot. This was my grandmother's house. She's still with me that way. It helps."

"You live here alone?"

"Mostly. My daughter's away at college. LSU. She'll be home for the holidays."

"I imagine it's been hard for her," Annie said. "Everything your family's been through."

"Yes. She had to live through all of that trouble with Robbie, her father and I falling apart, getting divorced. No matter how hard you might try, you can't really shield the younger child. They know what's going on. They absorb all that toxicity like a little sponge. Lisette always tried to be the peacemaker, bless her. She did everything she could to be the good kid, and the good kid always gets short shrift in these situations," B'Lynn said. "I always tried to be conscious of that, and I still failed as often as not.

"Of course, Robert lavished attention on Lisette as if she was his only child. Thank God she's a smart girl. Kids see right through us," she said, dipping a tiny spoon into an antique china sugar bowl and stirring it into her coffee. "Did Robert ever call you back?"

"No, ma'am."

She shook her head, scowling, and reached for her cell phone. Annie watched her pull up a contact and make the call, then wait for an answer. She rolled her eyes and mouthed, *Voicemail*.

"Robert, it's B'Lynn," she said. "I know you prefer to act like you don't have a son, but you do, and he's missing. The very least you can do is return the phone calls of the detective trying to find him. Imagine how you can bend her ear going on about how hard your life has been because of Robbie and your ball-busting ex-wife. She might even pretend to feel sorry for you, you narcissistic ass. Answer your damn phone!"

She ended the call and heaved a sigh as she set the phone aside. "Well, that felt good, anyway," she said, raising her mug to her lips. "To think I used to worship that man. The things my generation of women were raised to value . . . What a bill of goods."

She shook her head and sighed again. "His own father doesn't care that he's missing. Why would I expect anyone else to? I turn on the news this morning and all I hear about is Marc Mercier, Marc Mercier, Marc Mercier. Hometown hero. The savior of the youth football league. Missing three days. Everyone is up in arms about Marc. Robbie Fontenot barely gets a mention. His picture wasn't on the screen long enough for me to recognize him. There's so many layers of irony in that, I don't know where to start."

"It seems odd that they both happen to be missing," Annie said.

"Cops don't like coincidences. Robbie hadn't mentioned Marc to you?"

"No. Not at all. You have to understand. When Robbie got hurt, his life as he knew it ended. He lost his identity . . . and Marc Mercier stepped in and took his place on the football team, and the world kept on turning without missing a beat," B'Lynn said. "Don't get me wrong. Marc was a nice enough boy, even if he always did seem like he was running for political office. He was talented. Life gave him an opportunity, and he succeeded. But for Robbie . . . It was hard to watch. And nothing ever got better after that. It only got worse. So no, I don't see him seeking out Marc for any reason."

"It's ten years ago," Annie said.

"Ten years and how many stays in rehab? How many nights in jail? How many failures? How many disappointments?"

"Did Robbie blame Marc somehow?"

"Blame, no. Resent? How could he not?" she asked. "My God, I'm the adult, and look at me. I resent Marc for getting better news coverage than Robbie. How disgusting is that? If I were a better person, I would be calling his mother to offer my support."

"Do you know the family?" Annie asked.

"Not really, no. They weren't part of our social circle. Not to sound like an absolute snob, but doctors and lawyers mingle with doctors and lawyers. That's just how that is. Boring as hell when I look back on it."

"Those aren't your friends anymore?"

"No. Robert kept those friends in the divorce. I became much too real for them. Dealing with an addicted child strips away your social veneer. You just don't have any tolerance for pretentious nonsense. Anyway, you would have thought having an addict in the family was a communicable disease. They couldn't stay far enough away. What kind of friends are those, I ask you?"

"Not very good ones," Annie said. "Didn't you find a support network? Al-Anon? Or a church group or something?"

"Oh, sure, for a while. Al-Anon. No church group would have

me!" She laughed. "I'm too angry for them, too happy to call out God on his bullshit, pardon my language. I stuck with Al-Anon, but when the problem goes on and on and on . . . I got tired of the pity. After a while I just felt like a burden on the rest of them. A shining example of how not to succeed. I stepped away to give them hope."

And shouldered the burden herself. She was so small and delicate. How had she not been crushed by the weight of it all?

"You find your own way to tough it out," she said. "Or you walk away. Or it destroys you. Those are your choices."

"Are Robbie and his sister close?" Annie asked.

"In their own way. Robbie's very aware of how his problems impacted Lisette. But he's her big brother, even so, and she loves him."

"She hasn't heard from him?"

"She told me he called her on Halloween morning. That was their holiday. Robbie used to take Lisette trick-or-treating."

"And he didn't say anything to her about his plans for the evening?"

"She said no. I didn't mention it before because there was nothing to say."

"I'll want to speak to her anyway," Annie said. "Robbie was seen that night downtown at Monster Bash."

"Ah, well, that would be Lisette covering up for him with me, then," she said. "She's still his baby sister, but Robbie is a grown man. I realize he's not going to lock himself in a cell. He's going to live his life. He can go out if he wants to. I just have to hope he doesn't make a bad choice while he's at it. Who saw him?"

"I don't know," Annie admitted. "I had a text from another detective that Robbie had been seen that night in the vicinity of Evangeline Bank and Trust. I'll get more details later, and I'll be looking at surveillance video to see who he might have been with."

"Well, that's something more than we had, isn't it?" B'Lynn said, latching on to hope once again.

That cycle had to be exhausting. Soul draining.

"Is this the house Robbie grew up in?" Annie asked.

"Yes. It's been in my family forever. I inherited it from my grand-mother on my mother's side. We moved in here when Robbie was three."

Annie envied her that family history, and the traditions and memories that came with it. She had no idea who her mother's mother was, much less where she had grown up or how. Marie Broussard hadn't handed down any family heirlooms or traditions.

"Does Robbie normally spend much time here?"

"Sunday dinner every week."

"Your deal."

"We have a lot of unpleasant memories in this house," B'Lynn said. "But there are a lot of good ones, too. I want to keep build-ing on the good with him. So, Sunday dinner. Sometimes Lisette joins us. Sometimes my mother and stepfather join us. More often than not, it's just Robbie and me. We cook together. We have a nice meal. We play Scrabble and talk about everything except our prob-lems. We pretend to be normal in the hopes that one day it might stick."

"How does Robbie feel about that?" Annie asked. "Does he like it? Does he resent it? Does he participate or just go through the mo-tions?"

"He tries," B'Lynn said. "It's a journey, and we've been over some rough roads, but we're both trying. That's what makes this so hard, him missing now. I really thought we were making some progress."

"You said he thought he might have a line on a job," Annie said. "You don't have any idea what that was?"

"He didn't say, but I believe he was looking. He doesn't like hav-ing time on his hands, and he wants to pay his own way. He doesn't like being financially dependent on me. He feels like he's been a burden long enough."

"Does he still have a bedroom here?"

"Yes. He calls it the Time Capsule because I haven't changed any-thing about it in a decade."

"Can I see it?" Annie asked.

"Of course."

B'Lynn led the way up the oak staircase, the handrail worn as smooth as glass by a hundred-plus years of hands passing up and down. The old heart pine floors creaked and moaned as they made their way down the hall past a wall of ancestral portraits and photographs.

"Is there something specific you're looking for?" B'Lynn asked. "He doesn't spend much time up here except for the occasional Sunday-afternoon nap."

"I just want to be in his space," Annie said. "That house he's living in doesn't say much about him. Maybe I'll get a sense of something here."

"I've been doing the same thing," B'Lynn confessed, leading the way into her son's bedroom. "I find myself sleeping in here most nights since he's been gone. It makes me feel closer to him."

The room overlooked the front yard. The wall behind the queen-size bed was painted purple and stamped with gold fleur-de-lis. Sacred Heart high school colors. The rest of the walls were a rich cream. A thick purple rug covered much of the floor. It was a beautiful room fitted with everything a teenage boy could want—a good-size TV with a gaming console, a cushy recliner, a desk with a nice computer on it. The oak bookcases were loaded with books and keepsakes—a baseball glove, a collection of game balls from his football days, bobblehead dolls of his favorite players from various sports.

Annie picked a yearbook off a shelf and paged through it, finding a photo of Robbie Fontenot at sixteen or seventeen. Quite the teen heartthrob with his big dark eyes and shy smile. Young and bright and full of potential.

"What a cutie-pie," Annie said. "He must have had girls swarming around him like bees to honey."

"All he thought about then was sports," B'Lynn said, sitting on the edge of the bed to rest her sore ankle. "Girls were a baffling mystery he mostly shied away from. He dated a little bit, but no one serious. Much to the dismay of the young ladies."

"They didn't come calling when he was laid up after his accident? Girls that age usually love the idea of a wounded hero."

"Oh, they tried, but he didn't want anyone around, didn't want anyone seeing him that vulnerable. They gave up pretty quick and went on with their lives at school."

"That must have been a pretty lonely time for him."

"He pushed his friends away, then felt hurt when they didn't come back," B'Lynn said, picking at a loose thread on the purple comforter—a distraction from the pain of the memory. "He kept setting himself up for failure, then pointing to the failure as proof of why he shouldn't keep trying to succeed."

A self-feeding cycle of despair.

Annie sat down behind the desk. She wondered if there was any point in trying to get into the computer. Robbie had a laptop now, and only had access to this computer once a week.

"Did you get any useful information from our little thief?" B'Lynn asked.

"Not yet," Annie said, opening a desk drawer to find the usual assortment of pens and pencils, markers and paper clips. "I'm going over to see her after I leave here. See if I've managed to seed a little trust. I've done her a couple of favors now. Hopefully, she'll want to reciprocate."

"I hope she's appreciative," B'Lynn said. "She went right back to living her life, such as it is."

"How do you mean?"

"I couldn't sleep last night. I drove over past Robbie's, just in case he'd come back. Little Miss had company. I saw a man leaving her house about a quarter past one."

"I suppose we can't be surprised by that," Annie said, pulling open the bottom left drawer, a deeper drawer filled with a stack of old *Sports Illustrated* magazines. Funny they were kept in a drawer and not on the shelves of the bookcase with other similar collections.

"I can't help but feel sorry for her," B'Lynn said, "despite her attitude. I'm sure she came by that the hard way."

"I'm sure she did," Annie agreed. "I don't condone a life of crime, obviously, but some people have a harder road than others, and it isn't difficult to see how they end up the way they do. Your son is lucky he has you to fight for him."

She peered down into the drawer, looking alongside the stack of magazines to the bottom. Not the bottom of the drawer, she thought; it wasn't deep enough to be the bottom.

She pulled the magazines out a dozen or so at a time, setting them on the desktop until she had a stack a foot high. What had appeared at first to be the bottom of the drawer was an old dark stained wooden box, a finely crafted antique, about nine by twelve, and maybe four inches deep. Annie lifted it out of the drawer and placed it on the desktop.

"Oh, my," B'Lynn said, getting up from the bed. "That's my great-grandfather's writing box."

"Writing box?"

"That's what we always called it. It held his stationery and pens and an inkwell and so on. I thought it was down in the library."

There was a small, tarnished, ornate brass latch, but no lock. Annie took a deep breath and carefully worked the latch open, bracing herself to find a stash of drugs. But when she lifted the lid there were no pill bottles or plastic bags. The box was three-quarters full of cash. Twenties, fifties, hundred-dollar bills, all neatly stacked, banded together by denomination.

"What in the world?" B'Lynn muttered.

Annie fanned through the little piles, thinking there had to be a couple thousand dollars there. She looked up at B'Lynn.

"I have no idea," B'Lynn said. "Where would he get that kind of money?"

"I don't know," Annie said, but she had a strong feeling it hadn't come from anywhere good.

18

DOZER CORMIER WAS AS ADVERTISED: A MASSIVE INDIVIDUAL. Nick spotted him as soon as he got out of his vehicle at the construction site. Even from a distance, he dwarfed his co-workers by almost comic proportions. The sun had come out and shone off his bald dome as if it was made of titanium. Nick watched as he plucked a stack of two-by-fours off a flatbed truck and carried it to the house under construction like he was carrying a handful of yardsticks.

"Tommy Crawford?" Nick said, approaching the crew boss who stood at the cab of the flatbed, writing on a clipboard.

"Who wants to know?" The man looked up from under the wide brim of a straw hat, his eyes permanently narrowed against the harsh glare of the Louisiana sun.

Nick held his badge up. "Fourcade. Sheriff's office."

"Hell, there's never a cop around when you need one, and when you don't, here they come calling," Crawford said. He set his clipboard aside and reached out to shake Nick's hand. "Donnie called ahead to say you'd be stopping. You want to talk to Dozer, he said."

"Yeah. It shouldn't take long."

"Has he done something?"

"Not that I'm aware of. Is he the type?"

"Not in the main," Crawford said. "He's a good kid. He gets to drinking, though, he's been known to make some bad choices."

"I'm hoping he might be able to shed some light on where Marc Mercier is at," Nick said. "I understand they're buddies."

"Oh, yeah," Crawford said. "Mutt and Jeff. I saw on the news Marc's gone missing."

"You know him?"

"Marc? Sure. Everybody knows Marc. You think he's had an accident or something?"

"We don't know."

"They said on the news he'd gone out hunting. I hope he didn't fall out of his boat or something," Crawford said. "I had an uncle went teal hunting up on Catahoula Lake years ago, back when you could still hunt up there. Bent over the side of the boat to pull up his trolling motor, the string popped, and he lost his balance and went headfirst into the water with waders on. Those waders filled up and that was that. Another hunter saw him go in from maybe thirty yards away, but by the time he got over there, it was too late. It happens."

"It does," Nick said. "No sign of his boat yet, though. Hoping Dozer might have some ideas as to where he might have gone."

Crawford nodded and shouted across the yard, "Dozer! Dozer Cormier! Get your ass over here!"

"He's a good worker?" Nick asked as he watched the big man turn and start lumbering toward them.

"He's not a self-starter, if you know what I mean, but as long as I stay on him, he'll work harder than a rented mule."

"His drinking doesn't get in the way?"

He shook his head, rubbing at the beard stubble on his chin. "Almost never. He missed a couple days after Halloween. Too much partying at Monster Bash. He's been a little shaky since, but he'll be all right. I haven't said anything about that to Donnie. I want to give the kid a chance to sort himself out and get back on the beam, you know. He can be a damn *couillon* for sure, but he'll be all right."

"Whatchu need, boss?" Dozer asked.

He had to be six foot five or more, Nick thought, and well over three hundred pounds. A giant of a man with a close-cropped beard and mustache. He wore bib overalls that had to have taken an entire bolt of fabric to make. His hands were the size of catcher's mitts.

"This here's Detective Fourcade from the sheriff's office," Tommy Crawford said.

Dozer's face dropped. "I ain't done nothing!"

"Not saying you have, Mr. Cormier," Nick said. "You might have heard your friend Marc Mercier is missing. I'm hoping you might help me with some information."

"I ain't done nothing to Marc!"

He had a look in his small dark eyes like a horse on the verge of panic. No doubt that would be exactly what it felt like if he bolted—like getting run over by a horse.

"No one is accusing you of anything, Mr. Cormier," Nick said calmly. "I just want to have a chat. You want us to find Marc, yeah? Bring him home safe to his family?"

"Well . . . yeah . . ."

"Let's step over here in the shade. Might as well make this a little break from your day, right?"

"I guess," he said hesitantly.

They moved away from the worksite, and Dozer took a seat on a pile of building materials that had been stacked there for the purpose. Nick stayed on his feet, noting that seated, Dozer Cormier was almost at eye level with him.

"When did you last see Marc?"

"Oh, I don't know," Dozer said. "A couple nights ago, I guess. I don't remember exactly."

"You don't remember?" Nick asked with just a hint of incredulity. "He's your best friend. You spend a lot of time together the way I hear it, but you don't remember when you last saw him?"

"I don't know. It might have been Friday or it might have been Saturday. We had a few beers."

"Okay. Where?"

"Where?"

"Where did you have the beers? I imagine people saw you there. Someone will remember."

Dozer didn't seem to like that idea, that other people would have seen them together at a specific place and time. Nick could count the man's pulse ticking in his carotid artery on the side of his neck. He was pale beneath the flush high on his cheekbones, and a fine sheen of sweat was rising on his forehead.

"We went a couple places," he said. "I don't really remember."

"You seem awfully nervous, Mr. Cormier," Nick said quietly. "Why is that?"

"Me, I don't like talking to cops," Cormier admitted. "Y'all are always trying to trick people into saying things they shouldn't."

"I'm not trying to trick you, Mr. Cormier. I'm just gathering information. If you haven't done anything wrong, then I shouldn't be able to trick you into saying any wrong thing, right?"

Cormier looked at him like a deer in headlights.

"That's not a trick question," Nick said.

Dozer held still.

He was hardly the first person to react with nerves to being questioned. Nick knew not to read too much into it. People were wary of cops in general. He had learned to use it to his advantage.

"Let's do this," he proposed. "Why don't you just tell me about the last time you saw Marc, what y'all did, what kind of mood he was in."

"I told you, we went out for some beers."

"Was that Saturday night?" Nick asked. "He'd had a fight with his wife . . ."

"Yeah, maybe. They fight a lot. She don't like us going out."

"Does Marc get pissed off about that—her dogging him for going out with his buddies?"

"Yeah, for sure. She's always ragging on him. She's not from here, you know. She don't know how things are."

"So was he in a bad mood that night?"

"For a while."

"Did he ever talk about leaving his wife, getting divorced, anything like that?"

Dozer shrugged, his massive shoulders rolling. "Don't they all? Married guys. They're all the time bitching about their wives. I don't know why they get married in the first place."

"You're single, I guess."

"Yeah."

"Did Marc ever say anything about just packing it in, taking off, starting a new life?"

"Who doesn't?" Dozer asked.

"You didn't take it serious?"

"No. Everybody talks like that sometimes. Don't nobody ever do it."

"Did Marc say anything about what he was doing the next day?"

"He was going hunting with Luc."

"Did he ask you to go along with him?"

"No. Me, I don't like Luc. He's an asshole. I ain't gonna waste a day off with that guy."

"Why did you show up at the Corners, then, Sunday morning?"

Dozer startled like he'd gotten shocked. "What?"

"You were at the Corners Sunday morning," Nick said, "about seven, seven fifteen."

"How do you know that?"

"I'm a detective," Nick said.

"Why were you watching me?" Dozer demanded. "I ain't done nothing!" he said, pushing to his feet. "This is some kind of Big Brother bullshit!"

"If you haven't done anything, then why you don't want to answer my questions, Mr. Cormier?" Nick asked, letting his impatience begin to show. "This is getting tedious for me. Now, I can ask you to accompany me back to the law enforcement center, and we can have a much longer conversation about this, or you can find the spirit of cooperation right now. Do you want to have to explain to Donnie Bichon why you lost half a day's work being a goddamn *couillon* for no reason?"

Cormier shifted his weight from one foot to the other, his gigantic hands jammed at his waist as he looked left and right, as if scoping out an escape route.

"Marc was supposed to meet his brother at the Corners Sunday morning to go out to their hunting property," Nick said, trying to pull him back on topic.

"Then he probably did," Dozer said. "That's got nothing to do with me."

"He didn't," Nick said. "Neither of them showed up."

"Then maybe you ought to be talking to Luc, not me."

"You know they had a fight on Saturday. Marc gave him a black eye. Do you know what that was about?"

Dozer shook his head.

"Marc had a fight with his brother bad enough to come to blows, but he didn't say anything about that?"

"Nope. Ain't the first time that's happened."

"But he still planned to go hunting with him the next day."

"Yeah. So? They're brothers. That's what they do. That's how they are."

"What were you doing at the Corners?" Nick asked again.

"It's a free country," Dozer said. "I can go hunting, too. Me and half of south Louisiana. You asking all of them?"

"What were you hunting?"

"Deer."

"Did you get one?"

"No."

"What did you stop at the Corners for?"

"They got them good breakfast biscuits," Dozer confessed. "I got me a sack of them and went out in the woods. You can ask Sharelle Dupuis. She give me a hard time for buying so many."

"Those are good biscuits," Nick conceded, easing off on the pressure again. Dozer let go a sigh. "Have you heard from Marc since then?"

"No."

"Have you tried to call him?"

"No."

"Your best friend's missing and you haven't tried to call him?"

"I ain't got a cell phone right now," Dozer said. "I lost mine Halloween night. I can't afford a new one until payday."

"Sounds like you had quite a night that night."

He narrowed his eyes. "What's that mean?"

"You and Marc did Monster Bash," Nick said. "You must have partied some after. Your crew boss says you missed a couple days' work. That's a big hangover."

"It ain't against the law to get drunk."

"That all depends on what kind of trouble you get into while you're over the limit, yeah?"

Dozer looked past him. "Can I go back to work now?"

Nick said nothing for a moment, just to fuck with him. He pulled out a business card and tucked it into the chest pocket of the big man's overalls.

"You hear from Marc, you call me," he said. "Thank you for your time, Mr. Cormier."

Dozer started to move.

"One more thing," Nick said.

Cormier turned back around, scowling.

"Did you happen to see Robbie Fontenot on Halloween?"

"Robbie?" he said, as if he'd never heard the name.

"Robbie Fontenot. You went to school with him."

"No," Dozer said. "I ain't seen him in years."

And he turned and walked away.

Nick watched him go, trying to sort out the man's reactions and pick the truth from the lies.

His cell phone vibrated in his pocket. He pulled it out and looked at the text from Caleb McVay.

No go on the dental. Too much damage.

"Damn."

19

TWO THOUSAND FOUR HUNDRED FIFTY DOLLARS. WHERE HAD Robbie Fontenot come by $2,450, and why had he hidden the cash at his mother's house?

His paychecks from the lamp factory had gone by direct deposit to his bank account, B'Lynn said, not that he'd had a check in the last month. If he wanted to keep cash on hand, Annie supposed it wasn't all that strange that he hadn't wanted to keep it at his house in a shit neighborhood where his next-door neighbor was a thief and God knew what else went on. Where had the money come from was the pertinent question, and why did he want or need that much cash?

The obvious answer was that drugs were expensive and drug dealers liked cash, although some of them had taken to more modern forms of payment like Venmo, as weird as that seemed. If drugs were the answer, was Robbie keeping the cash to buy drugs or was he making the cash selling drugs? Neither answer was anything B'Lynn wanted to hear.

Annie felt the weight of that as she drove. The likelihood of this story having a happy ending was slim to none. She both hoped that Rayanne Tillis might have an answer and hoped that she wouldn't.

If she had an answer, the investigation would go forward in a direction that would end with Robbie Fontenot in jail at best and dead at worst. If she didn't have an answer, B'Lynn could hang on to a sliver of hope, and the thing about slivers was that they were usually painful and often left a scar. It seemed to Annie that Robbie Fontenot's mother had enough scars to last a lifetime. The look on her face as she'd sat on her son's bed, considering the possibilities of this latest discovery, had made Annie's heart hurt.

Barely twenty-four hours after coming back to work, she found herself up to her ears in emotional attachment to a case that had a snowball's chance in hell of ending well. As much as she loved her job, and as much as she was good at it . . . some days . . .

At least she wasn't thinking about her head injury.

She hit the blinker and turned onto Rayanne's block, trying to formulate a plan. How best to work the conversation in a way that would invite an exchange of information, not put the girl on the defensive, where she was almost sure to lie. It took time to build a relationship with someone as short on trust as Rayanne, but time was a luxury Annie didn't have.

B'Lynn had offered to pay Rayanne for any useful information she might have. Money was sure to be a motivator for a girl who had none, and any information she might have was more than they had at the moment.

Rayanne's manager at the lamp factory had said Rayanne definitely knew Robbie Fontenot. He had seen them interacting at work. To what extent that was a personal relationship or just workmates talking, he didn't know. He said Rayanne was friendly with the male employees. *Friendly* in italics. Friendly as in inappropriate. Friendly as in drumming up customers for her night job.

That reminded Annie of the condoms in Robbie Fontenot's nightstand, and she cringed a bit at the thought.

She pulled into the driveway behind Rayanne's piece-of-shit, falling-apart red Chevy Malibu, which looked like a homeless person was living in it. She glanced in the windows on her way to the house. The car was full of garbage and cast-off clothes. The front passenger window was broken and repaired with duct tape. The side mirror had come off. At least no one would bother stealing it, Annie thought.

She climbed the stairs to the tiny front porch and knocked on the door. No one came. At midday, there was no guarantee Rayanne was even up. She had no job to go to. B'Lynn had seen a visitor leaving her house at one-something in the morning. There was a good chance she'd spent the night getting high in celebration of not spending the night in jail.

She knocked again and looked around while she waited. Kitty-corner across the street, a heavyset elderly Black man was sitting on his porch in his dingy undershirt drinking a beer, his white hair standing straight up on his head like vintage Don King.

"Damn it, Rayanne," Annie muttered, knocking a third time.

Losing patience, she pulled the warped old screen door open and tried the interior door. It wasn't locked.

"Rayanne?" she called, cracking the door open. "It's Annie Broussard. Are you home?"

The silence that answered her raised the hair on the back of her neck. There she was again, walking into who-knew-what. Her heart beat a little faster.

"Rayanne?" she called again as she went into the house.

The front room looked the same as it had the day before. The smell was as bad as or worse than the day before, having added notes of weed smoke over the amalgam of cigarettes, rodent, and sour garbage.

Cockroaches scattered in all directions as she passed the filthy kitchen. Annie's skin crawled. How people lived like this never failed to amaze her.

"Rayanne?"

The term *dead silence* kept playing through her mind, over and over. Her heart beat a little harder.

"No, no, no," she muttered as she made her way down the hall, that sense of foreboding rising like a tide inside her. "Rayanne? Shit!"

The girl lay on the floor of the bedroom, half tangled in a bedsheet, still wearing her faded red Fuck Your Feelings T-shirt, naked from the waist down.

"Shit!"

Annie dropped to the floor beside the body and felt for a pulse. It was weak and thready, hard to feel with trembling fingers. She was barely breathing. Annie lifted an eyelid to see the pupil constricted to a pinpoint.

"Rayanne!" she shouted, shaking the unconscious girl. No response. She rubbed her knuckles hard against the girl's sternum. Still no response. "Rayanne, wake up!"

Her body was limp and cold as Annie rolled her onto her side. She had vomited at some point, a trail of puke already crusting at one corner of her mouth and down her chin.

"Don't you die on me!" Annie yelled, scrambling to her feet.

She fumbled with her phone as she ran down the hall and out the front door, dialing 911.

"This is Detective Broussard with the sheriff's office," she said breathlessly, running to her vehicle. "I need an ambulance ASAP at 2-1-7 Opelousas in Bayou Breaux for a probable opioid overdose. Subject is unconscious with a weak pulse and shallow breathing."

She yanked open the passenger-side door and popped the glove compartment, raking through the contents, scrambling to find the blister pack containing the Narcan plunger. Two tumbled out onto the floor. She grabbed them both and ran back to the house.

"Don't you die on me, Rayanne!" she shouted again, ripping the package open.

She dropped to her knees beside the girl and rolled her onto her back again, noting that Rayanne's lips had taken on a slight blue tint as the drug she'd taken suppressed her instinct to keep breathing. Annie tilted her head back, shoved the nozzle of the spray container up one nostril, and depressed the plunger.

This was the part where in the movies the overdosed person always came instantly awake, sat bolt upright, and started talking as if they hadn't been seconds from death. Rayanne Tillis did not sit bolt upright. She did not open her eyes. She did not suddenly take in a gasping gulp of oxygen.

Annie turned her onto her side and shoved some of the rumpled bedsheet up under her head, her own heart going a hundred miles an hour as she watched for the Narcan to kick in. Two to five minutes, the manufacturer claimed. Two minutes seemed like an eternity.

"Come on, Rayanne, you gotta wake up for me."

She stuck two fingers into the girl's mouth to clear away anything that might obstruct her airway, then used an edge of the sheet to try to wipe away the crusty remains of vomit from Rayanne's lips. She turned her onto her back again to begin mouth-to-mouth resuscitation, managing a dozen or so breaths before pulling away and gagging on the taste of vomit.

"Damn it, Rayanne," she muttered, ripping open the packaging for the second dose of Narcan. "Come on, come on."

In the distance the faint sound of a siren heralded the approach of the paramedics.

Annie felt again for a pulse that came and went, seemingly ducking out from under her trembling fingertips as death beckoned Rayanne Tillis. She tried to spit the taste of vomit from her mouth, then started in again on resuscitation. Another minute and help would arrive. Twelve more breaths.

And then came the organized chaos of the paramedics rushing in with their equipment and taking over with the speed and efficiency of an Indy 500 pit crew. Annie stepped back out of their way as they swarmed on Rayanne.

"What have we got here, Detective?"

"Rayanne Tillis. She's twenty-three with a history of drug abuse. I found her unconscious about ten minutes ago."

"What'd she take?"

"I don't know yet. She's got a history with opioids. Everything points to that."

"She looks like a meth head."

"That, too. Something for every mood."

"Did you give her Narcan?"

"Two doses. She's not responding."

"How long ago?"

"Maybe three minutes since the second dose."

"Shit, she's barely got a pulse."

"Hey, Rayanne, we need you to wake up for us!" one of them said, tapping the side of her face. He repeated Annie's actions, scrubbing his knuckles on the unconscious woman's breastbone. Rayanne didn't respond. "Come on. Come on back to us, girl!"

"She's going into cardiac arrest. Starting CPR!"

Annie stood and watched, leaning back against a wall, feeling drained and sick and useless as the paramedics worked to save the life of Rayanne Tillis—at least long enough to get her into the ambulance.

She followed them out of the house and watched them load her and go, siren screaming. As the ambulance drove out of sight, the adrenaline crash hit her. Feeling suddenly weak and lightheaded, she leaned over the rickety porch railing and threw up, her stomach trying hard to turn itself inside out as everything that had happened replayed through her mind at a dizzying speed.

She needed to sit down, but she needed to get the taste out of her mouth more as her stomach rolled again and again. She walked to her car on wobbly legs and fell backward into the driver's seat, bent over with her forearms on her thighs, breathing through her mouth, trying to slow her respiration as another wave of nausea crashed over her. She was both sweating and cold, and her pulse throbbed in her head like a drumbeat.

She had to go back inside to search for the drugs Rayanne had taken, but she needed a minute to gather herself. She grabbed her water bottle from the passenger seat, rinsed her mouth, and spat into the grass again and again, trying unsuccessfully not to think about her resuscitation efforts and the taste of Rayanne Tillis's mouth.

"You better live, Rayanne," she muttered, digging through the little travel kit she kept in the car for the tiny toothbrush and miniature tube of toothpaste. "I don't want to think I did that for nothing."

She was in the middle of brushing her teeth when Danny Perry arrived. She watched him walk up like some character in a TV cop show in his tailored uniform and mirrored sunglasses, wondering if he practiced that walk in a full-length mirror when he went home at night.

"Detective Broussard," he said, posing like an action figure a few feet in front of her. Backlit by the sun, the frosted tips of his spiky hair looked like little white flames atop his head. "Is there anything I can do to help?"

Annie rinsed her mouth and spat a few inches away from the toes of his boots. "Help what? What are you doing here?"

"I heard the call on the radio."

"Really? Where were you? Baton Rouge? The ambulance has been and gone."

"How's Rayanne? Is she all right?"

"No, she's not all right, you numbskull," Annie barked. "She OD'd. She died on the floor and had to be revived. I don't know that she'll make it."

"Oh, man, that's terrible."

"Is it?" She rinsed her mouth a second time, and he had to hop back to avoid the spray.

"What's that supposed to mean?"

"Nothing," Annie said, willing her legs to hold her up steady as she got out of the car. She still felt weak, and her head was pounding, but she didn't want Danny Perry towering over her.

"Are you all right?" he asked. "You look a mite peaked."

"Yeah, well, the senseless loss of life for a cheap high makes me sick," she said. "Do you have any idea who Rayanne's dealer is?"

"I don't think she's fussy. Last I knew, she didn't have any money, and I heard she owed a couple of people who weren't inclined to extend her credit."

"What about you?" Annie asked bluntly. "Are you giving her money? Is she your CI?"

"Me?" he asked, incredulous. "No! You met her. Do you think she'd be a source of reliable information?"

"I think even a busted watch is right twice a day. Maybe that's worth a few bucks here and there."

"Not from me."

"What about Rivette?"

"How would I know who his CIs are? Don't nobody share that kind of information."

"Well, she got something from someone."

"Yeah. She got a get-out-of-jail-free card from you, apparently."

"Mrs. Fontenot declined to press charges," Annie said. "That's hardly the same thing as giving an addict money for drugs."

"She probably traded a favor for a pill or two. That's what addicts do. Where there's a will, there's a way."

"Do you know any of her regular johns?"

"I wouldn't know if she had regulars. She's more of a crime of opportunity, if you know what I mean."

"A man was seen leaving her house late last night," Annie said, watching his face.

"Seen by who?" he asked. "You have a witness?"

"Yes, I do."

"Who?"

"Why do you need to know?" Annie asked pointedly.

Perry shrugged. "Just curious as to who's hanging around this neighborhood in the middle of the night. Did they describe this visitor, or do I not get to know who to look for?"

"White male. Average size. Wearing a dark hoodie."

"That's it?"

"It was dark. He was seen from a distance."

"Vehicle?"

Annie shook her head. "That's why I asked if you knew her regulars. I would start there if I had a list of names."

"Can't help you there."

"Because we only bother to prosecute the women and not the men who use their services," Annie said with disgust. "Do you know anything about Rayanne's family or where she's from?"

"She's from Henderson, I think. I don't know her people, though."

Annie sighed. "I guess I'd better go back into that mouse-infested roach hole and pick through her things. Try to find her phone or some clue who her folks are. They should know what's going on."

"You want help?" he asked.

Annie looked at him, both puzzled by and suspicious of his offer. "Hasn't your chief declared war on the SO?"

He shrugged. "He doesn't need to know. If that girl is at death's door and you want her kin to make it here before it's too late, there's no time to waste. What difference does it make what uniform I'm wearing? I'm standing right here."

Annie thought about it for a second. She had a hard time thinking Rayanne Tillis had a family who cared about her, but then she thought of B'Lynn, who would have given anything to see her son again, even if it was just for the last few seconds of his life. You never knew someone else's story or who might be heartbroken at the end of it.

"Okay, Hollywood," she said. "Let's go."

She grabbed a pair of gloves out of her bag and handed another pair to Danny Perry as they walked to the house.

"Brace yourself," she said, leading the way inside.

Danny shoved his sunglasses on top of his head and squinted at the smell. "Wow. About the only thing that could make this smell worse would be cat piss. Of course, maybe she wouldn't have mice, then."

"Let's start in the bedroom," Annie said. "That's where I found her. She's got a cell phone somewhere. And be on the lookout for drugs. If we can find what she took, that might be helpful."

"We don't need a search warrant for this?"

"It's exigent circumstances, but don't touch anything you don't have to."

"Oh, don't worry about that," he said. "I don't wanna touch the stuff I have to touch. It's unreal to me how people will live this way."

He pulled a ballpoint pen out of his shirt pocket and used it to move things around on the cluttered nightstand. "Animals don't live like this."

"Cockroaches and mice do," Annie pointed out, picking up the bedsheet Rayanne had been tangled in. Roaches scattered.

"Vermin. It's disgusting."

"All an addict cares about is getting high," she said. "Hygiene and housekeeping don't even make the list."

"Well, here's the drugs," Danny said. He turned around holding up a tiny plastic zip-top bag by one corner. "There's part of a joint, too."

"Where was it?" Annie asked, coming over.

He pointed with the pen to a spot on the nightstand between a can of Michelob Ultra and a dirty glass with an inch of whiskey with two cigarette butts floating in it.

Three white tablets with room to spare in the bag. Three pills left out of how many? Five, maybe. At thirty bucks per, minimum, that would have been $150.

"Where'd she get the cash for that?" Annie mused.

"Maybe she has a generous friend."

"I don't have any friends that generous—do you?"

She bagged the drugs and they kept looking for the phone, Danny picking through the mess on the dresser. Cringing, Annie got down on the dirty floor and looked under the bed. Dust bunnies, discarded underpants, a used condom. No phone.

A charger cord was plugged into the wall near the nightstand, stretched out as if maybe someone had yanked the phone off it on their way out of the room.

Maybe she had traded the phone for the drugs, Annie thought, getting to her feet, but that seemed doubtful. Why would someone take her phone? Because phones held a wealth of information. A little handheld treasure trove of potential evidence.

Her own phone vibrated, and she took it into the hall to answer. "Broussard."

"It's Chris Skinner, Detective. I'm just calling to let you know she didn't make it," the paramedic said. "She went into cardiac arrest a second time in the bus, and we couldn't get her back. The ER staff did all they could, but . . . she didn't make it. I'm sorry."

"Me, too."

Annie thanked him, ended the call, and heaved a sigh. All the urgency drained out of her, and whatever hope she'd held on to for Rayanne went with it, leaving her feeling empty.

Danny Perry watched her, waiting for her to speak.

"She didn't make it," she said quietly.

"Oh, man," he muttered. "That's our fourth OD in two weeks. And people keep taking that shit."

"Nobody thinks it'll happen to them," Annie said. "That's the bad lie they tell themselves every time they pop a pill or shoot up or whatever they do."

She sighed again and rubbed at the tension in the back of her neck.

"You can go, Danny," she said. "I'll close up here."

"You sure?" he asked. "I don't mind. I mean, you haven't found her phone yet."

"It's okay. You've got patrol and a prickly chief. I'm good here. There's no rush now. Thanks for your help, though."

She saw him out as if she was a hostess. When he was halfway to his radio car, she remembered her other order of business for the day.

"Hey, Danny. Did you happen to see Robbie Fontenot Halloween night at Monster Bash?"

He turned around, appearing to search his memory. "I don't think so."

"Someone saw him talking to a uniform near Evangeline Bank

and Trust," she said. "I'm gonna go look at the CCTV video from the area, but I thought maybe . . . I might as well ask on the off chance . . ."

She let the rest of the sentence trail off, giving him a chance to rethink his answer.

"You know, I might have," he said, shrugging. "There were only a few thousand people there that night. I try to do my thing as your friendly neighborhood po-lice man, you know. If I did see him, nothing stood out about it."

"Okay. Well, I was just hoping to get a read on what his mood was that night."

"Sorry."

"It was worth a shot."

Annie watched him get in his patrol car and drive away, wondering at his motives for showing up there. He'd gone right to the drugs and handled the package, potentially smudging any fingerprints that might have been left on the plastic bag. She didn't like the way her mind was bending, but it wasn't going that way for no reason.

A middle-aged woman was out on her porch next door in a sleeveless cotton housedress that showed off upper arms shaped like ham hocks, pretending to water a window box full of half-dead plants. Her gaze darted over in Annie's direction every few seconds.

"Ma'am?" Annie asked. "Do you know the woman who lives here?"

The woman just scowled at her with a face like a blobfish, then turned and went back inside.

Annie went back into the house, back to the bedroom to have one last look for Rayanne's phone. She stood in the doorway, looking around the shithole bedroom in this shithole house, wondering who would come for Rayanne's belongings. There wasn't anything in this house that shouldn't have been put in a dumpster and taken to a landfill. Would anyone from her family even bother? Would they come to Our Lady to claim her body or leave her there like a sack of trash for the parish to dispose of?

No matter how Rayanne had ended up in her life, she had once been someone's daughter, someone's baby. Had she been wanted? Had she been raised with love? Or had she been a mistake, an accident, the result of something brutal?

Annie tried to imagine what Rayanne must have looked like as a little girl with her straight-as-sticks hair and petulant expression. It was hard to imagine her as sweet or innocent, but she probably had been before the world had gotten hold of her. She had had hopes and dreams at some point in her life. No child had ever gotten up in front of their third-grade class and declared they wanted to grow up to be a junkie prostitute, but that was how her life had turned out. Dead on the floor of a shithole in a Fuck Your Feelings T-shirt and no underpants.

No one deserved that, no matter how poor their life choices had been.

"I heard she didn't make it."

Annie bolted at the sound of the voice and spun around.

"Jesus, Dewey! You gave me a heart attack! Don't you know how to knock on a door?"

"This isn't a social call, is it?" Rivette asked. He was in rumpled khakis and a wrinkled button-down that might have been the same outfit he'd worn the day before, though Annie wouldn't have been surprised to find his closet was full of identical garments. He didn't strike her as being long on imagination or fashion sense.

"You're lucky I didn't shoot you!" she said. "Though I suppose I shouldn't be surprised to see you, what with your favorite little toady having just left."

"Danny will be pleased to hear you think so highly of him."

"Danny knows exactly what I think of him. You make a good tag team. Are you here to express your condolences?"

"To you? Did you adopt Rayanne Tillis or put her in jail?" he asked. "Oh, wait, if she was in jail, she'd still be alive."

"Screw you, Dewey. I'm not the one who supplied her with drugs," Annie said. "Maybe you know something about who did. A witness described an unremarkable white male leaving here last night around one fifteen."

"I don't know anything about that. Or are you accusing me of killing a junkie hooker?"

"I didn't accuse you of anything. You're the town detective. You don't know who's dealing drugs right under your nose?

"And no matter who her dealer is, somebody had to be giving that girl money," Annie said. "Danny says it wasn't him. Was it you? We've all got our CIs."

He screwed up his round face like he'd smelled a fart. "Like I'd tell you who my CIs are! You can fuck right off, Broussard."

"She's dead now," Annie said. "You might as well tell me. What difference does it make?"

"Yeah. What difference *does* it make?" he asked. "She's dead now. You don't need to know anything about her."

"I'd like to know who her parents are," Annie said. "I'd like to let her relatives know what happened to her so they can give her a Christian burial. You want the parish to just throw her in a hole with two or three other indigent dead people?"

"I never said that! And why would I know who her parents are?"

"You are worse than useless, Dewey."

"And you are nothing but a pain in my ass," he returned.

"Speaking of," Annie said, "you ran straight to Chief Earl yesterday and tattled, didn't you? So predictable.

"How'd that work out for you?" she asked. "Did your chief enjoy getting his ass handed to him by Sheriff Noblier? I'm thinking there might have been some fallout there."

"No. Chief Earl was as appalled by your behavior as I was. And Gus Noblier being a pompous blowhard was no surprise to anybody."

"Well, then, everybody's happy," Annie said. "Good."

"Yeah, well," he said, disappointed that she wasn't offended. "You enjoy your nothing case, trying to find Robbie Fontenot, who is probably dead in a Lafayette drug house."

"Is that wishful thinking on your part?"

"Why would I want him dead?" he asked. "He didn't mean anything to me."

"Clearly not for all the effort you put into finding him."

"And what have you done?" he asked. "You ain't found him."

"I've done everything you didn't," she said, ticking the points off on her fingers. "At least people are aware of him today. People can call the tip line if they've seen him. He's on the NCIC database now. I've got his cell phone records coming. His car is listed as hot. You know, all the basics of running a missing persons case. You apparently missed that class at the academy, or do they even bother with schooling at the PD? Do you just send in your Wheaties box tops and get a badge?"

"I've been at this just as long as you, Broussard."

Annie stepped past him to get into the hall, tired of the smell of vomit and stale sex. She would have tried to open a window, but it was a good bet the windows had been painted shut years before.

"I need some fresh air," she said, walking away from him, going to the back door and out onto the rotting little porch.

"Why'd you let her go yesterday?" Dewey asked, following her. "I thought you had her red-handed stealing a TV."

"Mrs. Fontenot declined to press charges. What was the point, anyway? We got the TV back. And maybe I built a little faith with Rayanne.

"She used to work with Robbie Fontenot at the lamp factory," she said. "Did you know that?"

His expression said he didn't. That round face wasn't very good at masking surprise. And surprise tended to short out the brain circuits from asking obvious questions like how long did they work together, and did they actually know each other, and wasn't Rayanne high most of the time.

"Not just a junkie hooker after all," she said.

Dewey frowned.

"Why did you come here, Dewey?" Annie asked. "Obviously Danny Perry called you right up, didn't he? Why?"

"Why wouldn't I?" he returned. "This is my town. I should know what's going on."

"That's a novel idea. Or maybe you were afraid you left something here last night when you came to see Rayanne?"

Red rose in his cheeks as his temper began to heat up. "I was *not* here last night," he insisted. "I don't frequent prostitutes, and I resent you suggesting I'm some kind of dirty cop."

"Did I suggest that?" Annie asked. "I don't think so, but I'm glad to hear you're not, just the same."

"You're a really annoying person," he remarked.

"Yeah, well, my family loves me, so I'm good . . ."

She looked over next door at Robbie Fontenot's house and across the alley at the house with the security cameras, wondering if Dewey had even noticed that equipment. She bet not.

"A funny thing happened this morning," she said. "I found $2,450 cash money that Robbie Fontenot had squirreled away."

"What? Where?"

He couldn't stop himself from looking over at the house next door, making Annie think he had searched that house better than she had first thought.

"At his mother's house," she said. "Where do you think Robbie got that kind of cash? He's unemployed, and he didn't work there long enough to collect benefits."

"He's probably dealing."

"Maybe. But he's never had charges for dealing. He isn't on the radar for the drug task force. And I haven't found any product anywhere."

"Probably keeps it in his car," Dewey said.

"I suppose that could be. Funny how nobody seems to be aware of it, though. People who should know—drug cops, town cops, people who have arrested him on multiple occasions. Yourself, for instance," she said. "Everybody knows Robbie's drug history—which is as a user, not a dealer, but still, he might have graduated. People have an eye on him because of that history, but nobody knows anything about him dealing.

"You know," she said, "when I was going over his record, I kept thinking it was funny how he has never gotten caught for anything really bad. Charges were always bare minimum."

"Good lawyer," Dewey said. "He comes from money. His father is a prominent surgeon."

"Even so. I just keep thinking it looks like maybe he's useful to someone. Maybe he's been a good source of information. Maybe that's where some of that money came from."

Dewey said nothing. He had the body language of a man who wanted to leave, but he stayed out of a need to hear what she had to say next.

"I suppose I'll know more when I have that cash dusted for fingerprints," Annie said, and watched the color drain from his face. She turned and looked right at him, noting he was breathing a little faster than before. "Do you want to tell me something, Dewey?"

He shifted his weight from foot to foot and rubbed a hand across his jaw as he contemplated his options. There was no getting out of this if she had the money and the money had his fingerprints on it.

He ran a hand back through his bad haircut and sighed. "All right. I was throwing him a few bucks here and there for information. So what?"

"How much?"

"Fifty bucks here and there. Not no twenty-four-hundred dollars' worth! I don't know where he got all that!"

"For what?" Annie asked. "What kind of information?"

"What else? Drug deals and such."

"And how many drug arrests have you made off this information since he's been back in town?"

"A few."

"Do you think I won't check?"

"Information doesn't always lead directly to an arrest! You should know that."

"So, I'm supposed to believe your CI went missing and you have done basically nothing to find him. You put forth so little effort, his mother gave up on you and came to the SO. Are you a moron, Dewey?" Annie asked. "I don't understand how your brain works."

"I was looking for him!" he insisted. "I told his mother I was looking for him!"

"You told his mother he probably took off. You told me he's probably dead somewhere. Where in all this were you actually looking for him?"

He seemed to be having trouble getting a good deep breath. He couldn't stand still, the nervous energy winding up and up.

"Or do you not need to look for him because you already know where he's at?"

"I don't know where he's at!"

"But . . ." Annie prompted.

He shook his head, not at her, but as if he couldn't believe he was finding himself in this fix.

"You sure as hell know more than what you're telling me," Annie said. "You'd be a damned sight better off telling me all of it now than having to explain yourself to your chief and to Sheriff Noblier later. I'm thinking you wouldn't come out of that with a career intact."

"Oh, fucking hell," he muttered to himself, turning around in a little circle with his hands on top of his head. He was sweating now.

"I'm not trying to gloat here, Dewey," Annie said, "but I've got you by the short curlies. I'm not looking to ruin your life. My only obligation here is finding Robbie Fontenot. So, you might as well spill it."

He sucked in a big deep breath and let it go as he made his decision.

"He told me he could get me information on a ring of copper thieves," he said. "He wanted me to advance him two hundred dollars. I gave him one hundred. He said it might take a few days. When his mother came looking for him, I thought, *Just stall her.* A couple of days turned into a week. I figured he played me for a sucker and he just split. Maybe he did."

Annie said nothing for a moment. Dewey Rivette had let this go on for more than a week. Because he was pissed off. Because he thought he'd been played. If Robbie's offer had been genuine, Rivette had given him money for information on potentially dangerous people, then left him hanging out there because he was mad, and then told everyone who would listen that Robbie Fontenot was gone because he was a worthless drug addict.

"You are something else," Annie muttered, glaring at him. "You left your CI hanging over a hundred bucks. That's what his life is worth to you."

"I still say he left," he said, but without much conviction. He didn't believe that any more than she did.

"You really think he'd take off and leave twenty-four-hundred-fifty dollars in a box in his mother's house?" Annie asked.

He had the grace to look ashamed as he avoided her eye contact. "No."

"Me neither."

She turned to go back into the house.

"What are you gonna do?" Dewey asked.

Annie rounded on him, wishing she had some of her husband's ability to physically intimidate people. Nick would have left Dewey Rivette sitting in a puddle of his own urine. The best she could do was tell him the truth.

"Me, I'm gonna find Robbie Fontenot. And whatever happens to you, I don't really give a shit."

20

THE QUAIL RUN DEVELOPMENT ON THE FAR WEST SIDE OF Bayou Breaux had been one of Donnie Bichon's first successes as a developer. High-quality single-family homes of varying sizes situated on generous lots. Rather than razing the entire building site, the developer had left in place as many mature trees as possible and worked around them. The result had been to give a new development the feeling of an established neighborhood. A decade on, Quail Run looked like it had been there for a generation. And with its brick houses and manicured gardens, it looked a world away from Mercier Salvage.

Nick turned onto Quail Trace and muttered a curse. The street was clogged with local TV news vans, the sidewalk crowded with camera crews and reporters. Locals loitered on the outer edges of the media mess, taking it all in. Across the street, a pair of BBPD uniforms stood outside their radio cars, watching and chatting.

Kiki Mercier's on-air drunken tirade at Our Lady had chummed the waters for the press, her accusations against Melissa stirring their instincts for salacious sensationalism.

Nick hit his siren for a few quick blasts to chase the crowd out of his way and pulled into the Merciers' drive.

The reporters descended on him like a swarm of mosquitoes as he got out of his vehicle.

"Detective Fourcade!"

"Lieutenant Fourcade!"

"Have you identified the body?"

"Is the body Marc Mercier?"

"Are you here to notify the widow?"

"There is no widow I know of," Nick said. "We have not positively identified the body."

"What's taking so long?"

"Why is it taking so long?"

"Why won't Mrs. Mercier speak to us?"

"Mrs. Mercier is under no obligation to speak to you," Nick said. "If y'all had any decency, you would give the family space in this time. Now, stay off this property and do not harass this woman, or your next story will come from inside the Partout Parish jail."

Several of them started to follow him up the sidewalk toward the Merciers' front door. He turned and froze them in place with a look.

"I think most of you know I don't have a sense of humor with this kind of behavior. If you want information, go to the law enforcement center and wait. Sheriff Noblier will be speaking to the media later this afternoon."

"Is Melissa Mercier a suspect?"

"Do you think she killed her husband?"

"Who is the man who spent the night here last night?"

Nick shook his head in disgust and turned his back on them, going to the house and ringing the video doorbell. "Mrs. Mercier, it's Lieutenant Fourcade."

A moment later, the door cracked open and Will Faulkner looked out.

"Thank God," he said. "Come in, please. This has been insane. They've been here all day. Bunch of damn vultures."

"Mr. Faulkner," Nick said, stepping into the foyer.

"Do you have news?"

"Is it Marc?" Melissa asked, emerging from a room down the hall with a red-faced baby on her hip. "Did the dental records match?"

"No," Nick said. "They were unable to make a useful comparison. I'm sorry I can't give you any kind of closure here either way."

"What now?"

"Now we wait for the DNA results."

Melissa drew a shaky breath. She looked like she hadn't slept. Her blond hair was tied back in a messy ponytail. Dark circles ringed her eyes. Whether those dark circles were due to the stress, or the fussy baby, or Will Faulkner, he didn't know.

"This is a nightmare," she said, mostly to herself.

"Why don't we all sit down?" Will suggested, the genial host. "Do you want me to take the baby, Miss?"

"No. I've got her." She hefted the little one up on her hip.

"How old is she?" Nick asked as they moved into a family room where the television over the fireplace was silently showing news coverage of the outside of the house.

"Six months."

"Teething?"

"Yeah."

"She's not letting you get much sleep, then, is she?"

Melissa settled into the corner of a thick tufted love seat the color of caramel with the baby on her lap. "I wouldn't have gotten any last night anyway. That wind! I thought someone was trying to break into the house. And then I got this creepy phone call . . ."

"What was the call?"

"Well, it was nothing," she said. "No one said anything. I don't normally answer if I don't recognize the number, but it was the middle of the night. Who calls in the middle of the night? Emergencies, right? I thought maybe it was something to do with Marc. But I answered and no one said anything. It sounds stupid now, but it scared me. I already thought someone was watching me, and then that. I kept saying hello, but nobody answered, and I thought I could hear the wind and the trees over the phone. It freaked me out. I called Will and asked him to come over."

"You live nearby?" Nick asked.

"Yes. I'm just a few blocks away," Will said, perching a hip on the arm of the love seat beside Melissa. They looked like they were posing for a casual family photo. "I came right over. I looked around the yard, but I didn't see anyone. There was a loose shutter. That was probably the banging noise that woke her."

"Did you recognize the phone number?" Nick asked.

"No. It was a local number, though," Will said. "I called it back on Miss's phone. The call went straight to voicemail. Automated voicemail, you know. There was no name or anything."

"I'll need that number."

"Of course. Where'd you leave your phone, Miss? I'll go get it."

"In the kitchen," Melissa said.

"I was so rattled," she said to Nick. "I didn't want to be alone. Kiki had called about a hundred times last night, drunk, accusing me of everything from adultery to murder. I wouldn't have put it past her to come creeping around. I'm sure it sounds crazy, but I kept thinking she might come in and try to take Madeline. She's obsessed. It's unhealthy."

"More than the average grandmother?" Nick asked.

"If you've been around her for more than ten minutes, you know how she is about Marc. Marc this, Marc that. Maddie is an extension of Marc. You'd think he hatched her and I had nothing to do with it at all. That would certainly make Kiki happy if it were true." She laughed. "What am I saying? She's delusional and irrational. I wouldn't put anything past her."

"We think Kiki might have given this address to the media," Will said, returning from the kitchen with Melissa's cell phone. "Marc and Miss are unlisted. They rent the house from me. How'd they find this address without someone telling them?"

"Can't you do anything about those people?" Melissa asked. "They've been out there since this morning."

"I called the police," Will said. "But they're out there doing nothing."

"If the reporters don't come on your property and they aren't making a public nuisance, there's not much we can do," Nick said. "The sheriff is giving a press briefing in a couple of hours. They'll decamp for that. In the meantime, don't engage them. Their airtime is money, so if they're not getting anything for their trouble, they'll have to move on. Right now, they're mostly interested in you, Will."

"In me?"

"Mrs. Mercier's husband is missing, and another man spent the night in his house. Whatever your relationship may be in fact, the optics are not good."

"We're not sleeping together," Will said, looking him dead in the eyes.

"All they know is what they see and what they're told," Nick said. "Their imaginations fill in the blanks however they will. And people are all too happy to go down that road."

"This town," Melissa muttered.

"Is like any small town anywhere," Nick said. "Gossip is an Olympic sport."

"I was frightened," Melissa said, tears rising. "And I called the *one* friend I have in this shithole place!"

She started to cry, and Will Faulkner put a hand on her shoulder and let her lean into him. If they weren't a couple, they should have been, Nick thought. The ease they had with each other was natural. Faulkner was automatically protective of her and deferential toward her. It was hard to believe there wasn't something more to the relationship, but at the same time, they didn't seem to be trying to hide anything.

It was clear the Mercier marriage had been in trouble before Marc's disappearance. If Marc was, as Luc suggested, just off having a temper tantrum, he had left the door wide open for Will Faulkner and Melissa to find their way together.

Luc had suggested Faulkner was gay, but that might just have been his redneck bias against a successful, educated, white-collar city guy.

"This is the number," Will said, reading it off.

Nick typed it into a text to Wynn Dixon with *find out whose number this is ASAP*. Wynn responded instantly with a thumbs-up emoji.

"Do you have security cameras on the house?" he asked.

"Just the doorbell," Melissa said.

Will shook his head in irritation. "I called my security people this morning. They'll be here tomorrow to put cameras up."

"Have you spoken with any of Marc's friends?" Nick asked.

"The few that I know," Melissa said, wiping her tears away. The baby fussed and reached out a chubby hand, trying to grab the tissue. "No one knows anything. Or they're not telling me. I've tried five times to call his buddy Dozer. He doesn't answer. His voicemail is full."

"I spoke with Dozer today," Nick said. "He says he lost his cell phone Halloween night."

"I called everyone I could think of who might know Marc, even a little bit," Will said. "No one had any answers. A bunch of people saw him at Monster Bash, but that's more than a week ago."

"What about Robbie Fontenot?" Nick asked. "He and Marc went to school together. Do either of you know him?"

"I don't know him," Will said. "I know his mother to say hello. We've been trying to get her to let us add her home to the annual charity house tour for some years. She lives over on Belle Terre. Gorgeous old Queen Anne house. But she's a very private person. I don't know the son other than by reputation—which is not good, as I'm sure you know."

"Melissa? Have you ever heard Marc mention Robbie?"

She shook her head. "I'd never heard of him until the news yesterday. Is he somehow connected?"

"We don't know. They just both happen to be missing at the same time. So far, I've found no recent connection between the two," Nick said. "Will, if you can get me a list of the people you spoke to who saw Marc at Monster Bash, I'd appreciate that."

"Yeah. No problem," Faulkner said. "People keep asking me if there's a search party they can join."

"Until we have some idea where to look, there's no sense in organizing a search," Nick said. "For now, we've got the Wildlife agents and the sheriff's office boats on the lookout. The second we have some clue as to a specific area, we'll deploy all the search resources we have. We're in the process of getting Marc's cell phone records today. That might give us a starting point."

"I'll tell you what," Will said. "If Marc's not the one lying in the morgue, I will personally kick his ass when he comes back. Putting Melissa through this—and the rest of us . . . So irresponsibly thoughtless. And you know, as much as I like Marc, he can be spoiled and selfish, and here we are.

"I don't mean for that to sound like I wish him ill," he hastened to add.

"Of course not," Nick said. "It's normal, what you're feeling, that swing of emotions. Sometimes that anger saves you from despair."

The baby gave a little squeal of frustration and started to cry even as she tried to stick her fist in her mouth. Will plucked her off Melissa's lap and started walking her around the room, bouncing her on his arm like an old pro, making silly faces at her in an attempt to distract her from her discomfort.

Nick rose. "I'll have a look around your yard, then I'll leave you. If I get any information, I'll be in touch. And you both have my number if you need me."

He went out the French doors into the fenced yard and walked the perimeter. Tall hedges all around created a private retreat decorated with rosebushes and climbing vines. An old live oak gave shade—and cover, he thought. Someone standing in its shadows had a good view of the house with three sets of French doors and no draperies. At night with the interior lights on, it would be like watching a giant television. But if anyone had been out there the night before, they had left no obvious signs.

He let himself out a small unlocked gate near the garage. As soon as the reporters saw him, they started rushing up the driveway.

"Stop!" he barked. "Stay off this property. I'm not fucking around. I can have deputies here in two minutes, and your bosses will be dishing out bail money."

"There's police officers right across the street," someone pointed out.

"They appear to be largely ornamental," Nick said. "My deputies will be the real deal. Mind your manners."

He went to his vehicle and shut out their voices, starting the engine and kicking the AC on high just for the white noise.

His phone vibrated from the arrival of a text from Wynn. The name belonging to the phone number Will Faulkner had given him. The number from the call that had terrified Melissa Mercier in the middle of the night.

Robert Fontenot III.

21

THE CALL HAD COME TO MELISSA MERCIER'S PHONE AT 2:04 IN the morning.

"Why?" Annie asked aloud. "Why would Robbie Fontenot call her? Why would he even have her number?"

"She says she never heard of Robbie Fontenot until she saw him on the news last night," Nick said. "She was up when that call came in because she thought she heard someone trying to break into the house. Then she decided it was just the wind and a loose shutter. Will Faulkner says he walked around the yard when he came over—which would have been around two fifteen. He didn't see anything suspicious. I looked. I didn't see anything. But the yard is not secure, and there's no security cameras on the house."

"I think my brain has whiplash," Annie muttered, rubbing her forehead, wincing as she touched the bruise on her cut eyebrow.

They sat in the conference room of the Pizza Hut, where they had organized the whiteboards for each of their three cases. The room was filled with the intoxicating aroma of the building's namesake coming from a stack of boxes on the table. One veggie, one cheese, one sausage, one pepperoni. Four large pizzas for six detectives, but the boxes would be mostly empty before the night was over. Leftovers would be had for breakfast the next day.

"It looks like the phone has been turned off pretty much since Halloween night," Wynn said. "Location services are turned off. It pinged off that cell tower west of town last night for the one phone call and went dark again."

"So, maybe someone was there in that yard after all," Nick said.

"And he called Marc Mercier's wife, in the middle of the night, and said nothing," Annie said. "Why? Just to freak her out? And again, why?"

"I don't know," Nick said. "I wanted to put a deputy on that house tonight, but Gus shot me down. He's trying to play nice with Johnny Earl, who took exception to me saying his officers were largely ornamental."

"Truth hurts."

"I suppose they're capable of sitting in a car and watching a house all night, if that keeps the peace." He turned toward Wynn. "What about Marc Mercier's phone?"

"Dark since Saturday evening. No calls. Location services off."

"What was his last call?"

"To his brother at about six thirty in the evening."

"And then he turned his phone off," Nick said. "Why? Who does that? He went home for supper. He went out somewhere. He was supposed to meet his brother the next morning. Why wouldn't he have his phone on?"

"The world was better for us when people were ignorant about their electronics," Annie said, helping herself to a slice of sausage pizza. "Watch one *Dateline* marathon on TV and you'll know enough to turn your phone off if you're up to something."

"What's he up to, though?" Nick asked. "And what's your guy up to with his phone off?"

"Nothing good. I found a pile of money in a box in his old

bedroom at his mom's house. Twenty-four hundred and then some. A guy with no legit job."

"Is he dealing?"

"I haven't found any evidence of it or anybody to say it's so. Deebo doesn't think so. But I did get Dewey Rivette to confess he's been running Robbie as a CI. Although he swears he never gave Robbie all that money. And really, where would Dewey get that kind of cash to throw around? Fifty here and there. A hundred right before Robbie disappeared. That, I can believe. He claims Robbie told him he could get info on some copper thieves, then he dropped out of sight," she said. "And now he's driving around in the middle of the night, calling up the wife of a guy he went to high school with a decade ago? I don't get that."

"No one in Marc's world knows of any connection between Marc and Robbie in recent memory," Nick said. "But the Merciers are in the junk business. Everyone says they're on the up-and-up, but they may well know people who aren't."

He went to the whiteboard and wrote COPPER?? under both Marc Mercier's name and Robbie Fontenot's.

"The brothers had a fight Saturday morning," he said. "Came to blows. All Luc will say is that they disagree on how to run the business. He wants Marc gone so he can run things his way. Maybe what he wants to do isn't legal. Robbie Fontenot is shopping around info on copper thieves. Maybe that's the connection."

"It still doesn't explain why Robbie would call Marc's wife at two in the morning."

"*Mais non*. Did you look at any of that bank video from Monster Bash?" Nick asked.

Annie sighed her frustration. "I've looked at about an hour's worth so far. Do you know how many people were in that parking lot that night? Most of them in costumes. I counted five dressed as cops, which makes me wonder if what Donnie Bichon saw was even really a city officer. And the quality of the video isn't bad, but it's hard to make out faces the farther they are away from the camera. I can't say I saw Robbie Fontenot. I've only seen him in a photograph. I don't know how he carries himself, what gestures he uses."

"You might need to have the mother look at the footage," Nick said.

"I want to see the video from the camera on the other side of the parking lot first," Annie said. "The different angle might help.

"I asked Danny Perry if he saw Robbie that night, and he got cute about it. No, unless there's video, and then maybe he did, but if he did, it wasn't any big deal. He probably thinks he's protecting Dewey, but that ship has sailed. Dewey's gonna be working security at the lamp factory if I have anything to say about it. He put Robbie Fontenot in harm's way then turned his back on him."

"I asked Dozer Cormier if he'd seen Robbie Fontenot," Nick said. "He tried to act like he didn't know who I was talking about."

He turned to Wynn Dixon. "Wynn, when you go through the call logs, look for any contact between those three numbers: Mercier, Fontenot, and Cormier."

"Got it."

"We've got no legal cause to get Dozer Cormier's phone records, but his number will show up as incoming calls on theirs, at least."

Deebo Jeffcoat walked into the conference room looking like a vagrant in dirty, baggy trousers and an untucked flannel shirt, and made a beeline for the pizza. He took a slice of pepperoni and a slice of veggie and put the slices face-to-face, making a giant pizza sandwich.

"All my food groups right here," he said with a big, satisfied smile as he held his creation up like a prize, then lowered the pointy end into his mouth and took a bite big enough to choke a horse.

"Deebo, you have the metabolism of a fruit fly," Annie said. "I'm jealous."

"Well, there's gotta be some upside to being a scrawny runt," he said, wiping the grease from his scraggly beard with a napkin.

"I have something for you," Annie said, holding up the evidence bag with the drugs from Rayanne Tillis's bedroom.

Deebo set his supper aside and squinted at the bag, his expression sobering. "Where'd you get this?"

"I had a girl—a possible witness—OD this afternoon over on Opelousas near the Mardi Gras warehouse," Annie said. "Do you know what it is?"

"I know exactly what it is," he said, taking the bag and turning it over. "They're calling it Diablo, for the letter D on the pill. It's counterfeit Oxy that's coming up out of Mexico. It's laced with fentanyl. Bad, bad stuff."

"Where would a girl with no money come by that?"

"Santa Claus?" he suggested. "The Easter Bunny? The Great Pumpkin? This shit is expensive. Fifty bucks a pill so you can feel extra fancy while you die from it. They're not giving out free samples of this at Costco, I'll tell you that."

"So, if she didn't pay cash for this," Annie said, "then someone gave it to her for a reason. As payment for something, or as a lovely parting gift to send her on to the next life."

"This was the girl you picked up yesterday, caught stealing?" Nick said.

"Yes. Rayanne Tillis."

"Ah, man," Deebo said. "Rayanne's dead?"

"You knew her?"

"Picked her up more than once myself. She was no stranger to a jail cell. Possession, prostitution, shoplifting. Mean as cat meat, but she could be funny when she wasn't fucked up. That's a shame."

"Who would want to kill that girl?" Nick asked. "What threat could she be to anyone?"

"She was talking to me," Annie said. "Mind you, she hadn't actually told me anything useful yet. But now she never will."

"What could she know that would be worth killing her over?"

Annie swiveled her chair, contemplating what she was about to say.

"I was asking her yesterday about anyone she might have seen coming and going from Robbie Fontenot's house. I asked her had she seen the town cops going in there. I asked because I didn't believe they'd done much. And she said, 'Oh, yeah, 'cause I should rat out cops.'"

Everyone was silent for a beat. Finally, Nick said, "That's a serious accusation, 'Toinette."

"I'm not accusing anyone of anything," she said. "This is the sequence of events. That's what she said. This is what happened. A man was seen leaving her house last night about one fifteen in the morning. Someone brought her those drugs, and now she's dead. That's what I know."

"That could also be a drug buddy or a john she partied with, and she just lost the opioid roulette game this time," Deebo said. "Was there any sign anyone forced her to take those pills?"

"No," Annie admitted. "And she was still alive when I found her around noon. So the guy was long gone before she took the fatal dose. But if someone gave her those pills probably knowing full well how dangerous they are . . ."

"But that's not a secret," Deebo said. "Narcotics are inherently dangerous. It's not like she didn't know that. It's not like she thought she was popping breath mints. Addicts take drugs and die from it. That's just a sad fact."

"All right," Nick said on a sigh. "Let's put a pin in this for now and see what plays out. If it's about Robbie Fontenot, we're gonna get to the bottom of that anyway. What'd you find out about that drug house, Deebo?"

"That house is owned by a trust," Deebo said.

Annie squinted at him. "A falling-down house in that neighborhood is owned by a trust? Are gangs getting that sophisticated now?"

"Hell no. They just take what they want. Ravenwood Trust. The trustee is listed as a Kenneth Wood of Baton Rouge. That's as far as I got. There's no anecdotal information on any major drug dealing in that neighborhood. It's not like the old days when dealers staked out a corner and did their thing. Nowadays people text their orders and pay with Venmo."

"Y'all are gonna wanna kiss me full on the mouth!" Chaz Stokes announced as he walked into the room, arms wide, like a triumphant hero.

"Who's he talking to?" Wynn asked.

"Doesn't matter," Annie said. "No one here is taking him up on it."

"I'd do it on a bet," Deebo offered. "What'll you give me?"

"A punch in the mouth," Stokes said, scowling.

Deebo shrugged. "Your loss. I'm a really good kisser."

"I'd be waiting for something to crawl up out of that beard and bite me."

"Whatever you're into, man!" Deebo laughed. "Let your freak flag fly, Chaz Stokes!"

"You're hilarious, you are," Stokes said. "Have you eaten all the pizza yet, you human garbage disposal?"

"You snooze, you lose."

"What are we supposed to be so grateful for?" Nick asked.

Stokes pointed a finger at him. "Boss, I told you this was gonna come down to a chick, and I was right."

He dug a slice of pepperoni out of the box and sat down on the credenza.

"Marc Mercier was at that country bar, Outlaw," he said between bites, "on the south side of Luck Saturday night, dancing with the wrong girl, and her husband took exception. They had a little dustup."

"Is there video?" Nick asked.

"Oh, yeah. I emailed a copy to myself."

"Let's go see it."

Stokes wolfed down the last of his pizza on the walk back to the bullpen, then made a show of sitting down behind his keyboard like he was some kind of piano virtuoso sitting down to play at Carnegie Hall, cracking his knuckles before reaching for his mouse.

"This should be good," Deebo said. "Now the boss gets to see all the Pornhub emails Chaz gets sent to his work computer."

"Give me a little credit, please," Chaz said. "I've got a fake account for that."

"I catch you looking at porn in this office, you and your Johnson are parting ways," Nick grumbled.

"Damn, Nicky," Stokes complained. "No one ruins a joke quite like you."

He opened his email and clicked on the attachment.

The camera in the bar was situated high up on a wall, giving a broad view of the dance floor. People were dancing, smiling, laughing, passing a good time on a Saturday night as people in south Louisiana were wont to do.

"This is Marc Mercier, right here," Stokes said, reaching a finger toward the monitor.

He was dancing with a curvy little blonde, who was laughing and smiling, her thick braid bouncing over her shoulder down the front of her tight T-shirt.

"And here comes the angry husband," Chaz said, pointing to a male coming across from the far side of the room, making a beeline to the dancers.

He was tall, athletic-looking, with broad shoulders and trim hips. He clamped a hand on the girl's shoulder and yanked her back away from her dance partner, shouting something in her face. The girl cringed away like a whipped dog.

Annie felt a sickening chill run through her.

The angry husband surged in front of his wife to get in Marc Mercier's face. Mercier didn't back down. They were evenly matched for size. A pair of young bulls intent on squaring off. Words were exchanged but couldn't be heard. Then shoves were exchanged. The husband threw a punch, landing hard enough to snap Mercier's head around before a bouncer intervened.

"And who is this guy?" Nick asked.

Annie answered before Chaz could draw breath. "That's Cody Parcelle."

22

"THIS IS MY CASE," STOKES GRUMBLED. "I COULD TALK TO THE wife myself."

Annie rolled her eyes. "Her name is Tulsie, and I already have a relationship with her. If you weren't such a damn *couillon*, you'd see that this is a good thing. I'm helping you. You should mark this day on your calendar. I'm happy to leave Cody to you, but you won't get anything out of this girl. She doesn't know you."

"I talk girls into saying things all the time. I'm actually very good at it."

"Yeah. '*Ooh, ah, you're so good!*' doesn't really count."

"Very funny."

"I know you're a big hit with horny drunk women at the Voodoo Lounge, but I'm invested in this girl, Chaz. I don't want her withdrawing because she's feeling overwhelmed by a male detective she doesn't know."

"The least you could do was let me drive," he pouted.

"Oh, my God, you're such a child," Annie snapped. "You don't even know where we're going! And you're too much of a *tête dure* to ask for directions. We'd be driving around in circles all night. I should have made you and your ego ride in a separate car."

She hit the blinker and turned off the main road to the gravel road that led to the Parcelles' place. "Tulsie and her hired hand both told me Cody left for Houston Sunday morning. And he for sure gave her a beating as a parting gift. Now we know why."

"I take it this isn't the first time."

"No. I got called out here a while ago. She wouldn't press charges. I told her this morning she should think about leaving him. She didn't want to hear it."

"They never do. What's wrong with women, putting up with that shit?"

"Mostly they're more scared of what will happen to them without the guy than they are scared of the guy himself," Annie said. "You know, people have a hard time envisioning their own death. They don't really think it'll ever happen. It's like that OD I had today. That girl knew plenty of people who died taking drugs. She did it anyway. She never thought it'd be her dead on the floor. Tulsie still believes she can navigate around Cody's temper and keep the rest of her life in place."

The lights were on in the barn as they came up the Circle P driveway. Annie pulled in alongside the old white Chevy truck with the rusted wheel wells as the dogs came running, singing their song of greeting.

The Chicks were playing on the radio as she and Stokes walked in—"Set Me Free." Izzy Guidry was grooming the little palomino Tulsie had been riding in the morning. Tulsie was in the aisle struggling to unfold a stable sheet with her one good arm. She looked up with shock, her gaze darting from Annie to Stokes and back.

"Hey, Tulsie," Annie said. "This is Detective Stokes. Sorry to interrupt your evening."

"What's going on?"

"We need to ask you some questions about Cody. Is there somewhere we can go sit down and talk?"

"Is Cody all right?" Izzy asked, abandoning her task and stepping out of the grooming bay into the aisle. "Did something happen to him?"

"Oh, my God," Tulsie said. "Was he in a car wreck or something?"

"No," Annie said. "Nothing like that."

"Well, you can ask me here, can't you? We're trying to get the horses tucked in for the night. It's supposed to get cold tonight."

"I'll get their blankets on," Izzy said. "You can go in the lounge."

"Right," Tulsie said. "Okay. We can go right in here."

The lounge was directly across from the grooming area, a small room with barnwood walls and a grouping of a beat-up leather couch and a pair of armchairs, their worn upholstery covered with saddle blankets. The overhead light was a fake wagon wheel set with fake lanterns. Tulsie went to a corner of the couch and tucked herself into it. She looked terrified.

"You're scaring me," she admitted.

"I don't want you to be scared, Tulsie," Annie said, taking a seat. "You haven't done anything wrong. We just have some questions. We've seen a video from Outlaw, from Saturday night."

"Oh."

"Yeah. You wanna tell us what went on there?"

She gave a nervous little laugh and dodged eye contact. "Well, it wasn't what it looked like. It was just . . ."

"Just start from the beginning," Annie said. "You and Cody went out . . ."

"No, actually, it was a girls' night with a couple friends. Cody didn't want me to go, but it was my friend Celeste's night out to celebrate her divorce—which Cody didn't think was anything anyone should celebrate, so he was mad about it, and he didn't want me to go. But then I got mad, and I went anyway, which I shouldn't have done. I should have just stayed home. Cody's been working extra hours, nights lately, and he was tired, and I just should have stayed home with him. So, it's my fault what happened."

"So you and your girlfriends went dancing at Outlaw . . ."

"Yeah, and we were just dancing with a bunch of different people. Guys that we knew. It didn't mean anything. We were just having fun."

"So, you know Marc Mercier?" Stokes asked.

"I know him through Cody. The Parcelles do construction. They take down old houses and do remodels and stuff, so they do business with the Merciers all the time, selling them the salvage. Cody and Marc have been friendly since Marc came back to town. I didn't think he'd mind so much. We were just dancing."

"So why did Cody show up if he didn't want to go out?" Annie asked, already knowing the answer.

Tulsie shrugged with her good shoulder and looked down at a scratch on the leather couch, trying to rub it away with a fingertip.

"He doesn't trust you?"

She kept her head down, fighting the rise of tears. "He just gets jealous. That's just how he is," she said in a tiny voice. "It's just because he wants me all to himself. He doesn't want other guys thinking that they could have me, 'cause I'm his."

She was his, a piece of property, his toy to play with and no one else's. She didn't own herself, wasn't supposed to think or feel or do anything separate from him. She was a possession. As demure as she was being in her explanation, Annie had no doubt there was a side of Tulsie that rebelled, at least internally, a side that pushed at Cody's boundaries and probably even goaded him a little. She was a cute, sassy little thing with a flirty smile, and Cody Parcelle had not ground that out of her altogether. Yet.

"So Cody came looking for you," Stokes said. "And he and Marc got into it."

"It was so stupid," Tulsie said, rolling her eyes. "We were just having fun dancing. Marc's married, too. Nothing was gonna happen. But Cody had been drinking, and he gets mean when he drinks. He's not really like that."

"It looked like Cody hit Marc pretty hard," Stokes said. "And then the bouncer broke it up. What happened then?"

"They both got thrown out."

"Did they keep fighting in the parking lot?"

"No. Cody was just mouthing off."

"What'd he say?"

"Just dumb stuff. Dumb stuff boys say trying to sound tough."

"Like what?"

She hesitated, clearly not comfortable with repeating the words.

"We'll be interviewing other people who were there, Tulsie," Annie said. "You might as well tell us."

The girl swiped a tear from her cheek. "He told Marc if he ever caught him messing around with me again he'd kill him. He didn't mean it," she hastened to add. "He would never do that."

The guy who had beaten the shit out of her on more than one occasion would never be violent. Annie couldn't stop herself from shaking her head a little.

"Marc just walked away and left."

"And what did you and Cody do?" Annie asked.

"I went home," she said simply, though Annie was willing to bet there had been nothing simple about it. When they interviewed other bar patrons who had been there, they were going to say the couple had fought. Cody had probably ordered her to go home, and she had gone, knowing full well he wasn't done taking his anger out on her.

"And Cody?" Stokes asked. "Did he go home, too?"

"No. Not right away."

"What time did he get home?"

"Around two, two thirty."

Ample time for him to have gone after Marc Mercier to settle the demented jealous score in his head.

"Mrs. Parcelle, does your husband own a shotgun?" Stokes asked.

Tulsie pressed her hand across her mouth as if to keep from crying out and squeezed her eyes closed tight. She nodded.

"Do you know where it is?"

"In his truck," she said, her breath hitching unevenly. She pulled her feet up on the couch, tucking herself into a ball, making herself as small as possible.

"Have you talked to your husband today?" Stokes asked.

She shook her head. "He doesn't want me to bother him when he's away."

"We'll need his cell number," Stokes said.

Annie moved from the chair to the couch, to be a little nearer, a silent show of support. "We just need to talk to him," she said. "He'll need to fill in that timeline. If he hasn't done anything, it won't be a problem."

Tulsie started to cry in earnest, as if her world was ending right then and there. Annie slipped an arm around her shoulders.

"It'll be all right," she said quietly, though that seemed unlikely.

"Tulsie," she asked, knowing this was the moment to press, but hating doing it, just the same, "when Cody got home that night, did he hurt you?"

Nodding, the girl turned into her, buried her face in Annie's shoulder, and sobbed her heart out.

Dozer Cormier lived in a single-wide trailer in the Country Estates mobile home park halfway between Bayou Breaux and Luck. It was definitely in the country, but there was nothing estate-like about it. The collection of old mobile homes squatted over five acres like so many rusty metal toadstools. The most impressive thing about the place was that it had somehow managed not to be swept away by a tornado or a flood in forty-odd years.

Lights were on in Dozer's place. Nick pulled in alongside a nice tricked-out white Chevy Silverado pickup truck that was easily worth more than the house it was parked in front of. Good ol' boy priorities.

Dozer answered the door in boxer shorts and a Ragin' Cajuns T-shirt that didn't quite accommodate his belly. His eyes went round at the sight of Nick.

"Expecting company?" Nick asked, arching a brow at the getup.

"What the hell do you want?" Dozer asked. His breath reeked of beer and boudin sausage.

"I have a couple more questions for you, Mr. Cormier. May I come in?"

"Why?"

"Because me, I think you may not want your neighbors to look out their windows and see you being questioned by a sheriff's detective on your front porch. I've been all over the news lately. They might get the wrong idea about you."

"Fuck 'em," Dozer said, but he stepped back just the same.

The trailer stank of decades of cigarette smoke that had soaked into the acoustic tile ceiling and the cheap fake wood paneling. Dozer stood in the middle of the kitchen looking like a giant in a dollhouse. The seven-foot ceilings barely cleared the top of his bald head. For sure he had to duck to get through the doorways. He probably had to walk sideways to get down the hall to the bedrooms.

"Mr. Bichon, he's gonna be disappointed in you, Dozer," Nick said, nodding at the collection of beer cans on the kitchen table.

Dozer frowned. "Ain't against the law to have a beer."

"*Mais non*, it's not. But he's under the impression you're walking the straight and narrow during the week so you can give your best while working for him, the man who wants to take a chance on you. And here you are, clearly under the influence on a Tuesday night, and it ain't even hardly past suppertime. You gonna go through another six-pack before you pass out? Mr. Bichon gonna be sad to hear it."

"Why would you tell him?" Dozer asked, leaning back against the kitchen counter to disguise the fact that he wasn't quite steady on his feet.

"Because me, I'm an asshole," Nick said bluntly. "You don't give me some straight answers, I'm gonna fuck up your life any way I can."

"Answers about what? I already told you, I don't know nothing! I ain't done nothing wrong!"

"Really, though?" Nick asked making a face. "I think maybe I just haven't looked hard enough yet."

He looked down at the family room end of the trailer, where an enormous flat-screen TV showing *Wheel of Fortune* took up almost the entire end of the narrow room.

"You see, I pull up next to that fancy truck outside. That's gotta be what? Forty, fifty grand? And then I come in here and you got that big-screen TV. Watching football on that gotta be like sitting on the fifty-yard line. Those are some expensive toys. And I'm gonna bet you got a boat somewhere, too."

"So? I got a good job, me. Ain't none of your business how I spend my money!"

"Yeah, well, all these toys look like more than you make hammering nails," Nick said, though he didn't truly find it all that suspicious. Dozer Cormier wasn't wasting his money on his accommodations or on an expensive wardrobe. He wasn't wearing a Rolex or diamond-crusted neck chains. He didn't have a wife or children to eat up his income. He spent his earnings on the things that mattered to him—his truck and his sports—like many a young man in these parts.

"You got a second income, Dozer?" he asked, just to keep digging. Just to make him nervous. "You got a side job? You might be more ambitious than anyone gives you credit for."

Cormier looked away. "I don't know what you're talking about."

"Copper. That's what I'm talking about," Nick said, prowling around the room, making a show of looking at random pieces of mail on the kitchen table, spying a little burner cell phone half hidden by a take-out menu from a Cajun restaurant in Luck.

Dozer stepped over and snatched away a pile of junk mail. "Quit touching my stuff!"

Nick gave him a hard look. "You want me to go get a warrant and come back here in a bad mood?"

There was nothing in this house he had the least bit of interest in. Nor did he expect there was much worth finding with regard to his case. It was an empty threat made for no other reason than to make Dozer Cormier uncomfortable.

"I want you to fuck the fuck off," Dozer said, taking a menacing step toward him. Everyone Nick had spoken to had said Dozer could make bad choices when he was drinking, that he could get mean and reckless, and there he was.

Nick stood his ground and smiled. "You gonna try to intimidate me, Dozer? Because I'll tell you right now, I don't care that you're the size of a goddamn elephant. You don't scare me."

Cormier didn't know what to make of that. He had six inches and 150 pounds on Nick. How could a man that much smaller than him, and a dozen or more years older, not be intimidated by him?

"You can't bully me, Dozer," Nick said. "And no matter how mean you think you are, you will never in your wildest dreams be meaner than I am."

But he was just drunk enough to take another step forward. With two quick moves, Nick swept the big man's feet out from under him and landed him on his ass on the kitchen floor with a thud that shook the house.

"You just had to, didn't you?" Nick said, shaking his head. "Now we'll see if you're smart enough to learn a lesson. I'll give you that one for free, but you need to rethink your attitude here, Dozer. I guarantee you do not want me for an enemy."

"I wouldn't want you for a friend, either," Dozer grumbled, heaving himself up off the floor. He staggered a step to the table, picked up an open can of Michelob, and drained it.

"Why are you drinking so much?" Nick asked. "Your crew boss says you've been a bit off these days. He's keeping that from Donnie Bichon, you know. Giving you a chance to straighten up. Is something bothering you? You seem stressed. What's that about?"

"Nothing," Dozer said, scowling. It was clear he wanted to get physically away, but there was nowhere for him to go unless he retreated down the hall. Nick blocked his way out of the kitchen, and now he at least knew enough not to test that boundary again.

"Have you gotten yourself into something you can't get out of?"

"No."

"Are you and Marc mixed up in something?"

"No! Like what?"

"Here's the thing, Dozer: I'm looking for Marc Mercier, who runs a salvage business that for sure deals in copper. You work for Donnie Bichon, who tells me he's getting materials ripped off on a regular basis. And I'm looking for Robbie Fontenot, who told a cop he might have a line on some copper thieves. And as it happens, y'all know each other. And that all smells about as good to me as this house trailer."

"If you don't like it here, leave."

"Are you stealing from Donnie?"

"No!"

"And then there's Marc driving around in his fancy new Ford Raptor, pulling a boat I couldn't afford," Nick went on. "Is Marc dealing in stolen copper?"

"How would I know? I don't work for him. Ask Luc. If anybody's up to something, it'd be him. Marc's a straight shooter. Everybody knows that."

"Well, everybody says it, at least," Nick said. "What about Robbie Fontenot?"

"I told you, I haven't seen him."

"I know what you told me, Dozer. That don't mean I believe you."

"Nothing I can do about that."

"No, but you should know that my detectives are even now looking at surveillance video from downtown from Monster Bash. They will look at every store video, every bar video, every Ring doorbell video, every cell phone video taken by a citizen. And if they find even ten seconds of video with you, Marc, and Robbie together, you will have some serious explaining to do."

"We wouldn't hang out with him," Dozer said. "We ain't been friends in years."

"Because you ruined his life?" Nick asked bluntly.

Dozer looked at the floor. "That was an accident."

"Doesn't really matter, does it? Damage is damage. Does he hold a grudge?"

"I wouldn't know," Dozer said. "Can you leave now? I need to use the bathroom."

"I'm not done. You told me you went out with Marc Saturday night," Nick said. "Where'd you go?"

"I don't remember."

Nick took a big deep breath and huffed an impatient sigh. "Mr. Cormier, my people will go to every fucking rathole bar in this parish until they find out where you were Saturday night. But the more work you make us do, the less friendly I get. Now, did you go to Outlaw Saturday night with Marc?"

"No. I don't dance."

"How embarrassing," Nick remarked. "A Cajun boy who can't dance. How'd that happen?" He shook his head at the shame of it. "Did you talk to Marc after he'd been there?"

"I don't remember."

"Really? He got in a fight over a girl, got punched in the face, and he got thrown out of the bar. I think you'd remember him telling you that."

"Then he must not have."

"Do you know Cody Parcelle?"

"Yeah. What about him?"

"Cody Parcelle busted Marc right in the mouth for dancing with his wife."

Dozer shrugged. "Am I supposed to care?"

"You maybe should, yeah," Nick said, "'cause you're telling me you haven't heard from your best friend since Saturday night, when he apparently dumped your sorry ass to go dancing, and the last anyone saw of him was him getting punched in the face and thrown out of a bar, and now some people think he's lying in the morgue at

Our Lady with his face shot off with a shotgun. So yeah, me, I think you would care about that. You have a curious lack of response, Mr. Cormier. I wonder why that is."

"Maybe we're not as close as you think," Dozer said.

"Maybe you're the one killed him," Nick said, mostly just to see the reaction.

The shock on Dozer's face seemed genuine. "What?! No! No fucking way! Are you out of your head? Why would I kill Marc?"

"I don't know. Maybe you were mad he went dancing without you. Maybe you were mad he didn't invite you to go hunting Sunday. You've demonstrated to me here tonight that you have a temper when you drink, you're impulsive, and you don't make the best choices."

"Jesus fucking Christ," the big man muttered to himself, turning around in the kitchen as if to look for witnesses to this madness. "You're crazy, Fourcade."

"You're not the first to say it," Nick remarked. "But a lot of them that did, they're sitting in prison now. So the joke is on them, yeah?"

He smiled that unnerving, predatory smile.

A fine sheen of sweat glazed Cormier's bald head. "I need to go to the bathroom," he said, looking longingly down the dark hall.

The little burner phone on the table began to vibrate, and Dozer's face dropped.

"And there's that phone you told me you don't have," Nick said. He picked it up and tossed it across to Cormier, who caught it like he was catching a hand grenade.

"You really shouldn't lie to me, Dozer," Nick said. "That's not gonna work out for you."

Dozer stared at the phone like it might explode.

"Aren't you gonna answer?"

"No. They'll call back," he said stupidly.

"I bet they will," Nick said, moving toward the door. "If it turns out to be Marc, you give him my regards and tell him to call his wife."

23

"**THE FIGHT** AT OUTLAW TOOK PLACE AROUND ELEVEN THIRTY Saturday night," Stokes said, snagging the last cold piece of sausage pizza from the box. "They both got thrown out of the bar. They both went somewhere else. The wife went home. She says Cody got home around two, two thirty. Plenty of time in that window to get up to all kinds of mischief."

Nick poured himself a cup of coffee and took a long pull on it. He'd sent Annie on to pick up Justin from her cousin Remy and get him tucked into bed at a reasonable hour. She'd gone without argument, emotionally drained from the day. Nick had stayed to make some notes and get the debriefing from Stokes on the Parcelles. It was just the two of them now in the conference room.

"I tried calling Cody Parcelle," Stokes said. "The call went straight to voicemail and the mailbox was full. I tried calling the uncle in Houston, same thing. Tried calling the sales office for the auction, and they were closed for the night."

"If you can't get him or the uncle first thing in the morning," Nick said, "call the local sheriff's office there. They can send a deputy to the sales barn."

"You really think he'd kill a man for dancing with his wife?"

"I don't know. We don't know what the history there might be. Maybe that wasn't the first time. We know they did business together as well. Maybe he already had a beef with him. I know we need to talk to him."

"What about that business card on the corpse?" Stokes asked. "If that was an estimate Mercier gave—"

"I've thought about that," Nick said. "That could just as easily have been a price someone gave to Marc about something they wanted to sell to him as it was a price Marc offered someone else."

"But if Parcelle killed Mercier, do you think he just went on to Houston?" Stokes asked. "Just going on with his life like nothing ever happened?"

"People do. All the time," Nick said. "Murder is an anomaly. Some people would rather pretend it never happened than deal with the fact that they did something so terrible. Get rid of the body and go on with their lives. Hope nobody figures it out. After a while, they convince themselves it never happened, like it was just a bad dream."

"I'd get the hell out of Dodge and never come back," Stokes said. "I'm thinking I'd be long gone to Mexico."

"He might have done that, too."

"The place we found the body," Stokes said, "that's not but a few miles from the Parcelle place. On their way home from Luck. Still seems a careless place to dump a corpse."

"It's not a bad place to put a boat in the water," Nick pointed out. "If you wanted to take that body out and dump it, you can get to the middle of nowhere pretty quick from there by boat. Does Cody Parcelle have a boat?"

"I don't know. But we know Marc has a boat. Where's that at?"

"That's a good question. He went out with Dozer that night, and then he went on his own to Outlaw. He wasn't dragging that boat around with him all night, was he? Who would do that? Is there video from the parking lot?"

"Not beyond the immediate vicinity of the front porch. The place is made to look like one of those Old West saloons in the movies. It's got that wide front porch with an overhang that fucks up the camera angle. Can't see the comings and goings from the parking lot at all. Where was he at with this Dozer character?"

"Mr. Cormier is being coy about that, which makes me wonder why. There was an LSU football game Saturday night, so wherever those boys went, it's safe to say there were big-screen TVs. I'll start with sports bars tomorrow. I'm more interested in where he went after he left Outlaw.

"If that body is Marc Mercier, where did he get shot? Why was he only half dressed? He leaves Outlaw at eleven thirty. If we're saying Cody Parcelle shot him, and Cody got home a little after two . . . that's not that much time, really."

"So he leaves Outlaw," Stokes said, "goes to another lady, Cody shows up, BOOM!"

"And where is this other lady?" Nick asked, skeptical. "She sees her lover get his head blown off right in front of her, and she doesn't call the cops?"

"Maybe she's too scared to talk. Or maybe she's dead, too."

"*Mais, c'est fou.*" He shook his head, dismissing the idea. "That's some kind of crazy Hollywood movie shit. I don't buy it. You punch a guy in the mouth for flirting with your wife. You don't blow his head off with a shotgun. You don't track him down in the middle of the night and shoot him in the face. That can't be it."

Nick took another long drink of his coffee and sighed. "We don't even know if this body *is* Marc Mercier."

"When are we getting DNA results? They just gotta match the samples. How hard can it be?"

"With that lab in New Iberia? God knows," Nick said, disgusted. "I got a text tonight that they lost the goddamn sample. Bunch of *couillons* running that place."

"Somebody there was smart enough not to contact you during business hours," Stokes pointed out.

"If they think I'll be less angry tomorrow, they are mistaken,"

Nick said. "I hope Gus gets us out of that contract before he leaves office again."

"If this body *isn't* Marc Mercier," Stokes said, "then where is he? Why would he just disappear? He's running a business, big man around town, got a new baby. Why would he just up and leave?"

"He's fighting with his brother about the business; his marriage is a shambles. Is that baby even his?" Nick asked, thinking about Will Faulkner bouncing little Madeline on his arm as he walked her around the living room, so easy and natural with her. "If Luc has them in the stolen copper business, they could be mixed up with some unsavory people. Maybe Marc wanted out. Robbie Fontenot claimed he had a line on some copper thieves. That's our connection between them.

"I want a witness," he declared. "I want somebody saw someone dumping that body. Have you talked to any of those potential poachers?"

Stokes gave him a look. "Like I've had time to go track down swamp rat thieves today."

"Mr. Arceneaux gave you a list of names. Delegate. Sergeant Rodrigue would love nothing better than to track those miscreants down and haul them in here for questioning. Put it on him."

"*Mañana*, man," Stokes said, getting to his feet. "It's late. I'm outta here."

"I'll call him," Nick said. "He'll be out there and have it done before you get out of bed in the morning."

Stokes scowled.

"Don't pout," Nick said. "You had your chance. Now you can have your beauty sleep."

"Do I at least get to have my moment for making the Cody Parcelle connection?"

"*Mais* yeah," Nick said. "You had it, well done, and now the moment is over. Move on. We've got cases to solve."

"You're a heartless bastard, you know that?"

"Whatever."

"All right," Stokes said, giving up. "I'm outta here."

"Hot date?"

"With my own bed," he said, stretching his arms up over his head and twisting at a kink in his back. "I'm still seeing that body when I close my eyes. That's enough to make a man celibate. For a minute, anyway. You heading home?"

"I'll swing by the Mercier house first. Make sure those town boys are on duty, then go home to my wife and son. Try to be normal for a few hours."

"Nicky, you weren't ever normal, man," Stokes pointed out.

"*C'est vrai*," Nick said, turning out the lights as they left the conference room. "True enough."

It was after ten when Nick drove into the Quail Run neighborhood. The streets were quiet, residents tucked into their lovely homes, watching the late news on TV. The lights were on in the Mercier family room. Will Faulkner's BMW sedan sat in the driveway. He wasn't going to abandon Melissa Mercier just for the sake of appearances. If Marc Mercier was still alive somewhere, he was losing ground on his marriage.

Nick thought again about the scene in the Mercier living room, the picture of Melissa Mercier and her baby with Will Faulkner sitting on the arm of the love seat. It was difficult to imagine either of them killing someone, but it wouldn't have been the first time Nick had put handcuffs on the least likely suspect. People found all kinds of excuses to do the most terrible things.

The call to Melissa from Robbie Fontenot's phone . . . She claimed not to know him. Dozer Cormier claimed Marc and Robbie weren't friends. How would Fontenot have had Melissa Mercier's number . . . unless she gave it to him or Marc gave it to him? And why would Marc give his wife's phone number to a man he didn't associate with? Could Robbie Fontenot have a different role in this than anyone had considered? A longtime addict, out of work, needing money . . . $2,450 Annie had found in a box in his bedroom at his mother's house . . . What had he done to earn that money?

Murders had been committed for a lot less. And while Melissa Mercier had no reason to know Robbie Fontenot, Will Faulkner was a native to Bayou Breaux who admitted to knowing Robbie's mother. It wasn't a stretch to think he might know Robbie as well.

Nick turned these thoughts over in his mind as he circled the block of the Mercier house, looking for anything out of place, spotting the police department patrol car sitting down the side street from Quail Trace. The officer had a good vantage point to see any cars that might come prowling around. He wouldn't be able to see anyone approaching the house on foot from the rear, but he was just seconds away in the event of a 911 call.

Nick still would have rather had one of his own sitting on the house, but this would have to do. He drove past the patrol car on his way out of the development, briefly making eye contact with the officer at the wheel. At least he wasn't sitting there looking at his phone.

The fifteen-minute drive out of Bayou Breaux was usually decompression time, time to put the day's work in its compartment in his brain and shut the door for a few hours. But there was no escaping the endless questions in his head that night. The tangle of facts and theories spun around and around, moving like an elaborate three-dimensional shell game.

He tried to turn it off as he drove down the gravel road to his little piece of heaven on the bayou. The place had been a forgotten shambles when he'd bought it, an old-style Acadian house with rotting porches, all but swallowed up by weeds and vines. All he had cared about at the time was the peace of mind it gave him to be apart from civilization and a part of the natural wild beauty of this place. Reclaiming the house had been an exercise in catharsis. Then Annie had come into his life, and in the years since, with her as his partner, they had remodeled and added on, and turned the house into a home, and turned the surrounding property into a sanctuary. His blood pressure dropped every time he turned down the driveway.

Annie had fallen asleep reading to Justin and lay curled around him in his bed, the light from the bedside lamp glowing softly on her skin. Nick reached out to pick up the book, hoping not to wake her, but her eyes fluttered open. She blinked to focus and looked up at him with a soft smile turning her lips.

"Go back to sleep," he whispered, leaning down to kiss her forehead.

"No," she said softly.

She disentangled herself from their son, and Nick helped her up, taking the opportunity to hold her for a minute before bending down to kiss his son good night.

"Did I miss anything?" she asked as they closed the door and headed down the hall to their room.

"The lab lost Marc Mercier's DNA sample."

"No."

"I get to explain that to his family tomorrow. Two days and we still don't have an ID on that body. That's unacceptable."

Annie slipped an arm around his waist and leaned into him. "You don't control the lab."

"Clearly not. I feel like I'm not controlling much of anything right now," he said. "We've got a three-ring circus going on. That lab provides all the clowns."

"Well, for what it's worth, I do find the idea of you in britches and boots, cracking a whip, kind of a turn-on," she said, giving him a sassy look.

"Careful what you wish for, 'Toinette," he warned, pinching her bottom through the baggy plaid boxer shorts she liked to lounge in.

She scooted away, laughing as she went into their room. Nick darted after her, caught her, and wrapped her in a hug.

"How you doing, *bébé*?" he asked. "I know you had a rough day."

"There's an understatement," she said, looking up at him. "One dead witness, one battered wife, and my missing guy might turn out to be involved in something criminal."

"Past performance being the best predictor of future behavior, will that be a surprise?" he asked.

"No, but it will be a disappointment for his mom. I'm rooting for her in this. She's been through the wars for him. I can't help but want a good outcome for her."

"Don't get your hopes up too high, *chère*," Nick cautioned, stepping back.

"I know." She sat down on the edge of the bed, looking a little forlorn, then concerned as she watched him. "Do you know something I don't?"

"No," he said, stripping his shirt off and dropping it in the laundry basket. "But I have a question: Is there any history of violence in his record?"

"Violence? No. Why?"

"Just trying to make some sense of that phone call to Melissa Mercier and that pile of money you found. Add a missing husband into that equation . . ."

"You can't think she hired Robbie Fontenot to kill her husband," Annie said.

"I'm just trying to put puzzle pieces together to see what fits."

"What about Cody Parcelle?"

"One puzzle at a time."

"I thought you said the wife doesn't know Robbie."

"I'd say I didn't know him either if I'd hired him to kill my husband, wouldn't you?"

"I wouldn't hire anyone to kill my husband," she said.

"Glad to hear it."

"I'd kill him myself and dump his body parts in the swamp."

Nick chuckled. "Well, you are a Cajun girl after all, yeah? She's not."

"Do you get that vibe from her, though? That she'd want her husband dead and see it done?"

"No, but people are full of surprises, no?" he said, sitting down on the bed beside her to take off his socks. "I'm not sure what to make of that situation—her and Will Faulkner. They say they're not sleeping together, but they act like a couple. If they're having an affair, they're not doing anything at all to hide it, which makes me think maybe they're not. They're either absolutely genuine or they're the best liars I've come across in a while."

"I thought he was gay," Annie said.

Nick shrugged. "You're not the first to say it, but I think if he was, he'd be up front about it. He doesn't seem to care what people think at all. He knows tongues are wagging about him spending the night at the Mercier house, but he's there again tonight because he's not about to leave her home alone when she doesn't feel safe. She says he's her only friend here."

"He sounds like a good friend to have."

"Yeah. Like he'd do anything for her. Or would he do anything to have her?"

"I don't know," Annie said, getting up to turn down the bed, "but I can't think about it anymore tonight. This day's been sad enough. Take your shower and come to bed, Mr. Fourcade. I need your arms around me. The world will be just as messed up tomorrow."

"That's a fact," Nick said. "Trouble is a thing that has no end."

24

DANNY PERRY SAT IN HIS RADIO CAR EATING HOT AND SPICY pork cracklings out of the bag on his passenger seat. He was parked strategically on the cross street to Quail Trace, far enough down the block to not be easily spotted, thanks in part to the sparse street-lights in the development.

He had a good view of the Mercier house, which was closer to a corner light. It was a nicer house than any house Danny had ever lived in. That was Marc Mercier, though, wasn't it? Lucky son of a bitch. He always managed to come out on top, smelling like a rose. Everybody loved Marc, the golden boy of Bayou Breaux.

Danny had gone up to the door to let the wife know he was on duty, making a point of saying he had volunteered for the shift to keep an eye out for her safety. She was hot, of course, even if she hadn't gone to the trouble of putting on makeup or doing her hair. The girls had always fallen all over themselves to get to Marc.

Not that Danny had any interest in having a wife, himself. Why limit yourself to one pussy? he asked. Especially considering how many girls out there were hot to fuck cops. But having a classy babe like Melissa Mercier in the lineup would have been sweet, for sure. People said she was a bitch, but sometimes those girls were the wildest in bed.

The reporters who had clogged up the street earlier in the day had given up and gone. The rumor among them had been that Marc Mercier's wife was sleeping with her boss, but that didn't make a news story. Now, if the two of them had killed Marc to be together, or killed him for the insurance, *that* was a story.

Of course, they might have, he conceded. Though if they had, they weren't being very clever about trying to look innocent. Or maybe that was actually genius—to look so guilty, they couldn't possibly actually be guilty. He couldn't decide.

Anyway, he wasn't convinced Marc was dead. He could just as well have gone to Mexico to live like a king, looking out on the Gulf of Mexico while being serviced by black-haired beauties. What red-blooded guy wouldn't do that if he had the cash?

A white pickup truck came down the street from the entrance to Quail Run. Danny sat up straighter in his seat, hoping to see the tag number as it passed. It was after two in the morning on a weeknight. A town of mostly middle-class working people, the sidewalks of Bayou Breaux were generally rolled up by 10:30. People saved their late nights for the weekend. He held his breath as the truck turned down Quail Trace, but it rolled past the Mercier house and kept going.

None of the reporters that afternoon had admitted it, but Danny suspected one of them had been the prowler in the Merciers' backyard the night before. Trying to catch the wife in the act with her boss. They weren't going to be dumb enough to try it two nights in a row.

The alternate theory was Marc's crazy mother, who had been the one to suggest Melissa Mercier's affair with Will Faulkner, was trying to catch them at it. She seemed kind of old to be creeping through yards in the dead of night, but Danny had once seen her run across a football field and jump an opposing team player who had leveled Marc with a dirty hit, so she was probably capable of anything, even ten years later.

He ate the last of his cracklings and drank some Red Bull, then got out of his vehicle to take a piss in the bushes and do some jumping jacks. He needed to stay awake. These late nights were killing him.

He was still shaking the snake behind some azalea bushes when a car came from the opposite direction and turned onto Quail Trace. A blue Toyota Corolla, plainly visible under the corner streetlight.

"Shit," Danny muttered, tucking his Johnson away and zipping his fly.

He watched the car go down to the end of the block and take a left.

"What the fuck?" he muttered, getting back in his vehicle. He started the engine and rolled down the street, making the same left just in time to see the Toyota turn left again, circling the block.

Danny could feel his heart beating in his chest as his mind raced. His hands were sweating on the steering wheel.

He knew that car.

That was Robbie Fontenot's car.

What the fuck was Robbie Fontenot doing prowling Marc Mercier's neighborhood?

Danny had begun to think Robbie wasn't going to be a problem anymore. He had let himself start to believe Robbie Fontenot was dead, even though no one had come across his body yet. The pills should have done their job. Danny had put them in Robbie's hand himself. He'd done the same with Rayanne. A bonus for keeping their mouths shut. If they took the pills and died, that was on them, not him.

But there he was, watching Robbie Fontenot's car prowl this neighborhood.

What the fuck was he supposed to do now?

He killed his headlights and made the left, hoping he was far enough back to not be noticed. He could still see the Toyota's tail-lights as it made yet another left.

What happened if he let Robbie get out of the car and go into the Merciers' yard? If Danny got out and followed him, he might catch the guy, but then what? Arrest him? Take him in and run the risk that Fontenot might use what he knew as leverage?

What if he just shot him? he wondered. He could claim he thought Robbie had a gun and he shot him in self-defense. Really, he should be hailed as a hero for defending Marc's wife and kid. Who knew what a druggie like Fontenot was up to or after?

But police shooting people attracted a lot of media attention these days, and there would be a lot of questions and an investigation. And they were in the middle of a neighborhood where people had security cameras all over the place. He couldn't take the chance. He would be stupid to do anything there. He had to move this opportunity away from civilization if he could.

He stepped on the gas and flipped on his lights.

Ahead of him, the Toyota took off.

There was no way that thing was going to outrun a cop car, but Danny needed him out of the city limits, out of the way of witnesses. He eased off the gas, letting the Toyota get a good lead on him as they headed out of the development. He turned his light bar on but not his sirens, not yet. He didn't want to attract more attention than he had to.

Quail Run was on the western edge of town. Beyond the development was a state wildlife management area, the road winding through woods and swamp. Wilderness. No houses. No witnesses. All he needed was for the car to turn right at the end of the road instead of left.

"Go right, go right, go right!"

The Toyota turned right and took off.

Danny hit the gas. Now he turned on the siren, out there where there was no one to hear it except the driver he was chasing and the dispatcher as he keyed his radio and reported the pursuit. He accurately gave the make, model, and tag number of the Toyota but purposely misnamed the road they were on as his patrol car ate up the distance between the two vehicles. Any officer looking to join the chase would be heading to Cypress Canal Road instead of Cypress Island Road.

The night was dark as clouds slipped in front of the moon, and trees and black water swallowed up the land on both sides of the narrow, winding road. Danny ran his car right up behind the Toyota. There was nowhere for him to go, no shoulder, no side roads to turn onto for another mile or more. The Toyota started to skid into a hard left curve.

"Roll, you fucker, roll!" Danny muttered under his breath.

The patrol car swayed coming out of the turn but stayed right on the Toyota. He pressed the gas and pulled to the left, coming up alongside the car's rear quarter panel. If he timed this right, it would be perfect. He could turn into the Toyota to initiate a pit maneuver just as they hit the next curve. He had learned how to do it at the police academy, longer ago than he cared to think. There had never been any opportunity to put it to practical use inside the city limits of Bayou Breaux, but it wasn't hard to do. Just find the right point to move his car into the Toyota, just a tap, just enough to throw it into a tailspin.

The Toyota would flip, roll off the road and into the trees. An unfortunate accident. No one would be the wiser. At the speed they were going, there was no way Robbie Fontenot survived.

Danny took a deep breath. His heart was pounding like a drum. The adrenaline felt like rocket fuel coursing through him.

The next curve was coming up fast.

He needed to time this just right.

He started to turn his wheel.

A split second too late.

A foot too far back on the Toyota.

He pulled the wheel just a little too hard.

And it all went wrong.

The Bayou Breaux PD cruiser went off the road doing seventy, sailing into a swamp full of cypress trees.

The Toyota skidded sideways. The left rear wheel came off the pavement for a breath-catching instant, then came back down. The car straightened and ran clear, its taillights glowing red, until the night and the wilderness swallowed it whole.

25

ANNIE HELD UP HER BADGE AND NAVIGATED PAST THE LOCAL news vans and around the SO deputy's car blocking the way to the crash scene. She pulled over the best she could considering there was no shoulder to speak of on this road and parked behind a white state police patrol car as she got her first good look at the wreck.

Danny Perry's car had landed on a cypress stump. Its nose was smashed in like a cheap accordion up against the trunk of another full-grown tree. An incongruous sight in this wilderness, to say the least. Mother Nature: 1, police car: 0.

News of Perry's crash had come before first light, Nick having been alerted because the car Perry had been pursuing matched the description of a vehicle that had been reported stolen—Robbie Fontenot's vehicle—although the tags came back to another vehicle entirely.

Annie had hurried through her morning routine, grabbing a giant travel mug of coffee and a granola bar on her way out the door, leaving Nick to the parental duties of getting Justin up and ready for school.

She got out of her car now, jammed her hands in the pockets of her jacket, and hunched her shoulders against the damp chill. The temperature had dropped near freezing in the night. It would be another couple of hours before the sun gathered enough strength to do any good.

This was a place humans had no real business intruding upon. The road had been built on a human-made berm, splitting the swamp in two. On either side of the thin ribbon of asphalt there was nothing but water and trees. The early-morning sun filtered down through the canopy, pale, diluted, lemonade yellow against the shadowed black of the cypress trees.

A great white egret sailed in and landed on a cypress knee near the crashed vehicle, hunching its shoulders and folding its wings, curious about this unnatural metal creature lying broken in its habitat. The bird made its unmelodic, ratchet-like *gwok!* sound as if to protest. In the branches above, songbirds tried to drown out the noise with prettier tunes, unconcerned by the goings-on of the humans below them.

Annie started toward the state trooper, who was busy checking distances between evidence markers with a measuring wheel on a stick. Farther down the road, two black trucks from the Department of Wildlife and Fisheries sat side by side, blocking any possible traffic coming from the north, the Wildlife agents standing, watching, their breath rising in clouds as they chatted.

"Detective Broussard, Sheriff's Office," Annie said. "Good morning, Sergeant."

"Not for the officer driving this car, I'm afraid," the trooper said. He was a tall thirtysomething Black man who looked like he might have stepped out of a recruitment poster in his crisp dark blue uniform. The brass name tag on his jacket read GRANT. "Have you heard any update on his condition?"

"He's critical at Lafayette General."

"I'm surprised he's alive," he said, making a notation on his clipboard. "He had to be doing sixty or better to land where he landed. That was some nasty impact. Do you know him?"

"Yeah, I do."

"Is this just a courtesy call, then?"

"No," Annie said. "The vehicle he was pursuing might belong to a missing person I've been looking for. An older blue Toyota Corolla. The plates came back to a different vehicle, but I believe the officer knew the car. So what do you think happened here?"

The trooper drew breath to answer, then stopped, his focus going over Annie's shoulder. She turned to see Dewey Rivette running toward them, his hair sticking up like he'd just rolled out of bed. He stopped five feet short of them, puffing like a steam engine.

"I—just—heard," he gasped, bending over, holding his side. "What—the hell—happened?"

"Sergeant Grant, this is Detective Rivette from the PD," Annie said. To Dewey she said, "Dude, you need to start working out. Or did you run all the way from town?"

He narrowed his eyes at her. "This—isn't—funny."

"No, it isn't."

Dewey straightened with his hands jammed at his waist and stared at the wreck, looking like he might get sick.

"I was told—he was in pursuit—and—the guy—wouldn't pull over."

"Where was he supposed to pull over on this road?" Annie asked.

"He could have—just stopped," Dewey said, still gasping. "Was it—Fontenot's car?"

"Sounds like it," Annie said. "But the tags came back to a Ford Taurus."

She turned to the trooper. "You were about to explain what you think happened, Sergeant."

Grant nodded. "This is just preliminary, you understand. I have a lot of questions, but come look at these skid marks."

He led them to a cluster of evidence markers on the pavement.

"It looks to me like the two vehicles made contact here," he said, pointing. "The lead car skidded sideways. You can see the arc of the skid marks as the rear end of the vehicle slid away going toward the water, then straightened and kept going. The police vehicle veered to the right and went off the road at a high rate of speed and ended up where it did."

A chill ran through Annie that had nothing to do with the temperature as the trooper's words sank in. "You're saying the officer tried to run the other car off the road?"

"I'm just telling you the story the evidence is telling me."

"That can't be right," Dewey said. "Danny was just trying to pull him over. Maybe he was trying to pass and get ahead of him. Maybe the Toyota swerved into him."

"If that was the case, the police vehicle would have more likely been diverted to the left," Grant said. "He would have gone off the other side of the road. Or he wouldn't have gone off the road at all. He should have hit the brakes, but there's no evidence of that. I believe he was accelerating, not trying to slow down. It doesn't make any sense to me, but it looks like he might have been attempting a pit maneuver."

"There's no way you'd do that here," Dewey said. "It wouldn't be safe."

"Exactly," Annie said. "One or both cars would end up in the swamp."

If a pit maneuver was executed properly, the target vehicle generally spun sideways off the road. If executed at too high a rate of speed, there was too great a chance of rolling the target vehicle. No cop in his right mind would have tried it on this narrow, winding road, heading into a tight curve to the left, no less . . . unless rolling that vehicle into the swamp had been his goal.

"You can't say that's what happened," Dewey protested.

"I have more investigating to do," Grant admitted. "I'm just telling you how it looks at a glance. Those skid marks tell a story."

"Well, it's ridiculous," Dewey argued.

"That's beside the point. The evidence is the evidence," Grant said. "I'll sit down with the measurements and do the calculations. He should have had his dash cam on. Once we get the vehicle, that'll tell the whole story. And that video should have uploaded to your server at the police station, anyway, so there it is."

"If he had the camera on," Annie said.

"Why wouldn't he have the camera on?" Dewey asked aggressively. "Of course he did."

"And we'll also have the data recorder from the police car," Grant said. "Provided it wasn't damaged in the crash. That'll give us the speed, throttle position, brake usage. We'll put this together. It'll take a few days. I expect it'll take the better part of this day just to extricate the vehicle."

Never mind extricating the vehicle, Annie thought. She didn't even want to imagine the process it must have required to extricate Danny Perry from the car to get him to the ambulance, the time they would have lost just navigating the terrain while his life hung in the balance.

She had spoken to Sergeant Rodrigue on her way to the site, knowing he always had the scoop. He told her Perry had misspoken the name of the road, reporting to dispatch he was pursuing a possible stolen vehicle on Cypress Canal Road rather than Cypress Island Road, delaying support vehicles from finding him by precious minutes. Likely unconscious from the impact, he hadn't answered his radio calls as dispatch had tried to contact him for his correct location.

First responders had requested AirMed, knowing Perry would stand his best chance at the level-one trauma center in Baton Rouge, but there was no good place for them to land in this wildlife management area, and it was determined the most expedient choice was to send him by ambulance to Lafayette General, a level-two trauma hospital, and if they could stabilize him there, then chopper him to Our Lady of the Lake.

"This is a nightmare," Dewey declared, more to himself than to anyone. He looked at Annie. "This is on Fontenot."

"Oh, it's his fault Danny Perry tried to run him off the road?" Annie asked, incredulous.

"You don't know that's what happened!" Dewey barked. "Why didn't he just pull over?"

"Why didn't he?" Annie asked. "Out here in the middle of fucking nowhere in the dead of night? Why didn't Danny just follow him?"

"Why would Danny run him off the road?"

"To kill him is the first thought that comes to mind," Annie said.

"That's insane! You're accusing a police officer of attempted murder? What the hell is wrong with you, Broussard?" he demanded, then caught himself. "Oh, I forgot. You've made a career out of that."

"Oh, fuck off, Dewey," Annie snapped, irritated he would dredge up the ancient history of the time she had arrested Nick for assaulting a suspect. "I wasn't wrong then, and I won't look the other way for a bad cop now. I'm not the problem here. I'm not the one who tried to run someone into the swamp!"

Dewey's little eyes bugged out of his head. "Keep your voice down!" he ordered in a harsh whisper. "There are TV cameras rolling on this."

"The two of you can take this fight elsewhere," Sergeant Grant said in a stern voice. "I've got work to do here."

"Apologies, Sergeant," Annie said. "Thank you for the information."

She started for her vehicle. Dewey rushed up alongside her.

"Where are you going?"

"To do my job," Annie snapped back at him. "You might think about trying that instead of following me around like a lost puppy. Or are you stalking me, Dewey? Is that what this is? I'm sniffing around something you don't want me to find?"

"I don't like you accusing our officer of shit he didn't do. Danny's a good cop."

"It's not looking that way," Annie said, yanking open her car door.

"Where are you going?" he asked again.

She got behind the wheel and looked up at him.

"Lafayette," she said, and slammed the door, muttering *fucker* under her breath. She'd had more than enough of Dewey Rivette this week. Of course, now he was going to think she was going to Lafayette in the hopes of getting some kind of dying declaration out of Danny Perry. Good, she thought. She hoped the idea gave him diarrhea.

She turned her car around, glaring at him the whole time, and wound her way back through the growing mess of law enforcement vehicles, media vans, reporters, and gawkers. She needed to focus on the possible good news of the day: that Robbie Fontenot might be alive and well.

Danny had been sitting on the Mercier house when he spotted the Toyota prowling the neighborhood. That truth brought back the conversation she'd had with Nick the night before—his exploration of the seemingly wild possibility that Robbie might have been hired to kill Marc. She wanted to reject that idea out of hand, but she couldn't. What did she really know about Robbie Fontenot's state of mind? How could she know what he was capable of doing? She had two views of him: his criminal record and his mother's opinion. Neither of those things was the whole truth.

He was a man with no job and few prospects and by his mother's own admission could have been nursing a grudge against Marc Mercier for a decade. But would he kill a man for money?

That seemed like a big leap, but she couldn't stop seeing that pile of cash—$2,450. People had done the same job for a lot less. And that might have just been the down payment.

Where had he been headed, coming down that winding, dangerous road? she wondered as she turned onto the highway to Lafayette. That road through the wildlife management area went on for another mile or more beyond the crash site before coming to a T intersection that would have let him go anywhere. Or had he chosen that road thinking there was a chance that exactly what *had* happened *would* happen?

How could he have orchestrated that? This wasn't some *Fast and Furious* movie. Robbie Fontenot wasn't a trained stunt driver driving some mega-muscle car. He was a regular guy driving an old Toyota, being pursued by a souped-up cop car.

Annie really didn't want to think that Danny Perry was some movie villain rogue cop, either, but as Sergeant Grant had said, the evidence was the evidence. Or had Danny thought he could just scare Robbie into pulling over by bumping his car, then pulling back?

But he hadn't pulled back. He had been accelerating as the Toyota skidded sideways, and his cruiser had sailed off the road because he had miscalculated.

It was an easy mistake to make, she thought, recalling her own attempts at the pit maneuver when she'd been in training. You had to hit the target car in just the right spot. Too far forward and you could roll them. Too far back and they might be able to control the skid and keep going. Danny Perry had miscalculated, and the result had landed him in an ICU in critical condition.

She shouldn't have reacted, she told herself. She should have kept a poker face when Grant had been laying out his theory of the accident, but she hadn't been able to stop herself from reacting in front of Dewey. She had no way of knowing what Rivette's connection to any of this might be. She had no way of knowing yet if his story about giving Robbie money as an informant was true at all. He and Danny and Robbie could have all been up to their ears in something illegal.

What a mess.

She checked her rearview mirror as a car came up fast behind her, then checked its speed and dropped back a few yards. She couldn't see the driver. Was it Dewey following her? She could have called in to check the tags, but she didn't. She'd know soon enough if it was him. They were on a busy highway going to a busy hospital. Even if he'd had the cojones for it—which she doubted—Dewey wasn't going to try anything here.

The car stayed behind her as she left the highway for surface streets in Lafayette, navigating her way to the sprawling campus of the Lafayette General Medical Center, but kept going when she turned in at the parking area for the orthopedic hospital. Danny Perry would be in the ICU down the street in the main building. Annie had no need to go there. She wouldn't have been allowed to see him even if she'd thought she might get something out of him, anyway. And she had no doubt the waiting area would be populated by off-duty BBPD officers who would not welcome her intruding on their tribe.

She checked the directory as she went into the building and took the elevator to the floor where Dr. Robert Fontenot II had his offices. Several people were waiting in the chairs, reading old magazines and watching Food Network quietly playing on the television. Annie went up to the reception desk with a pleasant smile.

"Hi, I'm Detective Broussard with the Partout Parish Sheriff's Office," she said softly. "I need to see Dr. Fontenot."

"Do you have an appointment?"

Annie held up her badge. "This is my appointment. I'm so sorry to interrupt your day, but I need to speak to Dr. Fontenot regarding his son. And this needs to happen sooner rather than later. I promise it won't take long."

The receptionist's eyes went round. She popped up from her desk and disappeared down the hall behind her, returning a moment later to open the door.

"Thank you," Annie whispered as they walked toward Dr. Fontenot's office.

"I didn't know he had a son," the woman confessed in a whisper.

Annie just smiled.

"Dr. Fontenot will be right with you."

Annie glanced around the office as she waited. It looked like any other—a nice desk, a cushy executive's chair, a pair of generic armchairs for visitors, framed diplomas on one wall, and another wall with a gallery of photos presumably of patient athletes. On closer inspection, a fair number of the photos were of Dr. Fontenot himself participating in athletic events as a runner and a cyclist.

Annie had looked him up on the web. He was soap opera

handsome with chiseled features and black hair shot through with just the right amount of silver. Tall and lean, defying his age with athletics and a much younger girlfriend. As attached as she had become to B'Lynn, Annie had taken an instant dislike to her ex just on principle. There was B'Lynn all these years, struggling with Robbie and his addiction. And there was Dr. Bob, riding bikes in Italy and drinking wine with a honey twenty years his junior. Asshole.

The office door opened, and Bob Fontenot walked in looking annoyed and full of himself.

"Dr. Fontenot," Annie said. "I'm Detective Broussard with the Partout Parish Sheriff's Office."

He didn't offer to shake her hand, just gave her a look and walked around behind his desk. "You could have made an appointment and not disrupted anyone's schedule."

"And you could have returned my phone calls and spared me the trip up here, but here we are," Annie said bluntly.

He arched a dark brow. "Does Gus Noblier know how rude his detectives are?"

"Why don't you call him and ask?" Annie suggested. "I'm sure he'd be thrilled to hear from you. He had so many interesting things to say about you when I spoke to him about your son's case."

"As did my ex-wife, I'm sure," he said. He took a stance with his feet apart and his arms crossed over his immaculate white coat.

"She hasn't really had much to say about you at all, to be honest," Annie said. "I gather she's well used to having no support from you in a crisis. How many years have you been divorced?"

He didn't like having a woman clapping back at him. Robert Fontenot was the kind of man used to being treated like a prince. She could see him struggling already with his temper.

"Seven years. Not that it's relevant. I'm sure B'Lynn has told you, Robbie and I have no relationship, and haven't had in many years."

"She did tell me that," Annie said. "I thought maybe she was just trying to paint you in a bad light."

He looked away with a tight forced smile, a muscle working in his jaw. There was no comeback that didn't make him seem like an even bigger asshole.

"I'm not sure how I can help you here, Detective."

"Well, I have to touch all the bases, you know. Do my due diligence. Robbie hasn't tried to contact you at all? Not here or on your personal phone?"

"No. He knows better than to call here, and he doesn't have my cell number."

Annie let her brows sketch upward even though this was not news to her. "And do you have his number? I only ask because we're going through his cell phone records."

"No, I don't. B'Lynn might have texted it to me once. I would have deleted it. I'm sure you find that cold."

Annie said nothing.

"Do you have children?" Fontenot asked. "I'm guessing you do."

"I have a son."

"And you can't begin to imagine not supporting him, not loving him, not helping him no matter what," he said. "You haven't dealt with addiction."

"You don't know what I've dealt with," Annie said. "And it's not relevant anyway. It's your son I'm trying to find."

"I walked away," he said. "I'm not proud of the way that looks, but Robbie was destroying everyone and everything in his life, and there came a point when I had to say no. No more. I wasn't going to let him ruin my life as well as his own. Maybe one day, if he ever gets himself straightened out for good, we can try again, but I'm not betting on that. He's been to rehab more times than I can count. He'll bankrupt his mother."

"You don't contribute?"

"No. B'Lynn got a generous settlement in the divorce, and I got my freedom."

There were so many things Annie wanted to say, but she chewed them all back.

"I'm sure you've seen it in your line of work," Fontenot said.

"What addicts do, what they stoop to. Lying, cheating, stealing to get high. Robbie stole from his own family, hocked family heirlooms, stole from neighbors, from friends. And we had to keep making the excuses, making the apologies, begging friends not to press charges. It was humiliating."

And imagine what it was for your son, Annie thought. How desperate Robbie must have felt, how afraid he must have been. He was a child. And all his father cared about was how he looked to his neighbors.

"The last straw," he said, "was when he stole a prescription pad from my office, forged my signature, and sold the pages to other druggies. I could have lost my license to practice medicine. I had to call in every favor anyone ever owed me to get out of that one—including favors from your boss, in case he didn't tell you. That was it for me. I was done. I could have lost my livelihood."

"Well, lucky you," Annie said. "You only lost your child."

"I think we're done here," Fontenot said, stone-faced.

Annie nodded. "Yeah. I've certainly heard all I care to. I just have one question. You're a doctor. You knew the risks involved with those painkillers. Why did you let your son take them in the first place?"

"It's a perfectly safe drug if you don't abuse it."

Robbie had been seventeen with his whole world crashing in around him, desperately in need of the support of his parents, of this man he had probably idolized. And Robert Fontenot's answer had been to punish his son for being an embarrassment and an inconvenience when he could have prevented the tragedy from happening altogether.

Annie shook her head and started for the door.

"Not everyone is cut out to be a martyr," Bob Fontenot said, as if that was a viable defense.

"Or a parent," Annie returned, and walked out.

She wanted to go take a shower, to wash off the oily narcissism of Robert Fontenot. She knew it wasn't her job to judge this man or anyone else. And she certainly knew enough about the desperate struggle of families dealing with addiction to know that there were few good answers and too many tears, and people did what they thought they had to do to survive it. But this guy . . . wow.

Well, now she knew the whole story anyway, she thought as she got in her vehicle. The story Gus had let hang in the air with no explanation when Annie had spoken to him. The reason B'Lynn had thought she could appeal to him to take Robbie's case. No part of that story had ever made it into an arrest report, at least not one that had survived. Gus had killed it. A crime that would have warranted serious felony charges with serious prison time. Poof! Gone.

She wasn't sure how she felt about it. *Uneasy* was the best word she could come up with. It was like Gus had taken a truth and turned it into a lie, and everyone involved had just gone on with their lives. She wanted to be okay with it because she felt sorry for B'Lynn and Robbie, but that wasn't how the system was supposed to work. It was, however, how privilege worked, over and over.

Sometimes the ways of the world just drained the optimism right out of her. But there was nothing for it except to keep putting one foot in front of the other and hoping she could make a difference every once in a while.

26

"CODY PARCELLE ISN'T IN HOUSTON," STOKES SAID AS HE walked into the bullpen. "I talked to the uncle running that auction. Cody was supposed to be there Sunday afternoon. The uncle got a text from him late in the day Sunday saying he wasn't going to make it after all. No explanation, just that something came up and sorry he wouldn't be coming. The uncle was pissed—is still pissed. He said he tried to call him a couple of times, but the calls went to voicemail."

"Did he call the wife?" Nick asked as he poured himself a cup of coffee.

"No. He said she's useless, that she'd just say whatever Cody told her to say, so no real point bothering. He says he's too busy getting ready for this auction to give a shit what his asshole nephew is up to—those are his words, not mine.

"Border Patrol doesn't have any record of him going into Mexico," Stokes said. "I put a BOLO out on his truck."

"What's he drive?"

"A black Dodge Ram 3500 truck."

"Have you gotten anything back on those tire casts?"

"In two days? Get real, man. We'll be lucky if we get something back in two months."

"True enough," Nick said. "Come with me."

He rounded the counter and started for the front door.

"Where we going?" Stokes asked, falling into step.

"Going over to the jail. Sergeant Rodrigue has a couple of our reluctant potential witnesses in custody."

"No fucking way!" Stokes said. "Just like that?"

"I told you," Nick said. "Rodrigue and Mr. Arceneaux only had to go and wait. The thieves delivered themselves."

"They came right back to the same damn place?"

"Of course they did. They're like little racoons getting in the garbage. They're gonna keep coming back until somebody stops them."

"Not a rocket scientist among them, I'm guessing."

"*Mais non.* Lucky for us. Couple of dumb kids," Nick said. "I had Sergeant Rodrigue bring them over here so we can put the fear of God into them."

"Juveniles?" Stokes said with an evil chuckle. "This is gonna be like shooting fish in a barrel! Unless they've called lawyers," he added, frowning at the thought. "Have they called lawyers?"

"They're not under arrest," Nick said. "This is a noncustodial conversation. Their parents will be notified . . . eventually."

They went into the building, signed in, and surrendered their weapons at the desk. Rodrigue was babysitting the two thieves, standing on one side of the table in the interview room with his hands jammed at his waist. The overhead light gleamed off his bald dome. His massive mustache emphasized his ferocious scowl as he stared at them.

They couldn't have been more than fourteen or fifteen, Nick thought, scrawny, scraggly-looking with bad haircuts. They were dressed for hunting, their faces streaked with green camo paint as if they were going to war in the jungle. The pair of them sat on the far side of the little white table with their backs literally up against

the wall. Their eyes went wide as Nick and Stokes walked in. Stokes
pulled out a chair and sat down, leaning on the table, staring at
them.

"*Bonjour*, Sergeant Rodrigue. *Ça viens?*" Nick said. "What have
we here?"

"*Ça va*, Lieutenant Fourcade! Thieves is what we got here. Couple'a
goddamn thieves. Caught 'em red-handed, me and Alphonse, raiding his traplines, stealing his nutria."

Nick shook his head, staring at the boys. "That's low. Stealing a
man's livelihood. There was a time, was there not, Sergeant, when a
man could shoot a thief and dump his body in the swamp?"

"*Mais oui*. Some still might, if no one's looking. Who would be
the wiser?"

"*C'est vrai*. That's for true. Good thing you were with Mr.
Arceneaux. Do they have names?"

"Me, I call them Couillon One and Couillon Deux. Couillon One,
on the left, he's named Jimmy Munroe. And the other one is Owen
Olivier, who, I am sad to say, is Alphonse's nephew's stepson."

"*Bon à rien*," Nick muttered. "Stealing from your relatives. What
you got to say for yourself, *pischouette*?"

"I want a lawyer!" the kid blurted out.

Stokes let out a belly laugh, making them both jump.

"A lawyer?" Nick said. "Why you need a lawyer, *pischouette*?
You're not under arrest. Is he under arrest, Sergeant Rodrigue?"

"*Mais non*. Not until you say so, Lieutenant."

"Have you called their parents?"

"Not yet."

Couillon One decided to get bold. "We weren't doing nothing!"

Stokes slapped the table hard and barked, "Shut your mouth, Li'l
Rambo!"

The kid tried to jump back, hitting the wall.

"Don't waste my time with lies, boys," Nick said quietly. "That
will not work out for you. Do you understand me?"

They looked up at him like a pair of owlets. The Munroe boy was trying unsuccessfully to grow a goatee. His whiskers looked like strands of dirty cotton candy stuck to his little knob of a chin.

"This could be the worst day of your young lives," Nick said. "Or this could be your lucky day. Me, I'm not officially interested in your thieving. I'm looking for information. Y'all were raiding those same lines Monday morning, yeah?"

They glanced at each other, trying to decide if this was some kind of trap.

"Yes or no," Nick snapped. "Don't try my patience here. Were you there on Monday morning?"

The Olivier boy nodded. The Munroe boy hit him on the arm. "Don't tell him! We'll go to jail, dumbass!"

Olivier shoved him. "He just said he don't care about the stealing!"

"He's prob'ly a fucking liar!" Munroe said. "You can't trust cops!"

Stokes stood abruptly and started to reach across the table toward him. "You want me to take this one in another room, boss?"

"Not yet. Me, I'll give them one more chance," Nick said. "Were you in that same area early Monday morning?"

"No!" Munroe said. "I wasn't there."

Nick gave him a hard look. "If you're gonna ass up and lie to me, I could very easily change my mind about booking you today, Mr. Munroe, and leave you to sit in jail while the district attorney decides if you're worth his time. Is that what you want? All I have to do is say the word. Sergeant Rodrigue would be all too happy to see it done." He turned his attention back to the Olivier boy. "Did he tell you Mr. Arceneaux is a relative of his by marriage? Which makes him a relative to you, too, *pischouette*."

Olivier tried for a scowl that only managed to look like a pout. "Why do you keep calling me that? What's that mean?"

Nick shook his head and sighed. "Stealing from your relatives *and* you don't even speak the language of your own people. You have got a lot of improving to do, *pischouette*. You ask your *nonc* Alphonse what that word means after you apologize to him for raiding his traplines.

"Now, let's start again, shall we?" he suggested. "The two of you were out there Monday morning. You were in a boat, yeah?"

Olivier nodded, looking down at the table.

"I didn't hear you say *yes, sir.*"

"Yes, sir."

"What time were you there?"

"Five, five thirty. Alphonse, he plays cards with my uncles on Sunday night. He don't get up so early on Mondays."

"You know where we found that dead body, yeah?" Nick asked.

Olivier's eyes went wide again. "We didn't do that!"

"I didn't say you did. I want to know did you see anything?"

"It was dark!"

"There was a good moon still up then. Did you see anything at all?"

"We were a ways off," Olivier said. "There was a truck with its lights on, but we couldn't tell what they were doing."

"What kind of truck?"

"Couldn't tell. A pickup."

"Light or dark?"

"Dark."

Nick turned his gaze on the Munroe boy. "You can pipe up any-time, *tête dure.* Or I can let Detective Stokes take you and question you separately. You're not joined at the hip here."

The boy chewed a dirty thumbnail, weighing his options. Nick watched him, unblinking.

"Maybe he wants to spend the night here," Stokes said. "I'm sure we can find him a nice cellmate. Do you like big hairy guys, Li'l Rambo?"

Munroe gave Stokes the side-eye, then looked back at Nick. "There was two trucks," he said. "We come around the bend and I could see the dark truck off the road. It had its lights on. And there was a light one farther down on the road. Maybe white or silver. Hard to say."

"We figured it was drug business," young Olivier said. "We didn't want no part of that. I cut the engine when I saw 'em, and then we was in the tall grass and couldn't see nothing. I was afraid maybe they'd come and shoot us, but they didn't. They took off."

"Did you see them dump that body?" Stokes asked.

"No, sir. I swear."

"Did you see the people at all?"

They both shook their heads.

"Would you know these trucks if you saw them again?" Nick asked.

"No," Olivier said. "It was too dark, and we were too far away."

"One was a diesel," Munroe offered. "The dark one, I think. It was closer, louder. The other one had a gas engine."

Two trucks. Nick exchanged a look with Stokes. What the actual hell?

"You know your engines?" Nick said.

"My dad's a mechanic."

"You wanna be a mechanic, too?"

The boy nodded.

"You think you gonna get to be a mechanic if you keep stealing?" Nick asked. "You gonna learn to be a mechanic in prison, spend your time fixing farm equipment at Angola penitentiary. Would that make your daddy proud?"

"No, sir."

"What about you, *pischouette*? Why you think it's okay for you to take things don't belong to you?"

The boy hung his head. "Alphonse, he runs a hundred fifty traps. I didn't think he'd miss a few."

"That's not an answer," Nick said. "I don't care if he runs five hundred traps. He's doing the work, and he doesn't owe you anything. Why do you think you're entitled to his profit?"

"Just wanted some pocket money, is all," the kid mumbled, close to tears now.

"You want money, you earn it. You can't just take it out of

someone else's pocket, son. How has no one taught you this?" Nick asked. "You're gonna be men soon. You need to learn the responsibility that comes with that. Now, me, I don't wanna see either one of you back in here. You understand me?"

"Yes, sir," they mumbled.

Munroe looked up. "Will we have to testify in court? Against killers?"

"Probably not," Nick said. "You didn't see anything with any detail. You didn't see any faces. But this information is a big help to my investigation nevertheless, and I thank you. Sergeant Rodrigue will call your parents, and they can come get you."

They both looked horrified at the prospect.

"Can't we just go to school?" Olivier asked.

"No. We have to tell them we brought you in and why."

"Oh, man," Munroe groaned. "My old man is gonna whup my ass."

"Can't do the time, don't do the crime, Li'l Rambo," Stokes said.

"I'll tell them you were helpful to me," Nick said. "And I'll put in a good word with the Wildlife agent."

"What?" Olivier asked. "You said you didn't care about the stealing!"

"I'm not putting you in jail," Nick said. "I'm not charging you with anything. But you don't get off scot-free for stealing."

"But we helped you!" Munroe whined.

"And I thanked you for it. You do the right thing because it's the right thing, not because you think you should get something for it," Nick said. "I'll put in a word for you, but you're still gonna deal with the Wildlife agents, and you're gonna have to make it up to Mr. Arceneaux. That's only fair. No arguments. I'll see that done, myself if need be."

He turned to Rodrigue. "Thank you, Sergeant. They're all yours. Maybe you can explain to them how karma works while you're waiting for their mothers."

He nodded to Stokes and turned for the door.

"You're getting soft in your old age, Nicky," Stokes said as they collected their weapons and started back to the Pizza Hut. "You could have at least made them pee their pants."

"Well, God forbid you should ever become a parent," Nick said. "But if you do, you'll look at things different. They aren't bad kids. They're just dumb, thinking they're growing up to be badasses."

"Well, they're half right," Stokes said, chuckling.

"But look what they gave us," Nick said. "Two trucks."

"Yeah. What the fuck?"

"Cody Parcelle drives a black Dodge Ram truck. Luc Mercier drives a black Dodge Ram."

"But who the hell is the light-colored truck?"

"Dozer Cormier drives a white Chevy pickup, but I don't see how he would fit in that scenario. He doesn't get along with Luc. He knows Cody Parcelle, but if Cody killed Marc, I don't see Dozer helping him out. Marc's his best friend. Although he's certainly keeping secrets. I need to lean on him a little harder today."

"Oh, shit," Stokes said, stopping in his tracks.

Nick held up, looking at him. "What?"

"There was a white pickup parked outside the Parcelles' barn last night," he said. "Now, I know you can't swing a dead cat by the tail in south Louisiana without hitting a white pickup, but . . . This could explain why the body was half naked and why the lover hasn't spoken up. We know what time Marc Mercier left Outlaw. Tulsie Parcelle says she went home about that same time, but what if she didn't? What if she went and met Marc? Cody follows her, catches them together, *BOOM!* Then he beats the shit out of her and makes her go with him to dispose of her lover's body. He tells her to keep her mouth shut or this is what happens to her, too."

"That's a lot of puzzle pieces fitting together," Nick conceded.

He'd been looking at the possibility of a love triangle. Just maybe the wrong one.

"There's still loose ends," he said. "Where'd this murder take place? And where's Marc's vehicle?"

"They could have gotten rid of the vehicle after they dumped the body."

"A truck *and* a boat?"

"Let's ask her. Should I go pick her up?" Stokes asked. "Bring her in for questioning?"

"No," Nick said. "Not yet. Double down trying to find security video from the road between Luck and Bayou Breaux. Now we know the trucks we're looking for, and we have a tight timeframe for early Monday morning. I'd rather have that evidence before she comes in. If that's what went down, it'll be a lot easier to get the truth out of her if we can put proof right in front of her face."

"On it," Stokes said.

"Call me when you find something."

"You'll be the first to know."

Nick watched him go, then pulled out his phone and texted Annie.

27

"I ALWAYS LIKED ROBBIE," ELI MCVAY SAID, STIRRING HIS sweet tea. He was a slightly taller version of his little brother, Caleb, with the McVay trademark flame-red hair and pointy chin.

They sat at an outdoor table on the deck of a little café not far from the Lafayette Public Works department. The sun had grown warm enough to be pleasant. Down along a rambling little bayou a mob of white ibis were prancing around on their sticklike legs, grazing for bugs with their long, curved yellow beaks. It was a soothing view after the morning Annie had had.

They had already had their lunch, caught up on family news, talked about the upcoming annual Doucet family Thanksgiving weekend get-together—all the conversation essentials before Annie had asked a single question.

"He was a different breed of cat, for sure," Eli qualified, "but I liked him."

"Different how?"

"Robbie always marched to his own drummer. He wasn't just a jock. He had other interests. He was a reader. He followed the news.

He wanted to know about the world. He wanted to be some kind of documentary filmmaker or investigative journalist. I mean, the dude could have ended up in the NFL, for sure, but there was a lot more to him than football.

"He used to make all these videos on his phone and then post them on social media. Little news stories about stuff going on around school. Interviews with people—coaches, janitors, lunch ladies, teachers. He'd ask them all kinds of things. It was so odd because he was a quiet guy, himself. You didn't always know what he was thinking, and it was usually something deeper than the average teenager.

"Such a shame, what happened," he said. "He had a lot of promise. Drugs took that all away."

"So you were all good friends—you and Robbie and Marc Mercier?" Annie asked.

"Yeah, we were pretty tight up until Robbie got hurt."

"And Dozer Cormier?"

"Dozer was more Marc's friend. He didn't really fit our group. He wasn't the sharpest tool in the shed, you know? Or the most ambitious. But Marc would hang with him. I think they knew each other through their families somehow or family businesses or something. Me, I was interested in hot cheerleaders—I'm not gonna lie—and hot cheerleaders were not interested in having Dozer Cormier hanging around. Fair or not, he's got that kind of creepy giant vibe about him. A handy guy to have around if you wanted to intimidate somebody, that's for sure. Can't say we didn't make use of that talent more than once."

"And Robbie wasn't part of the group anymore after his accident?"

"Well, first of all, he was out of school a long time. He almost lost that leg, the injury was so bad. And then he didn't really want people around him. I'm sure he was in a major depression, but kids don't think about that kind of thing. He was out of sight, out of mind.

And that senior year is busy, you know? And by spring that year he'd already gone down the rabbit hole with the drugs . . ."

"I understand that was a particular problem for Marc—the drug thing?"

"Yeah, well, me and Marc were the DARE leaders, so we couldn't really be hanging around with a guy doing drugs and stealing and whatnot. And of course our parents didn't want us being around him."

"So that was the end of the friendship?"

He sighed. "Looking back, I wish I'd done some things differently, because I liked Robbie. I don't think I was a very good friend. But you know kids that age. We were self-involved and not really equipped mentally to navigate something like addiction. It was easier just to walk away, but that's not what friends should do."

"Do you think Marc might feel the same way?"

He shook his head. "I doubt it. Marc cut him off. Boom. Done. Of course, it was an awkward situation for Marc because when Robbie went down, Marc had to step in and take his place on the team, and the team went on and won the state championship. Marc ended up getting a scholarship to Tulane. That didn't really work out for him as far as football, but nevertheless there he was, and where was Robbie? In rehab or in jail. How do you get a relationship back from that? I don't know . . ."

He trailed off, looking down toward the bayou. The memories clearly bothered him. "Nothing was the same after Robbie got hurt. Not for any of us."

"Did you and Marc stay in touch after graduation?"

"Oh, not really," he said. "We went in different directions. Literally. He was in school in New Orleans. I was here in Lafayette. I'd see him time to time in Bayou Breaux, but not very often. Say hey. Have a beer. We didn't have much in common anymore. When we'd see each other all he wanted to do was play Remember When. And not to say we didn't have some good times, but that was high school. Grow up, dude, move on. Then he got married and moved up north somewhere. I was in Houston . . ."

Annie watched his body language. He seemed a little agitated, uncomfortable. Under the table, he was tapping his toe like he was keeping time to some music only he could hear.

"Marc's been back in Bayou Breaux about a year now, helping with his family's business," she said.

"Yeah, I know. It's been hard to escape the Saint Marc stories from home," he said with a forced smile. "Marc always did like to be a hero. Good for him."

"What?" Annie asked. "Do you think it's not genuine?"

"No, no, I'm sure it is."

"But . . . ?"

He shrugged. "After a while, it just starts looking like a politician kissing babies, you know? My dad once said, Marc's the kind of guy who would knock a bird's nest out of a tree so he could save the baby birds and get his picture in the paper." As soon as the words were out, he clearly regretted them. He made a face and said, "That's not fair. Forget I said it."

But he *had* said it, Annie thought. And not for no reason.

"And now he's missing or maybe dead, and here I am saying something like that. Jesus. Annie, you have permission to pistol-whip me for being an asshole," he said, his bright smile splitting his wide face.

"Being honest isn't a crime," Annie said. "I'd rather have you be honest than tell me some pleasant lie that doesn't help anyone."

"Most people think the opposite," he said. "Better a good lie than a hard truth."

"That philosophy might keep the peace at family gatherings, but it never solved a crime," Annie said.

"I suppose that's true."

"Caleb told me you ran into Robbie recently."

He nodded. "Yeah, I did, a month or so ago."

"How was that?"

"Awkward. I hadn't seen him in years. He looked good, though. He looked healthy. I was surprised. I didn't think he'd ever get clean. Frankly, I thought he'd be dead by now."

"What did you talk about?"

"Nothing. The standard pleasantries—how you doing, what you doing, where you living. I'm standing there feeling like a shit because what did I ever do to help him, and he's standing there feeling whatever because what's he ever done with his life but fuck it up? What's he supposed to tell me? That he just got out of rehab and he's working at the lamp factory? I made some stupid joke about him being an investigative reporter, and he said yeah, that he was deep undercover investigating police corruption in Bayou Breaux."

Annie's heart skipped a beat, and she sat up a little straighter. "Why would he say that?"

Eli shook his head and shrugged. "It was just a dumb joke. I said, what's that amount to? Them taking free day-old beignets at the back door of Melancon's Bakery? He laughed. I wanted to crawl in a hole. Next time I saw him, I just ducked around a corner."

"When was that?"

"At Monster Bash. I saw him talking to Dozer, and I thought, I don't want any part of that, another drunken trip down bad memory lane. No, thanks."

"What time was that?" Annie asked, her heart beating a little faster. Dozer Cormier had flatly denied seeing Robbie. Why would he lie about that?

"Must have been eleven fifteen, eleven thirty."

"Where?"

"Around Fifth and Dumas. I was leaving. I was parked in that lot down past Canray's Garage. I walked an extra block just to avoid them. I'm coming off here like a real asshole, aren't I?" he asked.

"You're not," Annie assured him. "We've all done it. Why make life hard if we don't have to?"

"Yeah, well, I looked at the two of them and thought, what the hell is that conversation gonna be anyway? 'Hey, Robbie, great to see you. Sorry I ruined your entire life'? I mean, Dozer became an alcoholic after that. He couldn't cope with what he'd done."

"Poor kid," Annie said. "It was an accident."

Eli said nothing. He looked down to the bayou again with a thousand-yard stare into the past. Annie could feel the tension in him, the need to say something pushing against the need to say nothing.

"I get the feeling you're holding something back here, Eli," she said.

He shifted on his chair and rubbed a hand across his lower face, as if he might just push any errant words back into his mouth.

"Just say it," Annie said. "I'm not gonna judge you."

He took a sip of his tea to buy time as he turned his options over in his mind.

"It's ten years ago," Annie said. "How much longer do you want to hang on to it?"

He took a breath as if to speak, then checked himself again, made a little face of frustration, and shook his head. Finally, he just said it.

"I don't know that it was an accident."

He blew out a breath that might have been relief.

"I know, it happened in front of fifty people," he said. "And no one ever said anything like that, but now I'm saying it. I was right there."

Annie sat still, waiting, feeling a little sick in her stomach. Around them, the few other diners who had chosen to sit on the patio went on with their lunches and their polite conversations, accented by the sounds of silverware clinking and the waitress topping off glasses of iced tea.

"There was absolutely no reason for what happened to have happened that day," Eli said soberly. "None. It was a routine practice. Robbie was in the red jersey. No one should have been anywhere near him. But there was Dozer, stumbling backward into him. And when he hit him, he twisted around and looked right at him as they went down. I'll never forget that for as long as I live. And the sound of Robbie screaming." He blinked back tears at the memory. "I was the tight end on the play. I was lined up maybe ten feet to Robbie's left. It still makes me sick to remember."

"Oh, Eli," Annie murmured. "I'm so sorry you had to go through that."

She'd known him all his life. He was a sweet boy. Fun, funny, smart, popular. She would have thought at the time that life was a breeze for young Eli McVay, if she had thought much about him at all. She'd been a patrol deputy at the time, fighting to gain respect in a department that thought women belonged elsewhere, not wearing a badge. To think at that same time Eli had been going through an experience so heavy, so sad, made her heart hurt for him.

"Robbie was *so* good," he said softly, emotion thickening his voice. "He was like watching a unicorn, the things he could do! The gods reached down and turned his arm into a thunderbolt, and he had wings on his feet. Everything was instinctual for him. It was like he could bend time, stretch it like a rubber band. Effortless. Easy.

"And there was Marc, sitting on the bench. And he was good. He was very, very good. But he was never gonna be Robbie. The college scouts would come around, and all they wanted to see was Robbie Fontenot. He was a legit five-star recruit. And of course, Robbie didn't need a scholarship—his family was loaded—but he was going anywhere he wanted on a magic carpet, a full ride.

"Marc needed that opportunity. He needed a scholarship. He wasn't going to any Division I school sitting on the bench. And his family were junk dealers. They couldn't afford to send him to Tulane or anyplace like it. But then Robbie went down, and all those doors opened right up for Marc.

"God help me for thinking it," he said. "But I always have, and I always will. I saw what I saw, and I know what I know."

"You think Dozer would do that for Marc?"

"I think Dozer *did* do it for him. And Dozer was no freethinker. He didn't come up with that on his own."

"Did he not like Robbie?"

"He liked Robbie fine, but he was loyal to Marc. He might have thought he owed him."

"Did you ever say anything to Marc about it?"

He shook his head. "No, but nothing was ever the same between us after that day. Maybe he sensed that was what I was thinking. I don't know."

"Did Robbie ever say he thought it was anything other than an accident?"

"Not to me. I can't imagine he didn't wonder, though. He was always the one had to get to the bottom of a story."

"Did you ever say anything to anybody about your suspicion?"

"I started to once. A few weeks after it happened. I was having a hard time dealing with it, and Coach Latrelle pulled me into his office. He was a good man. Still is. He asked me what was wrong, and I started to say *what if* . . . He didn't want to hear it. Nobody would have. By then Marc was already our team hero, and we were going into the playoffs. That's all anybody cared about, so . . ."

So . . . Robbie Fontenot had nearly lost his leg, an injury that set him on a path of self-destruction . . . and Dozer Cormier had become an alcoholic . . . and Marc Mercier had gone on with his life, gotten an education, met and married his wife . . . and Eli McVay had carried this terrible suspicion like a sliver in his soul all this time, festering, aching so that it could still bring him to the point of tears ten years later . . . all because a good lie was so much more palatable than an ugly truth.

People had wanted to believe Marc Mercier was a hero, just as they were happy to assume Robbie Fontenot was good for nothing once he'd fallen from his pedestal. The average human wanted life to be simple, cut-and-dried, black-and-white, but it almost never was.

If Eli's suspicion was correct, that Robbie's injury had been no accident, what did that mean in the here and now? What would ten years of rage built in jail and rehab and bitter disappointment do? Annie could only imagine the resentment. B'Lynn had suggested it, just based on the outcome of what had happened. How could Robbie not resent Marc? If he had somehow come to the conclusion that his injury had been intentional, how could that resentment not boil over? What if that resentment had become motive? Annie wondered as she drove back toward Bayou Breaux.

Nick had texted her to come back to the Pizza Hut as soon as she was done in Lafayette. He hadn't said why, nor had he answered when she'd tried to call him. She texted him back, including the piece of information she'd gleaned from Eli regarding Robbie being seen with Dozer Cormier at Monster Bash. He didn't respond.

She didn't want to try to imagine why he wanted her back at the PH. Her head was spinning just from that morning's revelations.

Danny Perry had tried to run Robbie Fontenot's car off the road into the swamp. Robbie had told Eli he was investigating police corruption. Just a joke, Eli said. Robbie wasn't a reporter. He didn't have a job at all. But he had a box full of money no one could explain. How much of that money might have Danny Perry's fingerprints all over it?

She kept going back to Halloween night.

Robbie had been seen talking to a town cop . . . or a party reveler dressed as one . . .

He had also been seen talking to Dozer Cormier.

And he hadn't been seen since—until Danny Perry had chased after his car leaving the Merciers' neighborhood.

If Robbie was driving that car, what was he doing there? And why had Danny Perry been there to intercept him? Danny had been working days—had worked that very day. How had he come to be there in the middle of the night? It wasn't like the PD didn't have a dog shift. The only way Danny got that assignment had to have been to volunteer for it, and why in the world would he do that when he had worked all day? Unless he thought there was something in it for him.

If Annie gave any credence to the possibility of Melissa paying Robbie to get rid of her husband, why this cloak-and-dagger bullshit in the middle of the night—calling her cell phone, creeping around the Merciers' neighborhood? Maybe if the wife wasn't paying what she owed him . . . But Melissa Mercier had no known connection to Robbie. Will Faulkner might have been the linchpin there, but they certainly didn't have enough cause at this point to ask a judge for a look at Faulkner's phone records or his finances for any unusual withdrawals of cash.

There were too many loose puzzle pieces, most of which would likely turn out to mean nothing. Murder almost always turned out to be depressingly, stupidly simple. A killed B because of money or jealousy or for revenge or in a fit of rage. The trick was sifting through the thousand pieces to find just the five or six that fit together to make the true picture of what had happened.

She turned into the law enforcement center parking lot, thinking she would begin again with the security video from downtown on Halloween night.

"Broussard!" Stokes called out as she walked in the door of the Pizza Hut. "How come you're never around when I need you?"

"Because I don't live my life for you?" Annie said. "Where's Nick?"

"I don't know. He got a text and left a little while ago."

"And since when have you ever needed me?"

"Since I found this video," he said. "Come have a look."

She rounded the counter and went to stand behind him at his desk. "If this is porn, I'm gonna kick your ass. I'm in no mood for your nonsense, Chaz."

"Well, this isn't gonna improve your mood any," he said. "We found out this morning there were two trucks at the dump site of our murdered guy. One dark and one light. This is a security video from a garage near the turnoff for that road. We lucked out. They've got a nice big yard light on that property."

He clicked his mouse and started the footage. "We know Cody Parcelle drives a black Dodge Ram, and there's a dark truck going by, could be a Ram. Can't see the plates, can't see the driver. And here comes our light truck right behind. Does that look familiar to you?"

An older white pickup with what looked like rust damage around the rear wheel wells.

The truck that had been parked in front of the Parcelles' barn.

Annie felt her heart sink. "Oh, man . . ."

Stokes pushed his chair back and stood. "We need to go pick up Tulsie Parcelle."

"And here I thought this day couldn't get any worse."

28

DOZER CORMIER HAD NEVER SHOWN UP FOR WORK THAT DAY. His crew boss had shrugged it off as Dozer being Dozer. Just more of the rough patch he'd been going through lately. The rough patch he'd been going through since Halloween, the night Robbie Fontenot had gone missing. Robbie Fontenot, whom Dozer had flatly denied seeing.

He had looked Nick right in the eyes and said he hadn't seen Robbie Fontenot in years when he had in fact seen him in Bayou Breaux little more than a week past. Why lie about it?

Of course, lying seemed to be Dozer's default mode when he was panicking. Confrontation overwhelmed him, and he automatically chose the quick lie over a truth that might trap him in something. Trap him in what, was the question.

Nick turned in at the Country Estates mobile home park. It was even more depressing in the light of day than it had been the night before with its faded, rusting old trailer houses and chicken-scratch yards of dirt and weeds and beater cars. He pulled in beside Dozer's Silverado. At least he was keeping his day drinking at home instead of endangering the public on the roadways.

Nick found him around the back of the trailer, snoring in a hammock strung between two sickly elm trees, a pile of beer cans on the ground beneath him.

"Dozer!" Nick yelled, and kicked the pile of cans.

The racket startled Dozer awake. The big man woke flailing and sputtering, clawing at the air, rocking the hammock. He twisted sideways, trying to escape some imagined threat, and dumped himself on the ground with a thud.

"What the fuck?" he said, groaning. "Goddamn it, that hurt!"

Nick watched dispassionately as Dozer struggled up onto his hands and knees.

"Me, I once got called to a death scene," he said, "where a man died in a hammock just like this one. He'd been dead a couple of days out in the heat. His head had swelled up like a watermelon, and his face turned black as pitch. Turned out he had passed out drunk and a rattlesnake had fallen out of the tree above him, landed on his face, and bit him, and he died right there."

Dozer looked up at him like he was crazy as he struggled to get his big feet under him and stand. He was dressed in his usual bib overalls with no shirt, one of the shoulder straps undone and hanging down. He shifted the denim suit around his bulk, tugging at his crotch. "Why the hell you telling me that?"

"Rattlesnakes are pretty good climbers," Nick said. "Most people don't know that."

"What are you doing here, Fourcade?"

"You should always be aware of what animals you might piss off, lest they bite you, Mr. Cormier. Myself, for instance," he said. "Me, I don't like being lied to, and I'm gonna have a bad reaction to that."

"I don't know what you're talking about," Dozer grumbled, sitting down on an old tree stump that had been sawed off at chair height.

"How drunk are you right now?"

"Not enough."

"You had better be sober enough to listen to me or I'll have a deputy here in five minutes to haul your ass to jail."

"Why? I ain't done nothing."

"Don't sell yourself short. You've managed to irritate the hell out of me today, and I've only just now laid eyes on you."

"This is harassment," Dozer said.

"You think so? Call a cop on that mysterious little cell phone you told me you didn't own, you fucking liar."

"You're mad 'cause I have a phone?"

"I'm mad because you keep wasting my time, Dozer," Nick said. "You think I want to keep coming out to this miserable shithole to talk around in circles with you?"

"Then don't."

"You told me you hadn't seen Robbie Fontenot in years."

"I haven't."

"And there you go again. I have a witness who puts you in the company of Robbie Fontenot Halloween night."

"He's a liar!"

"He's got absolutely no reason to lie about that. You, on the other hand, make a habit of it. Why is that?"

"It's none of your business who I talk to."

"Ah, well, see, you're wrong there, as usual," Nick said. "It is literally my business when the person you lie about talking to went missing on that very night."

"I don't know nothing about it," Dozer grumbled.

"Always so conveniently ignorant, aren't you?" Nick said. "Where did you go that night after you left Monster Bash?"

"Nowhere. Home."

"Really? Because I'm gonna go to every one of your neighbors here and ask them did they see you. And I'm gonna guess that even in this sorry place, at least one of them is gonna have a video doorbell, and we'll see if you were home or not."

Dozer frowned, his big face creasing like a bulldog's as he considered his next story.

"I was drinking with Marc."

"Where?"

"I don't know! I was drunk. Ask Marc."

"Ask Marc, who is also missing? Are you trying to be a wiseass here, *couillon*? 'Cause you're missing half that equation."

"Maybe I saw Robbie and I just don't remember," Dozer said, backtracking.

"Really?" Nick said. "You run into a guy you haven't seen in years, the guy whose life you ruined, and that just slipped your mind?"

"That was an accident!"

"Does it matter?" Nick asked, pressing on the old wound. "What happened happened. He could have been a superstar, but he became a drug addict because of you."

"That's not fair!"

"And you became an alcoholic," Nick said. "That's not fair, either, but here you are, a lying drunk sitting on a stump in the backyard of a shithole. You might want to reconsider some of your life choices, Dozer."

"Why are you doing this?" Dozer asked, looking miserable.

"Because I want the truth, and all you're giving me is one bad lie after the next."

Nick took a step back to release some of the tension between them. Dozer was red-faced, breathing hard, clearly emotional. Nick had just poked a sharp stick into an old wound that had never healed, a wound that had spent ten years in a state of festering infection. It was cruel, but he couldn't care about that. Dozer Cormier was at least sitting there in the flesh, which was more than he could say for Robbie Fontenot or Marc Mercier.

"You realize, Dozer, that we're living in the digital age, the age of communication, and there are cameras literally everywhere now, watching our every move," he said. "It may take some time, but I will go over every security video in town from that night, and I will find hard proof of you talking to Robbie Fontenot."

"So what if I saw him?" he said irritably.

"Why lie about it?"

"Maybe I don't like talking about him. Maybe I don't like remembering all that."

"Fair enough," Nick said. "But if you'd told me that from the start, we wouldn't be having this conversation now. See how the truth works?"

Dozer said nothing.

"You can't just bury it, Dozer, whatever it is," Nick said quietly. "You been trying to do that for ten years, and look at you. Do you want this to be the rest of your life? A drunk, a failure, trying to hide from yourself?"

"What do you care?"

"I hate waste. You have a life. You have people who care about you. Donnie Bichon, Tommy Crawford—they gave you a chance, they want you to succeed. You're just pissing it away because you can't resolve something you did ten years ago. You need to get right with that."

Dozer looked away and murmured, "I tried."

"Try again."

"I need to go," he said, groaning a little as he stood. He hitched up his overalls and fastened the loose strap.

"You think I'm gonna let you get behind the wheel of that truck?" Nick asked. "There's a dozen empty beer cans laying here. You get in that truck, I'll have to arrest you."

"Jesus fucking Christ," he grumbled. "Can you just *go*?"

"We're not done," Nick said. "When you went out with Marc Saturday night, where'd you go? And don't tell me you don't remember. You're too young to have Alzheimer's."

The big man huffed a sigh and lumbered around in a circle, cupping his bald head in both massive hands. "Goal Post."

"What was Marc driving?"

"What?"

"What vehicle was he driving that night?"

"His truck. What else?"

"Where'd he leave his boat?" Nick asked. "He left home driving his truck, pulling his boat. He was supposed to meet Luc Sunday morning at the Corners with it. He wasn't pulling that boat with him to every bar parking lot in town that night, was he?"

"I don't know. I wasn't riding with him. Who cares, anyway? What difference does it make?"

"Where'd you go after you left Goal Post?"

"I left at halftime and came home."

"Why you didn't stay until the game was over?"

"I was sick of listening to Marc complain about his wife, complain about his brother, complain about his life," Dozer said. "His life looks pretty damn good to me."

"And did Marc stay?"

"He was still there when I left, flirting with some blond girl."

"Tulsie Parcelle?" Nick asked, wondering if maybe there wasn't more to that story than an innocent dance at Outlaw. Maybe Stokes's latest theory of an affair wasn't so far-fetched.

Dozer shrugged. "I don't know her, and I didn't care."

"Does Marc like to play around?"

"He's a guy."

"Me, I'm a guy," Nick said. "I don't cheat on my wife. Does he?"

"*Mais*, I don't know. I mind my own business, me."

"You're not blind."

Dozer heaved a big beer-tainted sigh. "Girls like Marc. Marc likes girls. Whatever else goes on is not my business."

"Well, *not your business* might have got him killed," Nick said. "Unless you know something I don't . . ."

"Me, I don't wanna know nothing," Dozer said wearily. "That's why I drink."

"Did you see Luc that night?"

"Yeah. He was there. Another good reason to leave. Are we done now?" he asked irritably. "I've got another six-pack to start."

"Yeah, we're done," Nick said. "For now. Stay off the roads, Dozer. You want to drink yourself to death because you can't escape your own head, I can't stop you, but I don't want you killing someone else. The last thing you need is the death of an innocent person on your conscience."

"Yeah," Dozer said, looking away toward his house. "That's the last thing I need."

29

"**DO YOU** THINK SHE'D LIE FOR HER HUSBAND?" STOKES ASKED, glancing over at Annie.

He had insisted on driving this time. She had been happy to let him, though she almost hoped he would get lost, she was dreading this so. If this had gone down the way Stokes suggested, Tulsie was an accessory, voluntary or not.

"Yes. Absolutely, she would," she said. "One: she's scared to death of him. And two: she's scared to death to lose everything she's worked for."

"What about the hired hand?"

"I don't think she likes Cody, but she's loyal to Tulsie. There's nothing to say she would know anything about what went on Saturday night, though. She would have left after feeding the horses late in the day Saturday."

"Do you think Tulsie would have told her what happened?"

"I don't know. She's pretty ashamed. She might not have, but we should keep them separate."

"Agreed."

"Let me deal with Tulsie," Annie said. "This is gonna be really hard for her."

"That's why I brought you. I'm not a complete knothead."

Annie chuckled, glad for the second of relief. "Don't sell yourself short, Chaz."

"Very funny."

They pulled into the Parcelles' driveway and up to the barn. It was late afternoon, the sun already sinking low in the west, casting the barnyard in tones of gold and sepia. A couple of horses in pens near the barn raised their heads from piles of hay to look at them with casual curiosity. The dogs came running out of the barn, barking and baying their greetings.

The white truck that had been parked in front of the barn the last two times Annie had come there was gone. As they got out of the car, Chaz nodded in the direction of the house, maybe fifty yards away and partially obstructed from view by trees. The truck was backed in under the carport next to the house.

Country music was playing in the barn accompanied by the sounds of horses getting fed—buckets rattling, hooves banging on stall doors.

Izzy Guidry looked up as they walked in, her expression blank.

"Hey, Izzy," Annie said. "Is Tulsie around?"

"Nope. Can I help you?"

"I just have a couple more questions for her, is all. Is she riding?"

"No. She's home sick," she said, digging sweet feed out of a rolling cart with a big metal scoop. "She got a migraine. Been sick all day. Did you get hold of Cody?"

"That's the thing," Stokes said. "Cody never showed up in Houston."

"Seriously?" She took the scoop of feed to a stall where a black horse with a blazed face stood tossing its head up and down in anticipation of its dinner. "Where'd he go, then? Did he have an accident or something?"

"We don't know. He hasn't been in touch?"

She shrugged and dug another scoop of feed out of the cart. "He wouldn't call me."

"Tulsie hasn't said anything about him?" Annie asked.

"No."

"I'm just gonna go on up to the house and see her," Annie said. "It won't take but a minute."

"She's sleeping," Izzy said, going back to the feed cart. "She takes that migraine medication and it knocks her out. Can't she just call you tomorrow?"

"Did she say anything to you about what her husband did to her Saturday night?" Stokes asked.

"No."

"You weren't suspicious when you saw her looking like she'd been beat up?"

"I done been over all this with her," she said irritably, shooting Annie a look like she was a traitor or something. "She told me she got hurt getting bales down. It's none of my business what goes on between them. I'm just the hired hand."

"What can you tell me about that white truck up by the house?" Stokes asked.

"What about it?" she snapped, her eyes darting from Stokes to Annie as Annie stepped back toward the open door. Either she didn't want to be left alone with Stokes, or she didn't want Annie going to the house. Why was that? Annie wondered.

"Do you know who might have been driving that truck Sunday night?" Stokes asked.

"How would I know? Sunday's my day off."

Annie slipped out the door as Stokes continued his questions. A fat Welsh corgi dogged her heels as she walked up the driveway toward the house. Something felt off, she thought, her nerves raising goose bumps down her arms. Maybe Izzy just didn't like Stokes, or didn't like men, but she had come across as tense and anxious, which was different than the other times Annie had spoken to her.

Her own anxiety rose like a slow tide as she neared the house. There shouldn't have been any reason for that, she told herself. It was just the Ghost of Disaster Past. The anxiety was an oversensitive alarm she had to learn how to defuse. There was nothing dangerous about Tulsie Parcelle.

But even as she told herself that, her memory brought up the last person she had wrongly considered a non-threat.

She made one circuit around the white pickup, which had a couple of stuffed black garbage bags in the back. Raising up on her toes, she looked into the cab. There was a jacket and some dirty work gloves on the passenger seat, a few pieces of mail, a couple of discarded cash register receipts. An open can of Red Bull sat in the cup holder in the center console. Nothing out of the ordinary.

She left the truck and went up the front sidewalk, climbed the prefabricated concrete steps, and rang the doorbell. No one came.

Poor Tulsie, she thought, as she rang the bell a second time. She had been inconsolable the night before, sobbing to the point of gagging herself after she had admitted Cody had beaten her Saturday night. It wasn't any wonder she was sick. Her entire world was coming down around her, and it was about to get worse. She wouldn't be able to deny the video evidence. If she hadn't been in one of those trucks, then who had been?

Annie got down from the steps and went around the side of the house, peeking in windows as she went, seeing nothing of note. A typical living room with an oversize brown leather couch, a coffee table cluttered with magazines and a silver bowl overflowing with horse show ribbons. On the walls hung framed photos of horses in competition.

She went back around under the carport and climbed another set of steps to the kitchen door. Cardboard had been taped over a couple of broken glass panes in the upper half of the door. Annie peered in, getting a view of a messy kitchen. She buzzed the video doorbell, then knocked, feeling impatient. Maybe Tulsie was sleeping off her migraine medication, but she could have as easily taken an overdose and willed herself to sleep for eternity. Her life was a mess and not about to get better. It wasn't a stretch to think she might just want out altogether.

A wide deck ran the length of the back side of the house, with a gas grill and dining table and chairs right outside the sliding door into the kitchen. A patio lounge chair and a couple of swivel armchairs sat on the other end outside a second slider, along with another pair of stuffed garbage bags.

Annie went to the second sliding door and looked in at what had to be the master bedroom, squinting, willing her eyes to adjust. There were no lamps on in the room. Situated on the east side of the house, the room had little in the way of natural light.

Tulsie sat on the floor in the middle of the room with her back to the glass door, head down, shoulders slumped.

Unease ran like cold rain through Annie. She knocked on the slider. "Tulsie?" And knocked again. "Tulsie? It's Annie Broussard."

The girl didn't respond, didn't move.

"Tulsie!" Annie called louder, yanking the sliding door open.

The overwhelming smell of bleach nearly knocked her backward. Coughing on it, she went into the room, her focus on the girl, but her mind grabbing images like snapshots as she went—the bed stripped down to the mattress, a shattered mirror over a dresser, items that had been swept from the dresser and scattered on the floor . . .

The girl sat cross-legged on the floor, holding a bloody kitchen knife in her lap, tears streaming silently down her face, her eyes blank.

Oh, shit.

Her heart racing, Annie stepped slowly, carefully around the girl and crouched down into her line of sight. Tulsie had already cut both forearms a couple of times. In the wrong place and at the wrong angle to get the job done, but she was bleeding heavily nonetheless.

"Tulsie, put the knife aside," Annie said firmly but quietly. "You don't need that. I'm here to help you."

Tulsie didn't move, didn't acknowledge her. In her peripheral vision, Annie could see damage done to one wall from what looked like a shotgun blast, and blood spatter someone had smeared on the drywall in an unsuccessful attempt to scrub it away. The mattress was stained. Sections of the carpet had been cut out and removed. That was probably what was in the garbage bags, she thought, blood-stained carpet and other evidence of violence.

"Tulsie, why don't you give me that knife and tell me what happened?" she said, holding out her hand. "I know you probably think there's no way out of this, but that's not true."

"I can't do anything right," Tulsie murmured, looking down at her bloody arms. "Cody always says I mess everything up, and he's right. Look at me."

"Cody's an ass," Annie said. He was almost certainly a dead ass, though in the moment Annie couldn't begin to feel bad for him. He had beaten this girl senseless—more than once. And now his adoring little wife sat there, abused physically and emotionally, ready to end her own life over a man who had systematically destroyed her.

"Cody's dead," Tulsie murmured. "It's my fault."

"You have a right to defend yourself, Tulsie," Annie said. "A good lawyer will argue self-defense, and I don't know who in their right mind would blame you."

"I made him mad. I shouldn't have made him mad."

She was as pale as milk, and her eyes had a glassy sheen. She was going into shock.

"This isn't your fault," Annie said. It didn't matter if it was or it wasn't. All that mattered now was getting the knife away from her and getting her out of this house. "Let me help you, Tulsie. Set that knife aside, and we'll go get those cuts looked after."

"Everything is so messed up, Annie. I'm gonna lose everything. Everything I worked for."

"You're not gonna lose your life," Annie said, reaching out a hand for the knife. "Everything else can be fixed or replaced. It doesn't matter."

She tried to put the story together in her head. Tulsie had come home from Outlaw as ordered. Cody had come home and laid into her. She already knew this from what Tulsie had told them the night before. But that story had ended with Cody packing up and leaving for Houston the next day, when instead he had almost certainly died in this room that night.

"Let me have the knife, Tulsie."

"No. No. No . . ."

Annie leaned an inch or two closer. Tulsie pulled the knife up as if she might use it. Annie leaned back, her mind racing. What if this girl just snapped? What if Tulsie came at her with the knife? Could she get out of the way quickly enough? Would she draw her weapon? Would she use it?

Suddenly, splitting up with Stokes looked like a stupid, reckless decision. She had expected to find Tulsie ill and helpless, but desperate people did desperate things. They found wells of violence and self-preservation deep within. They tapped into physical strength they never knew they had. She had experienced that firsthand and had the scars to prove it.

Focus, Annie. Focus. She needed her full attention on the moment and did her best to shove her anxiety to the side.

"Put the knife down, Tulsie," she said. "Whatever happened, I'll help you."

Who else had helped her Saturday night? she wondered. Cody had to outweigh Tulsie by a good eighty pounds or more. And deadweight always seemed twice as heavy. Tulsie could never have moved him on her own. She had to have called someone to help her. Two trucks had gone out to that spot where the body had been dumped.

Stokes's theory had Cody killing Marc for messing around with Tulsie. Maybe he had the right puzzle pieces in the wrong order. Maybe Marc had done the deed and carried the weight. Maybe Marc was the one who had headed for parts unknown. They would sort that out later. Now the only thing that mattered was getting this girl the help she needed.

"Put the knife down, Tulsie," she said. "I'll help you any way I can."

The girl looked up at her, puzzled. "But what about Izzy?"

"What about Izzy?"

"She was only trying to help me," she said. She had begun to shiver. "She told him before . . . If he hurt me again . . ."

"Izzy shot Cody?" Annie asked.

"And I'd damn well do it again."

Annie looked up. Izzy Guidry stood on the deck in the open doorway, a handgun pointed straight at her.

30

THERE WERE NO SLOW NIGHTS AT THE GOAL POST SPORTS BAR, Louisianians being as sports obsessed as they were. Even in the middle of the week the bar was hopping. The building sat out on one corner of the parking lot shared by a newer strip mall that included a Rouses supermarket and an Ace Hardware, all of it built in the last ten years to service the trendier western neighborhoods of Bayou Breaux.

At a glance, it seemed like exactly the kind of place Marc Mercier would hang out—modern, popular with the upwardly mobile—and not the kind of place his brother, Luc, would frequent. But even a hard-ass like Luc Mercier had to succumb to the lure of college football on giant state-of-the-art TV screens.

A MISSING poster showing Marc Mercier was taped to the front door glass with HELP US FIND MARC! printed in big red block letters on a second piece of posterboard. The smell of hamburgers and onion rings filled the air as Nick walked into the bar. Basketball filled the TV screens.

The décor was industrial-meets-gymnasium with lots of exposed pipes and ducts in the high black ceiling. The two full-size bars on either side of the space were faced in corrugated tin. The floor was an actual blond wood gymnasium floor complete with the painted lines of a basketball court. The bartenders and waitresses were dressed as referees in black-and-white-striped tops with whistles hanging on lanyards around their necks.

Nick singled out the most senior bartender—a thirtysomething Black woman with LSU purple and gold braids woven through her hair. Devonta Williams. He recognized her as one of the parent coaches from Justin's T-ball league. She spotted him as he made his way toward the bar.

"Detective Fourcade!" she said with a big smile. "How's that little ballplayer of yours?"

"He's well," Nick said. "How's yours?"

"She's on to flag football now. That girl is as sports crazy as her mama. She runs me ragged. What can I get for you?"

"Nothing for me, Devonta, thank you," he said. "I'm here on business, I'm afraid."

"Is this about Marc Mercier?" she asked. "We put the poster up as soon as we got it."

"Do you know him?"

"Marc? Sure. He's in here all the time, holding court. Everybody loves Marc."

"So I hear. Were you working Saturday night?"

"Are you kidding me? LSU versus Florida? It was all hands on deck!"

"Did you see Marc that night?"

"Sure, he was in here. Him and his henchman, Dozer Cormier."

"Why do you call him that?"

Devonta shrugged. "It just always looks that way to me. There's Marc, all smiles, glad-handing everybody like a politician, and Dozer right behind him, the Bayou Bodyguard, looking like he eats iron and spits out nails. Don't nobody mess with Dozer."

"They were both here Saturday night?"

"Yep. Marc was here until the end of the game. Dozer left early."

"You're sure about that?"

"It was a madhouse in here, but I remember because Marc's brother was here, and it looked like the three of them were having words. I keep an eye on Dozer because he gets nasty when he's drunk, and I don't want no trouble in here. This is a nice place. We don't put up with fights and shit like that. You wanna ass up? Go elsewhere. I see someone making a problem, they're outta here," she said, gesturing like an umpire throwing a baseball manager out of a game.

"I heard Marc was flirting with a blond girl," Nick said.

Devonta laughed. "A blonde, a brunette, a redhead. My hundred-year-old grandma could come in here, and Marc would flirt with her, too. He's just like that. All charm. He don't mean nothing by it. He's sweet. He finds something nice to say to all of them, not just the pretty ones. All the girls love Marc."

"Did you recognize this blond girl?"

"No, can't say I did. Twentysomething. Hair like a mermaid. I think she was with a bachelorette party or something like that."

"I'll need to have a look at your security video from that night. Indoors and out."

"No problem," she said, letting herself out from behind the bar. "I'm manager tonight."

She caught the attention of the next senior bartender. "Kirk, you're up! I've got to go back to the office."

"Yes, ma'am!"

She led the way down a hall, pulling a set of keys off her belt and sorting through them for the right one to open the office.

"I sure hope you find him alive and well," she said. "I worry about all my customers, you know. I worry someone is gonna have just one too many and slip out of here without anyone the wiser. Next thing you know, y'all are fishing their car out the swamp with them in it."

"We'll hope not," Nick said. "He's got a wife and baby waiting on him."

"'Course the rumor is he's that dead body y'all found down the bayou, and that the wife and her lover did him in." She cut him a look over her shoulder. "Is there anything to that?"

"Not so far."

"Not that you'd tell me if there was," she said. "You're like the damn sphynx, you are."

She unlocked the door and let him into the office, going around behind the desk herself to wake up the computer and open the security program.

"Here you go. This is all the video from Saturday night. Eight cameras. Four inside and four outside. Good luck. I hope you find what you need to bring Marc home."

Nick thanked her and settled in at the desk.

"I'm gonna bring you a club soda and a veggie burger," Devonta said on her way to the door. "And I don't want any sass back from you about it."

"Yes, ma'am," Nick said, but his eyes were on the video screen, and food was the furthest thing from his mind.

31

"**GET AWAY** FROM HER," IZZY SAID, NEVER TAKING HER EYES off Annie. "Tulsie, come on. We're going."

Annie held her hands out to the side to show she had no weapon as she stood slowly. "She can't go anywhere but to the ER, Izzy. She's cut herself pretty bad here."

"I'll take care of her," Izzy said, stepping farther into the room. "I can bandage a horse, I can bandage a person. Come on, Tulsie."

"This isn't a scratch, Izzy. Come around and see."

"Don't think you can trick me," Izzy warned, but she took another step closer. Annie could see the concern in her eyes as she cut a quick glance at Tulsie, still not in a position to see the seriousness of her injuries. "Tulsie, what have you done to yourself? Are you all right?"

"I messed up, Izzy," Tulsie said softly, shivering. "That's all I ever do."

"That's not true," Izzy said, taking another couple of steps. She stayed to the far side of the room, trying to get an angle where she could see what damage Tulsie might have done to herself and keep an eye on Annie as well. "None of this mess is your fault. Cody did what he did, and he got what he had coming to him."

"You were here when he attacked her?" Annie asked.

Izzy shot her a glare. "I'm not telling you anything. I'm taking Tulsie, and we're getting the hell out of here."

"You're not," Annie said, taking a step back, trying to give Izzy more room to maneuver. "She's not going anywhere but the ER. And where would you go, anyway, Izzy? If you run, you're a fugitive. That never works out. You're better off staying. When you shot Cody, you were acting to save the life of your friend. People will understand that."

"He would'a killed her this time," Izzy said. "He said as much. The hell if I was standing by and watching that happen. He was a fucking bully, and he would'a never stopped. I *know*. I know *exactly* how that goes. Nobody ever did a goddamn thing to stop him, including you. He would'a killed her. Now he won't kill nobody."

"I'm sorry, Izzy," Annie said sincerely. "I can't make someone press charges."

"You should'a known she was too scared to do it!"

"I did know," Annie said. "But I can only do what I'm allowed to do."

"You're *useless*," Izzy said bitterly.

"I don't feel well," Tulsie mumbled. Her complexion had gone a bit gray.

"She needs to get to the hospital, Izzy. I don't think she'll bleed to death, but she's going into shock."

Izzy took another step around, still holding the gun on Annie, hesitant to look away. It was probably Stokes's gun, Annie realized. What had she done to him? Was he lying in the barn bleeding to death? Had Izzy somehow gotten hold of his weapon and shot him?

Izzy's eyes went wide, and she gasped as she finally saw the extent of the damage Tulsie had done to herself. "Oh, Jesus, Tulsie! What have you done?"

"Everything's wrong . . . and I can't fix it . . ."

"You need to let me call an ambulance," Annie said.

"I can't do this anymore . . ." Tulsie murmured.

Izzy crouched down in front of her. "Aw, Tulsie, no, no, no, no . . . Don't do this! Don't kill yourself over some stupid man. He never deserved you!"

"I just wanted someone to love me," Tulsie said.

"I know," Izzy whispered, fighting tears. She reached out and tenderly brushed Tulsie's hair back from her face.

"Please don't leave me, Izzy."

"I won't leave you," Izzy whispered. She set the handgun down on the floor and wrapped her arms around Tulsie's shoulders. "I'm right here. I'm not going anywhere."

She glanced back at Annie over her shoulder. "Call the ambulance. And tell them to hurry."

32

THE VIDEO QUALITY WAS GOOD, CLEAR. ONE OF THE BENEFITS of Goal Post being a relatively new establishment with a well-off group of local owners who enjoyed spending money to have the best of everything.

He found the camera that was focused on the area where Marc and Dozer had settled and watched the show. Devonta Williams had used the term *holding court*, and an apt term it was. Marc moved among his audience like an actor on a stage, with a big smile and big gestures, clearly basking in the glow of their adoration.

Dozer sat watching as Marc worked the room, looking like he would have rather been anywhere else on earth. This wasn't the kind of place for Dozer or the crowd he would have run with, Nick thought. He sat among the cute, stylish people like an ogre at high tea, too big, too rough, too ugly for them, looking miserable and angry as he drank his beer. He was an accessory for Marc, a prop, part of Marc's carefully cultivated image. Bayou Bodyguard, Devonta had called him.

Hell of a way to treat a friend.

Nick kept waiting for Tulsie Parcelle to arrive on the scene, thinking they might have hooked up at this bar before going on to Outlaw. She had been out that night with a group of girls, celebrating someone's divorce—a group that could have easily been mistaken for a bachelorette party, he supposed. But she never appeared. The blonde with the mermaid hair was no one Nick recognized, just another pretty girl with a big smile and a tight top, putting on a show for Marc. She was just one of half a dozen pretty young things swarming around in Marc's orbit that night.

Nick shook his head as he watched Marc work his charms. He thought of Melissa Mercier sitting at home that night with a teething baby, feeling abandoned on the eve of her birthday while her husband tried to hang on to his youth, putting on a show for a bunch of shallow people who were still impressed by the fact that he had been pretty good at throwing a football when he was in high school.

Who raised a man like that? He thought of Kiki Mercier and her adoration for her favorite child. Had she ever told him no? Had she ever taught him how to treat a lady? How to value other people? She had taught him that the sun rose and set on him, and that he could do no wrong.

Marc had no doubt found out—out in the real world, away from his past—that he might be able to get by on his looks and his charm to a certain extent, but that people who didn't have that frame of reference of Marc the Star Quarterback would have a different view of him, expect more from him, be less impressed by who he had once been. And what did that do to a man when he realized he had no substance, that he was just a fraud trying to skate through life on the thinnest ice of superficiality?

People were always saying what a great guy Marc was because again and again he stepped in when necessary to save the day. But now Nick wondered at his motives. Was he really a hero, or was he just addicted to the adoration of the people who saw him that way?

At one point in the video, Luc Mercier entered the picture. Luc, who had never once mentioned going to Goal Post or that Marc had.

He walked up to Marc's booth with a beer in hand and a scowl on his face. Angry words were exchanged. And there was the reason he had lied, Nick thought. He hadn't wanted to put himself in a bar having an argument with his brother, who had disappeared shortly after.

Dozer got up and left. Luc walked away. Marc downed his beer, then revved up the million-watt smile again and reimmersed himself in his pack of acolytes.

What had that conversation been about? Serious, contentious. The brothers had exchanged blows earlier in the day, then exchanged words that night. Nick had a hard time believing that was nothing but a disagreement over business practices—unless those practices were far outside the norm.

He kept wanting to go to the copper theft theory because that was simple and plausible. Junk dealers buying and selling stolen goods. But he had yet to find any evidence or hear anything about the Mercier brothers linking them to illegal activity.

What else would they have been so at odds about? Was it just the oil-and-water combination of a favored son and the family work-horse? Twenty-some years of jealousy and resentment coming to a head? Luc wanted his life back and his baby brother gone, but as Nick watched Marc bask in the glow of adoration, it seemed he had no intention of leaving.

Nick watched the video from that particular camera until Marc said his goodbyes, hugged half a dozen people, and headed down the hallway toward the back exit. He switched then to the exterior camera view from the back entrance and fast-forwarded to the correlating time stamp.

Marc came out the back door, heading to the area where bar employees parked. Nick scanned the first row of vehicles, looking for but not finding Marc's Ford Raptor truck. He could only see the first of two rows of parking, but he knew from driving around the building that this area backed up to a retaining wall where the garbage dumpsters were parked. If Marc had parked to one side of the lot, he would be able to exit without Nick seeing him. If he had parked closer to the other end of the lot, he would have to drive out right in front of the camera.

He waited impatiently for the Raptor to come around, but it never did. The only car to drive around the end of the parking area and past the security camera was a blue Toyota Corolla with some years on it.

Robbie Fontenot's car.

What. The. Hell?

Nick backed the video up and watched again. The car had no front license plate. Louisiana did not require such. But he froze the video as the car passed, trying to get a look at the rear plate. He jotted what he could see of the number on a Post-it from a pad on the desk, took a picture of the Post-it with his phone, and tossed the note in the trash.

He sat back and swiveled the desk chair. What the actual hell?

He ran the video back and watched it again. It was impossible to see into the car, impossible to see the driver or if there was a passenger. He couldn't see Marc Mercier in the vehicle, but if he wasn't, then where the hell had he gone? And if he was, what did that mean? Why would he be driving around in Robbie Fontenot's vehicle?

His phone pinged the arrival of a text from Annie.

Your DB is Cody Parcelle. Suspect in custody.
Details later.

Cody Parcelle was lying dead in the morgue and Marc Mercier was driving around in the vehicle of a man who hadn't been seen in more than a week. What the actual hell, indeed.

33

"SHE KNEW HE WAS GONNA LAY INTO HER WHEN HE GOT home," Izzy murmured. "She was terrified of him."

They sat in the same exam room where Kiki Mercier had slammed Annie into the cabinets just days before, Izzy sitting on the exam table in handcuffs while Tulsie was being tended to down the hall in the ER. Annie knew she was breaking about ten different rules bringing Izzy there, but she didn't care.

Despite Izzy's initial plan to run, Annie knew Izzy Guidry wasn't a flight risk. She wasn't going to abandon Tulsie. She wasn't going to do anything violent. Knocking the wind out of Stokes with the handle of a scoop shovel and locking him in the feed room was the craziest thing she was going to do that night. Technically, she was a killer, yes, but with a victim pool of one, and that damage had already been done.

She was maybe going to catch hell for it, but Annie felt this was her best option for getting the whole story, and more importantly to her, it was the humane thing to do for both Izzy and Tulsie.

"I reckon I shouldn't be talking to you," Izzy said. She looked so sad and so alone. She was beside herself with worry for her friend.

Her eyes kept going to the door, anxious for someone to come with news. She lifted both hands and tried to push her dark hair out of her eyes.

"I haven't read you your rights yet, Izzy, and that's for a reason," Annie said, moving to stand between Izzy and the door, to have her attention. "Until I do that, nothing you say to me is ever gonna make it into a courtroom. So, we're just two women having a conversation here. And nobody needs to know anything about it. You understand me?"

Izzy gave her a long, skeptical look. "Why should I trust you?"

"I want the best outcome. For Tulsie. For you," Annie said. "This is a shitty situation caused by a man who thought his wife was a piece of property for him to do with what he would. If I could have done anything within the parameters of my job to stop him, I would have. Our system let Tulsie down. It lets women down every day, and that's not right. If I can at least do something now to help, I'm going to."

Izzy took in her answer and sat with it for a minute, weighing the pros and cons of accepting her explanation at face value. Annie had a feeling Izzy Guidry hadn't had much call to trust anyone in her life.

"This wasn't the first time, you know," Izzy said. "This wasn't the first time he blew up on her in public, humiliated her, sent her home like a child. She knew he was coming and what would happen. And then he'd go sit somewhere and drink, and stew, and work himself up into it, knowing she was home waiting, sick with fear, afraid to do anything.

"He texted her that night when he was on his way home," she said. "Just to scare her. It made him feel like a big man, the fucker. I'll never understand guys like him or why women put up with them. Someone should'a kicked him in the balls until he was dead years ago. That's what he deserved."

"Did Tulsie call you?" Annie asked. "Or were you already there?"

"She called me. I told her the last time it happened to call me, and I'd come. I got there before he did. I thought if I was there, he'd leave her alone, but he didn't care. He was drunk. He said nobody would listen to me anyway, 'cause I'm just a piece of trailer trash from Eunice."

"Why didn't you call nine-one-one when you knew he was coming?" Annie asked.

Izzy looked at her like she was stupid. "Why? You never helped before. He hadn't committed a crime yet. Y'all would never have bothered to even show up."

Annie didn't bother to argue. She couldn't say for a fact Izzy wasn't right, and that truth made her feel sick.

"We locked the doors," Izzy said. "Hoping he maybe didn't have his key, and he didn't, but that didn't stop him. He was at the kitchen door, yelling, *I'll fucking kill you, you fucking bitch!* And he busted the glass with the butt of the shotgun.

"I thought he'd kill us both," she said. "He came in, yelling, waving that gun around. He used the barrel to knock everything off her dresser, then he left it there and started in with his fists."

"He started hitting her right in front of you?"

"I got between them, so he punched me first. Punched me in the stomach as hard as he could and knocked the wind out of me. Then he started in on her."

Tears filled her dark eyes at the memory, but she wiped them away and set her jaw, stubborn and defiant.

"My stepdad used to beat us," she said. "He beat my mother something fierce. Over and over. Years of that abuse. When I was sixteen and I finally got out of there, I said I would never put up with that shit from a man again."

She leaned over and put her face in her hands and breathed in and out, trying to steady herself.

"He was gonna rape her, too. Right in front of me!" she said, astonished still, days later. "I was laying on the floor, trying to get my breath, and he's taking his clothes off, pulling off his shirt, kicking off his boots. I remember thinking, thank God he's not gonna take to kicking her with those boots on at least . . . Tulsie was begging him not to. He just wanted to hurt her every way he could."

"Just because she was dancing with Marc Mercier?" Annie asked. "Or was there something more to that?"

"She never cheated on him," Izzy said. "Tulsie ain't that girl. She likes to flirt a little. Why wouldn't she? She's sweet and cute, and that's the only way she ever got any attention."

She covered her face again and fought hard not to start crying outright. Annie doubted many people ever saw Izzy Guidry cry. She was tough because she'd had to be, but she had a soft heart for helpless things.

"What happened next?" she asked, hating having to make the girl relive such a horrific event.

Izzy pulled in a shaky breath. "I managed to crawl away. He wasn't paying any attention to me then. Tulsie was screaming and crying . . . I finally got my feet under me, and I grabbed that shotgun. I managed to get pretty close to him before he turned around. I said something to him. I don't remember exactly what. And he turned around with that fucking smirk on his face . . . And for just a split second, he knew I was gonna do it, and it was his turn to be afraid. And I thought, now you know, you son of a bitch. Now you know what it's like to fear for your life. I could see it in his eyes. I could see it on his face. And then I pulled the trigger, and he didn't have a face no more."

She was breathing hard, sucking in deep breaths through her mouth and blowing them out like she'd just run a race. Annie came around to stand beside her and put a hand on her back, just to offer her some comfort, some support. She rubbed her back, the same as she did with Justin when he was upset at some injustice in his little world. She wondered if anyone had ever done that for Izzy, locked in a nightmare home life, her mother a victim over and over. What a horrible existence for a child.

Annie had her own unhappy memories from a childhood with a mother plagued by depression, but she had always had Sos and

Fanchon. She had always had people who loved her and valued her. She had never known what it was to feel unsafe or uncertain about her future. Even after her mother's suicide, she had never worried about where she would go or what would happen to her. She had never had to escape a nightmare or scratch out a living on her own.

"I need to call someone to take care of the horses," Izzy said, pulling herself out of the terrible memories to focus on something mundane, chores that needed to be done, animals that needed to be cared for. "They never even got their hay tonight. That's not right. Can we go back and feed them?"

"I'll have the deputies do it tonight," Annie said. "A couple of those boys have horses. They'll be fine."

"There's a chart in the feed room showing who gets what," Izzy said. "And they need to feed the dogs, too. And the barn cats."

"We'll take care of it," Annie assured her again.

Izzy looked up toward the door, the worry for her friend returning. "What's gonna happen to Tulsie?"

"I expect they'll keep her here for a few days," Annie said. "We'll stay and find out."

"Will she go to jail?" Izzy asked. "None of this was her fault. None of it."

"After you shot him, why didn't you call nine-one-one that night?" Annie asked.

It would have been a whole lot easier to sell a self-defense case if they hadn't disposed of Cody Parcelle's body. Looking at the case as it had happened, and trying to think like a prosecutor, Annie knew that Tulsie was an accessory after the fact, at the very least. Coming up with a scheme to get rid of her dead husband's body could have hinted at premeditation on his death.

"We were scared," Izzy admitted. "It was so horrible, and . . . Tulsie was hysterical. I kept thinking if Cody could just disappear, we could say he left for Houston and we just never saw him again."

"But you didn't move the body until Sunday night," Annie said. "Why?"

"I had to think it through. Saturday night there's always people out, even late. I was afraid someone would see us. And then the sun was coming up . . . We had to wait.

"And then it was so hard to move him! It was like trying to move a dead horse. I thought we were gonna have to cut him up, but I didn't have the stomach for it. I had to go get a dolly from the barn. We managed to get him loaded into the back of his truck and we waited until late, really late, and drove him down that road. Ain't nobody out that time Sunday night.

"I thought if we could get him in the water . . . There's usually gators around there. People feed them. Kids chuck hamburgers out there just to watch them eat. Idiots. But it had rained and I almost got stuck backing in, and then Tulsie hurt her shoulder worse trying to help me move him. And she was crying and throwing up . . . Everything went wrong. It took too long. It was getting on toward dawn, and then we heard a boat coming, and we just left him and took off."

"Why did you take two vehicles?" Annie asked. "We have the two trucks on a security camera—Cody's truck and that white truck in the driveway."

"We had to get rid of his truck," Izzy said. "We couldn't say he left and have his truck still sitting there. We drove to that big Love's truck stop outside of Lake Charles and left it there."

Annie refrained from heaving a big sigh, thinking this was going to be some heavy lifting for a defense attorney.

"What's gonna happen to me?" Izzy asked, her expression bleak.

It was the first time she had expressed any concern at all for herself in this mess.

"I'm gonna give you the name and number of an attorney."

The girl shook her head. "I can't afford an attorney!"

"Don't worry about it," Annie said. "She'll take your case, and she'll fight like hell for you. She'll work something out with you for payment. And I have a connection in the DA's office. I'll have a conversation with him."

Izzy's brow furrowed. "You're a cop. I thought you just arrested people."

"I want justice done," Annie said. "That doesn't always look the same."

She wished she could have done something before this train wreck had ended in death. It wasn't like she hadn't seen the disaster coming a mile away. She just hadn't envisioned it ending the way it had. She had worried Tulsie would be the one lying on a stainless steel table in the morgue, not Cody. She wasn't supposed to be relieved that it was Tulsie's husband who had ended up on the wrong end of a shotgun, but she was.

"Thank you," Izzy said. Tears rose in her eyes again. She was trembling like she was freezing. "I'm really scared."

Izzy suddenly looked like all the fear, all the horror of what she'd had to do, had risen up in a huge wave, and she buried her face in her hands and finally broke down sobbing.

Annie slipped an arm around the girl's shoulders. "Just know you're not alone in this, Izzy. People will help you. I'll help you."

She just wished she could have helped before it was too late.

34

"**YOU LET** THAT LITTLE GIRL TAKE YOUR GUN AWAY FROM YOU," Nick said. It was a statement, not a question.

They sat in the conference room, meeting to put the latest puzzle pieces together while the details were still fresh in the mind. It was just the three of them—Nick, Stokes, and Annie—the rest of the squad having already called it a night. Annie resisted the urge to glance at her watch, knowing her son was already tucked in bed at her cousin Remy's house. She tried to dodge the twinge of motherly guilt. She already had enough emotion weighing her down from the events of the day and evening.

Stokes pressed a hand to his chest and looked offended, ever the victim. "She attacked me! I couldn't see that coming! One minute she was scooping horse shit off the floor, and the next thing I know she's gone all lesbian ninja on me and rams me in the gut with the handle end of a shovel!"

"And we all know lesbian ninjas have superhuman strength," Annie remarked dryly. "Especially those little ones that maybe weigh a hundred pounds soaking wet."

Stokes cut her a look. "Let her ram you in the belly with a shovel. See how you do."

"Why would I?" Annie returned. "I would know better, for starters. And by the way, there's no reason to remark on her sexuality, of which you know nothing."

"Well, I don't know any regular girls that strong."

"You don't know any horse girls, then," Annie said. "You're lucky she didn't pick you up over her head and throw you somewhere."

"You're lucky she didn't shoot you," Nick said. "Desperate people do desperate things." He looked at Annie. "You're both lucky."

"I want her charged with assaulting an officer," Stokes pouted.

"Get over yourself," Annie shot back. "The only thing wounded here is your pride, and you had that coming."

Stokes looked incredulous. "Do I need to remind you she's a killer?"

"She shot a man who had assaulted her and was beating the shit out of his wife," Annie said. "Plenty of people will think she deserves a medal."

Nick arched a brow. "And you're one of them?"

"Pardon me if I don't shed a tear for Cody Parcelle, who thought it was his God-given right to beat his wife like a rented mule," Annie said, unrepentant. "He literally announced he was going to kill her before he broke the glass in the kitchen door. That'll be on their doorbell video, for sure."

"Do we know this wife doesn't have a big insurance policy on him?" Nick asked.

"I'll check into it tomorrow," Annie said, "but I doubt it. I doubt Tulsie would have ever done anything but take his abuse and blame herself for it. She was still saying tonight in the hospital that she shouldn't have gone out that night, she shouldn't have danced with Marc Mercier, she shouldn't have made Cody jealous, and on and on. She's terrified she's gonna lose everything they worked for. That doesn't sound like someone with a million bucks of insurance money waiting at the end of this rainbow. My guess is they live pretty hand-to-mouth. They're not rolling in dough from the horse-training business. Cody worked a day job with the family construction business doing demolition and remodels."

"That explains the Mercier business card in his pocket," Nick said.

"According to Tulsie, they did business all the time, selling salvaged materials to the Merciers."

"Well, I'm telling you," Stokes grumbled, "this whole mess is just another example of why not to get married."

Annie rolled her eyes. "I don't think you have to worry."

"You're gonna wind up on the wrong end of a jealous husband, is what's gonna happen to you," Nick said.

"We don't know that isn't what happened to Marc Mercier," Stokes said, pointing at the timeline on the whiteboard. "There's still a couple of hours unaccounted for between Cody Parcelle punching him in the mouth at Outlaw and these women blowing Cody's face off. He could have gone and done Marc in before he went home to beat the missus."

"He could have, but I don't think so," Nick said. "Our new wrinkle here is that I have video of Marc Mercier leaving Goal Post Saturday night, and the first car that leaves that parking lot after he walks out of sight is a blue Toyota Corolla."

Annie sat up like she'd been shocked. "What?"

"It's the same car Danny Perry chased out of the Merciers' neighborhood last night. So, if that's Marc, he's still alive."

"What the fuck?" Stokes said, tipping his hat back on his head.

"Robbie Fontenot's car," Annie said, feeling sick.

"Couldn't see the driver or if there was a passenger," Nick said. "Is there any reason to think the two of them would be holed up together somewhere?"

Annie thought of the conversation she'd had with Eli McVay about the accident he didn't believe had been an accident, about the rift that had come between the friends after.

"No," she said, a terrible sense of dread filling her. "Eli McVay saw Robbie talking to Dozer Cormier Halloween night, walking away from downtown, like they were leaving the party. That's the last anyone saw Robbie. He also told me he never believed what happened to Robbie was an accident. He knew Marc needed that opportunity to quarterback the team, to get noticed, to have a chance at a scholarship, and that Dozer was always loyal to Marc."

"Jesus," Stokes said. "He wrecked that kid's life to get a scholarship?"

"And Dozer became an alcoholic after that," Nick said. "And he's been drinking again. Heavy. Like he's trying to drown something."

"He's the weakest link, for sure," Stokes said.

"I pressured him hard today," Nick said. "I've got a deputy sitting on his place tonight. If he knows where Marc is at, I reckon he'll go there soon. There's a bunch of camps out on the far edge of that wildlife management area past Cypress Island."

"Where Danny Perry ran off the road," Annie said.

Nick nodded. "He had to be headed that way for a reason, yeah?"

"But if you go far enough down that road, eventually you hit that east-west state highway and end up anywhere," Stokes pointed out.

"That's true, but I'm thinking if that was Marc in that car, he's parked his truck and boat somewhere out of the way. Somewhere no one would bother to notice. I alerted the Wildlife agents to keep an eye out in that area, be on the lookout for those vehicles, but not to get too close if they see something. I don't want him spooked, and I don't want him trying to run in the dead of night. If he's holed up there, let him sit and think he's safe. Either Dozer leads us to him, or we send the marine unit out there tomorrow and see what we can see."

"If it's Marc, why is he riding around in Robbie Fontenot's car?" Stokes asked.

"The simple answer is he doesn't want to be seen in his," Nick said. "No one in his neighborhood would recognize that Toyota.

Maybe he wanted to have a look and see for himself if his wife is having an affair."

"And if he has Robbie's car," Annie said, "does he have Robbie's cell phone as well? If we eliminate the murder-for-hire plotline, there's no reason Robbie would have called Marc's wife in the middle of the night."

And if he had Robbie's car and Robbie's phone, then where was Robbie? She hated to voice the question, but she had to. "Why does he have that car at all?"

"No good reason," Stokes said. "If you ain't been seen in a week or more, but someone's driving your car around, it's probably because you don't need it no more."

"Eli told me when he ran into Robbie this summer that he made a joke about him being an investigative reporter, because that's what Robbie used to say he wanted to be back when they were in school," Annie said. "And Robbie said, yeah, that he was deep undercover investigating police corruption in Bayou Breaux."

"But he's not a reporter," Stokes said. "He's an unemployed drug addict."

"I know," Annie said. "But why would he say that? Even as a joke, why would he say that? I sent that cash I found to the lab to get dusted for prints. Dewey Rivette admitted some of it came from him, paying Robbie as a CI. Fifty here, a hundred there, he said. Where'd the rest of it come from?

"What if Danny Perry chased that car last night because he believed it was Robbie driving?" she asked, hating to say it out loud. "It looked like he tried to roll that car into the swamp. Why would he do that?"

"We'll ask him if he ever wakes up," Nick said. "Rivette said Fontenot had a line on copper thieves. Could Perry have been mixed up in that? If the Mercier brothers and Dozer Cormier are involved, if Danny Perry was involved in theft and fencing stolen goods, that's a big motive for any of them to get rid of Robbie Fontenot."

Annie thought of B'Lynn, sitting home hoping against hope her son was still alive. After all she'd been through, after she'd fought with him and for him and put all her strength into pulling him through his addiction and out the other side . . . After all of that, to find out he'd been murdered for knowing the wrong thing about the wrong people . . .

She pulled in a big breath and blew out a sigh, the last of her energy going with it as she swept her hair back from her face. "Man, this day just gets better and better."

"You want happy endings, you're in the wrong business, Broussard," Stokes said.

"Yeah. I used to be happy to settle for justice," Annie said. "This time, that's not gonna feel like enough. Not by a long shot."

"Don't tell me not to make it personal," Annie warned as she walked with Nick toward their respective vehicles.

"When have I ever told you that, 'Toinette?" he asked. "It's all personal if you care. And if you don't care, you shouldn't be on this job. It's too hard, and it means too much to just go through the motions for a paycheck. Best you can do is learn how to put it in a box and close the lid at the end of the day." He gathered her close and pressed a kiss to her lips. "Let's go home and do that, *bébé*. Try to get some rest. I have a feeling tomorrow is gonna be a day."

"You go ahead. I'll catch up," she said. "I'm gonna swing by B'Lynn Fontenot's and give her an update, such as it will be.

"You know, the first thing I thought when B'Lynn told me the story of her son was that he was probably dead of an overdose somewhere," she said. "I thought I was all set for a bad outcome, but now the closer that comes to being true, the less ready I feel to accept it. There's a part of me that wants to tell B'Lynn there's still some slim hope. Would that be a bad lie or a good one?"

"Either way, I'm sure she knows a lie when she hears one, good or bad." Nick brushed her hair back from her face and gave her a sad smile. "I know you want something good to happen for her, *chère*, but she hasn't just been down this road before; she's lived on it for a decade. She knows every monster. She's followed her son into every dark alley. She has, no doubt, prepared herself for the worst many times. It won't be your fault if that's the bad news you end up having to give her. She knows that."

That was an ironic truth, Annie thought as she drove to the Belle Terre neighborhood—that the woman she wanted to protect from her son's fate was better equipped to handle the truth than Annie was to give it.

The day had absolutely drained her. A low-grade headache was beginning to throb in the back of her skull, reminding her of the last time she'd made a late-night house call on a troubled mother of a troubled son.

This wasn't the same thing at all, she knew. The anxiety that idled in the background of her psyche these days began to rise to the fore now just because she was too tired to fend it off, not because B'Lynn posed any threat to her. Fatigue and her brain chemistry were a bad combination.

She parked in front of the Fontenot house and sat for a minute to pull herself together and push the anxiety back in its box. She wasn't in danger. She didn't need to be afraid. She wasn't alone. Nick had followed her in his vehicle—to assuage his own nerves as much as to assure her. They both had their scars to deal with from that night in September.

The neighborhood was aglow with expensive landscape lighting around the grand houses. Across the street, a man was walking his spaniel and talking on his phone. This was just an average night for the above-average people who lived there. Most of them were likely sitting in their living rooms watching TV, their thoughts far removed from drug addiction and police corruption and murder, unless that was the plot of a prime-time cop show.

Her legs felt leaden as she climbed the front steps to B'Lynn's porch. She wanted to just go sit on the porch swing and not ring the bell, but she pushed the button just the same.

B'Lynn answered the door in leggings and an oversize cashmere hoodie the color of moss, her hair up in a messy bun, a cut crystal glass of bourbon in one hand.

"You look like you could use this," she quipped, the worry in her eyes belying her tone of voice.

"I just wanted to stop by and give you an update," Annie said. "It's been a long day."

"Coffee, then? Tea?"

"Nothing, thanks. I won't be long."

"I saw the story about that police officer crashing in the swamp," B'Lynn said, leading her into a cozy front parlor with a fire in the fireplace and a pair of comfortable blush pink velvet love seats facing each other on either side of an antique mahogany coffee table that had probably been sitting there for a hundred years. Soft music played in the background. They each took a seat, B'Lynn curling her legs beneath her like a deer, both hands wrapped around her glass as if she took some comfort just holding it.

"That was Robbie's car he was after, wasn't it?"

"We think so," Annie said. "Although the license plate came back to another vehicle."

"You think the car's been stolen. Isn't that what they do with stolen cars? Change the license plates?"

"Sometimes, yes. It's something to do if you don't want a car recognized for one reason or another."

"You don't think it was Robbie driving."

"We have reason to believe someone else has been driving the car," Annie admitted. It was painful to watch the hope come and go from B'Lynn's face, like a faint little light brightening and dimming as it began to fail.

B'Lynn pulled in a big breath, bracing herself.

"I can't say who it might be," Annie said. "We don't know enough, don't have any concrete identification, but we're working on it."

"Well, that's more than anyone else has done," B'Lynn said primly, and took a sip of her drink. "Thank you."

"You don't need to thank me," Annie said. "I wish I had something better to report. At this point, I still have a lot of questions and not enough answers."

"I imagine you didn't get anything useful out of my ex-husband. He felt compelled to complain in a text that I had sicced you on him, like an attack dog. A mental image that brought a smile to my face, I have to say."

"He's quite the perpetual victim, isn't he?" Annie said.

"Oh, yes. Poor Robert, the star of every tragedy to befall our family. Not to say that he didn't suffer at the time. He did. We all did. Was he at all helpful to you?"

"No," Annie said. "He didn't have anything to contribute."

"That's the story of his role as a parent, right there in a nutshell: nothing to contribute."

"I confess, I have a hard time imagining you married to him."

"Me, too," B'Lynn conceded. "But that was a lifetime ago. I don't know who that girl was anymore. Not me, that's for sure."

"I also spoke with a guy Robbie went to school with," Annie said. "Eli McVay."

B'Lynn nodded. "I remember Eli. Nice boy. Nice family. How is he?"

"He's well. He's a civil engineer for the city of Lafayette."

"Good for him."

That had to be one of the ongoing injuries to an addict's parents, Annie thought: having to hear how well his peers were doing. Sacred Heart graduated crop after crop of kids who went on to be doctors and lawyers, architects and engineers. And every time B'Lynn Fontenot ran into one of those parents of the kids Robbie had gone to school with, she had to hear how well they'd done, because the kids were their one connection and the subject of the kind of small talk people engaged in at the grocery store or the bank or the charity events that were their common social life. And she had to relive over and over the awful, embarrassing truth of her son's life, which she would have to encapsulate in vague answers that didn't include words like *addiction* and *rehab* and *jail time.*

"He was telling me Robbie used to talk about becoming an investigative journalist," Annie said.

"Oh, yes. Or a documentary filmmaker. Or a sports photographer. After he retired from his stellar career in the NFL, of course," B'Lynn said. "He loved making little films on his phone. He had so many dreams, so much potential. That's what children are, you know—dreams and potential."

"You said he had talked about going back to school. Was that a focus for him? Becoming a reporter or a filmmaker?"

She smiled a sad smile. "He was so bright, so talented, such an incredible spirit. Who knows what he might have done if he'd had the chance.

"Oh, my God." She closed her eyes as if in pain, and when she opened them again, they were shining with tears she wouldn't let fall. "I'm talking about him in the past tense. He's dead, isn't he?"

"I don't know," Annie said, her throat tightening against her own need to cry.

"You're far too kind for this job, Annie."

"I'm gonna tell the truth, B'Lynn," Annie said. "I don't have a lot of hope for a good outcome here, but until I have proof otherwise, he's still alive to me, and I'm still gonna try to find him. And if the worst has happened, I'm still gonna fight to get you justice."

"I wish I believed there was such a thing."

"If someone has hurt your son, they'll pay for it."

B'Lynn shook her head. "That's retribution, not justice. If we lived in a just world, none of this would ever happen."

"I wish I had something wise to say," Annie said. "But I guess I haven't lived long enough to have wisdom."

"Honey, I'm old enough to be your mother," B'Lynn said softly. "And I don't have anything wise to say, either. Wisdom is something that never arrives until it's too late."

"I'm gonna go now," Annie said, pushing to her feet. If she stayed much longer, she was going to end up in a puddle of tears, crying on the shoulder of the woman she was supposed to be comforting. "But I'd like to come back tomorrow and go through Robbie's room properly, in case he might have left something else up there that could help us."

B'Lynn nodded as she rose. "I'll be here. Where else would I go?"

B'Lynn saw Annie Broussard to the door and thanked her again and gave her a hug because she looked like she needed it. *Pauvre 'tite bête*, her mamere Louisa would have said. Poor little thing, dragged unaware into the unending downward spiral of the Fontenot family. And for what? The ending to this story should have been obvious from a mile away. The only unknown there had ever been was the timing. Anything Annie Broussard could have done would only have postponed the inevitable.

All the time, and all the effort, and all the heartbreak, living and reliving the endless loop of Robbie's story, like Sisyphus pushing that damn boulder up the hill again and again, and none of it was going to matter at all in the end. He was gone. Just like that. She felt it with a terrible kind of certainty.

Annie didn't want to say it, bless her heart. She didn't want it to be true. But for the first time, B'Lynn felt her son's absence in a way she never had before. She thought about the night she had awakened in his bed, so sure he was in the house, and what he had said when she'd spoken to him: *You can't help me now. I'm so sorry, Mama.*

A dream. A hallucination. Wishful thinking. His spirit visiting her from the next dimension, as if she believed in such a thing. It didn't really matter, did it?

She locked the door and walked slowly through the house, sipping her bourbon and checking doors and windows, wondering why she bothered. What could anyone steal from her that meant more to her than what she'd already lost?

Feeling strangely numb, she went upstairs to Robbie's room, turned on the lamp on the nightstand, and sat on his bed, looking around at all the memorabilia of the milestones in his younger life, all the hopes and dreams that had never made it out of this room, and never would. No one would ever know what he could have been, the contributions he could have made, if only things had turned out differently.

What a strange feeling, to think that her child was dead but that the world continued to turn as if nothing had happened at all. The sun would come up in the morning like it always did. To think this happened every day to countless people, their grief ignored by most of the world. She wasn't even special in her pain. The fabric of her life was torn, a hole left where her son used to be.

How many times had she prepared herself for this in the past ten years? She had long ago lost count. Yet somehow, she still wasn't ready. How many times had she told herself in anger that it might actually be a relief, then felt sick with guilt for thinking it? Now the reality was here, and relief was not the emotion. Not at all.

She pulled her phone out of the pouch of her hoodie and dialed Robbie's number, just to listen to his voice message. She wanted to tell him that she loved him, that she forgave him, that she hoped he forgave her. But the mailbox was full, and she couldn't have left a message even if he had been alive to hear it. And somehow that seemed sadly perfect.

Restless, she turned out the light and left the room. She went back downstairs, grabbed a blanket from the TV room, and went out the kitchen door to sit on the back porch steps. Bundled against the damp chill of the night, she sat looking at the backyard in the dim silver moonlight and the ground-level glow of the landscape lighting. She stared out to the far reaches of the yard, where darkness crept in and stole her vision, hoping against hope to see his shadow there, just out of reach.

How many times had she sat on these steps, watching him play, watching him run, watching him practice passing the football, throwing spiral after spiral through the old tire that still hung from a limb on the oak tree, never once imagining how wrong it could all go, thinking only good things for a bright future? What a pleasant lie, a necessary lie, because the truth, as it had turned out, was just damn near unbearable.

Why did it have to all go so terribly wrong?

At least she had those good memories, she thought. At least she could close her eyes and remember when she had a beautiful boy and joy and hope. She could close her eyes and imagine him there, putting his arms around her, and she could tell him with her heart what a privilege it had been to be his mother.

35

HOW DID PEOPLE'S LIVES GO SO WRONG? ANNIE WONDERED. She stood at the bedroom window, looking out at the moonlight on the bayou. A stupid question. She was a front-row witness to the reasons every single day—the poor decisions; the unrealistic expectations; the addictions to drugs, to alcohol, to drama. The emptiness that needed filling. The anger that demanded release.

She thought of Rayanne Tillis, who had probably never caught a break her entire life, born in a hole of poverty and given a shovel instead of a ladder. She made all the wrong choices because no one had ever helped steer her toward better ones.

She thought of Tulsie Parcelle, the sweet girl who just wanted to be loved, and Izzy Guidry, the wounded child who had finally said *no more*.

She thought of B'Lynn Fontenot, who had once upon a time subscribed to the debutante dream of a perfect marriage, only to watch it all crumble around her when the foundation gave way. She thought of Robbie Fontenot, whom she had only met in the memories of the people who had known him. The much-loved golden child who had the red carpet cruelly yanked out from under him, then found himself trapped in the endless loop that was the struggle with addiction.

So many broken people. There were so many reasons their lives went wrong, a minefield of reasons. It was a wonder anyone made it from one end of the field to the other intact.

"Come back to bed, *chère*," Nick murmured, slipping his arms around her from behind. He pressed his cheek to the top of her head. "You're not gonna sleep standing up."

"I'm not gonna sleep," Annie corrected him, reaching a hand up to touch his face.

"You need to shut off that brain of yours. You're not gonna save the world tonight."

"Or tomorrow or the next day," she said. "That's the problem, isn't it? There's too many sad stories, and I can't rewrite the ending to any of them."

"That's not entirely true," he said. "Don't think you don't make a difference, 'Toinette. You can't bring back the dead, but you do what you can for the living. That will go further than you know."

"I guess I have to hang on to that. We can only do what we can do."

"*C'est vrai.* Come now. We've got another hour before the sun comes up. Come close your eyes at least."

His phone vibrated on the nightstand as they turned back toward the bed.

"Looks like your day is starting now," Annie said.

He picked up the phone. "Fourcade."

Annie watched his face as he took in the information.

"I'm on my way," he said, and ended the call. He met her eyes. "Dozer Cormier is on the move."

36

HOW HAD HIS LIFE GONE SO WRONG?

Dozer hadn't had a decent night's sleep since Halloween. Truth to tell, for longer than that. Way longer than that. The fatigue and the anxiety were weighing heavy on him. The alcohol that was supposed to numb the feelings only made him feel worse. People claimed they drank to forget. It never did that for him. It never had. That didn't stop him trying, but what was it people said? Doing the same thing over and over and expecting different results was nothing but stupidity. Something like that.

He didn't think he was a bad guy. People who didn't know him were scared of him because of how he looked, because of his size and the fact that he was bald and ugly. Some people thought that somehow meant he didn't have feelings, like he was an animal or Frankenstein's monster or something. They treated him like he was less than human, like he couldn't understand what they thought of him or didn't realize how used him. It made him sad. It made him angry. Anger made him dangerous, and when he was dangerous, people got scared of him, and that cycle went 'round and 'round.

He didn't have many real friends. Mr. Bichon was kind to him, tried to offer him advice. Tommy Crawford treated him decent enough. And there was Marc.

They'd been friends since their first day of football practice in seventh grade. Marc had singled him out and struck up a friendship. Dozer couldn't say he hadn't wondered why or hadn't suspected why—Marc was a quarterback, and Dozer was, by far, the biggest guy with the job of protecting him—but he had set all that aside in favor of feeling grateful to have a friend at all.

He wasn't so dumb as to think Marc considered him an equal. He was aware of the role he played in Marc's little dramas, but he had always reckoned Marc was as close to a real friend as he'd ever had or ever would, and Dozer was loyal as the day was long. Loyal to a fault. That, he could see now, was a problem.

All these years later, he was tired of being used. He was tired of being a drunk. He was tired of feeling like he was stuck in a loop of doing the same stupid shit, making the same stupid mistakes over and over.

Mr. Bichon always harped to him about the twelve steps and how you couldn't get anywhere by skipping any of them. Admit your mistakes and make amends. He couldn't even manage to get that right.

On Halloween night he had tried apologizing to Robbie Fontenot at long last, to do the right thing and to release himself from the weight of that guilt, and instead, Robbie Fontenot had ended up dead.

What a nightmare.

He started drinking more in a feeble effort to numb himself. He couldn't eat, couldn't sleep. That asshole Fourcade kept showing up, poking and prodding, trying to trip him up. Fourcade was smart and ruthless. Dozer was terrified to answer his questions because the detective could twist his words around and get him to say things he shouldn't. His stomach was constantly in knots just thinking about it.

He'd had it. He wanted this over, one way or another.

He had waited almost all night, because he figured Fourcade had a deputy nearby, just watching for him to drive out of the trailer park so he could pull him over for driving drunk. But he wasn't drunk now, not over the limit, anyway. And those night-shift deputies were about done and ready to head home.

Now was the time.

It was still dark. The morning was chilly with a light frost on the ground and a sheer veil of fog hanging in the air. He could see his breath as he went out to his truck. Lights were on in one of the other trailers nearby. The woman who lived there worked the breakfast shift at a truck stop on the highway to Lafayette. She would be leaving soon, too.

He pulled out the cell phone that he'd told everybody he'd lost and checked his traffic app where people always posted where they'd seen a po-po. Someone had mentioned a deputy on the road between Bayou Breaux and Luck, but that had been more than an hour ago, and no one had mentioned it since.

He needed to go. Marc was waiting. He was going to have to take his chances, because when Marc called, he had to jump to like a goddamn trained animal, he thought with disgust.

He started the truck and drove out of the trailer park.

How had his life gone so wrong? Marc wondered, as if he wasn't at all responsible for anything that had happened, and the answer had nothing to do with him other than giving him back what he thought he deserved. As if he was and always had been an innocent bystander, even though he knew deep, deep inside that wasn't the case.

And therein was the conundrum that was Marc Mercier—a brutally self-critical core wrapped in protective layers of narcissism and sociopathy as thick as cotton batting. A strange and useless being, desperate to save itself.

All he could think about now was how he was going to get his life back on track with no one the wiser about what a selfish, useless prick he was.

He would start that campaign today.

He knew he could only claim to be out of communication with the world for just so long before people decided he was an asshole, and he couldn't have that. People were looking for him. People were worried about him. His mother would be about to lose her mind. And Melissa . . . Well, did she even give a shit? He doubted it. Did he care? Not like he should have.

They had met at Tulane. His first taste of freedom away from home. His first chance to be anyone he wanted to be, not Troy and Kiki Mercier's favorite son, not the hero of Sacred Heart High School. It had been both exhilarating and terrifying to start from scratch where no one knew him, where he was just another student, just another rookie on the football team. All courtesy of a scholarship he shouldn't have had, but he hadn't thought about that at the time. He had only thought of himself. As usual.

All he had wanted at the time was out of Bayou Breaux, out of south Louisiana. It had been as if he could take a big, deep breath for the first time ever. He could reinvent himself, be whoever he wanted to be, aspire to whatever struck his fancy. For the first time in his life he had considered the possibilities of doing something new and different, going wherever he wanted to go. He didn't have to be tied to this place. He didn't have to be a junk dealer's son. He could have a future away from his brother's resentment and his mother's cloying pride.

In Melissa, he had met a girl unlike any of the girls he had known growing up. She was from a prominent family, from a place as different from south Louisiana as could possibly be. She was smart and sassy and outspoken. She had believed in him, believed in his potential, without ever having known Saint Marc of Sacred Heart.

He had grabbed that opportunity with both hands and left behind the idea of his childhood self like a snake shedding its skin.

The trouble had been that in his new life, he had felt as much like an imposter as he had in his old one. It wasn't really better; it was just different. The new Marc was just as much a phony as the old Marc, skating by on looks and charm. People were so happy to be fooled by a wide smile and a clever joke. They didn't care to look deeper, where they would have seen nothing, because he was as shallow as a puddle after a spring rain.

God, he hated himself and the mess he'd made of his life.

What the hell did he do now?

He sat on the deck overlooking the water. The eastern horizon had just begun to turn pink beneath a band of midnight purple sky. Wispy layers of fog floated above the water like so many ghosts traveling aimlessly from souls unknown.

The camp belonged to some cousin of Dozer's who lived up in Shreveport. The cabin was a single-wide house trailer raised up on pilings a good ten, twelve feet off the ground and wrapped around with a worn, weathered gray deck. The view off the front was beautiful—water like black glass studded with massive ancient bald cypress trees hung with ragged shawls of Spanish moss. He would have found it peaceful if the circumstances had been different.

He had come out there to get away, to think, to try to straighten out the mess in his head. He'd been a wreck inside since Halloween, a mass of nerves and fear and disgust. The tension between him and Melissa had become unbearable. The baby teething had ramped up the aggravation factor by ten. At work he'd had to contend with Luc's relentless criticism and bullying. They had finally come to blows on Saturday. Then he'd gone home to Melissa's bitching and yet another argument.

He couldn't take it. He didn't want to. He wanted out—of his marriage, of this mess, of his life—but at the same time, he was clinging to it all by his raw, ragged fingertips, terrified to lose any of it.

He had settled on taking a break for a day or two or ten. He brought his truck and boat out to Dozer's cousin's place and parked them, then took the Toyota and made his way back to town to be among people who thought he was great, who basked in his charm, who had no idea about the hollowness inside him. He could drink and dance and pretend for a few hours. But that hadn't worked out either, the evening ending with Cody Parcelle busting him in the mouth for dancing with his wife. What a fucking mess. What a fucking failure he was.

He had actually contemplated suicide for a minute, which was laughable. How could Marc Mercier kill himself? Too many people loved him. How could he deprive the world like that? The truth was, he didn't have the character to do it. He didn't have the balls.

He thought he might choke on his self-loathing.

He took a pull on the bottle of whiskey he'd found in a cupboard and tried to wash it down.

If he wasn't going to kill himself, then he needed to plan his next move. Dozer would be there soon. Things would happen. He would go back to Bayou Breaux, and he would find a way to do it as a hero because that was what was expected. Maybe he would say he'd been injured, that he'd lost his phone overboard . . . Maybe he would claim he had left a note with Melissa that he needed a little time to sort some things out, but that she must not have found it or accidentally threw it away, and that him "missing" was just a big misunderstanding. He'd only been gone a couple of days, holed up in a place with no TV, and in this scenario he had also lost his phone but hadn't worried about it.

He believed fully in his ability to spin a lie and in the gullibility of people who would be eager to believe him. But then what?

Part of him wanted to stay in Louisiana because it was familiar, because people bought the myth that was Marc Mercier hook, line, and sinker, and that was a comfortable role for him to play. Part of him couldn't stand the idea. The myth was a lie. He was a lie. He would be trapped in that lie forever if he stayed, trapped in this place with the memories and reminders of everything he'd ever done—not just the good, but the bad as well. But who was he if he wasn't here, and if the life he'd built with Melissa went up in flames?

She'd seen through him now, seen through to the real Marc, the liar, the fraud. She was done. He was sure she would take the baby and leave, despite whatever was going on between her and Will Faulkner. Friends, lovers, it didn't matter. Faulkner was just handy, someone to fill the space in her life her husband had already vacated.

Marc hadn't been able to resist going around the house at night to see if she was alone. He had even called once. He couldn't say why. To hear her voice? To scare her? To say something? Say what? How could he even begin? Faulkner had been there at the house that night, drinking wine and making Melissa laugh. He had gone at one point, but he came back fast enough after Marc's creepy, silent call from a phone that wasn't his, and he hadn't left.

That Melissa didn't even try to hide whatever that relationship was told Marc she was done with him. And he had to be done with her, because how could he stay with a woman who knew exactly what he was?

He took another pull on the whiskey, as if the answers he wanted were in that bottle. The pink band on the horizon had turned flame orange as daybreak neared, the color spilling down across the water like molten flame. The birds had begun to call. Dozer would be there soon. He had to get ready.

Nick picked up Dozer on the west side of Bayou Breaux, on the road everyone referred to as the Loop, skirting the new developments. He stayed well back, barely keeping the Silverado's taillights in sight.

There was no traffic to hide in at this hour, especially not where Dozer seemed to be headed, but a thin fog helped give him cover. He couldn't risk being seen, couldn't risk spooking Dozer. He would get one shot at this. Everything had to fall just right.

He drove Annie's old Jeep—the army-variety utility vehicle, small, black, devoid of any decoration. It in no way resembled a police vehicle. There were plenty just like it in the area. The kind of vehicle people used to head into the wild to off-road or to hunt. As soon as it was barely light, he cut his headlights.

The truck turned onto Cypress Island Road, winding through the stands of cypress trees. The road barely raised up above the water on both sides, and the fog gave a sensation of floating through the wilderness. They passed by Danny Perry's BBPD radio car, still perched where it had landed on a stump, its front end squished like an accordion up against the trunk of a tree. The area was still cordoned off by yellow tape.

Nick had a good idea where Dozer was headed. A Wildlife and Fisheries agent had tipped him off to some unusual activity at one of the fish camps—a vehicle covered with a tarp, a dim single light flickering in the house at night. No one would have thought anything of it come the weekend, but in the middle of the week, it was just enough to pique the interest of a trained eye.

The call had come late, while he'd been sitting outside the Fontenot house waiting for Annie. He knew the general area where the camp was located. There was one road in. Once Dozer turned down it, he was trapped, along with whoever was staying at the camp. Marc, Nick reckoned.

The question was why. Why would Marc Mercier have taken himself out there without telling anyone where he was going? He had left his wife without a word, left his child. His mother was beside herself with worry. Why? Why did a man who loved to be adored disappear? Something had become too much. Pressure bred the need to run away. The trouble with his marriage? The conflict with his brother?

But it seemed that Halloween had been the trigger. Something had happened Halloween night. Something involving Robbie Fontenot. In the days that followed, tensions had built, Dozer had started drinking, Marc and his brother had fought and come to blows. Marc had left his wife and child and gone out Saturday night as if he were a single man and never came home.

He had run away from something, but if he had meant to escape, he should have run farther, Nick thought. Justice was about to come calling.

37

DAWN WAS AN ORANGE HAZE IN THE EAST AS DOZER TURNED down the wooded path to the camp. The sheerest gauze of fog clung to the ground, giving a dreamlike quality to the scene, like a strange, distant memory. He had to stop for a moment as a buck deer stepped out of the brush and stood in the middle of the path, staring at him as if offended by his interruption. Eight points on the rack. On some other day he would have shot it, but that wasn't what he was there for.

The buck moved on. Dozer drove forward.

The camp looked abandoned. Marc had parked the Toyota next to the storage shed and covered it with a tarp. He had pulled his truck with the trailer and his boat inside the old metal shed, out of sight of anyone who might have had an eye open for it—deputies or Wildlife agents.

Dozer pulled in behind the car and parked and sat there. He didn't feel well. He felt sick at his stomach and odd, like his soul wasn't connected to his body. Nerves, he supposed. He had made a hard choice to do a hard thing. That was bound to come with nerves. He needed to change his life. That day. But he knew he wasn't the smartest guy, and Marc was an old hand at manipulating him.

He pulled a flask of Jack Daniel's out of the console and drank the whole thing down in a few gulps. His last alcohol. A parting shot for a little courage, and then he would be done. For good. He meant it this time.

Something Fourcade had said the day before kept coming back to him, playing over and over in his mind: *Do you want this to be the rest of your life? A drunk, a failure, trying to hide from yourself . . .*

No. No, he didn't. He didn't know what would happen after that day, but it would damn well be different from the purgatory his life had been for the past decade.

Marc came out of the house and down the steps.

Here we go . . .

Nick parked the Jeep and cut the engine, blocking the path that led back to the camp. A marked SUV from the SO pulled in crosswise behind him. Sergeant Rodrigue got out, carrying a long gun, his expression grim. Nick said nothing, just motioned for him to stay put. Rodrigue nodded.

Nick stepped off the path and moved into the cover of brush and trees, treading lightly and easily. He had grown up in these woods and on this water and in wilder parts of the basin than this. The terrain was familiar and comfortable. He had dressed in hunting gear—camouflage pants and snake boots and an olive drab pullover that blended into the moss-coated tree trunks. The moisture hanging heavy in the air softened the grass and scrub, allowing him to move through with minimal noise. The rich scent of damp earth and wet, decaying leaves filled his nostrils like heavy perfume.

An eight-point buck raised its head from nibbling on the leaves of a wild dewberry thicket and stared at him as he passed. Nick kept moving. Ahead and to his right he could see the camp through the trees—a rusty steel storage shed with a big pile of firewood maybe four feet high and six feet wide stacked along the side, a vehicle covered in a blue tarp, Dozer's Silverado behind it. An old house trailer stood in the distance up on pilings meant to save it in times of high water. Beyond the house, the water looked like a bright hot lava flow as the sun emerged from the horizon like a ball of fire.

He lifted his binoculars and zoomed in on Marc Mercier descending the stairs of the house. Across the way, Dozer got down from his truck. He was in his usual overalls under a camouflage hunting jacket, as if anything could disguise the size of him. He stood like a statue for a moment, then moved forward slowly, like a man going to his execution.

38

"**NO ONE** FOLLOWED YOU?" MARC SAID BY WAY OF GREETING, too tired and stressed for meaningless pleasantries. It was just Dozer. Social niceties weren't necessary.

"I wouldn't be here if they had," Dozer said irritably. "I'm not that dumb."

That was debatable, Marc thought, but he let it pass. He couldn't afford to have Dozer get a mood on. They had work to do.

"We need to get rid of that car," he said. "Fucking town cop chased me halfway out here night before last. Tried to run me off the goddamn road. I guess that's what they do to junkie thieves these days. Anyway, there's people looking for it now. It's gotta go."

"You got a junkyard," Dozer said stupidly.

"Are you fucking serious, man?" Marc barked. "I can't take that onto my family property! Jesus, Dozer! If somebody saw it there..."

Moron, he wanted to say, but he didn't.

Dozer shrugged. "Can't we just burn it?"

"No, we can't burn it! Someone will see the smoke. I think we should run it into the water and let it sink."

"Well, don't do it here," Dozer said. "Me, I don't want my cousin tied up with this. That comes right back on me."

"We'll take it somewhere else, then," Marc said. "Stick to the back roads. As long as it gets gone. The sooner the better."

"And then what?" Dozer asked.

"What do you mean?"

"You can't stay here forever."

"I know that," Marc snapped. "I'm working on a plan. I need to go home. People are gonna be pissed. I gotta figure out the best way to go back and not have everybody be upset and asking a thousand questions."

Dozer rolled his eyes. "You been gone for days. It's been all over the TV. You think people aren't gonna ask questions? Or you think they're gonna just throw you a parade, as usual?"

"What is your problem, man?"

"You're my problem," Dozer grumbled. "I got that detective, Fourcade, all over me like shit on a hog, asking all kinds of questions about you, about Halloween, about Robbie—"

"What's he know about Robbie?" Marc asked, a little shock of alarm going through him.

"Nothing. That's why he keeps asking."

"What'd you tell him about Robbie?"

"Nothing! He says someone saw us with Robbie at Monster Bash."

"Shit!"

"Yeah," Dozer said. "You're sitting out here doing nothing but drinking my cousin's booze while I gotta deal with that guy dogging my ass."

"Just keep your mouth shut!" Marc said, panicking a little at the idea that Dozer might have said something he shouldn't have. He was easily led, easily confused, and dumber than a stump. If he let himself get tricked into saying something . . .

"I told you, I ain't said nothing!" Dozer said. He was getting wound up now. His big ears were turning red. "You think I'm stupid? You think I'm just gonna up and say, 'Oh, you mean that guy we killed?'?"

"Jesus! Don't even say that out loud!" Marc snapped, looking around as if there might be people out there in the wilderness eavesdropping.

"Why not?" Dozer challenged him. "It's true. We killed a man!"

"It was an accident!"

"Was it?"

Marc felt suddenly cold. Dozer, for once, seemed sober as a judge, despite the smell of whiskey on his breath.

"You were there," Marc said. "You saw what happened. He came at me! And that was on *you*!"

Dozer nodded. "Oh, right. That was my fault. Everything is always my fault. It's never your fault, Saint Marc, is it? Nothing is ever your fault. You always got Dozer to pass it off onto, don't you?"

"What the fuck is wrong with you?"

Marc could feel himself hyperventilating. He was losing control of the situation, losing control of Dozer. That couldn't happen.

"You're the one just had to talk to him that night," Marc said. "You're the one had to say how sorry you were."

"Because I am," Dozer said. "I've spent ten years sick over what I did to him."

"It was an accident!"

Dozer wagged his head. "You probably even believe that now. You just went on like nothing ever happened, 'cause it didn't happen to you."

Of course he'd gone on with his life, Marc thought. That had been the whole point, hadn't it? Knock Robbie out of the way so he could get his chance. Of course he hadn't squandered it. He hadn't had any control over the extent of Robbie's injury. It wasn't his fault Robbie had gotten hooked on painkillers. None of that had been in his hands.

There was no point in talking about it now. They couldn't change what had happened even if they had wanted to.

He took a deep breath and gathered his wits.

"Look," he said, holding his hands up as if in surrender. "Let's just get this car gone. We'll sort the rest out later."

He turned away and went to pull the tarp off Robbie Fontenot's piece-of-shit Toyota.

"No," Dozer said.

Marc spun around. "What? What do you mean, no?"

"I mean no. You're the one went to college, and you don't know what no means? Oh." He caught himself. "I suppose you don't, since no one's ever said no to you, golden boy."

"What is your problem today?" Marc asked.

"You. You're my problem," Dozer said. "And I'm here to end it."

"What's that supposed to mean?"

"It means I'm done," he said. "I'm done being your henchman. I'm done being your stooge, Marc. I'm done trying to drown it all out with booze. You never even cared what that did to me, did you? You got what you wanted, and you got the hell out of here. What did I get? Stuck in a bottle, going nowhere."

"What was I supposed to do?" Marc asked. "I couldn't take you to Tulane with me! Was I supposed to take your SATs for you? Was I supposed to stop you drinking? What did you expect from me?"

Dozer stared at him with sadness and disgust. "Nothing. I served your purpose. That's all that mattered to you."

The thing was, Dozer wasn't wrong, Marc knew. He had used Dozer over and over because it was easy, because Dozer let him, because it did indeed serve his purpose to do it. He was such a piece of shit.

"I'm done, Marc," Dozer said, taking a step back. "That's what I come to tell you. I'm going to Fourcade and telling him everything, and what happens happens, but it's off my conscience."

Marc thought he might be having a coronary. His heart was suddenly banging in his chest like a fist trying to break through. He felt like he couldn't breathe.

"Are you out of your damn mind?!" he said, pursuing Dozer as he took another step back toward his truck. "We'll go to prison! And for what? Robbie's dead! He ain't coming back!"

"This is what I'm doing, Marc," Dozer said. "You do what you will. I'm sure you'll come out smelling like a rose. You always do. But this time you gotta do it without me. I'm done."

He turned and started to walk away.

Marc's brain was a scramble of animal panic and wild thoughts, grasping for ideas of how to get out of this. Maybe no one would believe Dozer. He was a drunk, and everyone knew he wasn't quite right in the head. *Who would believe him over me?* But this Detective Fourcade said he had a witness who put him with Dozer and Robbie that night . . . And there he was with Robbie Fontenot's car . . .

Oh, Jesus.

Oh, shit.

What could he do? There were three people living who knew what happened that night, and only two of them would never talk. The third had turned his back . . .

From the corner of his eye Marc caught sight of the red-handled axe lying on the firewood piled against the rusty metal shed. Without a second's hesitation, he grabbed it and swung it as hard as he could.

39

ANNIE DROPPED JUSTIN OFF AT HER COUSIN REMY'S IN TIME for breakfast and headed into the office early. Deebo had texted her that he had connected with Kenneth Wood of Ravenwood Trust and was getting access to the video from the security cameras on the house behind Robbie Fontenot's. She both hoped and dreaded it would give them something to go on—hoped for answers and dreaded what those answers might tell them.

B'Lynn had told her she was too kindhearted for this job, and that day she felt like that might be true. There was just so much sadness to unpack in these past few days. That Robbie Fontenot was dead was all but a foregone conclusion now, though she would hang on to the very last thread of hope until she absolutely had to let it go. She would have to go over to the jail that day to see Izzy Guidry and to the hospital to check on Tulsie Parcelle, hoping she could play a role in getting them if not a great outcome, at least a less terrible one. And she had yet to locate any next of kin for Rayanne Tillis, who lay dead in the morgue at Our Lady. It didn't please her to add a dirty cop to that pile of misery.

What a hell of a week this was. The kind of week that made her think about opening a flower shop or having another baby. Anything life-affirming to save her from falling into a pit of despair.

"Danny Perry didn't make it," Deebo said as she walked into the Pizza Hut.

Annie felt like someone had knocked the wind out of her. She gave him a look. "Could I get a 'Hi, how you doing, Annie' before the death notices, please?"

"Sorry," he said, having the grace to cringe a little. "I figured I might as well lead with it and get it out of the way, before you sit down and look at this video."

"You met with this Mr. Wood?" she asked, pouring herself a cup of coffee.

"Yes, ma'am. That house on Lafourche is his grandmother's house. She's gone into a nursing home recently and they needed to liquidate her assets so she could qualify for Medicaid. That's how it ended up in this trust, so it's still in the family. Mr. Wood had the security cameras installed on account of the sketchiness of that neighborhood. There's nothing much in the house, but he didn't want squatters or druggies or whatever taking up residence."

Annie pulled a chair up beside him and sighed as she settled in. "So what have we got?"

"I went directly to Monday morning," he said. "Who knows what else we might find going back, but I figured to cut straight to the chase and get it over with."

He brought the video up on his computer screen and made a sad face while he petted his scraggly beard as if for comfort.

Robbie Fontenot's back porch was some distance in the background, but there was no mistaking that the person unlocking the house to let Rayanne Tillis inside was a Bayou Breaux uniformed officer, square and stocky. Danny Perry.

It was what Annie had expected, but still she felt the weight of disappointment.

Deebo shook his head. "What the hell? I reckon we give him points for creativity, giving his snitch a bonus without dipping into his own pocket, right? 'Here, Rayanne, have this TV out of this guy's house. He ain't been around for a few days, and he's probably dead anyway.'"

"Ah, Danny," Annie murmured. "I was happier thinking you were just a fool."

"I'm gonna bet he was up to his ears in drug business," Deebo said. "Could be your Mr. Fontenot knew all about it."

Annie thought of the money she'd found in Robbie's bedroom, feeling sick at the idea that he might have been involved in the business. That was the last thing she wanted to have to tell B'Lynn.

"Thanks for getting this, Deebo," she said. "This gives me enough to get a search warrant for Danny's house, I should think."

"Well, good luck with that," he said. "Danny's house burned to the ground early this morning."

"What?"

"I heard it from a dispatcher. What were you hoping to find at his place?"

"Robbie Fontenot's MacBook," Annie said. "He made a joke to someone recently that he was investigating police corruption in Bayou Breaux, and he used to have a hobby of making videos, like documentary-type things. I'm gonna hope he saved some evidence for us."

"Annie, did he have an iPhone?" Wynn Dixon asked, peering around her computer screen.

"Yeah. I was told he used to make videos all the time on his phone. But we think his phone is with his car, wherever that may be."

"We can get a warrant for his iCloud content," Dixon offered. "If he was making videos with his iPhone, that automatically saves to the cloud. You don't need the phone or his computer. The content from all his Apple devices goes to his iCloud account."

"I hadn't even thought about that," Annie admitted. "He has an old Mac desktop sitting at his mother's house, too."

"If the operating system is up to date enough and if you've got his passwords, you should be able to access his content from that machine," Wynn said. "Even if you don't have the passwords, we can always hack into it. It'll just take longer."

"And that computer is sitting in his mother's house," Annie said, standing up. "We may not need a warrant at all."

She picked up her phone and texted B'Lynn to let her know she was on her way over.

40

NICK WATCHED THE ARGUMENT GO DOWN. HE WATCHED THEIR faces, watched their body language, the gestures. He watched Marc Mercier start to pull the blue tarp off Robbie Fontenot's Toyota, then turn to argue more with Dozer.

He was too far away to hear anything but the odd angry exclamation, but the one that counted most came through loud and clear: *We killed a man!*

He watched Dozer Cormier turn to walk away, and that fast Marc Mercier grabbed an axe off the top of the woodpile and swung it as hard as he could.

"Drop it! Drop it!" Nick shouted, bursting from the cover of the trees.

He drew his weapon as he ran, but the axe was already in motion, and the blade buried itself in the upper right quadrant of Dozer's chest as he twisted around at the sound of Nick's voice. He screamed and staggered sideways as the blade sank into his flesh, his momentum carrying the big man hard into the side of his truck. He flailed at the axe handle with his left hand, roaring like a wounded elephant. As the axe dislodged and fell to the ground, blood gushed in a torrent, and Dozer dropped to his knees.

Nick barreled into Marc Mercier with the force of a freight train, running him sideways into the wood pile.

"Get on the ground! Get on the ground!" he shouted, riding Marc down face-first, his knee between Mercier's shoulder blades, knocking the wind out of him as he landed.

"Marc Mercier, you're under arrest. And you had better hope to God that man doesn't die."

41

IT WAS STRANGE TO FEEL ANY KIND OF OPTIMISM, ANNIE thought as she pulled to the curb in front of the Fontenot house, but the idea of finding something on Robbie Fontenot's computer had rekindled the tiniest ember of hope inside her. Foolish, she supposed. Robbie had accumulated a pile of money doing something, and that something was quite possibly illegal. But the offhand remark he had tossed at Eli McVay stuck with her: that he was investigating police corruption. She was going to hang on to that tiny sliver of maybe, for Robbie and for B'Lynn.

A tan sedan was parked in the shade in front of the house next door, but Annie didn't think anything of it as she got out of her vehicle. Her mind was occupied, wondering if Robbie might have written his passwords down somewhere, or if B'Lynn might know them. She knew a few mothers who didn't allow their teenagers to keep their passwords to themselves. It wasn't hard to see B'Lynn as one of them, even if her son wasn't a teenager anymore. The computer on Robbie's desk dated to his school days.

She climbed the steps to the front porch, rang the doorbell, and waited. B'Lynn had said she would be home, had answered Annie's text with *OK*.

The heavy mahogany interior door stood open, which seemed a bit odd, but she might have wanted to let the fresh morning air in to lift the stagnant heaviness of her emotions from the house.

Annie rang the doorbell again as her anxiety began to stir. Slowly. Hesitantly. She tried to discount it. This was the Belle Terre neighborhood in broad daylight on a weekday. Next door, the neighbor's gardeners were swarming around with lawn mowers and Weedwackers. The strong smell of gasoline perfumed the air. Just a normal day.

"B'Lynn?" she called through the screen door. "It's Annie!"

The stillness of the place suddenly bothered her. What-ifs began to itch at the back of her mind. This woman had been through so much, all of it sad and crushingly disappointing. The night before she had come to the conclusion that the son she had fought so hard to save was very probably dead. She had spent the last ten years fighting for him, and just like that, her mission was over.

"B'Lynn?" she called again, trying not to imagine her dead by her own hand. "I'm coming in!"

"We're upstairs, Detective!"

We? *We who*? Annie wondered. Had B'Lynn's daughter come home? Or maybe she had called on her own mother to come for emotional support.

We.

And there was something in the way she had said *Detective*, with a certain formal emphasis . . .

Annie stepped back as she pulled the screen door open, and the tan car at the curb in front of the neighbor's house caught her attention. A tan sedan that had seen better days. Not the kind of car common to this street stocked with Mercedes and BMWs, but the kind of junker vehicles police agencies kept in their carpools for detectives to drive.

The tan sedan of Dewey Rivette.

What the hell?

"I'll be right up!" Annie called, stalling for time.

What was he doing there? Annie had relieved him of his duty. And why wouldn't B'Lynn have simply said he was there? Why wouldn't Dewey have announced himself?

She quickly called for backup to come, no lights, no sirens.

Her heart was thumping as she stood in the doorway looking into the gracious old home. Her sense of self-preservation told her to wait. Her concern for B'Lynn told her to go in. One part of her brain told her she was being ridiculous, that she'd known Dewey for years and there was no reason to be afraid of him. Another part of her brain recalled that car running up behind her on the road to Lafayette, and her wondering what might have happened if they hadn't been on a busy highway.

Then she remembered that Robbie's bedroom overlooked the street, and anyone looking out the window would see the sheriff's deputies pulling up. If there was a situation upstairs, she needed to be the distraction that kept the attention in the room.

"Annie?" B'Lynn called. "Are you coming?"

Her mouth as dry as cotton, Annie put her hand on the butt of her weapon.

"On my way!" she called, and went inside the house.

42

"**FUCKING HELL!**" STOKES MUTTERED, STARING AT THE SCENE in front of them: Sergeant Rodrigue straddling the prone body of Dozer Cormier, red-faced as he applied pressure to the massive wound in Cormier's shoulder.

"Go in with Mercier," Nick ordered. "Book him. Put him in an interview room and leave him alone, but don't take your eyes off him on the video."

"Aye, aye, boss," Stokes said, hustling off toward the marked SUV a deputy had already put Marc Mercier in.

Nick dismissed him, his attention on Dozer, who had turned an unhealthy shade of gray and lay wide-eyed with fear, gasping for air like a fish out of water.

"Dozer, can you hear me?" he asked as he knelt down beside him.

"I don't wanna die! I don't wanna die!" Dozer mumbled, terrified.

"The ambulance is on the way," Nick said calmly. "You gotta hang in there for us, yeah? You don't want Marc being the only one telling this story."

"He tried to kill me! He killed me!"

"You ain't dead yet," Nick said. "We're gonna get you to the hospital."

Rodrigue's pressure on the wound had stemmed the arterial bleeding for the moment, but the big man was drenched in red and he had begun trembling uncontrollably as his body reacted to the trauma. There was no guarantee he would make it to Our Lady.

"Dozer, look at me," Nick ordered, tapping his fingers on the man's cheek to try to keep him focused. "You need to stay with me here. Tell me what happened to Robbie Fontenot."

"He's dead," Dozer said, panting. "I wanted to make amends. Now he's dead."

He began to cry, for himself, for Robbie Fontenot. It was hard to say.

"Oh, God, I'm going to hell!" he wailed.

"No, you're not," Nick assured him. "You still have time, Dozer. You've got good in you. I know that. Who killed Robbie?"

Dozer moaned and writhed. Nick glanced up at Rodrigue, who was whispering the Rosary in French under his breath.

"Who killed Robbie, Dozer?" Nick asked again. "If you die on me now, you'll take the rap for it. Marc'll dump it all on you. You know it."

"Robbie punched him. Marc hit him back," he said, the words coming out in short bursts with his breath as he hyperventilated. "He fell and hit his head. Oh, my God, I'm dying! I can feel it!"

From a distance came the faint wail of an ambulance siren.

"Hang on, Dozer!" Nick barked. "The ambulance is almost here. You hang on!"

Dozer was sobbing now in the face of his own mortality. But that was between him and his God. Nick had other concerns.

"Where's his body, Dozer?" he asked. "Where's Robbie's body?"

"I dunno," Dozer mumbled. "Ask Luc."

43

ANNIE CLIMBED THE STAIRS WITH HER HEART IN HER THROAT and her hand resting on the butt of her weapon in her belt holster. She could see the open door to Robbie's room as she gained the second-floor landing. She could see B'Lynn standing a few feet into the room, near Robbie's desk. B'Lynn turned and looked at her, eyes wide.

"Annie," she said. "Detective Rivette has stopped by."

Annie approached the room, her feet as heavy as lead boots. She couldn't see Dewey, couldn't see if he was armed.

"He's brought a warrant for Robbie's computer."

"Really?" Annie said. "Why is that, Dewey? This isn't your case anymore."

"My investigation is ongoing," he said.

She got her first look at him as she came to the open doorway. His clothes were more disheveled than usual. He looked like he'd slept in them, if he'd slept at all. His limp brown hair was greasy and uncombed.

"You look like you had a hard night, Dewey," she said. She

remained in the hall, with her right side—her gun side—hidden from his view by the doorframe. "I heard the news about Danny. I'm sorry."

"Why are you sorry?" he asked. "Because he's not around for you to arrest him?"

"Because it's sad," Annie said. "How'd that go so wrong with him? I guess it's hard to see all that drug money floating around and not want some of it."

"I don't know what you're talking about," Dewey said. "Danny was a good cop."

"I just watched a security video of him letting Rayanne Tillis into Robbie Fontenot's house Monday morning, Dewey," Annie said calmly. "So, no, he wasn't a good cop. So if you've got some kind of misguided idea of trying to protect his reputation, you need to let go of that. Danny's gone, and whatever he was into is all gonna come to light. You need to get out of the way for your own sake."

He didn't react. He just stood there staring at her, his dark eyes a little glassy. She wondered if he'd heard her. For the first time, she wondered if he might be on something.

"We're getting a warrant for his house," Annie said.

Dewey laughed, an unexpected and jarring sound that couldn't have been more inappropriate. The hairs stood up on the back of Annie's neck.

"Why is that funny?"

The smell registered in her brain even as she asked the question: gasoline. She'd smelled it outside because of the gardeners next door, but this smell was in the house, in this room.

"What have you done, Dewey?" she asked, feeling sick.

"I'm just here to get this computer," he said. "I have a warrant."

"Let me see it," Annie said. He surely hadn't gone from setting Danny Perry's house on fire to the courthouse to get a warrant.

"It doesn't concern you," he said. "This is my case."

"It won't matter, Dewey," Annie said. "Whatever you've done, whatever you're trying to hide, you can't get rid of it. Everything on this computer is backed up to the cloud. My tech person is accessing that content as we speak," she lied.

Dewey didn't want to hear it. He wasn't thinking straight. He shifted his weight from one foot to the other and back, anxious, agitated.

"You need to leave," he said, raising his sidearm and pointing it at her, his expression stony.

Annie swallowed hard, her pulse racing. She didn't know what he was on or how volatile he might become. He was clearly desperate, cornered like an animal. Cornered animals lashed out.

"Why don't we let Mrs. Fontenot leave first?" she suggested, amazed she could sound so calm when she felt on the verge of panic. Her mouth was dry, her throat was tight. She felt like she couldn't breathe. She glanced at B'Lynn, who had placed herself between Dewey and the desk, protecting Robbie's old computer as she would have protected her son.

How had Dewey Rivette known this computer even existed? Annie wondered. If he'd been in this room before, how had he not found the box of money? Or had he just not thought to come there until she'd told him about finding the cash? And if Robbie had stashed the cash there, had Dewey wondered what else he might have hidden?

"No," Dewey said. "She'll call for help."

"Help is already here," Annie said. "Look out the window, Dewey. There's deputies waiting down below. I called for backup before I ever came in the house.

"You need to put the gun down," she said. "This is over. Whatever you've done, you're just making it worse."

He glanced over his shoulder toward the big bay window, and B'Lynn seized the chance to dash out the door.

Annie slipped her sidearm from the holster.

"What did Robbie have on you, Dewey? What'd he have on Danny? Was Danny dealing? Were you?"

He was breathing hard. His arm had begun to tremble from holding the gun up. Tears rose in his eyes.

"Just put the gun down and tell me what happened," Annie said quietly. "You look so tired, Dewey. Don't you just want this to be over?"

He let his arm bend and pulled his elbow against his side, the gun still pointed in her direction.

"Robbie was your CI," Annie prompted. "He found out about Danny. Why didn't you do anything about it? Because you were in on it? Or because you were a customer? Are you high right now, Dewey?"

Two big tears spilled down his cheeks. "I can't lose my job," he said, as if there was a snowball's chance in hell he was going to have a job after that morning.

"Was he blackmailing you?"

"He said he had video of Danny, and Danny was supplying me . . . He had us both. Jesus God," he muttered, shaking his head. "What a nightmare! I can't go to prison!"

"Did you kill him?" Annie asked, feeling sick at the thought.

"No!"

"Did Danny?"

"No! He—he gave him some pills. We thought he'd OD. We thought he probably had. And then Danny was chasing his car . . ."

He hadn't bothered looking for Robbie from the start of this because he not only thought Robbie was dead, he was betting on it.

"I can't go to prison," he said again. "I can't."

"Maybe you don't have to," Annie lied. "Put the gun down. You haven't hurt anyone. You're having a mental health crisis. You need help, Dewey. We can get you help."

He shook his head and spoke to himself. "My life is over."

Dewey had been caught in a trap of his own making, and there was a part of her that didn't want to have sympathy for him. But she sure as hell wasn't going to let him kill himself in Robbie Fontenot's bedroom in his mother's ancestral home. B'Lynn had suffered enough. Dewey Rivette could live to deal with the consequences of his actions.

He started to lift his arm again, to turn the gun toward his own head. He was crying so hard, he probably couldn't see her. His gun hand was shaking, waving his service weapon like a flag. Then his legs gave way, and he sank to the floor and curled into a sobbing ball, the weapon falling from his useless fingers, finished in every way.

44

NICK STOOD ON THE DOCK AT MERCIERS' SWAMP TOURS, watching the airboat glide in, the seats full of tourists delighted with their glimpse of this wild country he loved with all his heart.

Luc Mercier sat up on his perch, guiding the boat in, his eyes hidden by his sunglasses, but his full attention was on the sheriff's office personnel waiting for him—Nick and a pair of uniformed deputies stationed a few yards behind him. He took his time getting down, making sure the boat was tied off properly, before walking up.

"I don't reckon this is a social call, is it?"

"*Mais non*," Nick said quietly. He saw no need to make a show in front of the tourists, no need to embarrass the man or upset his loved ones. "I need you to come with me, Mr. Mercier. Your brother is already under arrest and in custody."

Luc's mouth twisted in a parody of a smile, and he looked off over the water. "And he threw me under the bus, did he? That's Marc. Our paper tiger."

"Me, I'm hoping you're not gonna make a scene in front of your sister," Nick said. "She doesn't need to see that."

"No," Luc agreed. "You'll give me a minute with her?"

Nick nodded. He watched Mercier go to his sister over by the ticket building and kiss her cheek and tell her he was going away for a bit and not to worry. Noelle Mercier smiled brightly and waved at Nick, her friend.

Nick had the deputies wait until they were on the far side of the vehicles to handcuff her brother and load him into the SUV.

It gave him no pleasure to take Luc Mercier away from his family and his business. Every part of this story was a tragedy that would go on and on because the Merciers' favored son had made a terrible decision when he was just a boy, desperate to be a hero. The wake from that choice was still rippling through lives a decade on.

"What are you doing?" Kiki shouted as she came running across the road, red-faced and wild-eyed. "Where are you taking my boy?"

Nick intercepted her with both hands before she could fling herself at the vehicle. She twisted out of his grasp and stepped back, fuming.

"What the hell are you doing?"

"He's under arrest, Mrs. Mercier," Nick said quietly. "Please don't make a scene. For the sake of your daughter."

Kiki's attention was on Luc now as he stared at her, stone-faced, from inside the vehicle. "What have you done?! What have you done to Marc?!"

She flung herself at the car, slamming her hands on the window and shouting at her eldest son. "If you hurt Marc, I'll kill you!"

Nick pulled her away and held on to her as the SUV drove off.

Despite the NO SMOKING sign posted on the wall, Luc lit up a cigarette and took a long drag on it, as if this might be his last for a while. He exhaled and shrugged. "What are you gonna do? Arrest me?"

"You don't want a lawyer present?" Nick asked, unbothered by the man flaunting a rule. That was the least of his sins.

"For what? To charge me money to tell me to shut my mouth? No, thanks."

"Your choice. Tell me about Halloween."

He tapped the ash off his smoke into a paper cup with a puddle of cold coffee in the bottom. "Marc called me in a panic. Eleven thirty or so. Said there'd been an accident and could I come. I wasn't far away, just down the street a ways at T-Neg's bar drinking. So I go, and there's Marc and Dozer, dressed up in costumes like a couple'a goddamn *couillons*, drunk. Dozer was crying. Marc was crying that his life was gonna be over . . ."

"Where was this at?"

"In the alley behind Canray's Garage. And there was Robbie Fontenot, on the ground in a bad way."

"He was alive?"

"Barely. There'd been a fight. Robbie hit Marc; Marc hit him back. Robbie fell and hit his head on a busted-up old concrete parking block. He wasn't gonna make it," he said, shaking his head at the memory. "The side of his head was caved in. He was barely breathing, having a seizure, foaming at the mouth. It was godawful."

"Why you didn't call an ambulance?" Nick asked.

"For what? So he could be a vegetable? So he could get to Our Lady and die there instead of in that alley? So my brother could go to prison? No. No. I couldn't let that happen. What would be the point?" he asked. "It was a stupid accident. It didn't need to get any more tragic than it was."

"What did you do?"

"I cleaned up the mess because Marc wouldn't. He couldn't suck it up and be a man and do what needed to be done. I put that poor bastard out of his misery, and I rolled him up in a tarp and put him in the back of my truck."

Like he was a stray dog that got hit by a car.

"What'd you do with the body?"

He sighed and looked away. "I stored it in a shed for a couple of days. I knew what needed to be done, but . . . I told Marc this was his fault and he should have to deal with it himself, but he wouldn't. We fought about it. More than once. In the end, I had to take care of the dirty work, as usual. I told myself it's just a carcass at that point, no different than a deer or a hog."

His voice thickened as he said it, and the muscles in his face tensed like the memory caused him physical pain. But he fought through the moment and pressed on.

He gave a rough, humorless laugh. "And all that time Mama's like 'Oh, poor Marc, he's under so much stress with work and his wife and the baby and all!' And how I should be more kind to him! And I wanted to say, well, your precious fucking baby boy killed a man. But I didn't. I just took care of it."

"Your mother didn't know what happened?"

Luc shook his head as he finished his cigarette, stubbed it out on the tabletop, and dropped the butt in the paper cup. His rough, stained workingman's hands were trembling a little as he lit up another, belying his calm demeanor.

"What'd you do with the body, Luc?" Nick asked again, knowing full well what the answer was going to be.

"I cut it up, 'cause I didn't want no body floating up to the surface. Better for everyone that he just be gone. I took it out to a place I knew there'd be gators. And that's what happened to poor Robbie Fontenot."

Nick let the silence hang for a moment as Luc lived with the memory and smoked his cigarette.

"You don't think he deserved better than that?" Nick asked.

A sad smile turned the corner of Luc Mercier's mouth. "We all deserve better, but what happened happened. I was raised that a man takes care of his family first and always. And I may resent the hell out of my brother, but blood is blood. The thing that stings is knowing he would never, ever do the same for me. But I can only control what I do and who I am. And I'll live with that."

Despite what he'd done—or maybe because of it—Luc Mercier

was not the worst person in this story, Nick thought. He wasn't sure there was a villain at all in the true sense of the word. People always wanted murder to be black-and-white, cut-and-dried, with a cartoon bad guy they could easily hate. But that wasn't always the case.

Luc had made his choices to save his family. Marc had made his choices to save himself. Dozer had made a choice long ago out of loyalty and had made his choice on Halloween thinking the truth would set him free from his demons. And their respective choices of lies and truths along the way were the connective tissue that wove the story together.

Nick left Luc Mercier and went across the hall to another interview room, where his brother, Marc, had been sitting alone, left to stew and fret for two hours. According to Stokes, he'd spent that time crying and puking into a wastebasket, pacing and pounding his fists against the walls.

Nick walked into the room, silent and stone-faced, and stood staring at Marc for a long moment. Mercier halted his pacing along the back wall and stood motionless, looking like a prey animal awaiting its fate.

"I've been waiting for hours here," he complained. "What's going on?"

"You might want to work on making peace with small enclosed spaces, Mr. Mercier," Nick said quietly. He took a seat at the table, turned his chair sideways, and crossed one ankle over a knee and sighed. "I watched you try to kill a man with an axe this morning, and I make an excellent witness at trial, if I do say so myself."

"I wasn't trying to kill him!" Marc protested, pacing again. "I just—I just had to stop him going. I needed to talk sense into him."

"An axe as a tool of persuasion," Nick mused. "That's . . . well, *overkill* is the word that comes to mind. And not that you've asked, but I'm told Mr. Cormier will survive his injuries. I'm going to speculate that his lifelong loyalty to you has perhaps run its course. You should also know that I've just come from across the hall, where I had a very illuminating conversation with your brother, Luc."

"Luc killed Robbie, not me," Marc said without a second's hesitation. "I just defended myself. What happened was an accident. Robbie threw the first punch. I hit him back, and he fell and hit his head. That's what happened. I didn't mean for him to die! But Luc said he was gonna die anyway, and I'd go to prison. For what? For an accident!"

A different sort of person would have asked for an attorney and said nothing more. But Marc Mercier had the narcissist's belief that his charm could talk him out of any situation, because it likely had more often than not all his life.

"Why did Mr. Fontenot punch you?" Nick asked.

"He had a wrong idea about something that happened a long time ago, and he blamed me, but it wasn't my fault! I never told Dozer to cripple him! It wasn't my fault he became a drug addict and threw his life away!"

"Why that night?" Nick asked.

Marc rolled his eyes. "Because Dozer was drunk and said something he should have kept to himself, and it set Robbie off, and shit happened. I wish it hadn't."

He put his hands on top of his head and turned around. His eyes kept cutting to the door, as if he was expecting someone to walk in and set him free.

"I moved back here to help my family," he said. "I can't believe this is happening to me!"

"That's an interesting choice of words," Nick said. "Because Dozer is the one that got hit with an axe, and Robbie Fontenot is the one dead and fed to alligators. This isn't happening *to* you, Mr. Mercier. This is happening *because of* you. Because of the choices *you* made. And when you go to prison, that will be because of what *you* did. And when your wife divorces you and takes your child and leaves, that will be because of the man you chose to be."

It became clear in that moment to Marc Mercier that he wasn't going to win Nick over, and he wasn't going to walk out of that room a free man.

"I think I should have an attorney now," he said.

"That's your prerogative," Nick said, pushing to his feet. "Unless you know one off the top of your head, I suggest you use your one phone call to reach out to your wife . . . and hope she answers."

"What's gonna happen to me?" Marc asked, his expression full of fear and a kind of disbelief that anything bad could happen to him at all.

Nick paused at the door and looked at him. "Justice, Mr. Mercier. Justice."

45

"IS HE EVEN SORRY?" ANNIE ASKED AFTER NICK HAD TOLD HER the tale of Robbie Fontenot and the Mercier brothers.

They sat on a bench under an oak tree in the meticulously tended gardens of Our Lady of Mercy. It was late enough in the day that the fairy lights had come on like lightning bugs in the tree branches and the ground lighting had come on along the paths. It was a place meant to give comfort, and Annie surely needed that after this day.

"For himself," Nick said. "I imagine other people's feelings are an abstract concept to him, for the most part. At least in comparison to his own sense of self-preservation. And I think deep down, he knows what he is. There's a certain fear at the core of him. He knows the Marc everyone loves and adores is a construction, a mask. The one person he could never sell that lie to is himself."

They had each come to the hospital separately as their last official task of the day. Annie to check on Tulsie Parcelle and talk to her about what would happen next for her and for Izzy, and to give her as much assurance as she could that there would be people willing to help them through it. Nick had come to see Dozer Cormier and take his statement about the things that happened that morning and the things that had happened on Halloween.

"That's a sad, screwed-up life," Annie said. "I could almost feel sorry for him if the context was different."

Nick nodded. "If I hadn't watched him hack a man with an axe in the attempt to save his own ass . . . Poor Dozer. *Pauvre bête.* All Dozer ever wanted was a friend. He was just a tool to Marc."

"Did he say why he picked that night to talk to Robbie?"

"I think it was a combination of opportunity and alcohol. Donnie Bichon had been pushing him to get right with himself, admit his wrongs and make amends."

"Ten years later."

"Took him that long to find the courage, I reckon. And I gather Robbie wasn't around here all that much over the years. They didn't run in the same circles. Whatever the case may be, that was the night."

"Timing," Annie murmured. "So many little pieces had to fall into place for those three people to all be in that exact spot on that night at that time."

She would have given anything to turn back the clock to that night and make Robbie turn left instead of right, leave five minutes earlier or stay ten minutes later. After all his struggles with drugs and petty crime; in and out of rehab, in and out of jail, in and out of the lives of his family; he had died in an alley at the hands of old friends because of a selfish decision made a decade earlier by a kid desperate for a future away from his past.

That the Mercier brothers had killed him and disposed of him like so much trash was unfathomable to her, even though she had seen such things before. At least the knowledge that she could still feel shock at what people would do to one another reassured her of her own humanity.

"How am I gonna get through telling B'Lynn this?" she asked. "She fought so hard for him for so long . . ."

"I'll tell her, *bébé*," Nick said, tightening his arm around her shoulders. "We'll go together, and I'll tell her."

"Thank you," Annie murmured, tucking herself into his side as close as she could get.

With the sun almost gone, the day had grown chilly. B'Lynn would have a fire going in the fireplace of her cozy, feminine sitting room, with soft music playing. She had already resigned herself to the idea that Robbie was likely dead, but intellectually accepting something and hearing that the worst had actually happened were two different things.

"I'm sure she thought having a police detective suffer a mental breakdown and threaten to kill himself in her home was the worst thing that would happen today," Annie said. "I can tell you I did not have that one on my shit show bingo card. Dewey Rivette. Who would have thought?"

"No one," Nick said. "We never know what someone else might be going through. We see what we want to see, what we know."

They had both seen Dewey as . . . just there. An average man, a mediocre cop. He was just a placeholder in life, like the character in a movie who didn't warrant having a name when the credits rolled, just a title, a label. Annie felt a little ashamed now that she had not bothered to know anything about him as a person.

"He told me he hurt his back about a year ago," Annie said. "He thought he could manage the pain meds. He only took them when he was off duty. But he built up a tolerance, needed more drugs. He wasn't sleeping, then he needed something to wake him up in the morning and get him through the day, and he still thought he had it under control."

That was the story of so many people. No one set out to become an addict.

"He was running Robbie as his CI. Robbie found out Danny Perry was dealing, then he found out Danny was supplying Dewey. Robbie had them both by the short hairs."

"That's where that money came from?" Nick said. "He was shaking them both down?"

"Yes, but he had an ulterior motive. Robbie told Eli McVay he was investigating police corruption. He said it as a joke, but Wynn spent the afternoon going over his computer from the house, looking at photos, videos, Word documents. He was gathering evidence. He was building a story. He kept a log of every dollar they gave him. He hadn't spent one red cent of it. He was building a case. He would have taken it to the media."

"He really was trying to turn his life around," Annie said. She shook her head. "And then he dies in an alley for no good reason at all."

"Life is under no obligation to make sense to us, 'Toinette," Nick said. "That irony never escapes me. Fiction has to be logical. All the loose ends of a novel have to tie up in a nice bow. But real life is messy and confusing and ugly, and it doesn't have to mean a damn thing."

He brushed her hair back from her face and looked into her eyes. "All we can do is write our own story and try to make our own happy ending if we can."

And appreciate every precious moment, Annie thought, because there were no guarantees of more to come.

She thought again of B'Lynn, imagining her younger, watching her little boy play in the backyard of the lovely home of her lovely family. No guarantees.

"Let's go, then," she said on a sigh. "Get the bad news over with, and go home. I want to spend tonight with my husband and my son."

46

B'LYNN DIDN'T ASK FOR THE DETAILS OF ROBBIE'S DEATH. SHE didn't want them. Not yet. Not ever, if she was honest. She didn't want to be sentenced to reliving his murder over and over in her mind for the rest of her life. She didn't want to be subjected to the endless torment of wondering if he had been aware of what was happening to him. Had he been afraid? Had he felt alone? Had he wanted his mother there with him at the end?

She couldn't stand thinking about it, not that there would be any avoiding the brutal details once the trials began, but that was in the future. For that night, she wouldn't think about Marc Mercier and all that he'd stolen from Robbie—his hopes, his dreams, his life. For that night, she would just sit with the knowledge that her son was gone.

For that night she could imagine that Robbie had just slipped away from this life and on to his next, whatever that might mean. She would try to comfort herself with the knowledge that at least after all the bad he had gone through, he had tried to do something good at the end of his life, and she could hope that he was at peace.

She thanked Annie Broussard and her handsome detective

lieutenant husband for their kindness and sent them home to their little boy. Five years old and full of promise. They were just starting that journey as B'Lynn's journey with her son was ending. She wished them nothing but the best.

She closed the door behind them and turned the lock, then went into her sitting room and poured herself a drink from the crystal decanter of bourbon and settled into the corner of the love seat closest to the fire. Her phone sat on the coffee table, blank and silent, waiting for her to make a choice.

Among the recent videos Robbie had made on his phone was a message for her. Annie had emailed a copy to her, for her to view when she felt ready. It was there inside her phone, waiting. All she had to do was open it and she could bring her son back from the dead, see his face and listen to his voice.

Her hands were trembling as she set her drink aside and picked up the phone. She opened her email app, touched on the message from Annie, and stared at the attachment.

What would he say to her?

She thought of every mistake she'd ever made as his mother and everything she'd ever done in an attempt to make up for those mistakes, and she hoped he'd seen the difference and forgiven her sins. She took a shaky breath and touched the screen.

Just like that, there he was, her handsome son, a little too thin, his face lean and drawn with dark eyes older than his soul should have been. Immediately a sheen of tears in her own eyes softened all the harsh lines and world-weariness.

"Hey, Mama," he said softly, his mouth turning in a sad smile. "If you're watching this video, then something bad has happened and I'm probably not around anymore. I just wanted this chance to say a few things.

"First, I'm sorry for everything I put you through. I know I dragged you down a dark road. I never wanted to go there, either. We both had better plans for me, but you know what people say about making plans and God laughing.

"Anyway, for whatever reason, that was the road I had to take. And I know I've thought it before, and thought wrong, but I believe this is the time for me to climb up out of that valley and breathe some fresh air and get a better view from a different path. So I'm trying to do something good and make something right. And even though it's probably turned out wrong, I hope you'll be proud of me for trying.

"I want you to know that even when I made bad choices and did bad things and told bad lies, I never stopped wanting you to love me. I never stopped wanting to be your son. And I know that no matter how angry, how disappointed, how hurt you might have been, that you never once stopped being my mom. You never once stopped fighting for me, and I thank you for that. If not for you, I would have been gone a long time ago. So, we made it out the other side, Mama. Know that. And that I apparently won't be going any further isn't failure. It's just what happened.

"I'm not sure what I really believe about where we go when we're done on this earth, but I once read that we're all just made up out of stardust and energy, and energy never dies; it just becomes something else. So we never really die, we just go back to the stars. Maybe that's what heaven is. I like that idea.

"So if I'm gone, go look at the stars and that's where you'll find me. That's where I'll be, shining down for you."

He smiled his sad smile, pressed a kiss to his fingertips, and waved. The video ended there, freezing on his goodbye.

B'Lynn sat motionless for a long while, staring at the screen, her fingertips touching his to keep the picture open. Their story was over, her heart broken and drained. No matter how badly she wanted to, she couldn't write another chapter and make a better ending.

Feeling as old as the world, she pushed to her feet and walked through the house, down the hall and through the kitchen, out the back door into the yard. She raised her phone to her lips and kissed her boy goodbye, then turned her face up to the clear night sky and looked for him in the stars.

GLOSSARY OF CAJUN FRENCH

arrête	stop
baw	Cajun slang for "boy"
bébé	This means "baby" in standard French, but the Cajun version is pronounced "beb" and is used like "babe," as a term of endearment.
bon	good
bon à rien	good for nothing
bonjour	good day
ça viens/ça va	How's it coming? / How's it going? This is a greeting that is also commonly given as the answer to the greeting.
c'est assez	that's enough
c'est fou	that's crazy
c'est triste	that's sad
c'est vrai	that's true
cher/chère	A term of endearment similar to "dear" or "sweetheart." It is pronounced "sha."
couillon	fool

dieu merci	thank God
fwa	diarrhea
je t'aime, mon coeur	I love you, my heart
mais	But or well. Often used for emphasis with yes or no.
maman	mom
mamere	mother
merci	thanks
merde	shit
mon ami	my friend
nonc	uncle
pauvre ('tite) bête	poor (little) thing
pischouette	runt
s'il vous plaît	if you please
tante	aunt
tête dure	hard head
tu es mon coeur	you are my heart

ABOUT THE AUTHOR

Tami Hoag is the #1 international bestselling author of more than thirty books. There are more than forty million copies of her books in print in more than thirty languages. Renowned for combining thrilling plots with character-driven suspense, Hoag first hit the *New York Times* bestseller list with *Night Sins*, and each of her books since has been a bestseller. She lives in California.